QUMRAN

www.jerrythenovelist.com

The author standing inside the mouth of Cave IV at Qumran.

Story Merchant Books
400 S. Burnside Ave. #11B
Los Angeles, CA 90036

www.storymerchantbooks.com

Los Angeles / Jerry Amernic

ISBN 978-0-9909436-2-4

Printed in the United States of America

Jerry Amernic

STORY MERCHANT BOOKS
LOS ANGELES / 2015

Jerry Amernic

Jerry Amernic is a writer who lives in Toronto. He has been a newspaper reporter and correspondent, newspaper columnist, feature writer for magazines, teacher of journalism, and media consultant. His first novel, *Gift of the Bambino*, was published in 2004. His most recent novel is *The Last Witness*, which is about the last living survivor of the Holocaust in the year 2039. *QUMRAN* is a biblical-historical thriller.

CHAPTER ONE

ONE

It was something that rendered all my earlier finds into nothingness. Not far from the mouth of one of the caves and buried in a shallow grave of dry desert sand was a human body wrapped in animal skins. The young Bedouin tribesman who found it had opened the wrappings, shrieked in horror at his numbing discovery and run off to tell the others. When word reached me, I was curious. From the hurried rambling description in a mixture of Arabic and broken English, it sounded like it could be a corpse of some kind, but one that might be very old.

The year was 1987 and the place the West Bank, just off the northwest corner of the Dead Sea near the ruins at Qumran, and I knew from past experience that artifacts found in the region were an archeologist's dream. Discoveries were made here all the time. This was the site of the Dead Sea Scrolls, a tiny forbidden zone that coughed up ancient relics of the past. The historical past. The biblical past. It was where the two met, and where interpretation of anything and everything depends on one's view of the world and our place in it.

There were countless caves, some of them a hundred feet long and with openings fifteen feet high. They were just east of El Buqeia and the Valley of Achor, and west of the Maritime

Plain that slopes down to the shore of the Dead Sea. For me this fragment of land and rock where the desert begins has always been the answer since it never lies.

"Come now!" the young Arab urged. He was a Taamireh Bedouin from the same tribe of nomads that discovered the scrolls in one of the caves back in 1947. Two thousand years of waiting was the reward and what a reward it was — an original record of the Old Testament, the history of the ancient Essenes — and now something else.

"Professor Marr, I want to go too," said Robbie Schueftan, my able assistant from the Hebrew University. He was a young Israeli whom I had selected from all my graduate students because he was the best of them.

Robbie and I left the protection of our tents and joined the two Bedouin shepherds. They said this corpse or whatever it was had been found right near the caves, and in their frenzy I thought they meant inside one of the caves. That excited me since so many digs had taken place there over the years, but no one had ever found a body before.

"What kind of condition is it in?" I asked. Robbie translated for his desert brothers who immediately unleashed a frenetic account of what they saw in the high-pitched rambling that is so typical of them.

"They say it is well preserved."

"Preserved?"

"Like a mummy."

"A mummy? What's it look like?"

"A man. It is a man. We should go see for ourselves."

We set off on foot from our makeshift camp on the West Bank of the Jordan River at the corner of the Judean wilderness, not twenty minutes by jeep to Bethlehem. Jeeps, of course, were for speed, but for an archeologist walking was better. There is less chance of missing something. Through the centuries walking has been the best way to travel this inhospitable terrain. But how far away was it? We trudged along the barren ground that was strewn with loose rock, followed the eastern bed of the Wadi Qumran and continued on to the ancient water spring of Ain Feshka.

It is a forbidding land. From the pinnacle of Mount Muntar

you can see an endless parade of rolling desert. The view is a breathtaking panorama that captures a third of the width of the State of Israel — Jerusalem, Bethlehem, Jericho, the Nahal Kidron canyon, the Hurkania Valley, and off in the distance the Dead Sea. That sea was the lowest place on earth and why anyone would live around it is a mystery, but for centuries — millennia — they have and still do. Pockets of Bedouin remain, carving out meager lives for their nomadic communities of sheep, goats and the occasional camel. They are protected from the blazing sun by their crude dwellings and tents.

But men of God live here too. Over the ages some sixty-five monasteries have been built in the Judean Desert, though only five remained. The most spectacular one is Greek Orthodox, and it's built right into the desert rock with beautiful stairways and a dome of blue serving as a stark contrast to the surrounding desolation.

It is a simple land of heat, rock and sand, and little else. But just the same, the stark beauty that abounds here possesses an element that soothes the soul. The desert, so devoid of distraction, puts the mind at ease while testing the very limits of the human body. The many wadis — dried-up river beds that speak of an earlier time of rushing waters — are reminders of the unexplained giving and taking of the Lord.

"They say it is just a little farther," said Robbie reassuringly.

"Where are they taking us?" I asked him. "All the way to Masada?"

My thoughts raced back to the fall of 1963 and the first excavations on the great rock fortress standing high above the shore of the Dead Sea. Masada. It was the last stronghold of Jewish zealots who had fiercely resisted Roman forces after the revolt of 66 A.D. Those Jews held out for seven years against the full brunt of Imperial Rome until they could defend themselves no more, but rather than surrender to pagan conquerors, they chose to take their own lives. A mass suicide of nine hundred and sixty men, women and children.

It had long stuck in my memory and not only because of the three-tiered palace of King Herod or the great collection of first-century Jewish and Roman coinage that was found, but because it was the first time my son joined me on a dig. He was only three, an innocent little boy with golden locks who was fascinated by all the climbing he could do amid the ruins. I had brought him then because I figured it wasn't too early to start learning something about the indomitable human spirit.

Finally, the two Bedouin stopped and pointed. The one who had found it started jabbering away in his native Arabic before clasping his hands together and falling in a heap onto the sands of the desert. Facing Mecca.

"They say it is just another hundred meters or so just beyond those rocks over there," said Robbie. "They do not want to go any closer. They are afraid of evil spirits."

I shook my head in disgust. Without fail, whenever I found anything important in the Middle East, there were always religious overtones laden with the fear of God. It didn't matter if it was Jews, the Arabs or even the Christians. This was holy territory and disturbing its sleep could arouse the wrath of the omnipotent One.

"If there are any evil spirits around this thing it couldn't be very old," I said.

Even on a November afternoon, it doesn't take long for the sweltering heat of the desert to drain the fluids from a man's body. Every few minutes we had to stop and drink. A long plastic bottle of water is a burden to carry in the desert, but smaller bottles don't last since you can down their contents in a single gulp. Water is precious in the exposed Judean wilderness — and a hat, of course. Without either of them you would be in serious trouble.

I didn't see it at first. There were only open spaces of desert sand interspersed with rocks. The caves weren't far off and here at the edge of the desert the first of the rock formations were easy to discern. I had to be careful for this was the natural habitat of the vipers and scorpions spoken of in scripture. Scorpions especially were ghastly creatures that I had long dreaded.

"Well where is it?" I asked, my breath growing short in the unbearable heat. "Are you sure they meant over here?"

Robbie nodded. "That is what they said. Around here somewhere. They said it was surrounded by darkness."

I looked up and absorbed the radiance of the mid-afternoon desert sun beating against my skin. "Surrounded by darkness? What's that supposed to mean?"

I soon found out. I didn't see it until I was almost upon it and even then I wasn't sure. From a distance what appeared to be a wall of black were only the shadows from a prominent ridge of rock. Just behind the ridge was a hole in the ground. It would have been easy to miss. I stopped, looked from side to side and took a few cautious steps. Then I saw it.

"My God!" I exclaimed.

Robbie's mouth just hung ajar.

It wasn't in a cave or even by a cave. But it was a grave, a shallow one, and there was no royalty buried here for this was no Valley of the Kings. It was six feet long and dug three feet into the sand. The body was on its back with the head tilted to the side, the hands crossed over the abdomen and wrapped in what seemed to be a very old and very dried animal skin. It *was* a mummy, the state of preservation incredible. I had never seen anything like it before. This was no skeleton lying in the grave.

It was a man.

The body was long and slender, and the animal skin had been disturbed, probably by the Bedouin, but it was a human being. With flesh. The skin, dried like that of a prune, encased the bones as if it were an elastic drawn taut. I looked closer and could make out individual pores on the face. Even the hair and fingernails were intact.

A numbing chill took hold of me, ignoring the desert heat that immersed us. I had seen corpses before — lots of them and some much older than this specimen — but there was something different about this one and it wasn't only the state of preservation, however remarkable that was. It was the look. The face. So sensual. Like a work of art. Soft and tender with perfectly chiselled features.

I could hear — feel — my heart throbbing inside my breast like a hammer pounding against a steel anvil. I looked into Robbie's eyes, then back to the two Bedouin who had rolled themselves into two human balls and were now chanting prayers to Allah, their ageless song casting a spell that filled the air.

"Robbie, what do you think?"

He shook his head and said nothing.

I dropped to my knees and gazed over our find. My hands made a sweeping gesture as if to behold a treasure that only a scientist could appreciate. Slowly, ever so slowly, my eyes searched up and down the body. I could tell right away that it was of great worth. Only once before had I seen a man so perfectly preserved and that too was courtesy of the hot dry sand. He was an ancient Egyptian who had stood the scientific world on its ear. He was also buried in a shallow desert grave, rolled up on his side in the fetal position and surrounded by pottery and flint knives from 3200 B.C., which made him *five thousand years old.*

But there was no pottery in this grave. There was nothing and that was strange, for the ancients — whoever these ancients were — always buried relics of the deceased with the body. Pottery. Weapons. Coins. Jewelry. Something. Anything. But there was nothing. This was a different find. A mystery.

The Judean wilderness isn't a likely place for an Egyptian mummy, so I figured it must be from a later era. But when? Then I noticed the hands. They looked so alive that I half-expected them to start moving. The fingers were slender and bony with long narrow nails. I took one of the hands in mine and felt the coarse texture of its skin. I wondered how many years, how many centuries, had passed since it was last touched by a human being. I examined the other hand, the left foot and then the right. Suddenly, a feeling of pure horror came over me and I gasped out loud.

"Professor Marr. What is wrong? What is the matter?"

Fear. Numbing fear. The kind that stills the blood. But I couldn't let go of the body. One of its raw hands was still hanging on to me, the fingers clasping mine as if possessing a life of their own. For a moment I thought I was in the presence of someone who was *alive*. Then my fingers relaxed and the solitary hand dropped to the sand in a gentle thud. I turned my head and stared off into space. Unblinking. Robbie would tell me later that I had a blank look on my face. Like stone.

"Professor Marr? Are you all right?"

"Another *Jehohanan*," I said.

"What did you say?"

"Only it's not *Jehohanan*."

"What are you talking about?"

Slowly. Mechanically. I got to my feet, emptied the scorching air from my lungs and looked across the infinite desert. This desert that has seen so much. It was a world unto itself, untouched by man, the elements or time, its naked beauty shrouded in mystery and echoed in the whispering wind. This primitive desert was forever.

My clothes, my entire body, were drenched in sweat, but I felt nothing. I was oblivious to the parched air passing through my lungs and the steam pouring from my mouth.

"Professor Marr, are you all right?"

"I've never seen anything like ... this ... before," I said to no one in particular. "We have to move it ... we have to study it ..."

"What? What is it?" said Robbie.

"It's from the Roman period," I said, my thoughts lost in the desert.

"How do you know?"

"I'm only guessing ... we have to analyze everything ... the skins it was wrapped in ... the cloth ... maybe a tissue sample ..."

"But why the Romans?"

I didn't hear him. My senses were still imprisoned by the emptiness and desolation about me. I felt so small and meaningless in this massive sea of nothing. There was only the soft breeze flowing over the frozen dunes. Finally, I broke the spell and looked into Robbie's eyes. I didn't want to say anything, not until I was absolutely sure. But I was a scientist, an expert, and knew about these things. In my own mind I was already sure.

"Robbie," I whispered.

"Yes Professor Marr?"

"I know how this man died."

"How?"

"He was crucified."

CHAPTER TWO

TWO

I knew this was no Lindow Man or hunter from the Bronze Age. The Lindow Man was a two-thousand-year-old mummy that had been found in a pool of peat bog in England. He was a spectacular discovery. His astonishing state of preservation was due to the absence of oxygen and acidity in the peat, and he had been the victim of a ritual murder. His throat had been cut and he'd received two blows to the head — that was clear from the skull fractures — but an even more startling find was the hunter who had been discovered in a melting glacier in the Alps. Otzi he was called. He had been found a few short years after we came across our desert mummy. He had been frozen in time for thousands of years, partly submerged in ice with his quiver of arrows, his axe, his sandals and his fur-lined leather clothing. When I first read about him I thought immediately of what we had found at Qumran, but the body buried in the sand near the Dead Sea wasn't really anything like Otzi. There were more similarities to 'Ginger,' the preserved man who also came to mind when I first laid my eyes on the Qumran mummy.

He was called 'Ginger' because of the color of his hair and he was an ancient Egyptian from the pre-dynastic period, which meant some time before 3200 B.C. He was perfectly preserved right down to the toenails and fingernails, and though his body had shrunk somewhat he was much more than a skeleton. There was no mystery as to why he had survived. He had been carefully wrapped in skins and buried in a shallow desert grave. The sand had absorbed the water from his body and preserved his remains.

Whoever buried Ginger prepared him well with flint knives and pottery to be used for the storage of food and drink during his journey to the next life. The ancient Egyptians believed that his spirit — his *Ka* — would be released at the time of death and then he would achieve what every man yearned for.

Immortality.

Was there a *Ka* with this one as well? I didn't know, but I did know it was the grave of a pauper. It had to be. There wasn't a sign of wealth or social status anywhere on the body or in the grave, for that matter. But even if he was a pauper it was obvious someone wanted to protect him from the passage of time. And what about the crucifixion if, in fact, he had been crucified?

I knew about crucifixion. As an expert on Roman history I was well acquainted with this ancient practice, a common form of execution reserved for recaptured fugitive slaves, army deserters, thieves and terrorists. It was a brutal way to kill someone, a slow agonizing death. Like all rulers through the ages the Romans used torture to extract confessions or issue warnings, but they never crucified their own. That was too demeaning. A Roman sentenced to death was beheaded, which was a far more dignified way to die. Even for a criminal.

Many civilizations practiced crucifixion — the Scythians, Persians, Phoenicians, Carthaginians — and all of them long before the Romans ever appeared. But the Romans were the masters. They crucified more victims than all their predecessors combined.

So this man was no Roman, but lived during the Roman Empire. The evidence was on his body. Those appalling wounds in the wrists and feet. They were little more than blackened holes now, but holes they were with dried blood all around them and the right size for a spike. What else but crucifixion could result in such wounds?

The Romans ruled this area for hundreds of years and

crucified so many insurgents that an official count was impossible. In one fell swoop they had lined both sides of the Appian Way with thousands of crucified slaves who had made the mistake of following Spartacus in his uprising against the Roman army. Another time, just outside Jerusalem, more than two thousand Jews were crucified under Varus, the Roman governor of Syria who had grown tired of their rioting. But no one had ever found the mummified remains of a crucified man before.

We didn't have much time and I was deathly worried about the Bedouin. They had been a nuisance when the Dead Sea Scrolls were discovered. They had taken the larger pieces and sold them in the marketplace for cash. Countless scrolls and fragments were lost. I didn't want that to happen now, so I had to work quickly. I drew a simple sketch of the grave with all its contents, which wasn't easy keeping one eye on the Bedouin. I trusted them as much as they trusted me. If only one enterprising tribesman decided to rip off the loincloth or pluck a few strands of hair or even a fingernail, and then gained money for his efforts, all would be lost and this find would quickly degenerate into a dog's breakfast. The mummy would be ruined. But for a few shekels they agreed to loan us a pickup truck with enough room in the back for a body.

Robbie and I waited for night to fall before bringing the mummy to the Hebrew University in Jerusalem where I taught. The university was high on the hill of Mount Scopus overlooking the Old City of Jerusalem. It was a city built on mistrust and we had to move in secret. How could we explain moving a preserved human corpse wrapped in animal skins across the occupied West Bank? The Israeli Defence Forces were everywhere. Somehow we managed to reach the university without being detected, but then another problem surfaced. The night watchman was at his desk inside the entrance. He asked why I was there at such an hour.

"I found a skeleton," I said. "Or part of a skeleton. Nothing unusual but I think it might have some archeological value."

"A skeleton?"

"Yes."

"An old one?"

"I think so. We don't know yet."

"Sign it in. You have the whole wing to yourself. No one is here. Just Professor Shimron."

That wasn't good. Eliraz Shimron was another professor of archeology who had employed Robbie until I offered him a few shekels more. She was an ambitious woman with boundless curiosity who insisted on knowing everyone's business. And she usually did.

"Then I have a problem," I said. "I don't want her to find out about this. Especially her."

"No?"

"Can I tell you a secret?" The night watchman nodded. "Professor Shimron and I have a little wager going. You see ... we're always trying to outdo each other … with discoveries I mean. We want to see who can find the most ... relics ... things like that ... and we're tied."

"Tied?"

"We have the same number. Of discoveries. But this skeleton I found puts me ahead. Only I have to study it first and I want to do that without her finding out."

"I see."

"It's a little game we play. Silly but we do it. Do you think maybe we can forget about signing it in? I don't want to leave any traces." He hesitated. "Tell you what. Just to show how appreciative I am, if this turns out to be something important I'll name it after *you*. What's your name?"

"Shlomo."

"Every find has a name and this one will be called Shlomo. Shlomo the skeleton. Who knows? I might even write a paper on it."

"Won't people wonder why you named it that?"

"I can name it whatever I want. Shlomo it is."

I winked at the night watchman who was full of smug satisfaction at his new status. He smiled at us, which Robbie and I took as an opportunity to go about our business. We wheeled the body-laden stretcher through two sets of double doors and then down a long narrow corridor, carefully avoiding the hall leading to Eliraz's office. All the other offices were closed and the lights off but for the solitary bulbs hanging overhead. It felt like a hospital emergency ward in the dead of night. But quiet. It was off hours and no one was around, but that made little difference to Robbie who kept glancing over his shoulder this way and that. After what seemed an eternity we got to my lab. We wheeled the stretcher inside and then I shut the doors and fastened the lock. We stood there staring at each other. Finally, Robbie spoke.

"I feel like we stole something," he said.

"Maybe from history we did, Robbie. But someone would have found it sooner or later. Good thing it was us."

I knew what would happen if this discovery got into the hands of someone else. It had happened with every major archeological find up for grabs in this region, and all because of the in-fighting that would arise from a mummified and apparently crucified corpse found in Qumran. First, the Israelis and Jordanians would claim it for themselves and then the university's lone research assistant of Palestinian extraction would say it belonged to her people. And then others connected to governments in Syria, Egypt or Lebanon would say the mummy had been tampered with and moved from its original burial place on their soil. Indeed, if anyone in Lebanon got wind of this, a powder keg could easily erupt with Shia Muslims, Sunni Muslims and Christians all getting into the act, and it would get very ugly as things usually do in this part of the world.

We removed the white cloak we had applied earlier in the desert and pried open the skin wrappings. There it was. There *he* was. We could do precious little but stare at the body in wonder and awe. Robbie studied the holes and dried blood on the wrists and feet.

"Professor Marr," he said.

I waved my hand to stop him. I didn't want to talk. I didn't even want to think. I only wanted to clear my mind and look at the facts, so I started examining the left wrist since that was the most obvious sign of a wound. I had never seen the mummified remains of a crucified man before. No one had.

"Robbie, you see this hole in the middle of the wrist? Right between the bones?" He nodded. "This is how I know it was the Romans."

"What do you mean?"

"They would place the hand of their victim on the wood and spread the fingers apart. The spike would penetrate the flesh but not the bones and that's exactly where this wound is." I looked at the other wrist. "Same thing here." I walked to the end of the table and inspected the feet. "You see this?"

Robbie leaned over, but wouldn't touch the body. I didn't know if it was because of fear or respect for the dead and I thought in some ways he wasn't much different from the Bedouin.

"There's a wound here right between the second and third toes but it's up towards the middle of the foot where the bones start to separate. Again no bones seem to be broken. That's how the Romans did their crucifixions."

Robbie turned his head away. He didn't want to look. "I thought they banged the nails right through the bones," he said, staring at the floor.

"No. There's a little spot in the bony part of the wrist. If the hand is flattened and spread out a nail can go clear through without hitting a bone. That way the hand is nailed securely to the wood and then the skin and flesh begin to tear and rip and soon the body can't be supported at all."

"But why?" he asked, still looking away. "Why did they do it like that?"

The answer was frighteningly simple.

"To maximize the suffering of the victim. The pain is ... unbearable."

"But I thought the nails went through the hands. Not the wrists."

"No it was the wrist and look, Robbie. You see the thumbs? See how they curl under the other fingers?" He allowed himself a glance. "There's a reason for that. When the nail penetrates the wrist it cuts right into a nerve. The pain is excruciating and it makes the thumbs fold into the palms. Just like we have here."

Sure enough, the hands were closed and crossed over the abdomen, the thumbs curled inward. Robbie turned to me and began to speak, nothing more than a whisper, so softly I could barely hear him.

"Professor Marr, I think we made a mistake. We are disturbing the dead. I think we should return … this … to Qumran and not tell anyone."

"You're not serious?" I said.

"Yes. I think we are making a mistake."

"But Robbie ..."

He shook his head from side to side. He was agitated in a way I had never seen before. I put my hand on his shoulder.

"You're forgetting something," I said. "We're archeologists, Robbie. Scientists. This is our job. We've got to ask questions and learn what we can. But first we have to clear our heads. We have to forget about folklore. About mythology. About God."

Robbie wasn't satisfied. "This is the Holy Land, Professor Marr. You cannot forget about God here. I have lived here all my life and if you have found something ... anything ... you will have to answer to many people."

I liked Robbie. He had been working with me for a few weeks by this time, and what had attracted me was his intelligence and keen desire to learn. But he had a good point. You can't divorce science from religion in the Middle East. It wasn't possible. There was too much history and too much pent-up emotion for that.

"Robbie, I hear what you're saying but there's no way I'm taking this back. I'm going to find out everything I can about this man. I have to. I am driven to."

"Driven?"

Robbie's English was good, but like many Israelis, even well-educated ones, he didn't pick up on many words, never mind the more subtle nuances and idioms of the language. Another thing about the way he talked was that he never used contractions, absolutely never, which gave his speech a slow and stilted pace. That was unlike most Israelis I knew. I found them to be a loud and emotional people. About everything.

"What I mean is we have no choice. Look, Robbie. Think of life as a puzzle. Sometimes we find a few pieces to put together. If we're lucky they fit and then again they might not. But at least we have to try to place them. We're scientists. Archeologists. We ask questions. Then we seek answers. If we don't, who will?"

Poor Robbie was breaking into a cold sweat.

"Settle down," I said. "Get hold of yourself. It'll be all right. Now look. This is what I want to do. I'm going to make a small incision."

"An incision?"

"Let me finish. I need a sample for carbon 14. I want to have it examined. But I don't want anyone else to know. Well maybe one person. A good friend of mine. He's Egyptian. A pathologist in Alexandria. The best one I know. I can trust him. Are you all right?"

Robbie was pale. He allowed himself a glance at the mummy. The wounds made him uneasy.

"Think of it this way," I said. "We'll have a Jew, a Muslim and a Christian all working together on this. Now what could be fairer than that?"

"And who is the Christian, Professor Marr? You?"

That made me chuckle. We both knew what a religious cynic I was and then — it was because of the intensity of the moment — the two of us suddenly burst into robust laughter. It was infectious, but didn't last long. When it subsided, Robbie still looked afraid. And what about me? Was I afraid? For his sake I pretended not to be and I would just go on pretending. But at least we could smile now and more than that we could sense a synergy operating between us. That was good. It was very good. We would need it.

CHAPTER THREE
THREE

Jamil Hassad was a man who did not look wanting for food. The head of pathological science at the University of Alexandria, he was a dear and trusted colleague of mine. We had kept in touch ever since our paths first crossed during the investigation of Egypt's Royal Mummies in the late '60s. He was a barrel-chested man with a generous mid-section. His skin was dark, darker than Robbie's even, and his hair as black as a night sky over the empty Sahara. His teeth were large and square, and conspicuous for the gaps between them. When he smiled the result was gleaming white ivory broken by lines that looked like shadows. It was a warm smile, but behind it was mystery and Jamil wore that mystery well.

He was a consummate professional who split his time between the university and the biggest hospital in Alexandria. He was also an Egyptologist whose interest in history had been piqued when he was asked to perform an invaluable medical service and examine the mummified remains of the pharaohs. The tombs of Ramesses II, Tuthmosis IV, Amenhotep I and others had been found in the Valley of the Kings just west of that great bend in the Nile not far from Luxor, the ancient city of Thebes. Jamil was a native Egyptian and proud of his heritage. When he studied the mummies of the pharaohs he wasn't merely lending his expertise to an archeological mission, but delving into his own lineage.

"Jamil, how good to see you!" I said, greeting him at the door to my office. It had been a long time.

"David, my good friend. How are you? You look weary."

Jamil's handshake was the first sign of his great strength. It was firm almost to the point of inflicting pain. He would grab your hand, stretch his wide thumb across it and compress your flesh as if it were in a vice. His voice was another sign of power. It was a deep voice that reached out and captured you. You were its prey.

"How is your wife Gita?" he asked. "Is she well?"

"She's fine, thank you. She's away at a conference right now but will be back in a few days."

"I trust you and Robbie got well acquainted in your drive from Ben Gurion," I said.

"Yes David, you have chosen well. He is a fine young man."

Robbie basked in the adulation.

"It must be three or four years since we've seen each other," Jamil said.

"I'm afraid so."

"When you called I knew it had to be something important. I don't get invitations to Israel every day."

"It *is* important. Very."

Jamil carried a small black briefcase that looked like the bag of a doctor on call and that's what he was. A physician. A specialist. On call. He placed his briefcase on the floor and took a seat. Robbie, always quick to observe those little niceties that demonstrate respect and courtesy for his superiors, remained on his feet.

"So David," said Jamil, "just what is it that brings me here? You said something about a discovery. Highly confidential. Near the Dead Sea. It sounds very intriguing."

That was a word that suited Jamil well. Intriguing. I told Robbie to shut the door.

"Jamil, I don't know how to begin. We ... Robbie and I ... found a mummy. It's not as old as the pharaohs you and I worked on but it's unique. We found it near Qumran. Not far from the caves."

Jamil was immediately aroused. He leaned over, his powerful hands clasped one another tight and he propped himself up on his elbows. "Tell me more," he said.

"It was the Bedouin who found it and when I saw it, well, I could barely believe my eyes. I've never seen anything like this before. There wasn't much time. We had to move it right away so we smuggled it to the university. In secret I'm afraid. It's in my lab now."

"But why did you have to smuggle it? Couldn't your university get permission to retrieve it?"

"No. I couldn't take a chance with the administration people. You see because of what it is and where we found it governments would get involved. Israel. Jordan. Maybe others. I didn't want that to happen."

"So what exactly have you found, David?"

"Well ... I was pretty sure when I saw it that it ... it ..."

"It what?"

I cleared my throat and searched for the words. "It didn't take me long to determine the cause of death."

"Which was?"

I hesitated.

"Cru-ci-fi-xion."

Jamil was transfixed. He opened his mouth and raised his eyebrows, and I noticed that one of them was higher than the other. "Crucifixion?" he said.

"Yes."

"A crucified mummy?"

"That's right."

"Are you sure?"

"Positive. I've studied the Romans for many years and I know their handiwork. Believe me Jamil, this man was a victim of crucifixion. Everything matches."

"And you dated it?"

"We took a bone sample and a sample of the animal skins."

"Animal skins?"

"That's what it was wrapped in. We did two independent C14 readings and they said the same thing."

"Which was?"

"First century."

Jamil eased his wide frame into the chair and took out a cigarette. "Do you mind?" he asked, not waiting for a reply. He lit up and blew out the smoke. "I know you don't approve of my smoking, David, but I find it a good way of relaxing especially when engaged in a discussion as heavy as this one is becoming. Talk of such morbid practices as crucifixion does that to me. I see human corpses every day. But crucifixion? That is a messy business." He motioned for me to continue.

"I want to take X-rays and maybe a CAT scan. But first let me tell you what we know. I think he was an adult. Young to early middle-aged. Mind you a CAT scan would give us good cross-section pictures of the bone structure and provide conclusive evidence about the cause of death. But Jamil I have little doubt about that. There is the collapsed position of the shoulder blades. The arms. The holes in the body where the spikes went."

Jamil was enraptured. "Remarkable," he said. "If what you say is true then what you have found is truly remarkable. It is a major discovery."

"Excuse me, Dr. Hassad," said Robbie, who if not in awe was at least in some trepidation of our visitor. "This is like investigating a murder. That is what it is. A murder. And an ugly one. Professor Marr has spent time with it ... alone I mean ... and that is not a pleasant experience. There are so many wounds. It is not a pretty thing to see."

"I'm sure it isn't," said Jamil, "but David I must ask you a question. You haven't told me how it was preserved. Was it natron? Like the mummies we worked on before?"

"No. I don't think so. You see … it's not Egyptian."

"No? Then what was the dehydrating agent?"

"Sand."

"Sand?"

"Yes. It was buried in the sand. In the desert. Three feet below the surface. Remember Ginger? The pre-dynastic mummy?"

"Of course. How could I ever forget?"

"Just like that."

"But in Qumran?"

"Yes. In Qumran."

"The climate wouldn't permit such a thing. It's too damp."

"That's what I thought."

Jamil stood up as erect as a soldier and if he was a soldier he would have been an officer. He snuffed out his cigarette. "I must see this discovery of yours. I want to examine this mummy ... alone ... as you have ... then we can discuss what we have here. Unfortunately I only have this afternoon and then must return to my commitments in Alexandria. Pathology doesn't allow much free time."

We left the office, and I led my two colleagues through the maze of weaving hallways and turns in the building. The double doors to my lab were locked. I grabbed a key and checked the halls. They were empty. Thankfully. No Eliraz. I opened the doors, told Jamil and Robbie to come in, and locked up behind me. The mummy was there on a table inside a plexiglass enclosure to prevent decomposition. It was air-tight, climate-controlled, filled with nitrogen and still partly buried in the same sand we found it in. It looked like a coffin, but one you can see through. I was about to remove the white sheet I had placed on top when Jamil raised his hand.

"Wait!" he said.

He put his bag on the floor and inched his way around the table. His eyes were riveted on the sheet as if he was immersed in some religious ceremony. I knew him as a deeply spiritual man, a Muslim who was learned in the teachings of the Koran, but he had to be. He was a physician who dealt with death every day. When Jamil was satisfied, he gave me a nod and with a sweeping gesture of his arm asked me to show it to him. I took off the white sheet and he just stood there looking through the clear walls of the mummy's tomb. I let him absorb it all for a moment before removing the top of the plexiglass. Then his eyes began to feast.

"Unbelievable!" he exclaimed. "It is magnificent! It is truly magnificent!"

For the next five minutes he said nothing. He examined the mummy first from a distance and then from up close, gradually earning his way in. I watched him feel the skin in his fingertips. Lightly touching the bridge of the nose. Placing his broad thumbs over the eyelids and raising them back to reveal two holes where the eyes had been. Even the eyelashes were intact. He sniffed as if sampling his first taste of a rare wine. He touched the brow of the face, and studied the long straggly hair and beard. He placed his hands on either side of the head and looked straight into the eyes as if conversing with the dead. Robbie, a look of incomprehension on his face, shot me a glance.

He was frightened.

"This man was a Hebrew," said Jamil, unruffled.

"Are you sure?" I asked.

"Am I sure? Look at his hair. It is the style of a Hebrew. There is no doubt."

"But Hebrews do not mummify their dead," said Robbie. "It is against Jewish law."

Jamil looked at Robbie from the corner of his eye. "That is true," he said, "but did you know that many years ago Sephardic Jews would take a small piece of a mummified human body to cure their ailments? It was called *mumia* which is the Latin root of the word 'mummy'. They would pulverize it, mix it with honey water and eat it."

Robbie put his hand over his stomach and a sickened look came over his face. "Ecch," he said in disgust. "I have never heard of that."

"But it's true my young friend. This was at the time of antiquity when bitumen was widely regarded as a potent drug for curing many things. The bitumen of the Dead Sea was called *mumia* too and it was used by the Persians and even by Arabs. By the twelfth century the Sephardic Jews of Alexandria had a prosperous mummy trade going. You I take it are Ashkenazi?"

"Yes."

"I never knew that," I said, and then lightly, "and I thought you were only a pathologist."

"Ha!" said Jamil. "My work allows me to meddle in many things." He issued a sly smile. "David, do you have any classes to teach today?"

"Not this afternoon. Why?"

"Is there something you can do to busy yourself while I examine this incredible man you found? Look, you had your time alone with him and now I want mine. Just give me thirty minutes. That should be enough."

Robbie shook his head. "I would not want to be alone in here," he said.

"And you are not the pathologist," Jamil said. "I am. Only to the dead do I reveal my innermost thoughts and that's because your secrets remain secrets with them. It is a business where rumors do not spread like wildfire." He turned to me. "Not like archeology."

Jamil had assumed center stage and wasn't the least concerned about asking me to leave my own lab. But I didn't care. I was glad he was here. I had absolute faith in him. He was a man who focused himself on the task at hand and if he wanted thirty minutes he would get it. I suggested that afterward the three of us go for dinner. I asked Jamil if he liked falafel, Israeli style. He patted his ample stomach.

"I enjoy Israeli food," he said. "In fact I enjoy many types of food. That is another vice of mine. But I don't know if I'll be able to eat after this."

"I know I will not be able to eat," said Robbie.

Jamil smiled and then he herded the two of us out of the lab. The excitement and anticipation were dripping off him like water from a man's chin in the desert. He couldn't wait to begin his analysis, but in private. Just before leaving I asked him a question.

"Jamil, why did you walk around the room like that when you came in? What were you doing?"

"I was getting in touch with this man's spirit. His spirit, David. But you wouldn't understand that. Would you?"

CHAPTER FOUR

FOUR

When Robbie and I returned to my lab, Jamil was without his jacket and tie. His shirt sleeves were rolled up past his elbows, pockets of sweat had formed under his arms and his black hair was pushed back at the sides from what I imagined were the countless times he had run his fingers through it. He had to hear us come in for Robbie made a point of clearing his throat, not once, but twice, while I dragged my heels so he'd be sure to detect the noise. We found Jamil standing by the window where for the longest time he just stood gazing out to the street below.

"Jamil?" I said quietly. "Jamil?"

It was as if I was trying to wake him from a deep sleep. Finally, he turned to me and his expression was one I will never forget. Subdued. Barren. Almost without life. Then, as if a switch was turned, the color rushed to his face and he welled up with energy. Bursting raging energy. He raised his arms and bellowed with all the voice he could muster.

"Allahu-Akbar! Allahu-Akbar! Allahu-Akbar! Allahu-Akbar!"

He cried this at the top of his lungs. Four times he cried it. And then more.

"Ash-ahdu-an-la-ilaha-illahah! Ash-ahdu-an-la-ilaha-illahah!"

Jamil!" I said, but there was no stopping him. He was caught in the ancient rites of Islam. The sheer force of his words ripped right through me. I could see his body growing in mass and strength. I could see his rippling muscles tensing firm in his arms, his veins surging with blood.

"Ash-hado anna mohammaden-rasulullah! Ash-hado anna mohammaden-rasulullah!

"Hayye-alas-salah! Hayye-alas-salah!

"Hayye-alal-falah! Hayye-alal-falah!

"Allahu-Akbar! Allahu-Akbar!

"La-illah-illalah!"

When he was finished, he looked at me. Completely spent. A man who had just emptied his very soul. He reached out and embraced me in the way that a man might latch onto a son or a brother. Then he whispered into my ear.

"David, no one has ever found the mummified body of a crucified man before. And you know more about crucifixions than anyone."

I nodded.

"Consider for a moment what you have here. With this discovery."

"What do you mean?"

"David, I am a physician and a scientist but I'm also a Muslim."

"I know that."

"Then allow the Muslim to speak."

I listened.

"The Muslim in me would say that with this discovery you have vindicated the scriptures." Then he grabbed me in his arms and I tried to break free, but Jamil was too strong. "The prophets all work together, David."

"Jamil," I said. "Let me go. Please."

He eased up and I slid from his grasp.

"Don't talk to me about scriptures and prophets, Jamil."

"But David ... it says in the Koran ... 'We believe in God and in that which has been sent down on us and sent down on Abraham, Ishmael, Isaac and Jacob and the tribes, and that which was given to Moses and Jesus and the prophets of their Lord. We make no division between any of them and to him we surrender.'"

"Dr. Hassad," said Robbie meekly, "what are you talking about?"

The mere force and presence of Jamil were enough to freeze Robbie in his tracks. Robbie even wore a look of apology for having the temerity to ask Jamil a question.

"What do you think I'm talking about?" Jamil said, glaring at him.

Robbie seemed afraid to speak and then he shrank like a shrivelling flower when dusk begins to take its light. But Jamil's eyes remained fixed on him.

"Well ..." Robbie began.

"Well what?" said Jamil.

"We found a mummy."

"Yes. A mummy."

"And Professor Marr thinks it was ..."

"Yes?" Jamil said impatiently.

"Go ahead Robbie," I said, trying to encourage him. "Tell him what you think."

Robbie felt about the size of an ant. He couldn't muster the strength to say anything at all. We waited. It was a long wait and the growing silence made me uncomfortable. But not Jamil. I didn't think anything could make him uncomfortable.

"Well?" Jamil said.

"We found a mummy," Robbie said, "that would appear to date ... approximately from the time ... of the Crucifixion."

No one said anything. We all just looked at one another. Then the color returned to Jamil's face and filled his cheeks. He put his hands in front of him and took Robbie by the shoulders. Then he raised his hands again.

"*Allahu-Akbar!*" he said even louder than before.

"Dr. Hassad ..." Robbie began, but Jamil only roared those words yet again.

"Allahu-Akbar! Allahu-Akbar!"

Robbie, petrified with this display of Jamil's power, waited until the Egyptian had composed himself. "Dr. Hassad, the Romans crucified many people. Thousands of people."

"So?"

"This could be any one of them."

"Yes it could but I can see how you are a disciple of David Marr. Are you not familiar with the New Testament?"

Robbie shot him a smirk. "I have little interest in the New Testament," he said.

"Forgive me," said Jamil. "I understand but despite your prognostications about the Christian world ..."

Then he stopped.

"David," he said to me, "do you have a Bible handy?"

I had a copy of the Gideons in my office, not that I ever looked at it. But I got it for him.

"It's in English," I said. "I hope you don't mind."

Jamil smiled. He could have gone through that book in any number of languages. For a Muslim he was well read in the scriptures. All of them. He was a man who possessed the uncanny ability of knowing something about everything. In fact, he seemed to know a great deal about everything. The Bible in hand, he wiped the tip of his forefinger across his tongue before whiffing through the pages with the look of one who knows exactly what he is searching for. Then he stopped and ran his finger down the page he had selected.

"And they spit upon him and took the reed and smote him on the head." He looked straight into my eyes. "St. Matthew. Chapter twenty-seven. Verse thirty."

His voice filled every corner of my lab as if it were an echo reverberating off the walls. He would say something and I would hear the words repeated. The same words. Over and over. St. Matthew. Chapter twenty-seven. Verse thirty. St. Matthew. Chapter twenty-seven. Verse thirty. St. Matthew. Chapter twenty-seven. Verse thirty.

Robbie edged closer to me. He was uneasy with everything Jamil said and did. Jamil moved to the end of the table and pointed to the head of the mummy.

"Note the markings all over the face," he said before returning to the Bible to find the next thing he wanted. "*And they clothed him with purple and platted a crown of thorns and put it about his head.* St. Mark. Chapter fifteen. Verse seventeen."

In my mind his words were repeated again.

"These are what appear to be dried blood stains on the

forehead and around the back of the head." Back he went into the Bible and came out with another passage. "*They brake not his legs*. St. John. Chapter nineteen. Verse thirty-three. I am certain David that your CAT scan and X-rays will show no broken bones in the legs. Judging by the appearance of the body I would conclude that the legs are not broken so we would appear to have a match here too and now, let me see, yes the very next verse. *But one of the soldiers with a spear pierced his side.* St. John. Chapter nineteen. Verse thirty-four. I am sure you noted the obvious wound from some very sharp instrument in the side … right … about … here."

His fingers pointed to a dried cut in the flesh. Robbie stared at me innocently. Jamil passed through the pages yet again.

"*The other disciples therefore said unto him we have seen the Lord. But he said unto them, except I shall see in his hands ... the print of the nails.*' St. John. Chapter twenty. Verse twenty-five. The horrendous markings in the wrists and feet you have already observed, David, and you are quite right. This man was crucified. I have examined the body and that is beyond question."

For a moment there was silence. None of us said a word. It was broken by the abrupt thud of Jamil closing the holy book and the sound shook Robbie with a start. Jamil put his hand on my shoulder, a faint smile on his lips.

"I am a Muslim who worships Muhammad and I know you, David, as a religious sceptic and perhaps it is fate that you called upon me now." Jamil shook his head from side to side. "David, we are both professionals. We have known each other a long time and if I didn't come here and see this for myself I never would have believed it." He shut his eyes and said something in Arabic, and then translated for us. *"And surely they slew him not but Allah raised him unto Himself.* Surah Nisaa. Verse one fifty-seven."

"Jamil," I said.

"David, remember I speak now as a Muslim. If anyone in the Muslim community hears a word about this you will have a grave problem on your hands. They would say you found the body of a great prophet. The very one you've been looking for your whole life."

"What is he talking about?" said Robbie.

"What I'm talking about is that your instructor has come full circle. I have known him for many years and consider him my good friend but I also know he is a stubborn man which is not an endearing quality in his profession. Yet in spite of his intransigence he remains one of the great archeologists of the world. One of the great scientists of the world."

"One of the great scientists of the world?" Robbie said.

"Of course he is."

"What do you mean?"

"Just what I say. Don't you know about this man who employs you?"

"Know what?"

"About his past."

"What about his past?"

Jamil tossed me a glance. "You mean you don't know about all the things he's done?" he said. "His discoveries? His *search*?"

"His search?" said Robbie. "What search?"

Jamil threw his arm over Robbie's shoulder. "Your friend David Marr is a great man but he is also a scoundrel for not telling you about his work. And he hasn't told you, has he?"

"You are talking about his reputation?" said Robbie. "He was at the dig at Masada? And Capernaum? And he did some work on the Dead Sea Scrolls?"

"Ha! He did some work on the Dead Sea Scrolls! Why this is the man who brought the Dead Sea Scrolls to the world my young friend. If not for him they would still be in those mountain caves of Qumran along with the worms and other vermin that infest the wilderness. He was there when the first scrolls were discovered. He took those caves apart with his own hands and the discovery of that ancient papyrus was what pointed him in the direction of his life's work."

"Dr. Hassad, what are you talking about?"

Jamil looked at me, but my eyes said nothing. "It was just after World War II. When Palestine was partitioned by the United Nations. He was the first person from the West to see the scrolls. He was only a student but he was the first scholar to study them and realize how valuable they were and ever since then he's been searching. Searching for some connection to the God he has always denied. Trying to rekindle the faith he so desperately wants to believe in. Did he tell you about the Shroud of Turin or his adventures in the United Kingdom with the Holy Grail?"

Robbie shook his head.

"How can I begin? David Marr is a man who needs proof to believe in anything and he is so reluctant to believe but his work leads him to questions and these questions puzzle the living hell out of him. It all began with the Dead Sea Scrolls. They intrigued him because he realized people actually sat down and wrote the books of the Old Testament. They were *real*. Then there was the story of Christ's chalice, supposedly a myth from the Crusades, but a lot of blood has been spilled over a myth. Do you know he actually held what is alleged to be the Holy Grail in his own hands? And the shroud. When it was finally unveiled in Turin David was one of the scientists on the investigation team and he played a key part in that investigation. But now he can deny himself no longer for his life has come full circle. Hasn't it, David?"

I looked at Robbie with apology in my eyes. But my words were directed to Jamil.

"Jamil," I said, "Robbie is right. The Romans crucified thousands of people. People who were whipped and beaten before they would bear the cross."

"I have noted the marks on the body," Jamil said.

"Yes but the biblical Crucifixion wasn't unique. There is still a possibility … a strong possibility … that this man was a slave. Or a Nubian."

He dismissed this with a wave of his hand. "David, you toy with me. This man was a Hebrew. You have dated the body to the first century. Don't tell me about slaves and Nubians." He came closer and whispered into my ear. "Surely you realize that many learned men would claim this to be the body of a prophet. A descendant of King David who himself was descended from Abraham. A forerunner of Muhammad. A messenger from God!"

I threw up my hands in disgust. "God," I said. "Listen, I've been cursed with God my whole life. He always gets in the way of my work."

"David, you cannot deny Him. Just gaze upon this incredible

find of yours. There are voices out there ... a great many of them ... who would call this the very proof you've been looking for."

"Proof? What proof?"

"Everything matches with the scriptures."

"If everything matches with the scriptures, Jamil, then there is only one conclusion. It's a fraud just like countless other frauds through the ages. This is no different."

"But have you asked yourself this question? Why would anyone want to preserve the body of a common slave or a Nubian from two thousand years ago? It wasn't custom. It wasn't custom for the people of the time. Someone wanted to preserve this man or they wouldn't have taken the time to bury him in the sand. They knew what they were doing and they wanted him to be found and now he has. David, this is no simple matter and you delude yourself if you think it is. A moment ago you witnessed the reaction of Jamil Hassad the Muslim and now you will witness that of Jamil Hassad the pathologist. I cannot begin to tell you how secret this must be. For your own good. Why, if anyone finds out about this there's no telling what they would do."

"Who are you talking about?" I said.

He put his hand on my shoulder.

"All you have to do is study history. Christians can be a fanatical lot and the Jews too." He looked at Robbie. "Even more so I'm afraid. And the Muslims ..." He sighed. "My own people are the most obstinate, the most subservient and the most fanatical of them all. Have you considered what would happen if any of them found out about this?"

I shook my head. There hadn't been time to think about it.

"Look," he said. "What if the Jews find out? Then the State of Israel finds out and it would respond in due course but at least it would be a response from a government so things wouldn't move too quickly. I assure you though the Department of Antiquities would want to see what you have here. Now what if the Muslims find out? Any Muslims. Then it would be an unorganized response, a religious response which is much more dangerous. Then there is the matter of the Christian authorities."

"Christian authorities?"

Jamil thought for a moment, his hand resting on his chin. "It is one thing keeping this from governments but quite another keeping it from the Church. It has spies everywhere."

"What do you mean the Church?"

"The Vatican."

"The Vatican," I said. "An institution of higher learning."

"David, don't tease me. Don't you remember when we worked on the pharaohs? There were many people who didn't want us to research anything at all. They were content with history and had no desire to look into it and question the record. You will find such people in the Christian community and in the Jewish community and in the Muslim community. I guarantee it. You have to be careful. This is the Holy Land. Remember? There are extremists running around. Lots of them."

He looked at me with that unyielding face of his, a face that would intimidate anyone with its undaunted conviction. Again, he put his hand on my shoulder, and shook his head back and forth.

"When I think what you have found. What you have found! It's a discovery that could have repercussions through the world. But I must warn you. I must warn you because you are my friend. Tell no one about this. Absolutely no one! Not a soul."

"What about the Bedouin?" I said.

"Don't worry about the Bedouin. They are the least of our fears. They are a people who are afraid of their own shadow. But you and Robbie must remain quiet. For your own safety. Something as important as this must be dealt with the right way or it would be nothing short of disaster."

With that he stopped and looked right into me.

"David, you worked in Qumran a long time ago. You were in those caves and you found many things there. Important things. And not everyone liked what you found. Did they? Those scrolls upset a lot of people. But now … with this … why there is no telling what we can learn. I only pray that Muhammad watches over us. *Allahu-Akbar.*"

CHAPTER FIVE

FIVE

Palestine, 1947

Muhammad adh-Dhib was a young Taamireh Bedouin whose name meant 'the wolf.' It was late winter, the air was cold and the cheap leather sandals on his feet didn't cover his toes, but an old jacket shielded his shoulders and back from the wind. A white headdress was draped around his head and the only disarming thing about him was the long knife under his belt. He had been minding his goats in the foothills of the Judean plateau when one of them strayed near a cliff not far from the Dead Sea. The animal picked its way up the scarred rock face that erupted from the ground like an old skeleton yellowed with age. Up near the top about twenty feet high was a hole big enough for a man to enter. He called after his goat, but it continued on its way, stuck its head into the black opening and ventured inside. He hollered, but the goat disappeared.

Keeping one eye on his flock, he gave chase. It took a few minutes for him to climb the same rock face that the nimble goat had mastered in seconds. At the mouth of the cave he called for it again, but saw nothing, so he picked up a stone and threw it into the cave. There was a loud SPLUNK. That wasn't the dead sound of rock on rock, but more like metal. He walked in. It was dark. He called out to another shepherd to join him. They were the first people to set foot in this cave in two thousand years.

Inside were tall clay jars with cracks all over them and on the top heavy round lids. Muhammad the Wolf placed his hands around the edge of one of the lids and turned it. He lifted off the top and the odor that came from the jar made him cover his nose. He put his hands inside only to find deep in the jar scrolls of leather wrapped in linen cloth. They were brittle at the ends. Partly decomposed. The two Bedouin carried the scrolls outside the cave and unrolled them. They discovered manuscripts written in a hand they didn't know. Perhaps it was something of value, they thought, and commodities of value were important for they were contrabanders who smuggled goats, sheep and other goods into Palestine from Transjordan. They had been on their way to Bethlehem to sell their wares on the black market and had brought their herd of goats to the ancient water spring of Ain Feshka.

They opened more jars, took what scrolls they could and showed them to a merchant in Bethlehem who pronounced them worthless. After being refused a sale by three other merchants, they found their way to a businessman who said he would buy a few scrolls for twenty pounds. It was Saturday, the day of the weekly market in Bethlehem. Seven days later the two Bedouin were back with more scrolls to sell.

Word got around that something had been unearthed from a cave near Qumran and when the young student of Middle Eastern antiquities heard about it he was aroused. David Marr was in Palestine for the first time and it didn't take him long to fall in love with this ancient turbulent land. His knowledge of Arabic was non-existent but for a few essential words and phrases. *Baksheesh* was the most important word of all.

His thick brown hair and full beard fit the erudite look of a student. He had chosen to focus his studies on the Middle East, that old tormented land where for some reason unknown to him God had shown himself through the ages. It didn't take long while trekking through the barren rock-hewn monotony of the wilderness around the Dead Sea to see why God had been manifested here. The region was a rugged landscape devoid of color. An unending mass of rock with jagged hills, sparse vegetation and little water for sustenance.

The ancient Hebrews called it *jeshimon*, which meant 'desolation' and *tsia*, which meant 'wasteland'. It was a lifeless world if not for the birds of prey, snakes and scorpions. Another student, a Jewish girl from New York, was always telling him the correct Hebrew words for everything and she summed it up well when she said, "Nothing but monotheism could come from such a place."

Gita Levitt had a way with words. She wore her straight, dark hair parted in the middle, hanging well below her shoulders. She came only to his chin. Her skin was soft, she had striking hazel eyes and the figure of a goddess. She and David were both studying at the Hebrew University. Like David, she wanted to be an archeologist and like David she was drawn to the Middle East, but as an American Jewess she felt a yearning for the land that was above the purely curious and intellectual magnet that had attracted him.

"Palestine is the land of my people," she told him, "and one day we will return. Next year in Jerusalem is a lot closer than you think."

The first trip they took together was to the oasis of Ein Gedi. They bathed in its crystal waters that were said to possess qualities of healing. The sparkling spring-fed waterfall delivered an exhilarating taste of comfort. Ein Gedi had been providing such pleasure to weary travellers since ancient times. It was here where David first relished the spectacle of near naked women frolicking in the latest bathing-suit phenomenon known as the bikini. It was two years after the defeat of the Nazis and their Axis partners. None of the women in bikinis did the style any justice, but Gita was different. David imagined how such a sparse fabric would cling to the curves of her body. It was at Ein Gedi where they heard of the scrolls.

They immediately contacted their teachers at the university. Then, in the roundabout way that investigators must often wade before locating someone who can offer assistance, they were led to the tribe of Bedouin shepherds. The shepherds were busy building what market they could in the ancient scripture trade, but Gita didn't want to approach them. They were Arabs and she didn't trust them. That didn't bother David and when he offered five pounds to one who claimed to know Muhammad the Wolf personally, he had his guide.

The guide took them along a dusty road with the remains of buildings that had been damaged in skirmishes. Jerusalem, not far to the west, was on the verge of exploding as Arabs and Jews were jealously guarding their areas. The Jewish quarter was under martial law and violence had already spilled throughout the region.

In the descent to the Dead Sea they could feel the throbbing pressure in their eardrums as the ground dropped to four hundred meters below sea level. The lowest place on earth. Gita, constantly sticking her fingers in her ears to alleviate the discomfort, mentioned the Roman Emperor Vespasian and how he once ordered members of his Tenth Legion — and only those men who couldn't swim — to be thrown into the waters of the sea with their hands tied behind their backs so he could see them rise to the surface. Gita knew her biblical lore. She pointed out Mount Nebo, the hill where Moses had rescued his people from Egypt only to wander forty years in the desert. The history of the area absorbed them both and then they saw something emerge from under a rock. It gave Gita a start and she uttered a sharp cry.

It was a scorpion and for something so small it aroused great fear. The creature looked almost plastic and was so lifeless it didn't seem real, but then it raised two pincers and began its slow methodical movement. It created the same kind of shivering sensation one gets when thinking of insects crawling all over the skin. Gita whispered into David's ear about "the great and terrible wilderness with its fiery serpents and scorpions."

"What are you talking about?" David asked her.

"Deuteronomy," she said.

The Bedouin told them to stop talking and reached for his gun. All the Arabs had guns. The scorpion's deadly pincers were in front of its body ready for battle, so the Bedouin inched his way to this ancient dweller of the desert. Instinctively, the scorpion raised its tail up over its body, poised for attack, the sting with the killer poison in the tip. Then the Bedouin stomped it into the ground with his boot before firing a resounding blast into the hapless thing.

David and Gita looked at each other uncertainly as the sound of the gunshot reverberated across the desert.

Unruffled by the encounter with the scorpion, the Bedouin spoke as much English as they did Arabic. Then he led them away from the road toward the cliffs where the scrolls had been found. It was late in the afternoon.

For the benefit of their guide, David banged his hands on his pockets and said 'baksheesh.' He pointed in the direction of Jerusalem where he was living, brought his hands together and then stretched them wide apart over his head. "More baksheesh," he said. "You take us to caves. More baksheesh for you."

The Bedouin, a young shepherd who spent more time doing business in the black markets of Bethlehem and other towns than he did grazing sheep and goats, got the picture. He motioned to the cliff just ahead and started jabbering away in Arabic. David nodded, pretending to understand, figuring he had him on side now with the offer of more money. Then he and Gita followed the guide up the wall of craggy rock to the same hole where Muhammad the Wolf, something of a legend now among the local Arab tribes, had chased after his goat. David helped Gita up the last step to the front of the cave and they walked in. They didn't take ten steps when they saw a pair of clay jars two feet high and ten inches in diameter. The tops were missing.

The Bedouin said something. David feigned comprehension, pulled out his flashlight and went deeper into the cave. It wasn't long before he saw an old Roman coin on the ground with a prominent 'X' stamped on the surface.

"Gita! Look at this!" he said excitedly. "This must be from that Tenth Legion you were talking about. And look over here!"

He picked up three more coins and wiped them off. Each one was stamped with the Latin words *'Judea Capta'*. He showed them to Gita.

"Judea captured," she said, subdued. "That would put them in the reign of Titus some time after 79 A.D."

David looked at the coins and thought about them being two thousand years old and he wanted to scream with euphoria at the enormity of such a discovery. But her eyes wore only sorrow.

Judea capta, he thought, and he could tell that deep within her beauty she carried the torment and anguish of her people.

"I feel strange here," she said, gazing at the walls of the cave. "It's like a part of me has been here for a long time. But I've never been here before. Weird isn't it? *Judea capta*."

David learned a lesson just then that he would carry with him for the rest of his life. It had to do with history and the fact people do not forget suffering and misery. Even through the centuries.

"I'm glad you brought me here," Gita said. "I feel a part of this place. Like I belong here. In this cave. With these old coins."

David thought he understood. "Let's see what else we can find," he said.

The deeper they went the more they learned of the people who had lived in the cave. It was undisturbed. Untouched. Everything left in the very place where it was dropped. There were ancient picks and javelins tarnished with age. There were chisels, buttons, needles, combs and simple trinkets that looked older than anything Roman. One of them was a small piece of flint. David wiped it with his thumb before blowing away a thick layer of powdery dust.

"This is bronze," he said. "It's a flint knife. It must be from the Bronze Age. That would make it from 3,000 or 4,000 B.C."

The Bedouin pointed to the side where there were lots of fragments of manuscripts and potsherds. David aimed his flashlight, rushed to the edge of the cave and fell to his knees. Some of the fragments were so small they had only one or two characters on them, but others were six and seven inches long, and appeared to carry the remnants of wide columns of writing.

"This is Hebrew!" Gita exclaimed.

They found more manuscripts. David was crawling on his hands and knees to even more startling discoveries. Pieces of manuscripts were everywhere. There were almost complete pages of them, everything written in the same ancient Hebrew.

"Can you read any of this?" David asked her.

"No," she said. "It's different from modern Hebrew but there are people who can. Do you think we can grab a few pieces?"

David was already lining his pockets with fragments, searching for larger pieces. He didn't have to look long. Inside the third jar was a scroll. He unravelled it. It was almost six inches wide and a foot long. The scroll had two full columns of writing. David couldn't read a single letter, but even without Gita he recognized the language as Hebrew because of the unmistakable square squat-like letters with the occasional stem leading straight up. The letters sat on the parchment like living relics from the past.

"I wonder what it says," he said. "God only knows how old it is."

Gita smiled at his choice of words. He rolled the scroll back into the cylindrical form it had slept in for so long and reapplied the linen covering. The Bedouin guide motioned with his head to the mouth of the cave. A trickle of daylight was still coming from the opening, but soon darkness would fall.

"I think he wants to go," Gita said.

"Not yet," said David. "There's too much to see in here."

"I have an idea," she said. "Why don't we spend the night? It would be an experience spending a night here just like people used to." Suddenly her face lit up. "Hey. We could pretend we're hiding from the Romans!"

David looked up at her. Palestine was hot during the day, but night was different. It would be cold and not a sliver of light would seep in from the opening of the cave.

"I don't think that's a good idea," he said.

"Why not? Are you afraid?"

"Afraid?" But of course he was. The thought of spending a night in the cave terrified him. "What about scorpions? And snakes?"

"We could make a fire. They don't go near fire."

David thought of his simple flat in Jerusalem. It wasn't much, but it had appliances, a bed and a window.

"Well I'm staying whether you do or not," she said impetuously. "And all this time I thought you were a man. I'll stay even if I'm going to be alone."

David took stock of the facts. Gita Levitt, a breathtaking Jewess whom he had admired from afar before scrounging up the courage to introduce himself, wanted him to spend the night with her in this hovel of a cave. On the other hand, he could think of a thousand better places than this.

"We'll be cold," he said.

Gita turned to the Bedouin. Putting her hands together and placing her head on them in the universal sign for sleep, she pointed to the ground and closed her eyes. The Bedouin mumbled.

"David, how do you say 'blanket' in Arabic?" she asked.

David was still on his knees, which were getting sore. Crawling around on cave floors did that. He took out his dictionary, focused his flashlight on the pages and looked up the word. *"Bat-taan-ee-yaat,"* he said awkwardly.

"Battaaneeyaat? Maaya battateen fi el jeeb," the Bedouin said.

"What?" David said.

"Jeeb. Jeeb! Car!" the Bedouin said more with his hands than his voice. He made as if he were grasping a steering wheel.

"Car?" said David. "You have a blanket ... *bat-taan-ee-yat* ... in the car?"

The Bedouin nodded. *Baksheesh,"* he said, his palm open and his fingers snapping. It was the one word that required no explanation. David tossed two pounds sterling to the young Arab who rushed off. When he was gone, David got to his feet, stretched out his legs and massaged his knees. He wasn't tall, but still he towered over the diminutive Gita.

"I guess you'll go when he gets back," she said.

"No, I'll stay. If you're crazy enough to spend the night in a place like this I can't leave you alone. Can I?"

She broke into a huge grin. "But don't you think it will be exciting? We'll be just like people thousands of years ago."

Soon the Bedouin guide was back with a pair of sleeping bags. He threw them to Gita, then turned to David and opened his palm. *"Baksheesh,"* he said, demanding more money. David flicked him two more pounds sterling. "Morning I come," the Bedouin said, hitting the middle of his chest with his thumb. And then he was gone.

When the last of his footsteps disappeared, David and Gita were alone in the cave. She took comfort knowing this was where Jews once took refuge from the Romans. Dusk was fast approaching, but she didn't mind. She looked for the flattest area she could find, laid out the two sleeping bags side by side and went to collect kindling. Not far from the mouth of the cave, loose branches and twigs were about, and when she returned she had enough for the night.

"Here," she said, throwing David a lighter. "Can you make a fire?"

Night came and the only light sneaking into the opening was from the full moon. The two of them prepared for sleep. It was March and the air was cold. The fire created some warmth if you were close enough to feel the heat, but it also painted eerie shadows that danced on the walls and ceiling of the cave, and soon their eyes were riveted on the spectacle. Ghosts — spirits of those who dwelt here long ago — were performing an ancient ritual. The cave was huge with lots of hiding places for old manuscripts.

"I'm glad you stayed," Gita whispered, her body curled up inside her sleeping bag. "Hey why don't we pretend we just returned from a hunt? We just cut up a carcass and are cooking it over the fire."

"We must be husband and wife then," David said.

"We could pretend we are."

"Then we should be in the same sleeping bag. Shouldn't we?"

She ignored his comment. "Don't you think it's strange here?" she said. "In the same place where the Hebrews hid from the Romans. I bet they hid from the Assyrians and Babylonians too."

"Who?"

"Jews. They ... we ... were here in the wilderness. Nomads without a home. Here in Judea. So many people tried to get rid of us."

"They're still trying to get rid of you."

"You're right. But they won't. They'll never take us from this land. Never."

David wondered what it was like being so attached to a place that it's part of you. To feel the veins and bones of your feet sink into the ground, and mesh with the dirt and rock below. He had never felt like that about anywhere, but Gita did.

"This land is important to you. Isn't it?" he said.

"It has been for four thousand years. That's a long time. It rubs off after a while."

"*Four thousand years*." He said it slowly, his voice trailing off at the word 'thousand'. He thought if you said it fast it didn't matter, but once you got lost in the words time would begin to scratch away at you.

"Four thousand years ago Abraham led the Jews into Canaan," Gita said, "and ever since that day this land has been important to Jews. Ever since that day other people have been trying to get rid of us. First the Assyrians. Then the Babylonians. Then the Persians, the Greeks, the Romans, the Arabs and then the Crusaders and after them the Turks." With each name she ticked off a finger. "And now we've got the British on our backs but hopefully they'll leave soon."

"You want them to go?"

"Of course. It's not their land. They don't belong here."

"But Gita when the British leave Palestine all hell is going to break loose."

"I'm not worried. God is on our side."

"But he's on the Arabs' side too. Isn't he?"

"The Arabs? Who cares about them? What do they call him? Allah? I'm not talking about Allah. I'm talking about Yahweh. Adonai. God."

"But don't the Arabs also have a right to the land? They've been here a long time too."

"Everyone knows we were here first. God knows it. He chose us. It's in the Bible."

Her mind was made up about everything, but he found her alluring. Gita was a woman, yet part of her was a girl. A child-like innocence poured from her.

With the smoke from the fire filling the cave, the air wasn't as fresh as before and getting colder. David shuffled around in his sleeping bag.

"Maybe Christians hid from the Romans in this cave too," he said.

"Maybe. The Romans couldn't stomach anyone who didn't worship their gods."

"So they were intolerant to the Jews then? The Romans I mean."

"I guess so. Hey you ever heard of the Essenes? They were Hebrews who lived apart from other Jews two thousand years ago. They were supposed to live around here. Near the Dead Sea. I know about them from Pliny and Josephus."

David had a blank look on his face.

"Really David, I can't believe it. You want to be an archeologist but you have to catch up on your reading. Pliny and Josephus were writers from the first century."

"So what about these people? What did you call them?"

"Essenes. They probably lived in this cave too. They were ... outcasts ... who had their own community."

"Because they didn't go along with conventional Jewish thinking?" She nodded and David paused for a moment. "So you mean other Jews were *intolerant* to them?"

She glared at him, at a loss for words, but not for long. It wasn't possible to keep her from talking for long. David sensed a slow stubbornness rising within her.

"No matter what you say we were still here first," she insisted.

"But Gita it doesn't matter. You've got two people fighting over the same land. Land both of them have been in for thousands of years. That's the trouble. And now there's going to be a war. When the British leave there's going to be a war."

"Then it will be very bad for Jews in all the Arab countries," she said. "They ... we ... will need our religion more than ever."

"Why?"

"Because everyone needs something to help them through the day. Like the Bible. It has rules. The Torah for me. The Gospels for you."

"Gita, I don't see how you can believe in anything after what Hitler did to the Jews."

"It's not easy but maybe that's what it's all about."

"What do you mean?"

"Faith. Keeping the faith even when it's hard to believe. Isn't that what the Bible is all about?"

"I don't know."

"You know what? I think you David Marr are an atheist." At first, he didn't reply. "You *are* an atheist?"

"Well to go on preaching intolerance seems pretty stupid to me."

She looked at him incredulously. "You mean you're not even

a Christian?" she said.

"Not even a Christian?"

"You know what I mean."

"Look Gita, archeology makes a lot more sense than religion. Take those coins we found. You can feel them. Touch them. Put a date to them. They're real. That's what I like about it. You dig up facts. Clues about earlier civilizations. Really ... when you think about it ... it's a lot more *logical* than religion."

Gita turned onto her back, her arms crossed tight.

"Are you upset?" he said.

Nothing. No answer just to spite him. She stared into the blackness of the cave where wisps of smoke from the fire disappeared into the air. Their sleeping bags were only a foot apart, but now a huge gulf separated them.

"David," she said finally, "one day I'm going to make you believe. It's just so … *illogical* ... to use your word ... to believe in nothing. Why that's the most *illogical* thing I've ever heard. Mark my words. One day you'll reach out and touch the spirit of God."

The two of them were surrounded by the numbing overpowering silence of the cave. It wasn't like camping in a forest by a river or lake with the waves gently crashing soft against the shore, the sound of birds and other creatures of the wild stirring the senses. There was nothing. Absolutely nothing. It was the perfect quiet of emptiness.

"Gita," David said, "you're shivering. We should zip our sleeping bags together."

She looked over her shoulder. Shy. Uncomfortable. Then suddenly she sat up with a start, falling on him with her arms around his neck.

"What's wrong?" he said.

"Did you hear that?"

"What?"

"A voice," she whispered, looking around in the dark. "I heard something."

"The Bedouin?"

"No. Not him. It was a different voice. Deeper. Powerful. Kind of scary. But not scary." Her arms still around him, her eyes darted through the shadows of the cave. "Maybe it was God," she said, her lips almost touching his ear.

He put his arms around her, leaned her onto her back and saw her face shimmering in the light of the fire. He pulled up the cover of the sleeping bag around them and she was no longer a bold archeologist out to experience a night with the spirits of her ancestral past. Now she was just a frightened little girl watching fire shadows jumping around in the blackness.

"I heard a voice," she said. "I didn't imagine it."

He drew himself in close and found her lips. It wasn't a long kiss, but it was the first. She laughed modestly and he kissed her again, more passionately this time. He slipped his hand under her clothes and massaged the smooth marble skin of her back. He took her face in his hands and soon he was on fire. A moment more and their bodies were entangled. She was beautiful and nothing else mattered in this place of eternal time.

It was the middle of the night — just when he wasn't sure — since the hours melded into one another in the way that clouds pass through a morning mist. But her words seemed foreboding and something told him he would never let go of her.

"I'm going to teach you, David Marr," she said with conviction. "I'm going to teach you."

"You're going to teach me what?"

"About life."

CHAPTER SIX

SIX

There were many problems with the Qumran mummy that couldn't be explained. It was unlike anything ever found in the desert. The head didn't face west, which was the practice of the Egyptians, so it wasn't them. It wasn't buried in the fetal position, the most common method of burial, and there was no pottery or anything else to help with an identity. But the biggest mystery was that it wasn't found in Egypt or anywhere along the Nile Valley, but just off the Dead Sea where the climate shouldn't allow for the preservation of human remains. It was too humid. There was too much rainfall. So I began to wonder if it was buried somewhere else and then moved.

"Where are the nails?" Robbie asked. "If this man was crucified there would be nails. No?"

I told him the Romans removed the nails after a crucifixion since they believed the nails possessed healing powers for such ailments as epilepsy.

"So that is more evidence for a Roman crucifixion?"

I said it was and thought of my one earlier encounter with crucifixion. It was the first time I ever knew true fear from an archeological find. It was 1968, a year after Israel had captured Jerusalem in the Six Day War. Bulldozers were clearing an area in the Old City for a new apartment block on a rocky hillside north of the Damascus Gate. The site was a Jewish burial ground dating to the time of the New Testament, so the Department of Antiquities and Museums organized an excavation. Inside the tombs we found fifteen stone ossuaries — caskets full of bones. I had never seen so many bones in one place before. There were skeletons of thirty-five Jews from just before the revolt of 70 A.D. — eleven men, twelve women, twelve children. We examined their remains and learned that three of the children had died of starvation, one had been killed from an arrow in the skull, an old woman had succumbed to a blow from a club or a mace and a youth had been burned to death on a rack Another woman had also burned to death. It was easy to tell from her charred bones.

We found all this in the ancient burial caves at Giv'at ha-Mivtar and were sure a crucifixion had taken place because one of the iron nails was intact. It was ghastly. The nail was eighteen centimeters — as long as my hand. It went right through the heel bones of the victim's feet with enough left over to secure a hold on a cross. We assembled the full skeleton and produced a man whom we estimated to be twenty-four to twenty-eight years old. He was five feet, seven inches tall. His bones showed no sign of manual labor, so we figured he was from the upper class. His name, incised in Aramaic on the stone ossuary, was *Jehohanan*, which was pronounced Ye-ho-he-nun.

The wooden cross had two pieces — the upright *stipes crucis* and the horizontal *patibulum*. The condemned man was placed with his back over the *stipes*, his hands nailed to the *patibulum*, the nails carefully driven between the carpal bones of the wrist. His feet were nailed directly to the upright.

Our later experiments with cadavers showed how hideous crucifixions were. When the hapless victim was suffering on the cross, his head would tip forward blocking his thorax, so the only way of breathing was to shift his weight to the nail supporting his feet. But then he would soon fall back, exhausted, and die very slowly from asphyxiation.

In this case the nail was hammered through the feet with one blow, the free end extending beyond the second foot. A second blow and the end of the nail was curved back, as if there was any chance of escaping. What made it even more gruesome was that his feet had been amputated, a macabre find for the uninitiated. And why? As with most things Roman there was a logical answer. After Jehohanan expired the two iron nails at the top were removed, making his body fall forward to the ground. The only way to get his corpse down from the cross was to cut off his feet and that's what they did. We found the evidence — the nail — in the bones of his feet.

It all brought home the stark horror of a Roman execution. It was real. It happened. Thousands of times. I got so sick that my stomach started to rebel, but managed to control myself and avoid vomiting, which wouldn't have made a good impression on my colleagues. But still this was a first. The skeletal remains of a crucified man.

There were also other times when I had reason to be afraid. During the early excavations of the caves in the Judean Desert I saw things that would make people tremble. An expedition organized by the Israeli government and Hebrew University explored the valleys between Masada and Ein Gedi. We made fantastic discoveries in Cave 1, which wasn't easily accessible since the opening was a fifty-meter drop from the top of a steep wall of rock. Below the opening was another two hundred and fifty meters of sheer cliff face, so the only way in was with ropes and a paratrooper's harness. We figured people in ancient times used a narrow track along the rock to get in, but it was worn away. When we finally got inside we had to crawl around on our hands and knees, but had to be careful because the roof might collapse. We put wooden beams up to support it.

The lowest stratum of the cave yielded hearths and fireplaces, and there were many layers of ashes and debris about. We found Chalcolithic and Roman potsherds, fragments of glass vessels, textiles, charred wood, animal bones and one gruesome find. A human skull. I remember grabbing what was left of it and mimicking those sober words of Shakespeare's Hamlet — "Alas poor Yorick, I knew him, Horatio." The Israelis with me didn't know what I was talking about, but it seemed to embody the ephemeral nature of life and led me to a profound conclusion. No matter who we are or what we are — peasants, common slaves, kings — we all wind up as equals.

Later in that cave we found five human burials. They were the most terrifying things I had ever seen. The skeletons, undisturbed through centuries, were wrapped in linen and leather clothing. We found the remains of human hair, rotted skin and dehydrated parts of internal organs. It was grisly. I had never seen the insides of a man exposed like that. But at least these people had died natural deaths. Not like in Pompeii.

On August 24, 79 A.D., the volcano Vesuvius erupted and a black cloud descended over a community of ten thousand people. The area was immediately blanketed with more than fifteen feet of volcanic debris. The next day hot gases and ash surged along the ground at seventy miles per hour — suffocating, burning and burying everyone in its wake. In time all the bodies decayed, but they left behind detailed cavities in the compacted ash. In the nineteenth century a scientist filled these cavities with plaster and recreated the actual forms of Pompeii's victims in their final moments. When I first saw the two tangled bodies of a mother and child it made me weep. We estimated that one-fifth of the inhabitants perished, but not in vain because they left us a three-dimensional photograph of life as it was.

It wasn't fear that I experienced then, but sorrow for the victims who were simple people going about their routine domestic tasks when disaster struck. But it wasn't until Jehohanan that the stark reality of man's brutality to man reared its ugly head for me. This man, what was left of him, had been *crucified.*

Then there was the mummy at Qumran, which was even more remarkable. Unlike the skeletal remains at Giv'at ha-Mivtar, its feet and body were intact. No organs were removed. Nothing was tampered with. Except for the wrist and foot wounds there was only the deep gash in the side. But what did it mean?

"He was stabbed when he was on the cross. During his crucifixion," Robbie said.

"It probably wasn't unusual," I said. "On the other hand maybe he was wounded before his crucifixion. When he was captured."

That was when Robbie brought up Jamil. "Professor Marr, you think very highly of your Egyptian friend Dr. Hassad. He said how secret this must be or it could be dangerous. People will jump to conclusions."

"Only a fool would jump to conclusions," I said.

"The world is full of fools."

Robbie was right. The world was full of fools, and it didn't matter that biblical history and *history* were different commodities. One was the result of observation and documentation by writers — witnesses — while the other was a simple record written by authors we can't identify. We aren't even sure when they wrote it. We know only that their information originated in stories related *orally* from one person to the next and that wasn't very scientific.

There was also the delicate matter of the Temple of Luxor, a rather sticky point for any Christian. It shot so many holes into the foundations of the religion that any truly discerning individual would have to stop and question what it was all about. This ancient temple, which still stands intact, displays through intricate artwork the very stories of the New Testament. The only problem was that the temple was built in 1700 B.C. and it didn't depict the story of Jesus but the Egyptian god Horus. Still, it's all there to see — the angels announcing the impending birth to shepherds, the nativity scene, the three wise men kneeling before the infant deity, the virgin mother with baby, the Resurrection. Indeed, the parallels between Horus and Jesus are too numerous to ignore.

"Robbie, the only thing on my mind right now is what we can learn from this mummy. What it means in terms of science. Have you thought about that?"

He shook his head.

"Think! We found a man from two thousand years ago. His body is well preserved."

"So?"

"We have technology today that can tell us a lot about him. With modern science we can learn more about him ... more than any book ... any *Bible* ... could tell us. Like a forensic examination. We could learn about his death … why he died … how he died."

Now that excited me.

"X-rays? CAT scans?" Robbie said.

"Yes. We could look right inside his body. Maybe find the cause of death. Something about his diet. Any ailments he had. We could even identify his DNA. But there's a problem. It's this place. The Holy Land. When you apply modern technology to the study of human history … well … you have a dangerous elixir."

"A what?"

"Sorry Robbie. A dangerous ... formula. I mean what if we prove the history books are *wrong*? Or the Bible is wrong. Think about that. That's what happened when I was studying the Royal Mummies with Jamil. We ran into all kinds of trouble with the Egyptian government. They said that …"

"What Professor Marr?"

"Ne sutor ultra crepidam."

"What?"

It was Latin. I translated for him. The cobbler is not to judge of things above the sandal.

Robbie didn't know what I was talking about. "I am afraid I do not understand the English either," he said.

"It means, Robbie, that shoemakers should stick to making shoes."

"Shoes?"

"Look, I was an archeologist. They didn't think I should get into this stuff. The point is the Egyptians didn't want us to mix with their history. But with this discovery there is so much we can do. I mean now."

"We would need help. Someone in forensics. A pathologist."

"Jamil is a pathologist."

"Could we not get someone else? Someone here in Israel?"

"You won't find a better pathologist than him."

Before returning to Alexandria, Jamil had reminded me about all the troubles we encountered with the mummies of the pharaohs. We had created quite a stir in Cairo back then. Our findings led us to believe that some of the pharaohs had ruled during periods that didn't match with the historical record and at one point we were told to stop our work. Cease and desist. The government didn't like it. Egypt was a poor chaotic country and its long history was one of the few sources of national pride that remained. But we continued.

Despite Jamil's concerns about our story getting out, I had to examine this find in more detail and needed help. While he pointed out the similarities to scripture, there was no way I could be swayed by biblical records to establish the identity of a corpse. All I knew was that we had a mummy — a remarkable mummy and obviously a victim of Roman crucifixion — but that was it. I tried to think as a scientist and when I thought like that everything was clear and logical. You start with questions, and then proceed to observation and analysis, and if you're lucky you get some answers. You discover what is left of a human being and make conclusions based on your findings. But life isn't always that simple.

"We have another option," Robbie said.

"What's that?"

"Take it back to Qumran."

I couldn't believe he would want to do that. Just return this mummy to the sand and let its secret be sealed beneath the desert forever? What kind of scientist would do such a thing?

"Robbie, have you ever wondered why I work in the Holy Land?" He shook his head. "I'll tell you. Because it's the source of inspiration for hundreds of millions of people. It's the cradle of Judaism, Christianity and Islam, the three great monotheistic religions, and each one thinks their way is the only way. They all think of this land as their spiritual soul and because of that it's just been ripped apart in bloodshed. Right through history. And it's still going on today. It's all about race and religion and hate." I could see Robbie didn't like my little speech, but I had to get it out. "The funny thing is I feel drawn to it. It has a way of filling the space in me."

"What do you mean?"

"There's this big empty space inside me that wants knowledge and the more I learn … the more I feed it … the more it wants."

"You are attracted to the violence of the Holy Land?"

"Maybe. But I think I just want answers. There are so many questions. That's why I'm an archeologist, Robbie. It gives me an insight into all the death and devastation wrought by God over the years. It never ceases to amaze me that bloodletting is the result when people look at life differently than others. History books are full of it. The *Bible* is full of it. Masada might be the best example of all. When I think of young Jews committing suicide because of a stubborn belief in God I see how irrational man can be when his life hangs in the balance. It makes no sense. I'd sooner believe in Zeus than have a machete-wielding pagan kill me and my children. Wouldn't you?"

"I have principles, Professor Marr. My religion is one of them."

"And I'm a scientist, Robbie. A man who deals in facts. And logic."

"You use that word a lot. Logic. I think it is a poor substitute."

"For what?"

"For faith."

"Faith? There's little room in my mind for faith. I lost that a long time ago."

Robbie wasn't satisfied. He didn't like my response, but then he surprised me. *"Homines quod volunt credunt,"* he said, quoting Julius Caesar. The Latin meant 'men believe what they want to'. That was good. I smiled at him sardonically.

"Inter urines et faecae nascimur," I replied, and he tried to decipher it.

"Inter urines ..."

I had to help him out. "It's about life and anatomy, Robbie. It means 'we are born between piss and ... well you know ... *faecae*."

Robbie, as formal as any young Israeli you could meet, was alarmed when he figured it out.

CHAPTER SEVEN

SEVEN

"David, what have you got in there?"

It was Eliraz. Trouble.

"Nothing. Why?"

"Come on I'm not stupid. I know something is going on."

"What are you talking about?"

"That night. You and Robbie brought a stretcher in with something on it. I saw you. So what have you got that's so important you have to bring it in at night when no one's around?"

"Huh?"

"I was in my office. I saw the two of you go down the hall. You didn't see me but I saw you."

That was Eliraz. A spy if there ever was one.

"Well ... I ..."

She could tell that I wasn't doing very well and it wasn't only because of running into her, but where I had run into her. Just outside my lab. The doors were shut behind me. But there was no time to lock them.

"You've got something in there, haven't you? What is it?"

My hands were fidgeting behind my back. Absolute denial would get me nowhere. "Yes I've got something."

"Well?"

"Well what?"

"What is it?"

"Eliraz, does the word 'confidence' mean anything to you? Did it ever occur to you this may be something that doesn't concern you?"

She smiled. "Everything around here concerns me. I'm going to be department head one day. You know that as well as I do. Why keep secrets from me?"

"It's confidential."

"Why?"

"I can't tell you."

Eliraz was a good archeologist who thought she was special since she was a native Israeli. She was born after the War of Independence, the only woman in the faculty who was a true *sabra*, and she wore this honor blatantly like a medal around her neck. Because of this she felt she was at least three up on me. First, she was a Jew and I wasn't. Second, she was a citizen of Israel and not only that, she was born here while I was a foreigner. An outsider. And third, she — an ardent feminist — was a woman.

Whenever I ran into her I had the distinct impression her eyes were cutting right through me, heaping scorn on me for being a North American male, as if that was why I attained any success. I didn't like her, but respected her abilities. She had published papers in the most prestigious publications, including the Israel Exploration Journal, and getting in there was no easy feat. I decided to change my approach. I would resort to deceit.

"All right, Eliraz. I'll tell you. You'll probably find out anyway. It's a skeleton. We got it from Alexandria University."

"Alexandria University?"

"Yes," I said not as convincingly as I wanted. "It's a trade. We gave them one of ours and they sent us one of theirs."

"Why would Alexandria University want to trade with you?"

I shook my head in mock frustration. "Eliraz, you forget. I have contacts there. I studied the Royal Mummies. Remember? It was a long time ago but I kept up my contacts. You need friends in this business."

"So what did they send you? An offspring of Ramesses?"

"Eliraz, if it's related to Ramesses I promise you'll be the first to know."

"Why didn't you sign it in?"

"I beg your pardon?"

"I checked. You didn't sign anything in that night. Why not?"

This woman was impossible.

"I must have forgotten. We were in a hurry."

"So why the big rush? What's so important about a skeleton? And why would a university send it here late at night?"

I shrugged. It felt like an interview. With a reporter. She would have been good at that.

"At least tell me how old it is," she said.

"It's nothing pre-dynastic," I said with a sigh.

"If it was the press would be in here right away."

I trembled at the thought. "I guess they would but I don't think they'll find this too interesting. It's only a skeleton, Eliraz. An Egyptian skeleton. You wouldn't care much about that would you?"

"Because it's Egyptian? Why not? Some great finds have been unearthed in the Nile valley. You should know. So are you testing it?"

"What?"

"Your … skeleton."

"We're doing some tests. Look you're wasting your time. It's just a skeleton. Like hundreds of other skeletons we've had in here. Excuse me but I have to run."

She gave me a look full of profound disbelief in everything I had said. She didn't buy it, not for a second, and I had every reason to fear her. She had allies in the highest circles of the university and I had no doubt she would be department head one day. Eliraz had the credentials. She was bright, dedicated, an excellent teacher and had built an impressive track record in publishing. All this was crucial for success in the field and her being a woman was a plus too. Eliraz, for all her nose-to-the-grindstone approach to things, wasn't unattractive. She was about forty with short black hair, a slim but full body and an airy confidence that made up for any shortcomings she may have had. What made her especially dangerous was being a woman who knew how to get what she wanted. When I turned to leave she grabbed my arm.

"David."

"What is it, Eliraz?"

"Don't ignore me so much."

"Ignore you? What do you mean?"

"You heard me. I'm much too valuable to be ignored. Especially by a man."

CHAPTER EIGHT

EIGHT

Palestine, 1947-1948

"Young man. Are you aware of the magnitude of these scrolls of yours?"

"They're old aren't they?"

"I should say they're old. There is almost a complete Book of Isaiah here!"

"There is?"

"Are you familiar with the Nash Papyrus?"

"The what?"

"The Nash Papyrus. It's the oldest Hebrew manuscript ever found. Dates from the second century. But what you found is even older than that."

David had been sure about the scrolls from the moment he saw them and now someone agreed with him. Professor Eli Solnik was an archeologist at the Hebrew University in Jerusalem. For four months David had taken them to one expert after another only to have them dismiss the scrolls as worthless. But he, a student no less, knew they were important. They had been rolled up, sealed in linen wrappings and put in clay jars that looked very old. But no one believed him. Until now. Professor Solnik was a godsend.

"Can I buy them from you?" he asked.

"I haven't thought about money," said David. "I was only interested in the scrolls for their historical value."

Professor Solnik laughed, preferring not to believe so innocent a reply. "They are much older than the Masoretic text which until now was the oldest Hebrew Bible ever found. But that's only from the ninth century."

David nodded, but he had no idea what Professor Solnik was talking about.

"Why it's even older than the Alexandrian Septuagint!"

"What's that?"

"The Alexandrian Septuagint is a Greek translation of scripture that is said to have begun in the third century and finished approximately two hundred years later. There is one other form of scripture that is also very old. Saint Jerome's Latin Vulgate from the fourth century. But what you found is older."

Professor Solnik's kindly face was hidden by a greying beard. His right hand kept scratching away at the roots as if trying to extricate the mass of hair from his chin.

"I don't think you understand the immensity of these scrolls," he said. "You see all our knowledge of the Bible has been based on those translations that I mentioned. But now we have this!"

He slid back his chair and rose behind a desk overflowing with a mountain of paper. David wondered how he ever found anything in this ramshackle office. The top drawer of his filing cabinet was half-opened with chewed-up files. The walls were covered by book shelves, some of the books upside down, and open books were on the floor. In front of his desk was a table covered in documents with files and paper everywhere.

His state of dress was just as chaotic. An old sweater smelling of mothballs was draped over his slight frame. His pants needed ironing and his shoes were scuffed beyond repair. He was a small man, five and a half feet tall with a slight stoop to his back, and when he sat in his chair he looked like he was framed by all the paper surrounding him. David could imagine him standing before a congregation leading a service in one of Jerusalem's old synagogues. He could see him in a long black robe with a skullcap on his head, a holy book in his hand.

"You won't sell them to me then?" he said.

"To tell you the truth, Professor Solnik, I didn't even realize that I owned them."

"You found them, didn't you?"

"Yes. Well that's not really true either. The Bedouin found them. Then I heard about them and hired a guide and went to look for myself."

"But it was you who took these scrolls from the cave?"

"That's right."

"So you own them."

"You mean whoever finds an artifact is automatically the owner?"

"That's about it. Those Bedouin friends of yours have been selling fragments of manuscripts in the markets around Bethlehem all summer. I would rather these things were in my hands or yours than theirs or somebody else's who doesn't realize their value. Or care for that matter. I don't think any Arabs would be concerned with old Hebrew text. Why are you smiling?"

"I'm amused by the fact that finders keepers applies to old scrolls but not to Palestine itself."

"What do you mean?"

"I mean you said that by finding the scrolls I'm their rightful owner. If we applied that argument to the land, well, the Jews were here first but the Arabs have been here for hundreds of years and they say the Jews should go."

Professor Solnik looked at David askance. His right hand began scratching away at his beard. "You feel the Jews should leave Palestine to the Arabs?" he said.

"No I didn't say that. What I meant was ..."

"I don't think Americans who have no understanding of this part of the world should so easily pass judgment on Palestine."

"I'm not American. I'm Canadian."

"What's the difference? How long have you been here?"

"About a year."

"About a year. In four thousand years come back and talk to me. Then I'll have more respect for your opinion."

He said it quickly as if it had been rehearsed. David had noticed this with Jews in Palestine before. Any question about their laying a stake in the land and they changed into snarling cats. There was something about this business of four thousand years that translated into 'ownership.' David first sensed it with Gita and she was from New York.

Professor Solnik's demeanor was changing from gratitude and thanks to offense. David had to change his tack. The man was insulted, but David couldn't lose him. He was the first person, the only person, who believed in his discovery.

"I'm sorry, Professor Solnik. I didn't mean to offend you. Maybe I'm mixing where I shouldn't."

"I should say so."

"Do you think we can find out who wrote the scrolls?" David said, trying to move on. "Aren't they the rightful owners?"

"That would be fine if people lived for two thousand years but unfortunately they expire sooner than that. Since you're so concerned about the question of who owns them let me put it this way. There's a law in Palestine that says all archeological discoveries must be reported to the Department of Antiquities. But with all the trouble these days it's almost as if there is no government in Palestine. No government. No law."

"But there *is* a law?"

"The UN is going to vote on what to do with Palestine. The English are getting out. They're going to leave the Jews and Arabs to fight it out for themselves. So if there are more scrolls in that cave we should get them as soon as possible. Soon we might not have a chance and wouldn't it be terrible if those other scrolls, scrolls that may be even more important than the ones you found, were destroyed?"

"Can I take you there?" said David. "Would you go with me?"

This was what Professor Solnik wanted to hear. "I was hoping you'd ask me that. Of course I'm just dying to go there. Do you know the way? But without the Bedouin. They're Arabs. It would be dangerous. You wouldn't be afraid?"

"No."

He led David to his door and they agreed to go the next day. They wouldn't tell anyone. But the kindly scholar had one more comment, which he made with the utmost of paternalism. "You seem to be a bright young man, eager to make discoveries, and you could see something in those scrolls that others with far more experience couldn't see. That means you passed the first test of archeology ."

"What's that?"

"Experts and I use that word lightly always reject great discoveries. They refused to absorb the significance of the early digs at Pompeii and Herculaneum even though stratigraphical results showed that ancient cities were found. They couldn't accept the deciphering of cuneiform for what it was until many years passed and now they fail to see the importance of these scrolls. But you saw it right away and you're only a student and that's because you have an open mind. You would do well to keep it that way."

"Thank you."

"It wasn't meant as a compliment but advice. Stick to the facts and don't let politics muddy the waters of your brain and you might have a future in this work."

....

On November 29, 1947, the UN passed a resolution to partition Palestine and create two states — Arab and Jewish. But the entire Arab bloc voted against it and the whole lot of them walked out of the Assembly Hall at Flushing Meadow, New York. Nevertheless, a special commission was struck to watch over the region and report to the Security Council should the Arab nations make good on their threat to fight a Jewish state arising in Palestine. A few blocks away, the St. Nicholas Arena on West 66th Street was filled to capacity in an emotional rally applauding the UN decision. Moshe Shertok, head of the Political Department of the Jewish Agency for Palestine, took the podium and paid tribute to the countries that voted in favor of the resolution.

"This is the first time the UN and the civilized world have decided to create a new state," he said. "Its creation is a challenge to the world to keep faith with us. The Jewish responsibility is not a bed of roses. Every step is fraught with danger but Jews throughout the world must support the Jewish state."

....

Professor Solnik was a man of intelligence, conviction, and as David would learn, great courage. Hostilities between Arabs and Jews broke out the day after the partitioning of Palestine, but the venerable scholar wanted to find the rest of the scrolls. He wanted to find missing portions from the Book of Isaiah and talked about finding more of the 'Habakkuk Commentary,' which he said could have enormous impact on not only Judaism, but Christianity. He said it was from the first century and was about the threat from the Romans, at least, as perceived by whoever wrote this.

When David took him to the cave they found more fragments, but by this time the Bedouin had unearthed new samples in other caves and sold them. The road to Bethlehem was a dangerous place since thoroughfares between towns in Palestine were under attack. The Arabs were trying to isolate the Jews by cutting off their communications links to Tel Aviv, and buses were being stopped. It was a time when those with guns shot first and asked questions later. Professor Solnik was right about there not being enough time to find all the scrolls, but they did get through to Bethlehem and wound up purchasing more scrolls from merchants there. The cost was fifty pounds.

Back in Jerusalem Professor Solnik immersed himself in the manuscripts and the more he saw the more excited he got. There was indeed almost an entire Book of Isaiah. There were also fragments and whole columns from the 'Habakkuk Commentary' and portions of something called the 'Manual of Discipline,' which he said could have enormous repercussions on the Christian world. He said another work called the 'Genesis Apocryphon' was a literary commentary on the Book of Genesis. There was also a poem about the fall of Babylon, which he said was even older than the other writings, maybe as old as 500 B.C. He learned this by showing samples to various experts and was told that no one had lived in these caves since just after the time of Christ. He took photographs of specific passages before sending them to people as far away as the Yale Divinity School.

"You trust this with Americans?" David asked him.

"Sometimes Americans are our friends," he replied. "Now is a particularly good time."

"But why Americans?"

"Because they are godless people. Look, the Arabs already have many scrolls. Who knows what they'll do with them? And at least one Christian businessman bought a few and if those wind up in Rome we may never see them again. So we have to make sure that what we have finds its way to America or the truth may never be known."

"How many scrolls do you think there are?"

"Hundreds."

Professor Solnik told David that the seven scrolls they had found or bought, depending on your point of view, must be smuggled out of Palestine. The New Year came and went, and with each passing day and escalating violence, he grew more agitated. Finally, he decided to go public and call a press conference. He would tell the world about the *Dead Sea Scrolls*, as he began to call them.

In January the Arab Legion was shelling the Jewish sections of Jerusalem every afternoon. Professor Solnik called his press conference at the offices of the Jewish Agency right in the middle of the area under siege. He said this way the press could report on the scrolls and the bombing. There was a long table with scrolls laid out and a dozen chairs on the floor, David and Gita sitting in the front row. When Professor Solnik saw the Jerusalem correspondent for *The New York Times*, he called the gathering to order, adjusted his glasses and began to read.

"Thank you for coming. This is not the easiest way to make an announcement but I feel it is necessary. I am Professor Eli Solnik and I am an archeologist with the Hebrew University. I have called you here to tell you about an incredible discovery we made in caves near the Dead Sea."

No sooner did he begin that an explosion shook the room. It was like an earthquake had hit, but then it passed. The unruffled academic continued.

"We have found the most ancient Hebrew manuscripts ever discovered. They are scrolls ... the Dead Sea Scrolls ... and from our research I can tell you they are the oldest biblical writings ever found. Some of them date to the first or second century B.C. and maybe older than that. We found almost a complete Book of Isaiah and another work that was previously unknown."

"What do you mean unknown?" asked one of the reporters.

"And who are you?" Professor Solnik said.

"I'm with *The Biblical Archeologist*. From Oxford."

The man had a strong English accent.

"You came all the way from Oxford?"

The man shook his head. "Afraid not. I'm a correspondent stationed in Jerusalem. I've been here the past two months but I was curious when I heard about these scrolls."

"Well thank you for coming. Now where was I? I lost my place."

Professor Solnik returned to his text, searching for where he had left off. Even with reading glasses, his vision wasn't good. With every interruption, and there were would be many that afternoon, he would move his finger up and down the page looking for what he had last said.

"You said something about a work that was previously unknown," the English reporter said.

"Ah yes here we are," said Professor Solnik. "What was that?"

"You said something about a work that was previously unknown."

"Oh yes," he said looking up. "Well we're still a little confused about what this mysterious work is called but for lack of a better title I will call it 'The War of the Children of Light Against the Children of Darkness'. You can consider it about good and evil."

Just then another shell burst, louder than the first. The journalists, most of them foreign correspondents soon planning to leave the city, looked out the window.

"Please. Please!" Professor Solnik said. "Don't worry. Their aim is terrible. They couldn't hit us if they tried. This won't take long. Now as I was saying I don't have time to go into great detail about the writings but I can assure you these scrolls will enrich our understanding of the Hebrew world at the time before the destruction of the temple."

"What temple is that?" asked the reporter from *The New*

York Times.

"What temple?" said Professor Solnik. "Why *the* temple. The temple built by King Solomon."

Because he was so close, David could hear the old archeologist muttering under his breath something about Americans.

"King Solomon?" the reporter said.

"Have a look at Kings One, chapter six, verses one to thirty-seven," Professor Solnik said. "It's all there. All the dimensions."

"And what year was that?" said the reporter, jotting down these Old Testament references.

"What year?" said Professor Solnik. "70 A.D. The Romans did it. You want the name of the emperor who was responsible?"

"Yes please. If you have it."

"Nero."

"Thank you."

Professor Solnik shook his head, adjusted his glasses and once again searched for his place. "Now where was I? Ah yes. Here we are. As I was saying these scrolls are important for our understanding of Judaism and also for the very nature of Christianity."

"What do you mean by that?"

The Englishman again.

"Give me a minute and I'll tell you," Professor Solnik said. "I believe these writings or most of them were made by a group of dissident Jews called Essenes. The evidence is overwhelming. The only writings we had about Judaism before the destruction of the temple ..." He glared at the reporter from *The New York Times* "... in 70 A.D. ... came from outside writers and we have translations and translations of translations that were preserved by Christians. But now with these scrolls we have literature written by a group of Jews at the time when the temple was still standing. This is important. The time I'm talking about was just after the latest books of the Old Testament were created and just before and during the time when Christianity came into being. I think the complete deciphering of these scrolls will enrich the world's understanding of Judaism at the time when Christianity arose and help us more clearly understand the New Testament and early Christianity."

"But what is there to more clearly understand about early Christianity?"

The Englishman.

"Plenty," said Professor Solnik, glancing up from his notes. "Look, I don't have to quote the Gospels to you but there are many things in these books that are inconsistent."

"Like what?"

"I'm not here to discuss the New Testament but there are many discrepancies in the Books of Luke, Matthew and Mark and the Book of John is completely different from the other three."

"How?"

"How? The very genealogy of Christ himself differs from one book to the next. There are differences in the date of the Last Supper. The Book of John omits the Eucharist entirely and both John and Matthew mention nothing of the Ascension while the others do. There are also discrepancies in the four Gospels as to the very nature of Christ's mission."

"So who do you believe?" said the American reporter.

"That is your question, not mine," said Professor Solnik, shooting the reporter a look of contempt. "My point is these scrolls can shed light on the world at this time because we simply don't have any other biblical writings that survived from the period."

He glanced across the room. The Englishman was making copious notes. Next to him was a man of darker complexion. Professor Solnik thought he might be native to the region. A Jew or an Arab. He couldn't tell. Sometimes it was hard to tell.

"What's all this about the Children of Light and the Children of Darkness?" asked the American.

"First let me tell you what we know about the Essenes." Professor Solnik returned to his text, searching for the right place. "We have the writings of Pliny, a Roman, and Philo and Josephus who were Jews. Josephus was an Essene and at different times of his life belonged to the three principal sects of the Jews. The Pharisees, the Sadducees and the Essenes. He says the Essenes renounced pleasure and material goods. They had nothing to do with trade and commerce. They didn't marry and didn't permit women in their community but adopted other peoples' children and refugees and this is how they managed to perpetuate themselves. They wore plain clothing and ate simple foods and lived on the west shore of the Dead Sea. They were a simple people who according to Philo were farmers, shepherds, beekeepers and artisans. Unlike most people at the time they had no slaves. They shared what they had. And they were very clean ... always washing themselves ... always dressed in white. Unlike other sects of Jews they paid strict attention to the Sabbath and didn't believe in animal sacrifices and because of this they were excluded from the court of the temple in Jerusalem. They believed that at the time of death virtuous souls went to a pleasant hereafter somewhere beyond the sea while evil ones went to a place of torment and eternal suffering. This is how they lived and we can see a strong resemblance to early Christians. But we must keep in mind that we're talking about a people who were thriving long before the appearance of Christ."

He raised his head. "It's my personal opinion that John the Baptist and maybe even Jesus were members of the Essenes."

"That is hearsay," said the Englishman. "Nowhere in the New Testament is there any mention of the Essenes."

"True but nowhere in the New Testament is there any description of the Resurrection but you don't regard that as hearsay, do you?"

The diminutive archeologist knew his Bible and his familiarity with the books of the New Testament, for a Jew yet, was not lost on those present.

"I'm not here to find holes in the scriptures but to shed light on them," said Professor Solnik, returning to his text. "In these Dead Sea Scrolls, in the Manual of Discipline, we learn about the world being divided into two groups. Each is dominated by a Spirit of Darkness and a Spirit of Light. The followers of the Spirit of Darkness, the Children of Darkness, are denounced. They are, without a doubt, the Romans. So what we have here is an isolated sect of Jews, the Essenes, who share this doctrine of human brotherhood, who even have the practice of a ritual washing much like baptism, who have a form of communism ..."

"Communism?" said the American reporter, aghast.

"Communism. Call if communalism if you like but in Acts,

chapter two, verses forty-four and forty-five it says 'and all that believed were together, and had all things common, and sold their possessions and goods, and parted them to all men, as every man had need'. What's that sound like to you? These people lived like monks and shared traditions just like traditions in the New Testament. The similarities are so great we can't ignore them."

"And you think John the Baptist and Jesus were Essenes?" said the American.

"According to the Bible John baptized Jesus where the Jordan River flows into the Red Sea. This is where the Essenes lived. The ruins of their monastery are there today and there is a cemetery with graves. What's unusual about these graves is that nothing was buried with these men. No ornaments or weapons or funeral objects. Only bones. In some of them we found small fragments of jars and why they're in some graves and not others I don't know but the fragments have been dated to the first century B.C."

"So how long did these Essenes live there?"

"We believe from the second century B.C. to 68 A.D."

"How can you say 68 A.D. with such certainty?"

Professor Solnik raised his head to face the upstart American. "Because my good man that was the second year of the Jewish revolt against the Romans. We have found Roman coins from the year 68 A.D. in the Essene ruins at Qumran and that is when the Romans destroyed the monastery. Mind you not far away we also have coins stamped with the mark of the Tenth Roman Legion which was a few years later." Professor Solnik removed his glasses, shrugged and opened his hands for effect. "Look, it all fits. It makes sense. It's the role of an archeologist to find artifacts and try and place them in the context of human history and that's what we're trying to do with these scrolls. But there is more I must tell you." He reapplied his glasses and began searching through the text. After what seemed an eternity he found his place. "Some of the writings we deciphered from scrolls called the Habakkuk Commentary mention a *Teacher of Righteousness*, a priest who was said to have divine revelations, a man who was a leader of note."

"Jesus?" said the American.

"I don't know."

"What year was this?" asked the Englishman.

"One biblical scholar says it was written in 41 B.C. which was three years after the death of Julius Caesar."

"Then it couldn't be Jesus."

"Probably not," said Professor Solnik. "There is some thought that the *Teacher of Righteousness* could be John the Baptist but the year would seem to be early for him too. We're not sure who this *Teacher of Righteousness* is but the point is a definite theology runs through these scrolls and this theology goes right to the New Testament. One portion even mentions a 'last judgment' at the end of time when the Messiah shall divide the world and this, of course, had no basis in Jewish scripture. Another point is that the town of Bethlehem isn't far from the site of the Essene monastery so it's fair to assume that Jesus, if he wasn't a member of the Essenes himself, may have been influenced by them."

"That is enough!" The outburst was from the British reporter. He shut his notebook and pointed a wavering finger at Professor Solnik. "You sir are meddling in the most filthy slime imaginable! You announce a so-called discovery and assume the entire Christian world order must be rewritten in order to subscribe to your beliefs. Two thousand years of evolution of human thought and morality are suddenly dismissed with a wave of your hand. The Bible called it blasphemy and that's exactly what it is! You have a nerve calling us here for something so ridiculous."

"I beg your pardon but this is an important discovery. You consider yourself a journalist, don't you?"

"Yes and I'm also a Christian and this kind of nonsense doesn't deserve to be reported in *The Biblical Archeologist* or any other publication. We're here to report news! Not hyperbole." He turned around to address the other reporters. "I urge everyone here to get up and leave and not give this man the satisfaction of reporting on something that has no basis whatsoever."

No one moved. David, who had been enthralled with Professor Solnik's presentation, suddenly felt for him. He looked so fragile and small.

"Well I won't have it," said the British reporter who proceeded to rip up the notes he had taken before throwing them on the floor.

"What kind of journalist ignores facts?" Professor Solnik said. The comment stopped the Englishman in his tracks.

"What facts? You don't have any facts. Some scrolls were found in a cave. So what? That proves nothing. How do we know they weren't written last year? Or ten years ago? How do we know someone didn't plant them to make some kind of political statement when a war is breaking out in Palestine?"

"That's a good point," cried a voice from the back.

"It's strictly coincidence that the scrolls were discovered when all this trouble is taking place," said Professor Solnik. "Believe me I would much rather conduct a press conference without bombs bursting all around us but that's how it is."

"I think the only reason you called us here was to get some attention about the shelling."

The man seated next to the Englishman got to his feet. "Excuse me," he said. "I have a question. Will these scrolls affect the Islamic world in any way?" Professor Solnik asked who he is. "My name is Hayam Ashrawi and I am from *Muslim World*."

"That's a good question. There are many similarities between some of these works and what's in the Old and New Testaments. What effect this may have on Muslims I don't know other than the fact the Koran has been greatly influenced by both Judaism and Christianity. Since the philosophy that runs through these scrolls is consistent with early Christian philosophy I assume that would have some bearing on one's understanding of the prophet Muhammad as well."

"But could it change our understanding of the Koran?" asked the man.

"It could."

Just then a deafening barrage of explosions poured in from the street and everyone started rushing for the door. The American was the first out. Before long the room was empty except for Professor Solnik, David and Gita. Professor Solnik shook his head and sighed.

"This was a mistake," he said. "I shouldn't have done it. I thought they would want to know."

"But it'll be in *The New York Times*," Gita said.

"That fool wouldn't know the Old Testament from the New

Testament. I can only imagine what his story will look like."

"At least he'll have a story," said David.

"Maybe. I don't know. But we should get out of here before this place goes up in smoke."

Out on the street there was a building in ruins and it made David think twice about Professor Solnik's comment concerning the poor aim of the Arabs. They tried to figure which way to go.

"East," Professor Solnik said. "That is best. Don't worry. It's almost five o'clock. They always stop at five o'clock." A few minutes later they got to his car. "Can I take you some place?" he said to David. "Your apartment?"

"We'll be all right," said Gita. "We can walk. Why don't you go home and get some rest? I thought you did a great job. You were wonderful!"

"I did my best but now I must collect everything at the university. These scrolls must leave this area immediately. We can't take a chance and leave them in Palestine. Here take these two that I brought with me. I didn't even get to show them."

"What about the other ones you have?" said David.

"They're in my office. I'll have them shipped to the States. It's the only place where they'll be studied fairly. Just so you know I tucked them behind my filing cabinet next to the wall. So what about you two? It's not safe here anymore."

"We're leaving soon," said David. "I'm going to New York with Gita. She said I can stay with her while I look up some of the people you told us about."

There was an uneasy moment as the old and new generations came together. It was broken by Gita.

"It's all right, Professor Solnik. David will stay with me until he finds a place of his own." She put her arm around David. "He's going to be a great archeologist someday. Just like you."

"Of that I have no doubt," Professor Solnik said. "And so will you my dear."

"I'll be sure to write you from New York after we speak to your contacts," David said.

"Those people can help you learn more about the scrolls. Did I give you a list of names?"

"Yes you did."

Professor Solnik smiled again and Gita gave him one of her own. Then she put her arms around his neck and hugged him. It was supposed to be a hug from a girl to a grandfather. But he didn't take it that way. He didn't know how to take it.

"Hey I have a wife," he said, embarrassed.

"It's all right," said David. "We won't tell her."

When Gita let go Professor Solnik laughed, shaking his head from side to side. "You will do all right," he said to David. "You have *chutzpah*."

"What?"

"*Chutzpah*."

"*Chutzpah*," Gita said. "It means ... guts ... nerve ... class ..."

Professor Solnik raised his hand. "There is no direct English translation for *chutzpah*. It's just *chutzpah* and either you have it or you don't but you have it. That's the main thing." He shook David's hand. "Make sure you get those two scrolls out with you. I wouldn't want to leave them lying around. You can see how many open minds there are when it comes to religion and history. Be sure to write me from America."

....

The next day classes at the university were cancelled. It was clear now that once the British left Palestine and a Jewish state declared itself, there would be all-out war and no Westerners wanted to stick around for that.

Five days after the press conference David and Gita were ready to leave for Tel Aviv. Then they would take a ship across the Atlantic to New York and what David would do then he didn't know. It all depended on the scrolls. He figured the two he had would create a stir, but he didn't know what to expect. The only thing he knew was that they were a great find worthy of a place in history. Everything else was a blur.

Then there was a phone call. The voice on the line was short of breath.

"Come over here right away. To my office. At the university."

It was Professor Solnik.

"Please hurry."

David and Gita didn't have much time. Their ship was leaving in three hours. They gathered some last-minute things and with luggage in hand — not much considering — they headed off by bus to the university where they made their way to the archeology department. Professor Solnik's door was shut. David rapped on it, waited and rapped on it again. No response.

"I don't think his hearing is that good," Gita said.

The door wasn't locked, so David turned the handle and pushed the door open. Professor Solnik was in his seat buried among his papers. His face was on the desk and he looked asleep. His glasses were on the floor. The lens was cracked.

"Professor Solnik," said David. He saw that the room was in even more disarray than normal. He edged toward the desk and almost stepped on the glasses. Professor Solnik lifted his head. His mouth was cut, blood spattered all over his beard. He had bruises and welts around his eyes.

"My God!" said David. "What happened?"

"Would you get me some water please?"

Gita went to a water fountain and came back with a cup filled to the brim. "Let me wipe your face," she said.

"No. Please. Let me drink. Thank you."

"What happened?" David said.

"Two men came. Arabs. I think one of them was at the press conference. They wanted my scrolls. They said the prophet Muhammad commanded them to take the scrolls so I told them to get out and they shut my door and hit me. Then they hit me again. They tore my office apart but I wasn't going to tell them where the scrolls were."

"Behind your filing cabinet?"

"They didn't know that. I told them I didn't have any more scrolls but they didn't believe me. I think they hit me again after that. I can't remember. But my jaw is sore." He rubbed the side of his face.

"Why didn't you call someone?" Gita said. "An ambulance."

"I had to wait until you got here. That's more important. Here. David take the scrolls with you. Take them to America. They'll be safe there. You must get them out of here right now."

"But ..."

"Hurry. There isn't much time. Who knows? Those men might come back. Please!"

David reached behind the filing cabinet and found the scrolls just like Professor Solnik had said. One by one he fished them out. There were five. "I can't take all these," he said. "Where will I put them?"

"Swallow them if you have to but you must take them. It's the only way to save them."

Professor Solnik told Gita to grab the leather bag that he kept across his chair and David to put the scrolls inside it. David did as he was told, but only two or three of them would fit, and he didn't want to force them or crush them. They were much too valuable for that.

"There isn't enough room," David said. "I can't take them. There's too many."

"Too many?" said Professor Solnik. "These may be the only scrolls from that cave that will ever amount to anything. You have to take them. Use your arms."

David put two scrolls under each arm while Gita took the other three. The two scrolls from the press conference were already stashed away in David's luggage. That made seven in all, seven scrolls from the hundreds found in the caves.

"But how can I carry them on the boat?" David said.

"Buy another bag if you have to. Wrap them up with a rope. I don't care how you do it. Just do it." Professor Solnik grabbed David by the collar. "Listen to me! You want to be an archeologist, don't you?"

"Yes."

"Then take them with you! These scrolls may be the greatest archeological find in history! Do you understand?"

"What about you?" David said.

"I'll be all right. Now the two of you get out of here. And hurry. There isn't much time."

"But we can't leave you like this. It's not right."

"The only thing that's right is you take the scrolls with you. They're the only thing that matters. They matter more than me and they matter more than you. We are just their servants. Now go!"

The scrolls tucked under his arms, David walked to the door, turned and looked one last time at this man who understood the value of these old manuscripts and who was courageous enough to speak the truth.

Good-bye," David said.

Professor Solnik shook his head. "No. There is a better word to use. A much better word."

"What's that?"

"Shalom."

CHAPTER NINE

NINE

Sometimes when I was deeply embroiled in a lecture I forgot my students were Israeli. Most of them had passable English, but they didn't know many words. I was reminded of this in every class.

"Professor Marr, what was the Piltdown Skull?"

"It was a hoax."

"A hoax?"

This was one of those times.

"That means it was a fraud. A lie."

"Who did it?"

"We aren't sure."

"Why did they do it?"

"We're not sure about that either but we have suspicions. You see science is never static. It's always moving. New discoveries are made all the time and with each one we learn a little more about ourselves and the world we live in. But sometimes our thinking is tied to theories and people can subscribe to a theory with such fervor they'll do anything to see that their ideas aren't challenged."

I had to stop. I was getting ahead of myself. They wouldn't know words like 'subscribe' and 'fervor'.

"The Piltdown Skull was found in 1912 in England. The skull

of a man was found beside a jawbone that looked like it was from an ape. It had human-like teeth that were flattened at the top which would indicate a man's diet."

"Or a woman's," said one of the girls to modest laughter.

I lowered my head and peeked out over the tops of the glasses. I wore them only for class.

"Or a woman's. At the time this discovery seemed to prove the great *missing link* between man and ape had been found. You've heard about the *missing link*? The theory of evolution developed by Charles Darwin more than fifty years earlier? By the time of the Piltdown Skull it was widely accepted by science. So widely accepted that someone planted this phoney skull to prove that Darwin's ideas were right."

"Didn't Darwin say man came from apes and our brain was an expansion of the ape's brain?" another student asked.

"Yes he did but if man evolved from apes I doubt we had an ape one day and a man the next."

"I know some men who are still apes."

It was the same girl who had offered her insight a moment earlier and it immediately threw the whole class into an uproar. I didn't appreciate the outburst, but at least these first-year dunderheads were getting absorbed in something. I dismissed the remark.

"Whoever planted the Piltdown Skull wanted to show that a creature ... part man, part ape ... really lived. To solve the *missing link*. A few years later and just a few miles from where this skull was found another skull was discovered. Again part man, part ape. But there was a problem with the Piltdown Skull. It didn't fit other examples of hominids that were found in places like China or South Africa. Hominids?"

I looked around. This they understood. They were archeology students.

"These examples implied that man evolved from a common ancestor of both man and ape so somebody was missing the boat here. It wasn't until forty years later that the Piltdown Skull was shown to be a fraud. A lie. Scientists learned that the skull and jawbone were of different ages. The skull was a real fossil but the jawbone turned out to be from a modern orangutan and its so-called man-like teeth were filed down. And the skull and jawbone were artificially stained so their colors would match and make everyone think they were from the same thing. But for many years people believed the Piltdown Skull was the real thing. And why? Because scientific thought at the time *wanted* to believe it and that's where we as archeologists have to be careful."

I stopped talking and paused. Something was actually sinking in here.

"Whenever someone comes up with a new idea and has evidence to support it he's going to be attacked because he's going against other ideas. If human history shows us anything it's that changing an idea is hard to do. People hang on to their ideas like they hang on to their children. They don't want to let go even when fact stares them in the face and that's why men and women who go into science are important. That's why archeologists are important. Because they can tell us about our past. Where we come from."

"Where did we come from?"

Now that was a good question.

"How about Adam and Eve?" someone said and a few of them laughed.

"What's so funny?" I said. "If you asked everyone in the world if they believe in Adam and Eve a lot of people would say yes. So we can't dismiss it lightly. That's the trouble Darwin got himself into when he published *The Origin of Species*. Up to then people thought the world was only a few thousand years old. The only thing we had to go on was the Bible so Darwin's thinking really upset the applecart."

"The what?"

I shook my head. How careless of me.

"I mean it went against existing thought and it did more than that. It was a radical change, as radical as the idea of the earth being round and not flat or the earth revolving around the sun and not the other way around. People were ridiculed when they first developed these ideas. People were even killed for them. But today astronauts send us back pictures of the earth and anyone can see it's round so we accept this. But other ideas, ideas that maybe you can't see, are harder to accept.

"Not long before Darwin a man found a few pieces of flint when he was digging in gravel pits in France. He found them in the ground at the same level as the bones of extinct animals. He assumed they were man-made and were made at the same time as those extinct animals. He was right. But it took over twenty years, not until after Darwin came out with his ideas, before anyone believed him. And then you know what happened? People started digging up flint knives all over the place and they all agreed that mankind was much older than the Great Flood."

"So ideas had to be changed?"

"That's right."

"So the more we learn the more we find the Bible is full of lies?"

"I never said that. But sometimes scientists discover things that require a drastic change in how we think about ourselves. Anyone ever heard of Willard F. Libby? He was an American who discovered radiocarbon dating. Now we all know what that is. He even won the Nobel Prize for it but at first his ideas were challenged. The funny thing about Libby is that when he set out to search for natural radiocarbon his first tested sample came from the sewage system of Baltimore and the sample was from … human excrement."

They all looked at me in wonder.

"Ex-cre-ment?" one of them said.

I thought for an uneasy moment. "Waste. Human waste."

"Waste?"

"Feces?" I thought of my earlier conversation with Robbie, but Latin would only get me blank stares. It was no use. "Oh dammital," I said giving up. "Shit! Human shit!"

There was a moment of silence as the class made the quantum leap necessary and then they all burst out in laughter. When they settled down I continued.

"We talked about carbon 14 dating before and we know it's an important tool for archeologists. Unless you're lucky enough to excavate a city that was destroyed by a volcano ..."

"Like Pompeii?"

"Yes. Like Pompeii. Or unless you excavate a place that was burnt to the ground by an army and get to see the remains of an ancient civilization you have to dig through layers and layers of ruins that make up a tel. Each layer in the tel corresponds to a different period of time and that's how you learn about the people."

"Wasn't carbon 14 used to date the linen wrappings of one of the Dead Sea Scrolls?"

That was close to home. I nodded.

"And wasn't it used to date some of those old mummies?"

"What mummies?"

"The bog people?"

"Yes. That's right."

"Are you going to use it too, Professor Marr?"

"What do you mean me?"

"For your skeleton?"

"My skeleton?"

"The one you found."

"What are you talking about?"

"Professor Shimron said you have an old skeleton from Egypt in your lab and you might let us look at it. She wants to book a day when both classes can get together."

Damn her. Damn the woman. She had crossed the bounds of decency.

"Really? Well I'll have to speak to Professor Shimron about that."

Now I was really getting paranoid about Eliraz and the more I thought about it the more I realized she was the kind of person who would go to any lengths to get what she wanted. She was a woman, an inquisitive woman, and more than that she was a scientist. Just like me. That was the problem.

"Class dismissed."

CHAPTER TEN

TEN

"Professor Marr. Can I see you for a moment? There is something I have to tell you."

It was Robbie. I told him to come in and shut the door. He seemed uncomfortable, but then seeing Robbie look uncomfortable was the new normal.

"I just had a visitor. Someone who used to study here."

"Who?" I said.

"His name is Levi Ashkol and he is trouble."

I said to take a seat. Robbie then told me about this former classmate of his, Levi Ashkol, who used to be an archeology student at the university, but one day he quit. Just like that. Robbie said he found the scholarly route too bureaucratic and slow for his needs, and his needs were a lot different from Robbie's.

The way he told it, Levi Ashkol had abandoned his studies to join Elad, a group devoted to removing Palestinians from the Muslim Quarter of Jerusalem's Old City. As Robbie explained, the organization was full of activists who were determined to wrest properties owned or occupied by Palestinians by any means. They had an extensive network of informants and collaborators who helped them identify Palestinian homes for sale in the Muslim Quarter. They would make their move and offer to buy the property at an inflated price, a price the owners would find hard to refuse, but sometimes a family did refuse.

It didn't matter. A few days before Robbie told me about this character, it had been in the papers. A family had been living in the same house for forty years. Through three generations. They were Palestinian refugees who had come from Haifa in 1948 during the first Arab-Israeli war. They were woken up in the middle of the night when men with sub-machine guns broke through their front door and smashed in their windows. The men pulled every member of the family from their beds and ordered them out, even the grandmother, a woman in her eighties. When the family was outside shivering on the porch, they collected all their furniture and threw that out too. Then they set up a makeshift flagpole outside the house with a blue-and-white Israeli flag flying from the top.

The group had ties to government. When they resorted to kicking a family out of their home, they would come armed with titles and deeds to the property, which was now owned by this umbrella group called the Ateret Cohanim. Then they would sell the home to Jews and in this way hundreds of Palestinian families were uprooted and replaced. But this incident was particularly nasty since all the men in the family had been beaten by these thugs.

Their leader was Levi Ashkol.

"What does he have to do with us?" I asked.

Robbie told me Levi was once a serious student who, just like him, wanted to be an archeologist, but then he got mixed up with a bad bunch. It had happened during his military duty with the Israeli Defence Forces.

"When he was in the army he was stationed for a few months in Silwan, the Palestinian village not far from the Temple Mount," Robbie said.

"I know Silwan," I said. "Many artifacts have been found there. A lot of stuff from the Early Bronze Age. Ninth century BCE."

"And that is the trouble. In Levi's way of thinking that is evidence for Jews living there during the Kingdom of David. Long before any Palestinians arrived. He believes the land was stolen from his people."

"So he's a fanatic," I said. "But I still don't see ..."

"Professor Marr. He asked me if I know a man named Ismail."

"Who?"

"I do not know him but Levi said he works at the university. In our department. With the cleaning staff."

"Ismail? Wait a minute. I know a young man with that name. Ismail Abbas. He's here all the time. He comes to clean up. What about him?"

"Levi said Ismail works for him."

"What do you mean?"

"He said he works for him.

"But Ismail is a Palestinian."

"Yes. He said they have Palestinians who spy for his group in the Muslim Quarter. They tell them when a house comes up for sale. I guess they get paid. But Levi said Ismail does something else for him too."

"What's that?"

Robbie stopped talking. He pursed his lips together. He often did this when he didn't want to speak the words that were about to come.

"Levi said Ismail tells him about all the archeological discoveries we make. Just in case something shows up at Silwan."

"But we haven't found anything at Silwan."

"That is not the point, Professor Marr. Levi ... Levi Ashkol ... said this man Ismail works with the cleaning staff ... that is his full-time job ... and he seems to know what we do."

"What do you mean he knows what we do?"

"Levi said antiquities are important to his group and they always want to know what is going on around here." Robbie stopped for a moment. "He said they have eyes and ears in the department."

With that Robbie raised both his hands and touched his two forefingers to his eyes. Then he did the same thing with his ears.

I got the message.

"And he said it is not only Ismail. He said there are others too."

"But Robbie, Ismail doesn't work here anymore. He left the other day. Someone else took his place."

"Another Palestinian?"
"I think so."

CHAPTER ELEVEN

ELEVEN

It was just past five in the afternoon and I was returning to my office to finish marking some student assignments due at the end of the week. Down the hall a young man was lingering outside my lab, playing with a chain of keys. At his feet were a mop and a bucket of water. The moment he saw me, he stopped what he was doing.

"Can I help you?" I said, approaching him.

He wasn't a student, but looked about the same age. He was my height, but very thin with a wide nose and a slender round chin that was full of stubble from two or three days' growth. His black eyebrows were full and thick, his eyes dark, and on his lips he wore this look of quiet self-assurance. I had never seen him before.

"Can I help you?" I said again, a little louder this time.

"I am the cleaner," he said, his English more than passable.

"You are cleaning staff?"

He nodded. Just once.

"I am new," he said.

"Oh. You're the one who took over from Ismail?"

The single nod again. It was bizarre the way he did it. More of a military shrug. But he was a civilian.

"I'm Professor Marr. This is my lab."

With that his face went blank, as if I had just revealed some secret. He started jingling the chain of keys.

"I was going to clean up," he said.

"But you don't have a key to my lab on that chain. Do you? You only have a key to my office. Right?"

He looked confused or at least he was trying to look like that.

"Didn't anyone tell you?" I said.

"Tell me what?"

"That you can't go in there."

"No."

"I see."

We weren't getting off to a good start.

"I'm sorry," I said, extending my hand.

He just stood there. Frozen. Numb. Not knowing what to do. And then he offered me his hand in return. It was limp, a normal handshake for this part of the world.

"Your name?" I said, my voice reaching.

"Mahmoud."

Mach-mood.

"You are Palestinian?"

The single nod again.

"I was surprised that Ismail left so suddenly," I said. "What happened to him?"

"He got another job," he said with a shrug. "More money."

I asked him to come down the hall to my office and he did, reluctantly, as if he was short of time, but not before he mentioned the mop and the bucket. I told him to leave them where they were, that we wouldn't be long. When we got to my office I unlocked the door and told him to take a seat in the chair opposite my desk. He looked nervous when I shut the door behind me.

"This is your first day?" I asked.

"Yes."

"I gather you have an interest in archeology if you want to work in a place like this?"

"I was looking for a job."

"So you don't have an interest in archeology then?"

No response.

"Where are you from?" I asked him.

His eyes were studying me now.

"I was born in Silwan," he said.

"Silwan is a very old community. I know it well."

"You do?"

"Yes. And where exactly in Silwan are you from?"

His eyes were on me still, but I sensed a softening. Just a bit.

"Wadi Hilweh."

It was a Palestinian neighborhood in the village. Very old and very poor. And totally neglected by the Israeli authorities, as were all Palestinian communities in the area.

"My people have lived there for thousands of years."

"Thousands?"

"We were the first people in Silwan."

"Well a lot of different people have lived there," I said. "Let's see now." I started rhyming them off one by one. The Assyrians, Babylonians, Egyptians, Greeks, Romans, Arab Canaanites. And the Jews.

"We were there before the Jews."

It was the first thing he said with any authority.

"I know about Silwan," I said, "and all the things they found there but it's not always easy to date them and match them with the right period and the right people. Sometimes it's very difficult to do that. Many Jews think it's part of the original Kingdom of David and any artifacts that turn up are proof of Jewish existence. Historically I mean."

He sat in the chair, clenching his fists, a young man who looked not much more than a boy.

"How old are you?" I asked him.

"Twenty-four."

He looked younger than that.

"The Jews wants Silwan because it's near the Al Aqsa Mosque," he said.

"You think so?"

"El Ad makes trouble for us."

El Ad was an organization that had been established to build new settlements for Jews and to zero in on local Palestinian neighborhoods. El Ad wanted the Jews in and the Palestinians out. It had the State of Israel on its side, and the army and the local police, while the Palestinians had nothing. Except their homes. He kept talking.

"They kick Palestinians out and move in Jews. Then they change the street names from Arabic to Hebrew."

"Yes I know that and I don't agree with it."

"You don't?"

"No. I think it's wrong to kick people out of their homes just because they happen to be Palestinian. A home is a home. But some people see it differently. My wife for example. We've talked about it many times."

"She is Jewish?"

"Yes."

"And you are Jewish?"

"No." I shook my head. "I'm not Jewish. I'm just an archeologist."

"But you work for them. For Jews?"

I had never thought of it that way. I was a visiting professor.

"To tell you the truth I work with a museum but I'm teaching a course here right now. But I work for the university. I don't work for the Jews."

"It's the Hebrew University, isn't it?"

"Yes."

Case closed or so he figured.

"*Mahmoud*," I said, "let's talk about you. You got yourself a job at the university so in your way of thinking that makes you complicit, doesn't it? I mean you're working for the Jews too. Aren't you?"

"I needed the money. All I do is clean."

"I see. Well I have to do some marking but if you need anything let me know. And if you see Ismael say hello for me. I always liked Ismael."

The single nod.

"And you'll stay away from my lab. Right? No one is allowed in there. And you don't have a key anyway. Do you?"

He looked at me stone-faced.

"No key," he said.

That was my first meeting with Mahmoud.

CHAPTER TWELVE

TWELVE

At night the desert is so dark and still it's hard to believe you are with the living. There is nothing above but the stark emptiness of the heavens and the only thing to hear is the sound of your feet sinking into the sand. If the moon is out like it was this night, you can make out the rolling lines of the dunes, but those lines are not sharp and precise. Nothing is sharp and precise in the desert. Especially at night.

Robbie and I were returning to the site. To Qumran, or Kirbet Qumran, as it's called. The name is Arabic and it means 'the ruins at Qumran'. Since the 'Q' is pronounced as a 'K,' Kirbet Qumran achieves the effect of alliteration. The ruins are near the spring of Ain Feshka at the northwest corner of the Dead Sea, less than a mile from the shore and not far from the plain cut by the wadi that drains the Buqeia valley. From a distance the caves, those same caves where the scrolls were discovered many years earlier, sit like solitary dots in the wall of cliffs. This was where that mysterious sect of Hebrews called the Essenes lived in their monastery and this was where they buried their dead.

The best record we have of them is from the scribe Josephus who described their sacrosanct way of life and their ostracism from the other Hebrews. When the area was excavated in the early 1950s there was suspicion that the Bedouin had planted the manuscripts in the caves themselves only to begin selling them later, but archeologists proved this story false. Similar manuscript fragments were found in many caves in the area and the pottery in those caves was identical to that found at Qumran. The pottery was from the first century. The stratigraphy pointed to several phases of occupation in the region, beginning with the ancient Israelites in the eighth century B.C. But the Essenes didn't make their mark until the second century B.C. and over a period of two or three hundred years they thrived.

This was where we found the mummy. But on this particular visit to Qumran there was a difference. We weren't on a journey inspired by the rambling of some Ka-fearing Bedouin who thought he had found an ancient grave. No. This time we were going back to look for clues to see if there was something else, but we had to be careful because of those same Bedouin. They were the ones who first found it and now they knew it was important. At least, it was to us. Our ace in the hole was their fear, which kept them at a distance. But I still knew the Bedouin could be opportunists like Muhammad the Wolf and others who once developed a scripture trade with the Dead Sea Scrolls. If there was money to be made with this find they would make my life miserable.

We parked our jeep and grabbed the simplest instruments of excavation. A shovel for digging. A trowel to scrape away the earth from anything we find. Two paintbrushes to brush loose dirt from exposed artifacts. A screen to catch small items that the trowel missed. Like beads. But I didn't expect to find any beads here. We also brought a bag filled with bottles and cotton. If we were lucky enough to find something it would have to be cleaned and put inside a bottle. The cotton was for packing. We had other things too, important things like tools to help us find artifacts that may have been hidden for hundreds or even thousands of years. We had an electromagnetic metal detector and a long rod with a T-bar handle. That was my probing device.

"It was over there by that ridge," Robbie said.

We followed the same route where the Bedouin led us before, along the eastern part of the Wadi Qumran and toward the ancient water spring at Ein Feshka. There was that mysterious wall of blackness again. We stepped behind the ridge and stopped. The hole in the ground where we found the mummy was covered with the loose dirt I had shovelled from our last visit. No one had been here since.

"Here we are," said Robbie, dropping his load and removing the shovel from his shoulder. He looked around. There was nothing to see but darkness. I lowered the metal detector and probing device to the ground.

We would do a standard grid excavation. Nothing fancy. The grave site would be divided into small squares, the sides of each square a foot in length. At the corners we would place wooden pegs to be used as reference points for surveying and then we'd dig out the squares one by one, leaving behind the narrow unexcavated strips in between them. The site measured six feet by four feet, so we'd have twenty-four squares in all. Under the circumstances, I thought this was the best method. It was fast and I had the feeling that time was not on our side. I measured the site and placed the wooden pegs into their respective positions.

"All right, Robbie," I said. "Start digging around the edges." He took the shovel and made a motion to begin, but something stopped him from disturbing the ground. "What's wrong, Robbie?"

He was uneasy.

"Professor Marr," he said. "What if this is holy soil? Maybe we should not touch it."

Just then I thought of Robbie in the same light as the Bedouin and wasn't impressed. I shook my head and took the shovel from his hands. I began to dig and something came over me. As I prepared the site for excavation I abandoned every rule of archeology I ever knew. Preparing a site meant slow digging and caution, so as not to destroy anything near the surface, but I attacked the site with venom. Rage. Some strange and powerful force that I didn't even know was inside me.

"Professor Marr," Robbie said, putting his hand on the shovel. "Be careful."

"Eliraz suspects something," I said, making stabbing thrusts into the densely packed sand below the surface. "One of her students is in my class. She told him we found a skeleton and that I'm going to show it to them. Her class and mine."

"Why would she say that?"

"You tell me. You worked for her, didn't you?"

"She is a persistent woman. That is for sure."

"She must not find out about this, Robbie. I don't want her to find out!"

"But no one knows except you and me. And Dr. Hassad."

"The Bedouin know."

"But they will not ..."

"They will not what?"

I stopped digging and looked at him in the eye. It must have been painfully obvious what was going through my mind.

"You think I will tell her?" he said. "Why would I do that?"

"I don't know," I said, resuming my thrusts with the shovel, but this time not going as deep into the dirt. It was an awkward moment. I was accusing Robbie of something that hadn't even happened. But I had to be sure.

"I think you should be more worried about your friend Dr. Hassad," Robbie said.

"Jamil? I'm not worried about him. Besides isn't he the one who said not to tell anyone?"

"So you think I might tell Professor Shimron but not him? Is that it?"

"I didn't say that."

"You have little faith in me, Professor Marr. That is your problem. You have little faith in anything."

"Robbie, I'm sorry if I insulted you but I want to make sure she doesn't find out. She's the type to snoop around. You know that. And she's watching us. She's watching our every move. Trying to trap us. We can't let her do that."

Robbie looked at the grave site. It was marked with fresh droppings of the dirt and sand I had just dug up. "So what should we do?" he said.

"For the time being nothing. I won't tip my hand. I'll just pretend Eliraz isn't a factor. I'll play coy with her."

"Coy?"

"Oh damn it, Robbie, when are you going to learn to speak English!"

It was a curt remark and I regretted it immediately. I stopped digging, rested my arms on the handle of the shovel and took a deep breath. It was almost evening, but still very hot even for this time of year. I grabbed a bottle of water and drank it down.

"Professor Marr, you are forgetting something," said Robbie. "You are in my country. I am not in yours."

"Yes," I said, wiping my lips. "You're right. I'm sorry. I shouldn't have said that. The last few days have been hard. I haven't been getting much sleep."

Gita had returned from her conference the night before and I didn't mention anything to her. But she could tell I was ill at ease. She could always tell that. I blamed it on fatigue.

I nodded to Robbie in a way that apologized for my being a man with human frailties. I wanted to say something reassuring to him, but didn't know what. All I could do was let out an exasperated sigh and get on with my digging. After ten minutes there were twenty-four holes in the ground and nothing in them but sand. Only sand.

Robbie took the electromagnetic detector and began sweeping it across the grave site this way and that. If anything of metal was under the surface and not too deep we would find it. I was sure of that because of how the body was found; any objects related to the burial would be no more than three feet in the ground and in or near the site. But we found nothing. Over and over I told Robbie to sweep across the grave and no matter how much I dug and how often he made a pass over the holes the device remained deathly silent.

"There is nothing here, Professor Marr. We are wasting our time."

"Just a few minutes more. Let's try again."

It was no use. We found nothing. Robbie started getting ready to go. He packed up the metal detector and probing device.

"Come on," he said. "I do not like it here. I have a bad feeling about this place."

Robbie started walking away in the direction of our jeep while I started packing up the tools. In frustration I grabbed the shovel and made a few angry jabs at the dirt. There was a noise. A scratch. My ears were trained to pick up sounds that aren't expected in a dig since it could mean something. I stopped, threw the shovel to the ground and fell to my knees, my tired knees worn out from years of crawling around on dirt floors and rock foundations. I tore away at the sand near where the head of the mummy had lain. It was maybe two feet below the surface. The edge of what appeared to be a piece of wood was jutting out. At least, it looked like wood. I touched it with my fingertips. It was brittle. I retrieved my shovel and carefully dug deeper around the immediate area, then began to scratch away with my bare hands.

"Professor Marr! Are you coming?"

It was Robbie. His voice was off in the distance now.

"Just a minute! I'll be right there!"

I clawed away at the dirt, breaking my nails, gnawing the skin off my fingers. But I didn't care. There was only the burning desire to discover.

"And there followed him a great company of people and of women which also bewailed and lamented him."

It was a piece of wood. Old brittle wood. Marked with the scarred indentations of age. In the middle of it was a weathered iron spike from another era. The Romans, no doubt. I eased it out from the sand and turned it over.

"And he bearing his cross went forth into a place called the place of a skull which is called in the Hebrew Golgotha."

I knew right away what it was. A plaque. A *titulus*. Used by the Romans to describe the crime of their victim. And it was acacia. That was the kind of wood they used. Then the shivering began. First in my lips, then inching its way to my cheeks before spreading to my jaw. Soon my whole head and neck were shaking.

"And when they were come to the place which is called Calvary, there they crucified him and the malefactors, one on the right hand and the other on the left."

There were letters on the wood. Big ancient letters of languages no longer spoken. I recognized them right away and the fear that gripped me at that moment was a fear I had never known before. Not in the caves of Judea. Not at Pompeii. Not even at Masada or Giv'at ha-Mivtar. My teeth were rattling and my eardrums pulsating, and I couldn't stop it. The writing was in Greek and Hebrew and Latin. The Latin of the Imperial Roman Empire. And if this was really happening it meant the words of

Matthew, Luke and John were wrong. They were all wrong. But not Mark. It meant Mark was right. It took me a few seconds to do the translation.

"*And the superscription of his accusation was written over THE KING OF THE JEWS*".

Those were the words of Mark and that was the message on this piece of wood — this ancient piece of wood — with an iron spike, a Roman spike, running through it. *Rex Judaeorum*. THE KING OF THE JEWS. That's what it said. I was numb. Completely numb. I had turned to rock.

CHAPTER THIRTEEN

THIRTEEN

"David, you look terrible. What's the matter?"

We were sitting at the breakfast table. Gita had just returned from her conference the night before. It was the same night when I got back from my latest visit to Qumran with Robbie. We were renting an apartment in Jerusalem during my stay as a visiting professor and she had been away for a few days. But now she was back.

"I'm a little tired," I said.

"You were up all night."

"I couldn't sleep." I looked at her. "Maybe I was just happy to have you back."

She laughed. "A nice thought but I don't buy it. Something's bothering you. What is it?"

"Nothing."

"Is it your students?"

"Maybe. There's always one or two who are a real pain. Here in Jerusalem it's no different."

"Is it work? Something with your work?"

"No."

"What is it then?"

"Nothing."

Gita and I had known each other for forty years. There isn't much you miss when you've been around somebody that long. If I was on a dig and saw something particularly gruesome or upsetting, she would know as soon as she laid eyes on me. She wouldn't have to ask. It had happened too many times now. She also knew when I was lying.

"Listen, if something is bothering you so much it occupies your mind through the night I want you to tell me about it. Okay? I'm only your wife."

I said okay and then asked about her conference. It was a scholarly gathering and had to do with the recent discovery of the ancient city of Bethsaida, a place mentioned in the New Testament. Gita said the only interesting thing about the conference was the session about Bethsaida possibly being built on an even older city dating from the Old Testament. Then she told me about the camp.

"One day we had a free afternoon so a few of us did a little exploring," she said. "We wound up going through one of those refugee camps. It was horrible. The way those people live. The poverty. So many children running around with nothing but the shirts on their backs. I don't even think they have electricity. I never saw anything like that before. It was terrible, David."

"Since when are you so concerned with Palestinians?"

"They're children, David. No one should have to live like that. When we were leaving a few of them starting throwing stones at us. They couldn't have been more than five or six years old. I can only imagine what they think about us in places like that."

"Us?"

"I mean Jews. You have little kids living like that and the only thing they know ... the only thing they learn ... is what they're told."

"They learn to hate. It's easy when you have nothing."

"That's the trouble. Golda Meir bless her soul said it right when she said peace will come when the Arabs love their children more than they hate us. Everything starts with the children."

A lot of trouble was brewing. It had started when four people, all of them Palestinians, were killed in a refugee camp in Gaza when a military truck driven by an Israeli got out of control and hit a car. People said it was deliberate. There were riots in the camp, which brought out the Israeli army, and soon things were boiling over in the West Bank and East Jerusalem. Young Palestinians, even children, had taken to throwing stones at Israeli soldiers.

They were calling it an *intifada*.

CHAPTER FOURTEEN

FOURTEEN

The official name is a Languedocian scorpion. Native to the Mediterranean region, it lives a life of solitude and is one of the largest in the scorpion family, growing to three and a half inches long. Three and a half inches of tawny yellow poison. Enough to kill someone. Most people don't know that the scorpion is related to the spider, although it more closely resembles a lobster, but while lobsters are dim-witted creatures no one would take a scorpion lightly. With five stick-like legs on either side, it moves quickly. Like an overgrown insect. The scurrying motion and small front claws are more than enough to send shivers down your spine, but the real danger is that tail with the venom in it. There are hundreds of species of scorpions and some much better known than this one, but the Languedocian is to be feared, which is why I used it for experiments.

It's probably the inherent violent nature of man within me, but I was told there is some spectacle when a Languedocian scorpion is placed inside a glass jar with a poisonous spider, so I wanted to see for myself. I would have settled for a tarantula, which is relatively easy to trap, but a biologist I know explained that the tarantula — he called it the *Lycosa Tarentula* — isn't dangerous and isn't even that poisonous. That was news to me.

He suggested the *Narbonne Lycosa*, which he said is more nimble and far more potent than a tarantula. I got a few specimens, followed his instructions and put sand on the bottom of the jar to allow the combatants a good foothold just so everything begins equally. I have since seen what happens many times and it always ends the same.

Both the scorpion and Lycosa are equipped with poisonous fangs and the Lycosa is infinitely more agile. When the two creatures are placed in isolation, the spider has all the dexterity necessary to leap onto the back of its adversary and attack at will, which is exactly how it kills much of its prey, even prey larger than itself. The first time I tried this little scenario I thought the scorpion, which is slow to react to danger, would be at a disadvantage. I figured the giant spider would jump onto it and deliver the fatal stroke before fleeing. But it didn't happen like that and it never does.

What happens is that the Lycosa stands there, half-erect, opening its poison-bearing fangs, an insect vampire daring its opponent to make a move. And the scorpion does. It approaches with short quick steps, the ever present pincers in front. Then it seizes the spider with those two-fingered pincers and holds it at a safe distance. The spider protests by opening and closing its fangs, but it can't bite. It can't move. It can't do anything.

The scorpion wastes no time delivering the coup de grace. Its curved tail lifts up, comes down over its head and thrusts the deadly sting right into the spider's exposed breast. This isn't the clean sting of a wasp or a bee. The knotted tail of the scorpion with the sting imbedded deep inside its foe pushes and shakes without mercy. The sting lingers, caught in a frenzy of excited palpitation inside the hapless Lycosa, as more and more poison escapes and flows through its body. Only a little poison is enough to kill the spider, but the scorpion isn't satisfied. It releases an orgasm of venom. Once the spider receives this flow of poison, it draws up its legs and dies.

It happens like this every time, without fail, and I feel almost guilty when I watch it again and again knowing what will take place, but there is something in that glass jar that compels me to watch. Over and over. Maybe I'm hoping for a different conclusion. Maybe I'm thinking how this battle encapsulates life itself. But the fact remains that the Lycosa is killed so convincingly and so overwhelmingly, while the scorpion lives on to kill again.

"Ecch. What have you got there?"

The voice came from behind me. I turned to find Eliraz peering over my shoulder.

"How did you get in here?"

"Your door was open."

"It was?"

Impossible. I always locked it and especially now, but then I remembered. I had just brought in two glass jars, each with a new spider, and must have been so preoccupied that I forgot to shut the door.

"What are you doing with those terrible looking things?"

There was nothing to hide, so I stepped aside to give her a better view. "A spider. A very poisonous spider. With a scorpion. Inside a jar. They can't escape. One must kill the other. But the scorpion always wins."

"How awful. Look at that thing. Is it dead?"

"You mean the spider?"

"Yes."

"It's dead."

"What's it doing now?"

"The scorpion?"

"Yes."

"Watch."

The feast begins instantly. The scorpion starts consuming its dinner, beginning with the head. It's always the head. Eliraz couldn't stand it.

"Oh my God," she said. "That's sickening. How can you watch like that? Are you crazy?"

"But look what it does."

She glanced back at the jar to see the scorpion move in close to the spider, taking a chunk of the head before swallowing small mouthfuls. A chunk at a time. A swallow. A chunk. A swallow. A chunk. Like a machine.

"It's going to take all day at that rate," she said.

"It does take all day and all night too. At least twenty-four hours to eat the whole spider. Everything but a few bits of the legs that are hard to digest. I know. The last time I did this I left it there at night and when I came back in the morning it was still eating."

"Where on earth does it put it?"

"I don't know. You wouldn't think it could eat so much, would you? But it does."

The mummy was at the far end of the lab, inside the plexiglass with the white sheet on top. Eliraz would see it when she turned around.

"Is that your skeleton from Alexandria University over there?" she said.

"Yes."

"I see you have it all covered up."

"That's right."

"Special box?"

I nodded.

"Afraid it might catch a cold?"

"Very funny."

"So can I have a look?"

"I'd rather you didn't."

"Why not?"

I didn't know what to say. Could I plead the rights of ownership? What difference would that make to her?

"Come on, David. I'm dying to see it. Just let me have a look."

"No. It's ... messy. Bones ... everywhere."

"So what? I've seen lots of skeletons before and I'm sure it's not as sickening as what you keep in your little jars. Let me see it. Why won't you let me?"

"You just can't."

"But why?"

"Eliraz, you're in *my* lab. My lab! I didn't ask you in."

"The door was open."

"I must ask you to leave."

She looked again towards the mummy. "It looks like a long box from here. Is that what it is? Or a coffin maybe? Why would you put a skeleton in a *coffin*?"

The mere mention of the word made me uneasy and what made me so uneasy is that I had thought of this myself. Leave it to Eliraz to mimic my innermost apprehensions.

"Come on, what's the big mystery? What have you got in there? It's not a skeleton. Is it?"

I put my hands on her shoulders, nudging her to the door. "Eliraz, I want you to get out of my lab. Right now. Out." I pushed her gently. My hands on her arms. She was almost out of the room when she caught me by surprise. She reached up around my neck and pressed herself against me. I was dumbfounded.

"Eliraz ... what are you doing?"

"Come on, David. I see how you look at me."

"What?"

"A woman knows when a man wants her."

"What!"

"I know. You're a married man. So where is your wife? Back home? Thousands of miles away?"

I thought the whole thing was so ridiculous that I wanted to laugh. I was supposed to laugh, wasn't I? Eliraz was much younger than me and if anyone in the faculty — the staff, the students — even hinted at such a thing they would have been badgered unmercifully. But nothing seemed to faze her, certainly not the fact that I was married. Her hands on my neck, she began to rub my skin and then she slid her fingers across my mouth. Her nails were red like those of a witch and a dangerous witch at that, one who carries around a blatant sexuality.

"Actually Eliraz, my wife is not back home. She was away at a conference but she just got back. She's here in Jerusalem."

Eliraz didn't seem to care.

"You're a lonely man, David," she said. "Your work consumes you. It's not good."

I should have pushed her out, thrown her out, and got rid of her once and for all. But I didn't. I let her stay there. That was when I caught the scent of her perfume and felt trapped by it like the poor Lycosa had been with the scorpion's venom.

"Won't you just let me have a peek?" she said, her fingers scratching the back of my neck.

"It's nothing, Eliraz. Just a skeleton. I don't see why you're so interested. It's nothing."

"If it's nothing there's no reason why I can't see it. Is there?"

"No except I don't want you to."

"David, I know something is going on around here. I'm not stupid."

I took her hands and removed them from me. Unfortunately, this required more courage than it should have.

"We have to talk," she said.

"About what?"

"We just have to talk. We never do. We always ignore each other and that's silly. You know perfectly well that you and me are the best people in the department. We shouldn't be enemies. We should be friends. We should talk about our work."

"Oh? I think you just want to talk about *my* work."

With that she began stroking my wrist, her red fingernails clawing my skin like the cat that she was, only this one was tall and erect with sharp features. Everything about her was crisp and sure. There were no rough edges with Eliraz. She was intelligent, determined and alluring, especially when she wanted to be.

"David, you have no idea how highly I regard you. Professionally I mean."

"Oh?"

"For all the things you've done. I know all about you. The digs at Pompeii. Masada. Herculaneum. How the Department of Antiquities thinks you're some kind of superstar. I'm insanely jealous. Did you know that? Because you're so *good*. It's not easy for a foreigner to be held in such high esteem in a country like Israel. I remember that paper you wrote for the *Israel Exploration Journal*. It was magnificent."

"Which one?"

"The one on crucifixion."

I blinked.

"What was the name of that man? The skeleton? That was crucified?"

"Jehohanan."

"That was some discovery. I think you have a sense for the morbid that I don't have myself."

"What do you mean?"

"All your research on the Romans and crucifixion. I could never do that. You must like this sort of thing. Why else would you spend so much time on something like crucifixion? Now take me. I find that just a little too grotesque. But I admire you for what you do. And your little game here with the scorpion and spider."

"Game?"

"Experiment. It's not something I would do. I prefer dealing with the aesthetics and social aspects of ancient cultures. Especially where it concerns women. How they were treated by their men for example."

"How *were* they treated, Eliraz?"

"For the most part pretty rotten. Not much different from today, is it?"

"You tell me."

"I really don't think you want to hear about my ex, do you? I could fill your ear with him. He was a bastard if there ever was one. But typical for an Israeli man. They all treat their women like dirt. They live in this macho world and think we owe them something. The funny thing was ..."

"What?"

"He wasn't a good lover. Not very good in bed."

"Eliraz ..."

"Eliraz what? You asked me, didn't you? He just didn't have it. That's all."

What on earth could I say? She looked at me, still stroking the sensitive underside of my wrist, her feline eyes about to pounce.

"I could never figure out men like that. They think they're God's gift to women and they can't even perform! I bet you're not like that. Are you?"

Eliraz was going for broke. How I sympathized with the Lycosa.

"There is this *thing* with Israeli men. A militarism about them. Maybe it's this country. But they just can't seem to relax and treat a woman the way she wants to be treated. Gently ... with tenderness ... but men like you aren't like that. I bet you treat your women much better."

She was flirting with me. It was only information she wanted.

"There were some things he wouldn't do," she said.

"Who?"

"My husband. He was very ... conservative ... in bed I mean."

My mouth hung ajar. The scorpion's venom had just been inserted.

"Look," she said, "why don't we get out of here and go somewhere where we can talk? About our work."

"*Our work?*"

"Yes."

"You mean crucifixion? Scorpions? Things like that?"

....

I had been in my lab for several hours and needed a break. I also needed to get Eliraz out of there, so I agreed to go with her. She said we would go for coffee. It was against my better instincts, but I went along.

"Where are we going?" I asked once she began driving us to west Jerusalem, away from the Old City.

"Relax. It's not far. I live near here."

I started fidgeting in the seat beside her. She took me to an area with apartment buildings everywhere. Her apartment. There was a sly smile on her face. I asked about the coffee and when we were inside her place she said she would brew a pot.

"I think you should know that in me you have met your intellectual match," she said. "I'm a very good archeologist."

"I know."

"But I'm an even better *lover*."

That was it. I felt I was in the company of a harlot. Eliraz had sometimes looked the part of a harlot, but I didn't know she could act like one. She went into the kitchen and I began asking myself what the hell I was doing in her apartment, so I pretended I wasn't. I closed my eyes and imagined I was in Pompeii. More than two thousand years ago. Where two narrow streets crossed in the most densely populated part of town. The *lupanar*. It meant 'brothel' and it was a two-storey building at the corner. On the upper level were cubicles with couches and cushions draped all over them. I imagined I was in one of those cubicles with a girl. There was nothing secretive or illicit about it. I was a visiting sailor and she would replenish me after my long trip from some far-off port. I don't know if I drifted off, but the next thing I knew

Eliraz was there with two cups of coffee. She put the coffee down and began stroking her hair. It was sultry the way she did it. That was a word I would never associate with Gita. Gita wore her natural beauty with a reserved modesty, which always made her so appealing. The thought of her brought me back to reality.

"You've always given me the impression you think you're better than me," Eliraz said. "That I'm inferior to you. But I'm not."

"I never thought you were."

"No? You come here to teach. The superstar that you are. You take the biggest lab in the faculty even though you're only here a short time ... and then you shut everybody out just because you found something spectacular. You're making a mistake. I'm going to be department head some day. That's my ambition."

She smiled confidently. I noticed there wasn't a glimmer of shame or shyness about her. I wondered how many men she had made love to since her divorce. I suspected many.

"You should take me more seriously," she said. "You could use a friend like me. We think alike. We do."

"How is that?"

"We are both *intense* individuals."

"Intense?"

"Yes. You even carry your intensity around with you. In your work. I can see it. And you carry other things around with you too."

"Like what?"

"Sadness. I can't explain it but it's in your eyes. Some scar that you wear. There's a sadness about you. I can see that too. A loss of some kind maybe? A longing for something you can't have?"

If Eliraz was a knife she was cutting right through me. She may have planned to seduce me to get what she wanted, but first she would bare me emotionally to make the conquest complete.

"I know about losses, David. My marriage went up in smoke after eight years. Eight years! That was a good part of my life so I'm at a loss too. You see we have something in common. But you haven't told me what ails you. Maybe I can help."

She pushed her cup away with a fearless look in her eye.

"Eliraz," I said.

"What David?"

"I know you just want information from me."

"How do you know that? You don't give yourself enough credit."

"I could almost be your father."

"But you're not."

"Look. If you want to talk ... we can talk."

She took my hand in hers. "I don't like being left out. You've got something in your lab and you won't tell me. That means it's important."

"What do you mean I carry a sadness around with me?" I said, trying to change the subject.

"I saw it the first time I met you but now there's something else. Fear. Only the fear came after your ... skeleton. Listen you're wrong to keep this to yourself. Who do you know in this country? What contacts do you have? I know a lot of people. Important people."

"I have contacts."

"Here? In the Israeli government?"

She was right. My contacts were strictly with academics and any involvement with government was merely the passing correspondence of a bureaucrat or two.

"So who do you know, Eliraz?"

"People. At the Department of Antiquities. People with power. They could help you."

"Like who?"

"David," she said with a smile, still playing with my fingers. "Believe me when I tell you this but I've made a career out of knowing who's important. I have connections. Right to the top. I can get through the bureaucracy."

"You mean you've brought politicians here?"

Eliraz was not impressed. She let go of my hand. "You're making a mistake," she said. "For all your achievements you're still a foreigner in Israel. You think you understand but you don't. You don't have it inside you. Israeli blood I mean."

"Israeli blood?"

"That's right. I'm talking about fighting for a nation. Giving your life for a country. Have you ever had to do that? Knowing your enemies surround you and would love to eliminate you.

You shouldn't keep secrets from me, David. Especially at a time like this."

"I thought there was a peace process going on."

"There is but it's fragile. Have you ever heard of the Ateret Cohanim?"

I nodded.

"They're a fanatical group of Jews who want to get rid of all the Arabs in Jerusalem. Every one of them. They say Jerusalem belongs to the Jews and only the Jews. Some people think they're as bad as the Fatah."

"Are they?"

"I don't know but they have a point. The Palestinians are trouble for everybody. On the other hand even the Palestinians have a beef. If someone took my home I'd be pretty upset too."

"Eliraz, I haven't met many Israelis who think like that."

"Maybe not. But the geography creates a lot of problems. You have the Jews and the Western Wall and a few feet away the Muslims and their Dome of the Rock which is on the site of the original temple altar. The Ateret Cohanim want to build a *new* temple there. They already have a seminary in the middle of the Arab Quarter."

"That's like rubbing the Arabs' noses into the dirt."

"And what do you think the settlements on the West Bank are doing? Those aren't settlements. They're permanent. Some rabbis talk about building a synagogue right on the Temple Mount. In the sanctuary. Between the two mosques."

"But that place is sacred to Islam."

"Of course it is. And then some Palestinian would blow himself up along with the mosques and the Arabs would blame it on the Jews. It's insane. But it's always insane. Could you imagine what would happen if they destroyed the Western Wall?"

"I wouldn't even want to think about it."

"Well I hate to tell you but we're almost there. So down goes the Wall and then down goes the Dome of the Rock."

"That would lead to a holy war. A jihad. It would make the Ayatollah's revolution look like nothing."

"But it can happen. These people ... the Fatah, the Ateret Cohanim ... they use religion, the religion of their enemies, to get what they want. The problem is when people like that start to wage war they drag everybody else in too. There are fanatics on all sides."

With those words Jamil's warning came back to haunt me. I could hear his voice as if he was in this very room, urging me not to tell anyone, urging me not to tell Eliraz. But she was the first Israeli who ever spoke to me like this. The faculty members didn't talk to foreigners about such things — among themselves maybe, but not to me — and I realized then that maybe it had been a mistake to ignore her for so long. Maybe there was more to Eliraz than the prying scheming woman I always took her for.

"I can help you, David. I'm an Israeli. I know how the people think. But like you I'm an archeologist. I know how *you* think. You couldn't have a better go-between than me so if you found something you should tell me." She reached for my hands again. "You have nothing to fear from me. By the way ... *acacia* ... what's that about?"

I wasn't sure that I heard right. "What did you say?"

"Acacia." She saw the perplexed look on my face. "When I was in your lab I saw your notebook. It was open and there was only one word on the page. *Acacia.* That's a tree. Some type of wood. No?"

I didn't say anything. But I didn't have to.

"It was written in big letters with a question mark after it." She caught the hesitation in my eye. "It has something to do with your discovery, doesn't it?" She had my hands in hers, playing with them. Teasing.

I tried to pull away, but she wouldn't let me.

"I bet these hands of yours have touched a lot of artifacts, haven't they? Tell me. What is the most fascinating artifact they ever held?"

"Fascinating?" I said. "Well as far as popular culture goes I guess that would be the Holy Grail."

"I beg your pardon?"

"The Holy Grail. You know. The chalice of Christ."

"What are you talking about?"

This time I pulled my hands away. This woman made me uncomfortable.

"What do you mean the Holy Grail?" she said. "That's a lot of nonsense."

"Some people don't think so."

She shook her head. "You really are a man of mystery, aren't you? With this hurt that you wear all the time. I can tell you know. You can't hide it from me. And the Holy Grail?"

I wish I could have told her, if only to tell someone. The only ones who knew about the Qumran mummy were Robbie and Jamil, both of them men who were sometimes overbearing about their heritage. I still hadn't mentioned anything to Gita.

"I was in England in 1967," I said, Jamil's words of warning dissolving into the air. "It was the year of the Six Day War."

"A wonderful year. One of the most memorable in the history of my country."

"It was a memorable year in my country too. Our centennial."

"You're Canadian, aren't you?"

I nodded.

"Yours is a young country."

"Yes and that can be a problem. A young country often lacks its own culture."

"Culture takes *time*. As an Israeli archeologist I know that as well as anyone. Now tell me about this Holy Grail business. And your *whatever it is*. What did you find that's so important you have to lie about it? What is this skeleton all about, if that's what it is, and what does it have to do with acacia wood?"

I didn't want to say anything. Really I didn't. But the words started to come. "All I can tell you Eliraz is that I found something ... important ... but potentially ..."

"Potentially what?"

"Cataclysmic."

"Cataclysmic? My but you're sounding very biblical all of a sudden."

"Maybe but I can't think of a better word."

"Cataclysmic? That's a flare for the dramatic. You make it sound like Armageddon is right around the corner."

My thoughts reverted to the words of the holy book and the warning of the battle ... the *great battle* ... yet to come. "Armageddon," I said. "The final judgment. I'm starting to think it might really happen."

Once again she took my hands in hers. "Why do you feel that way? About Armageddon I mean."

I sighed, not wanting to talk, but the words kept coming. "It's just that all my life I keep finding one reason after another why God can't possibly exist."

"Then that's what separates you from other people in the Holy Land, David."

"How's that?"

"All the people here … the Jews … the Christians ... the Muslims ... they all think they've found him. So tell me about this Holy Grail of yours."

CHAPTER FIFTEEN

FIFTEEN

England, 1967

David Marr was back in Israel after leaving Cairo where he and Jamil Hassad had been examining the Royal Mummies. He had been away from the family for too long, and decided to take them to England for a holiday. But on the morning of June 5th something happened. Egypt had amassed an army of eighty thousand troops along the Sinai border where they stood nose to nose with Israeli forces. Who fired first no one knows, but the third Arab-Israeli war since creation of the Jewish state nineteen years earlier had begun.

Gita said it happened for a reason. The family had left Israel for England a mere twenty-four hours before the conflict broke out and she figured God wanted to protect them from harm. David preferred to think of it as a coincidence. In science, he knew there was cause and effect, but in the world and especially the Middle East, things were more like a soup. Sometimes the potion reached a boil.

When the fighting started, they were in Cornwall on their way to Tintagel Castle, which was little more than a pile of medieval rubble sitting on a cliff overlooking the Celtic Sea. The castle was said to be the birthplace of King Arthur and their seven-year-old son Brian wanted to see it. He was a vivacious boy with full cheeks, a telltale sign of Levitt offspring. Also with them was their daughter Jennie who was going on two.

Gita was buying tickets for a tour of the ruins at the aptly named King Arthur's Castle Hotel. Everything in Tintagel, a village whose claim to fame was the legendary king, was about King Arthur. There was King Arthur's Café, King Arthur's Country Inn, and King Arthur's Bookstore, and David had to chuckle when the guide told the story about the infant Arthur being tossed over the castle walls to the sea below. As the illegitimate son of a local king, the bastard Arthur was deemed better off discarded, or so the guide said. But Arthur was saved by Merlin who just happened to live in a cave by the water's edge. The whole thing didn't wash well with Gita, who immediately deduced the age of Tintagel's ruins.

"These castle ruins are from Roman times," the guide said. "In our museum you can see Roman pottery and coins that were dug up from below the castle."

"This castle isn't Roman at all," said Gita. "Historians place its origin in the thirteenth century when it was built by Earl Richard of Cornwall, the younger brother of King Henry III. Judging from the ruins maybe there was a Roman monastery of some kind but the castle isn't Roman. It doesn't even look Roman."

"This castle is the birthplace of *Ah-thuh* himself," the guide insisted.

"Can't be. The legend of Arthur and it's only a legend puts his birth in the late fifth century which was at least seven hundred years before the castle was built."

"And how are you so learned in the story of *Ah-thuh* and the Romans?"

"I'm an archeologist."

"American?" She nodded. "An American who knows more about English history than the English. Well please don't ruin it for the others. They are here to see Roman ruins and that's what we are going to show them."

Gita, itching to do battle, had no patience for people who

changed history to suit their needs, like the people of Tintagel. It was abundantly clear to David that the place depended on tourism to stay afloat and if there were historical inaccuracies along the way, so be it. But that wasn't good enough for Gita. To her, history shouldn't be bent. David thought it best to take her by the hand and lead her away. And he did.

Little Brian had joined them on trips before. He remembered Masada and the Acropolis as having a lot of rock while Pompeii was boring with no big buildings to speak of, but Tintagel castle and its grounds were something else. Brian liked the zigzag path that cut into the cliff by the shore and the steep steps leading from Merlin's cave. Tourists could wander inside the cave and feel the spirit of Merlin casting his ominous shadow over the rock, and the whitewater crashing against the shore provided the sound effects. But it was in the castle's Great Hall where Brian immersed himself in the legend of Camelot, and the hall was great indeed, a quarter the length of a football field. After the visit, the family passed a shop where David spotted a newspaper with the headline 'Israel-Egypt battle erupts.'

"It won't be a long war," David mumbled to the woman behind the counter who pointed out that the Arabs greatly outnumber the Israelis. "Maybe so but the Israelis have the best armed forces in the world," David said. "Besides, Reuters picked up something from Cairo radio that said forty-two Israeli planes were downed right away and that can only mean one thing. The Arabs are being annihilated."

The woman asked if they had been to Glastonbury and said their young one would like it. She added that *Ah-thuh* was buried in the abbey. "They say the abbey is where the Holy Grail is kept," she confided as if divulging a great secret.

During lunch, Gita asked the waiter about the Holy Grail and he confirmed that it was kept within the walls of Glastonbury Abbey. "In 1191 they discovered the coffins of King *Ah-thuh* and Queen Guinevere. They also found the scourging post and the very scourge used to flog Christ himself. They even found the two sponges offered him when he was on the cross as well as actual pieces of the cross and rubble from Mount Calvary."

"But isn't that a long way from Calvary?" said Gita.

"Yes but there used to be great pilgrimages to Glastonb'ry. The abbey was closed in 1539 when the last abbot was hanged and quartered."

David asked Brian if he would like to see where King Arthur was buried and he said yes. So off they went to see where the legendary king, who presided over the region to this very day, wound up.

....

He was born just past midnight in the coldest February anyone could remember. When the doctor said it was a boy, Gita's pain at giving birth immediately turned to joy. And so, now they were now a family. But what would they call him?

"He's a very special person and deserves a name as special as he is," Gita said. David waited. "Micah was a Hebrew prophet from the eighth century B.C., a Morasthite during the kingdom of Judah."

"Micah?" said David. "I don't think so. Not for my son. How about Michael? That's a nice name. It's also a name that won't make the kid hate you when he gets older." Gita said no, and then she offered another choice. Jeremiah. "No son of mine is going to be named Jeremiah," David said. "Or Moshe if that was the next one on your list."

"I would never name our son Moshe. Its origins are Egyptian."

David almost threw in the towel and was ready to accept Joshua after rejecting Nehemiah, Isaiah and Zechariah. David figured everyone would just call him Josh. But he didn't like that name either. "If you want a biblical name why not just call him John?" he told her.

"John! That's a Christian name. The *most* Christian name. We can't call him that."

When the morning of the eighth day arrived and the baby was still without a name, something had to be done. He was going to be circumcised. Gita had insisted and wanted a rabbi to do it while David preferred a doctor. They settled for a doctor with a rabbi present.

"The name?" the rabbi asked when he was about to begin.

Gita looked at David and blurted out the compromise.

"Brian."

It was no one's first choice or second for that matter, but David felt that one day his son would thank him. It was much easier the second time around four years later when David settled the issue up front. He had prepared a list of boys' names and girls' names, although Gita had refused to consider any boys' names at all.

She liked Esther and Rachel while he leaned to Elizabeth and Sandra. They finally struck a chord with Jennie. Gita had always liked that name. She loved the book *Portrait of Jennie* and the movie with the same name starring the actor Joseph Cotten. Gita was crazy about Joseph Cotten. She thought he was Jewish.

"Fine," David had said. "Jennie it is. But what if it's another boy? Then what?"

"This one will be a girl," she said and somehow she knew.

....

A hundred and twenty miles west of London and twenty miles inland from the Bristol Channel was the town of Glastonbury, and in the center of town were the ruins of an old abbey. The local commerce of this community revolved around an execution said to have taken place two thousand years ago, but on this day all the talk was about war in the Middle East. Fighting was raging everywhere. Israel had taken several Arab towns and claimed that it had destroyed the air forces of all the Arab states. The first thing David did in Glastonbury was buy himself a copy of *The Times of London.*

"If the Israelis destroyed those air forces the war will be over in days," he said.

"I hope so," replied Gita, "and they should keep any land they take in Gaza and the Sinai."

Little Brian had no interest and wanted only to see where King Arthur was buried. Everyone said it was around here somewhere. The abbey in Glastonbury dated from the seventh century and, according to the story, local monks said they found the coffins of Arthur and Guinevere five hundred years later, which led to a massive flow of money from King Henry II.

That brought tourists. Then came discoveries pertaining to the Crucifixion, resulting in even more monies from London, but nothing related to the Crucifixion was ever verified.

"Lots of sizzle and no steak," David said, which prompted Brian to ask about food, so Gita took the children to lunch while David went looking for the mysterious monk whom, it was said, was entrusted with keeping the Holy Grail. All fingers pointed to an old man sitting behind a desk at the entrance to the abbey.

On top of the desk in front of the man were two jars, each filled with money. One was for tickets to explore the ruins and the other was teeming with donations to the nearby church. David paid for the tickets and was asked to make a donation, so he contributed more to the cause. Then he said he would like to see the Holy Grail.

"That will be quite impos'ble," said the monk. "Tis not for public view. Do you have an int'rist in the Holy Grail sir?"

"Yes and the burial of Arthur too."

"Ah good King *Ah-thuh*. You say burial as if you are a learned man."

"Let's just say I'm a student of religious history."

"Well that is most in'tristing sir. But if *Ah-thuh* is buried here I'm afraid I haven't the foggiest idea where his remains might be but the Grail is quite another matter. Do you wish to know about the Grail?"

David said he would.

"Some forty years ago my eldest uncle who was a deacon in the Church was given the Grail to watch over. Tis quite a fanciful story as to how it got here. As you know the Grail was the chalice of the Last Supper and after the Cruc'fixion it was passed into the hands of Joseph of Arimathea who filled it with the blood of the Saviour after he was removed from the cross. This sacred blood conferred upon the Grail a magical quality of healing. For many years Joseph's family were the keepers of the Grail. It was his brother-in-law a man named Brons who carried it to England and became the Fisher King and so the line continued until the time of the Crusades and Galahad who himself was a direct descendant of Joseph."

David turned to walk away and the old monk asked if

something was wrong.

"Well," David said, "ever since I've been here I've heard lots of stories but I still haven't seen anything."

"Well seeing is believing as they say and in light of your gen'rosity in assisting our church I am going to give you a special treat. Have a look at this."

He put a chalice on the desk. David could tell immediately that it was ancient.

"Why this is fantastic," David said. "Where is it from?"

"A place called Antioch."

"This is the great chalice of Antioch?"

The monk's face lit up. "You know about the great chalice of Antioch? Why you most def'nitely are a learned man. A most learned man indeed."

Antioch was an ancient city in southern Turkey. In 1910 workmen digging in ruins found a huge cross and two silver chalices. One chalice wound up in a museum, but the whereabouts of the other one had long remained a mystery.

"There is a horrible dent in the side," David observed.

"Tis thought that it occurred a long time ago when the silver was still flex'ble but time has made it so brittle that no attempt has ever been made to restore it to its orig'nal form."

The chalice was a work of art with ornate biblical figures connected by weaving stems and leaves. David absorbed its weight in his hands.

"It looks like Roman chalices," he said. "The truncated bowl. The short stems. The detail."

"Quite right and if you turn it here you can see the figure of Saint Mark. That over there is Saint Matthew and this is Saint John. Some scholars have dated it to the fourth or fifth cent'ry and others say it is even older but a man named Eisen ..."

"Gustav Eisen."

"Yes ... Gustav Eisen ... claimed it was the Holy Grail itself."

"He was referring to the inner cup. The reliquary. In Rome in the Arch of Titus there are chalices like this and in the frescoes of Pompeii too. I think this chalice does date from Roman times."

"Yes," said the monk, greatly impressed. "And you see over here? This is Christ the man. Look at that detail, will you?"

"It might even be older than the fourth or fifth century. I wouldn't be surprised if it dates back to the first." David put the chalice back on the desk. "So is this the Holy Grail?"

The old monk was about to respond when Gita showed up with the children. Right away Brian's eyes were drawn to the chalice.

"What's that?" he said, reaching out to touch its narrow base. The chalice tipped over and starting falling to the floor, but David was quick to catch it in mid air.

"Thank God!" said the monk, who wasted no time putting it back inside his desk before waving his finger in front of Brian's nose. "You gave me quite a start there young fellow. You really shouldn't grab things that don't b'long to you. And you sir I am etern'ly grateful to for coming to the aid of this valuable art'fact. Would you care to see our church? I don't norm'ly send people there but you see this chalice in front of you is not the Holy Grail at all but merely another very old object from the time of the Romans. But if you wish to find out about the *real* grail I can steer you to someone."

"What's going on here?" Gita said.

"The Holy Grail is in the church?" David asked.

"No. I merely said a gentleman there can assist you. Would you like to meet him?"

"Where's King Arthur?" Brian demanded.

"Just a minute Brian," David said. "Yes I would like to meet him. Where is he?"

"Follow the path from the abbey ruins to the church. Tell the man inside that Brother Randolph sent you. And I do thank you for your contr'bution. Have a pleasant day sir."

David told Gita to take the children through the ruins of the abbey while he was going to the church. They parted ways. David followed the narrow pathway and went inside the modest building. The church was dark and in the shadows was a man dusting off the benches by the pulpit.

"Excuse me," David said. "Brother Randolph told me to see you. About the Holy Grail?"

Another monk. He said his name was Brother Henry. David introduced himself.

"Mr. Marr, while you were walking over here I was on the phone with Brother Randolph. So tell me. How do you know about the great chalice of Antioch?"

"I'm an archeologist who specializes in Roman history and I'm interested in these legends about the Holy Grail."

"Well what are you interested in, Mr. Marr? The legends or the real thing?"

"I beg your pardon?"

Brother Henry sat on a bench in the chapel and told David to sit next to him. "The Grail does exist. But not here. This would be much too dangerous a place for it but it does exist."

"How do you know that?"

"I will tell you but first I have a question. You could tell that the chalice with Brother Randolph was of Roman vintage so I presume you're a man who knows his history and who can recognize fact when he sees it." David nodded. "What do you know of Joseph of Arimathea?"

"Not much I'm afraid."

"We don't know much either. According to the Gospels he was a disciple of Jesus who went to Pilate and begged for the body of Jesus after the Crucifixion. Pilate granted him the body."

"That's ridiculous."

"Excuse me?"

"It never happened."

"Why do you say that?"

"Because according to Roman law a crucified man was denied all burial. He was just crucified and then the vultures finished him off. Except for the feet. The Romans would have hacked off his feet."

Brother Henry gave David a look of profound disbelief.

"That's how they did these things," David said.

"Not in this case."

"Well ..."

"May I continue? There has been much written about Joseph of Arimathea and how he came to be the keeper of the Holy Grail. There are many stories and not all of them agree."

"Which is just like the four Gospels."

"Mr. Marr, you are quite the religious cynic. Well permit

me to be so bold as to assume that there was a Jesus and a Last Supper and that Jesus and his twelve disciples all drank from the same cup. Some allege it to be the cup that caught his blood when he was on the cross. It is said that Joseph brought the cup here to Glastonb'ry."

"Your colleague said his brother-in-law brought it."

"No it was Joseph. People do get their stories mixed up. For many generations the cup was protected but when Henry VIII came to the throne he made things very difficult for the Church. So the monks took the cup to Wales where it was kept by the same family for hundreds of years but earlier in this century a replica was made. Like the real cup it had powers but unlike the real cup they weren't powers of healing. Instead, whoever owned it or even came into contact with it was faced with a great affliction."

"A curse?"

"If you will. We traced the owners of the replica over the years and the stories of accidental deaths, unfortunate mishaps, in one case a murder even, are rather frightening. But we did manage to obtain the replica and now we keep it in this church so it will cause no more grief to anyone."

"And the real cup?"

"The Holy Grail is in Rome under the care of the pontiff." Brother Henry lowered his head and smiled. "It is so obvious that it really is the safest place and all these tales that go back to the Crusades are really nothing but wild conjecture that can only add to the safety of the real grail."

"How do you know it's real? Has it been dated?"

"Oh yes."

"By who?"

"Mr. Marr, surely you know the Church employs scientists, men like yourself who are familiar with dating techniques. Believe me it has been dated. It's authentic."

"But even the great chalice of Antioch may be as old as the first century and you don't think that's the Holy Grail, do you?"

"It isn't but the one in Rome is. It is but a humble carpenter's goblet. Very simple and plain. Just wood. Why would a poor man like Jesus have an elaborate gold or silver cup?"

"And the one here? The replica? It's exactly the same?" The

monk nodded. "Can I see it?"

"Why would you want to? Do you wish to experience a personal tragedy?"

"I don't believe in curses. I'm an archeologist."

"David, we've been looking all over for you." It was Gita. She was pushing Jennie's stroller with Brian ambling along behind, but he stopped in his tracks when he got to the door of the church. It was dark. The monk sensed the problem and flicked on the light. David did the introductions.

"I am Brother Henry. Delighted to meet you. Gita is a Jewish name, is it not?"

"Yes."

"And Marr? That doesn't sound Jewish."

"It isn't," David said.

"I see."

"We were talking about the Holy Grail and the curse of the replica," David said, Gita permitting herself a sly smile as Brian cowered behind her.

"I don't put much stock in Holy Grail stories," Gita said.

"I don't put much stock in them either," said Brother Henry. "Only one in fact."

"The one you told me?" said David.

Brother Henry patted Brian on the head. "A fine looking lad you have there. A fine looking lad indeed. And that little one. What's her name again?"

"Jennie," Gita said.

"Jennie. My but what a priceless vision she is. How old is she?"

"Two. Almost."

"Is that right? Well I must say she has to be about the most beautiful child I've ever seen. Those eyes." He looked at Gita. "Just like her mother's."

"What's this about a replica of the Holy Grail?" Gita asked, feigning interest.

"Tis not a very pleasant story. Not a pleasant story at all. On one hand you have something with so much goodness and on the other something that is so detestably evil. But there is something I didn't tell your husband about the replica."

"What?" said David.

"Mr. Marr, I don't mean to alarm you or your lovely wife. But we do have requests to see the replica and we always try to deter people. Unfortunately some have seen it."

"And?"

"Well in every single case the person who came into contact with it ... has experienced something absolutely horrific in their life soon afterward. And the real tragedy is it always involves ... children."

CHAPTER SIXTEEN

SIXTEEN

Dear Jamil:

Please accept this cable. I am indebted to the High Priest Herihor who as you know was responsible for rewrapping the mummies of the Royal Family and moving them to safety back in the Twentieth Dynasty. If not for him and his foresight we would never have had the opportunity to study your 'ancestors' as you like to call them. And worse than that, you and I never would have met.

Thank goodness for Herihor.

Jamil, I feel so alone. There is no one to confide in. I am a man in my own world and it's a lonely world. Sleep has become a thing of the past. Every night I go to bed and close my eyes but my mind is never at ease. It never stops and what happened two nights ago I must tell you but first I have to tell you something else.

It happened a few days ago when Robbie and I went back to the site at Qumran. It was the very place where we found that mummy. But this time we brought our tools, even my metal detector, and I don't know what I was expecting to find but we didn't turn up anything. Robbie got very frustrated as he kept passing the metal detector over and over the site with nothing showing up so after a while we decided to pack it in. Robbie left in a hurry and was already on his way back to our jeep, leaving me to dig around in the dirt with my shovel. Then I found something. What I found, Jamil, was an old piece of wood that looked like it was fossilized. It wasn't, of course, but the moment I saw the letters I knew what it was. It was a Roman 'titulus'. The kind they used on a cross. How can I be sure? There was a spike through the middle of it and it was identical to spikes used in a Roman crucifixion. As for the wood, I think it's acacia which was often used for a titulus. But it wasn't the wood that captivated me. It was the inscription.

That titulus bears the Greek, Hebrew and Latin letters of the inscription 'King of the Jews'. That's right. 'King of the Jews'! It's crazy, isn't it? I looked at those letters by that age-old gravesite in the desert and thought of you, Jamil. I could see your face. I really don't know what any of this means but one thing I do know is that I'm frightened like a little child who needs his mother. I'm afraid to tell anyone about this except you, Jamil. I haven't even told Gita. I haven't told her anything.

So what about our find? And what does this titulus mean? The only answer I can come up with is fraud. A fantastic forgery just like so many others over the centuries. I could never use the scriptures as evidence for an archeological find but with this piece of acacia it is all becoming rather strange, isn't it?

I have to tell you that after finding that piece of wood I started to read the New Testament. The four Gospels. The Book of Mark, as I'm sure you know, is quite explicit as to what the actual words on the titulus said. There is nothing mentioning the languages they were written in but in the other books there is. Matthew states, 'This is Jesus the King of the Jews' but on that piece of acacia, that Roman titulus, I didn't find the first four words of this line. Only the last four. The Book of Luke is different again. Luke says the words were written in Greek, Latin and Hebrew and what it says is 'This is the King of the Jews' and like I say I found only 'King of the Jews'. The Book of John is different again. It cites the words 'Jesus of Nazareth the King of the Jews' and it also refers to those same three languages.

So we know the Gospels don't agree. They are not exact, Jamil, and I am anything but an exact man myself. Especially now. Please excuse my rambling but on the surface it would appear that I found something that corresponds to the scriptures — or at least to one of the books. Mark.

Now let me tell you what happened two nights ago. I haven't told anyone about it, not even Robbie. Gita, of course, knows I was up all night. It was just after our second visit to the site. I wasn't planning to tell Robbie about the inscription since he was already a bundle of nerves. The mummy scares him but in a different way than it scares me. Anyway, when I got back to the jeep Robbie could tell something was up so I showed him what I found. His face went white like a ghost.

I don't know if it was a dream or what. Maybe some kind of hallucination. I said good night to Robbie. I told him to go home and get some sleep and that was what I tried to do. I went home and went straight to bed. I must have had insomnia for an hour or two and then I saw it. Or him. There was a man in a white robe standing barefoot at the end of my bed! I was asleep or half asleep because I didn't see him at first. But I heard him. Or I heard something. It was the wind, just like the wind that blows in the desert but this wind was right in my bedroom. Maybe I was dreaming. I don't know. But I felt like my whole room was caught in some kind of whirlwind. The sound was so sharp I remember thinking it couldn't be a dream. I remember that sound so clearly even as I write to you now. I don't know if my eyes were open or closed but at some point they must have been open because this man suddenly appeared. He just looked at me and opened his arms as if he was coming to take me away. He said nothing. Not a word. But there was an expression of comfort on his face and it was the face of that mummy. And he was alive!

There is more. I don't know how to tell you but this thing is turning my life upside down. I want to study it in more detail and wish you were here to help. There is no one else I can trust. At some point we really must do a forensic examination. I keep thinking of a DNA analysis. What would it turn up? I don't know but I'm sure of one thing. If word gets out we'd probably be besieged with requests for cloning. Remember the Cairo businessman who wanted us to clone that tissue from Ramesses II? He was an educated man but he really thought we could clone tissue and make another pharaoh.

As for my dream, well, it started with this sensation of winds whirling about and it got to the point where I felt like I was freezing to death. My hands were cold so I stuck them under my pillow. I pulled the blankets over my head until I was buried under them just like a little boy having a nightmare. I remember seeing lots of lines, lines of I don't know what, but they were all around me and I could see them even though my eyes were shut. Do you know the sensation? Your eyes are shut yet you see shadows and things moving in front of you? Have you ever felt like that? Then this face appeared and then a whole body. It was all white, a faded kind of white, and at first I couldn't see his feet but then I realized he had no feet! Like Jehohanan. Nothing was moving. But his hands were outstretched and his fingers were wide apart as if he was beckoning me and then the entire vision started getting bigger and bigger until the whole room was filled with him and I was terrified. Absolutely terrified.

I know I wasn't sleeping, Jamil. I was conscious. I even remember waking up. The next thing I know I was looking at a rock that was being rolled away from the front of a cave. It was Christ's tomb. And there was a man's face. I kept seeing this face. He had a full beard and long hair but no eyes. Just holes. Like the holes in the eyes of that mummy. Then his body began to rise right there in front of me. His hands were open and I think he wanted to take me away. It's crazy. I was petrified and then he just disappeared into the ceiling. I know that because suddenly he was gone and I was left there shivering in my bed with nothing but the wind.

There is something else I must tell you. A woman was there too. The Bible says Mary Magdalene saw that the stone of the tomb was moved. I suppose this woman could have been Mary Magdalene except she had the face of someone I know. A professor at the university and not only that. She's a woman who suspects something. She asks a lot of questions. I told her I've got a skeleton from your university but she doesn't believe me.

So what do you make of all this, Jamil? Did I just imagine it or have I gone completely over the edge? Do you know of any Egyptian gods who can decipher dreams and their impending portent? Do you? If anyone would know, it's you. You are the expert for this sort of thing. You and your precious Koran. Maybe it's time to consult Muhammad the prophet. What would he advise?

Your troubled friend,
David

CHAPTER SEVENTEEN

SEVENTEEN

Eliraz looked like she had been crying. I could hear her on the phone from the hallway — her door was open — and there was obviously a heated discussion going on because all of a sudden she slammed down the phone and started whimpering. She was still wiping her eyes when I stuck my head in.

"Are you all right?" I said.

I could tell she was embarrassed.

"Sure. Sure," she said. "It's nothing."

"Anything I can do?" I said.

She gave me a soft smile. It was the first soft thing I had ever seen from her.

"If you must know that was my beau," she said. "Make that ex beau. We're finished. Done. He found somebody else he likes more than me."

"I'm sorry."

The sad smile again.

"It's not your concern. It's just me and my sorry life that's all. I just can't seem to make a man happy." She looked up at me. "Am I too old?"

"You're a lot younger than me."

"Am I not attractive?"

I smirked.

Third time now for that smile of hers.

"I'll be all right," she said, and then under her breath but just loud enough for me to hear, "at least until I find something to do with my life."

Eliraz was an accomplished woman, professionally speaking, but it seemed that her man problems, whatever they were, had been getting the best of her. It was just that she always had so much to prove to everyone. It was a competition.

"Nothing important going on in your life these days?" I said.

"Nothing with real *meaning*."

"What kind of meaning are you looking for?"

"Something that gives me a reason to get up in the morning."

"Your work doesn't give you that?"

"Sometimes."

"Aren't you the one who's going to be department head?"

She pushed back her chair.

"You don't understand, David. With everything going on in Israel right now my work doesn't seem all that important. Not really. Have you seen the news? This *intifada* thing is getting worse every day. Boys are throwing stones at our soldiers and the whole world is watching. We look like the bad guy."

"I know."

"But the real crime that doesn't get out is the killing going on by the Palestinians. Killing other Palestinians."

"What do you mean?"

"If they suspect someone is a collaborator they kill them. No questions asked."

"I haven't heard anything about that."

"Why would you? What do you watch? The BBC?"

"How do you know this?"

"Oh David. That's what I mean about you being a stranger in this country. You don't know what's going on. Maybe you're just too preoccupied with that *skeleton* of yours."

That was something I didn't want to talk about and certainly not with Eliraz.

"What can you do about Palestinians killing other Palestinians?" I asked.

"I don't know. We Jews have our hands full just trying to get them from killing us. They hate us so much."

"And why is that?"

"Why? Because we took their land or so they say. But it's more than that. They hate us because we're Jews."

"That would be a tough nut to crack," I said with a sigh.

"What do you mean?" she said.

"I mean teaching them not to hate Jews. How do you do that?"

"I don't know. It's such a vicious circle. But I think you have to get them when they're young."

It was strange, but Eliraz was starting to sound a lot like Gita and I couldn't think of two women who were more different even though both of them were Jewish. But I remembered what Gita had said about that refugee camp.

"Get them when they're young?" I said. "How can you?"

"I don't know. But let me think about it."

CHAPTER EIGHTEEN

EIGHTEEN

It was him again. Mahmoud. In the hallway just outside my lab.

"Hello," I said from a distance.

The mop and bucket of water were on the floor by his feet. He looked up. I walked down the hall and with my every step he seemed to stiffen. By the time I was next to him he was little more than a statue.

"What are you doing?" I said.

I reached over and turned the handle of the door leading to my lab. It was locked. I looked him in the eye. But he only looked away.

"What are you doing here?" I said.

"Cleaning."

"Cleaning what?"

"The floor."

"But it's not wet."

"I'm just starting."

"Here? In the middle of the hall? Why would you start in the middle of the hall?"

"That's how I do it."

"But that doesn't make any sense. Anyone who's mopping up the floor would start at one end of the hall and work their way down. How else can you do it?"

He was uneasy.

"I start in the middle. First I do this half and when it's dry I do the other half."

"I see."

He wouldn't make eye contact with me. Not if his life depended on it.

"That's an odd way to clean the hall," I said. "Different."

"I am different."

That may have been the first thing he said that was the truth.

"Your name is *Mahmoud*," I said. "Right?"

The single nod.

"That was an interesting chat we had the other day," I said. "When we met I mean. About your village. Silwan."

Now he looked at me. For the first time.

"Yes it was interesting," he said.

"And you're with the cleaning staff?"

The nod. We both stood there looking at each other.

"Who else do you work for?" I said.

"What do you mean?"

"How about the Ateret Cohanim?"

Immediately, his mouth went ajar. I had just hit a chord and could sense his body going into retreat. I decided then that confrontation wasn't the best approach.

"Look," I said, "I don't begrudge you getting a job so you can scrape some money together but those guys are something else. I understand your friend Ismail was working for them. Is that right?"

He didn't reply, but started to fidget this way and that. If I was an investigator, my suspicions would have been aroused. More than aroused.

"I have to go," he said.

"Cleaning?"

The nod.

"Look I'm not accusing you of anything but I wonder ..."

"What?"

"Why would a Palestinian want to work for those characters?"

Now his eyes were burning right into me and he was getting

more uncomfortable by the second. He looked like someone who was trapped inside a cell and couldn't get himself free.

"I have to go," he said again.

I raised my hand.

"Come with me," I said.

I thought he was going to object, but he didn't. He followed me down the hall to my office. Like before I opened the door and told him to sit down. I took the seat opposite him behind my desk. He looked afraid. But this time I left the door open.

"I want to ask you something," I said. "You hate the Jews for what they're doing to your village. Right?"

He nodded. Once.

"We ruled the village for over a thousand years," he said.

"We?"

"But the Jews have been there only twenty years and now they want everything."

"You mean the settlers?"

The nod.

"Listen I agree with you where those settlers are concerned. I don't think they should be there either. But unfortunately the situation is political."

"Everything is political."

"I guess you're right."

He was skinny. He looked almost malnourished. There was something about him that made me sympathize with his plight, that made me understand or at least want to understand what he was doing and why he was doing it. But he had to realize that dealing with extremists wasn't the answer.

"What were you doing outside my lab just now?" I said. "This is the second time I found you there."

Nothing.

"Can I see that key chain?"

I thought he would put up a fuss, but he didn't. He handed it over. There were lots of keys, all of them clearly labelled, but the only one that had anything to do with me was the one to my office. Where we were sitting right now.

"There's no key to my lab here so why do you keep hanging around there? That lab is private. No one has access to it but me and my research assistant Robbie Schueftan. Have you met Robbie?"

"No."

"Well you should. Robbie is a smart guy and he can tell you a lot about artifacts. Assuming you have an interest in such things. Do you?"

He shrugged.

"I want to ask you something. Do you know a man, an Israeli, named Levi Ashkol by any chance?"

He gave me the big freeze again. But this time it lasted longer. Finally, he said, "Who?"

I didn't buy it for a minute.

"He used to be a student around here," I said. "He's one of those characters who's trying to get all the Palestinians out of the Old City."

Mahmoud was moving uneasily from side to side.

"I believe your friend Ismail worked for him. Oh he was a cleaner during the day but he gave Levi information about anything that turned up at Silwan so I imagine he got a little extra cash for that."

He was listening intently to everything I said.

"I didn't know about it at the time and if I did I would've been pretty angry. With Ismail. The crazy thing is he was a Palestinian himself."

"Maybe he needed the money."

"Betray your own people for a few shekels?"

"It's not as simple as that. I know Ismail and he's a good man. Maybe ... maybe he was helping his people."

"Helping them? How?"

"Maybe he was finding out things. From long ago."

"What do you mean?"

"I mean if he learned about things that were found at Silwan ... things that once belonged to Muslims ... then ..."

"He could build a case against the Jews?"

"Yes."

"So it's a trade-off then? On one hand you ... or Ismail ... do some snooping around for Levi Ashkol so he can use it against the Palestinians ... and on the other hand you build a case against the Jews."

"Maybe."

"A trade-off?"

"Life is full of such things."

"How do they pay you? You give them information and they pay you the same amount each time? Or does it depend on what you tell them? The better the information the bigger the payoff?"

No response.

"*Mahmoud* ... what makes you think we found something? And what makes you think *I* found something?"

Nothing. Then he just stood up. He said he had to go. I asked him what he had to do that was so important.

"I have to mop up the floor in the hallway and the offices."

"My office? Here?"

The nod.

"But not my lab. You don't have a key to my lab."

"No."

I lowered my head in a bow of sorts and he gave me one in return. Then he opened the door and left.

CHAPTER NINETEEN

NINETEEN

Robbie had never seen the photographs of Jehohanan before. I had taken them many years earlier with the first discoveries at Giv'at ha-Mivtar. The most remarkable pictures were those of the bone with the nail running through it. At first, it wasn't clear to the uninformed eye. After all, it was only an eight-by-ten, black-and-white photograph with some thick metallic *thing* flattened on top, protruding from both ends of this mysterious grey matter. Only when you learn that it is human bone pierced clear through by a spike does the stomach begin to churn.

"What is this?" Robbie asked.

"Jehohanan," I said.

"I know. But what are these?"

I turned the picture sideways, so it would be easier to see. "This is the spike and this is the calcaneum bone. From his right foot."

"And this?" he said, pointing to the section of bone pierced by the spike.

"Sediment," I said. "Ferreous and calcaneum sediment." He looked at me. Perplexed. "It's sediment, Robbie."

"I know what sediment is but that other word?"

"Ferreous? That's iron. From the nail. You get deposits of iron mixed with bone just where the nail penetrates the bone. The bone itself is calcaneum and right below it is a sliver of wood. Probably acacia."

"From the plaque? The titulus?"

I nodded. He was still confused, so I elaborated. "Look. If I labelled everything it would look like this. Ferreous and calcaneum sediment here. Bits of wood over here. A limy crust on top of this big bone."

"That is a bone?"

"The tuber calcanei. On the right foot. And as you move across ... or down ... you have the sustentaculum bone … on the left foot … then the tuber calcanei … the left foot itself … and finally at the end … what's left of the nail … with wood fragments all over the place."

All the grisly details were clear now. He looked at the picture and grimaced.

"Robbie, maybe you'll get a better idea with these."

I pulled out two old sketches of mine. The bigger one was of a man nailed to a cross. His arms were stretched wide across the *patibulum*, the nails through the wrists, the legs bent outward at the knees, the feet flat against the upright of the cross. The second sketch was a close-up of his feet showing how the big toe of the left foot rests across the big toe of the other foot, so both feet are pressed together. The nail went through solid bone. The calcanei.

"Professor Marr," said Robbie after studying the pictures, "did you enjoy working on that dig?"

I was well aware of Robbie's feelings about crucifixion. For him the stark evidence of man's brutality to man was something that dulled the senses. It was a page to be turned and ultimately forgotten. But a student of history can't do that. Of course, I was just as repulsed as he was, but the sorry plight of our friend Jehohanan possessed more for me than mere revulsion. It was an adventure in the macabre and not only that. It told us something about ourselves.

"I wouldn't call it enjoyment, Robbie. It was a job. But when we found Jehohanan, well, that was something else. He was the first crucified man ever found. Or skeleton anyway."

"And now we have a man. A complete man."

"Yes. The only thing left is to identify him."

"You were able to identify Jehohanan because his name was inscribed on the stone?"

"That's right."

"We have an inscription with this man as well. Do we not?"

He was referring to the *titulus*.

"Robbie, citing the Bible as evidence isn't very scientific. Yes we did find a *titulus*. Most victims of crucifixion had one."

"But not just any *titulus*."

"I know what we found. But we still have a lot to learn."

I looked him square in the eye. I was beginning to think this discovery might be the parting of the ways between us. It was just too much for him. At times, I thought he was going to resign. I thought that when we were back at the site in Qumran and especially after we found the *titulus*. The look of horror on Robbie's face said it all. But I didn't want him to quit on me. I needed him. I needed his energy and his insight into the Holy Land. After all, he was one of them.

"Robbie, listen to me. We're going to identify this man but we're going to do it scientifically. Jamil can help us do the tests. He'll be back soon."

"I do not know if that is good news or bad."

"You don't like Jamil, do you?"

"Professor Marr, to be honest he gives me the ... the ... oh ... what is that word you use?"

"Word?"

"When something rubs you the wrong way. It gives you the ... the ..."

I thought for a moment. "It gives you the creeps?"

"Yes! That is it. Dr. Hassad gives me the ... creeps. Big time creeps!"

Big time creeps? Robbie had coined a phrase all by himself. I laughed.

"I guess he does that to some people but he's still the best pathologist I know. He has a lot of experience with blood."

"So what now? You want to extract DNA?"

"I'd like to."

"I know someone else who could help you do that."

"Who?"

"Professor Shimron. She did undergraduate work in microbiology. Specialized in cell structure."

"She did? I never knew that."

"Yes. But you do not want to use her. Do you?"

"Robbie, we have to be careful. The more people we involve the greater the chance for trouble. Remember what Jamil said. It could get dangerous."

"But what if she studied the blood for us? We do not have to tell her where it came from. We could give her a sample."

I hesitated.

"But why not? Do you know how to isolate DNA? Do you know how to analyze it?"

"I'd need help. I was hoping Jamil ..."

"If I had to choose between Professor Shimron or Dr. Hassad I would rather have Professor Shimron. I worked with her. She is good. Now your Dr. Hassad is another matter. I met him only once." He paused.

"What is it, Robbie?"

"I think he is too sure of himself."

"Brilliant people are always sure of themselves."

"I still think Professor Shimron could help us. At least with blood testing. Besides she is right here in Jerusalem and Dr. Hassad is in Alexandria. This would be faster."

Robbie was right. It would be faster.

"Okay," I said. "Tell you what. I'll give Professor Shimron a call."

"You will?"

"Yes but for the blood test only. Then when Jamil arrives maybe we'll have something to show him. But for the tissue samples I want to study … the skin … the strands of hair … we must use Jamil. He's done a lot of work with rehydrating tissues. From mummies. He's the best person I know for stuff like that. And there's another thing in his favor."

"What is that?"

"He's a Muslim."

CHAPTER TWENTY

TWENTY

Six Day War, 1967

On the morning of June 7 Israeli paratroopers reached the Western Wall in the Old City and hoisted the Israeli flag on the summit. Facing the hallowed stones that dated back to the time of Solomon, the battle-weary troops put their hands on those aged blocks and prayed. The Temple Mount and Western Wall had been in the hands of the Jordanians since 1948 and Jews had not been allowed to visit, but now they were back. The Chief Chaplain of the Israel Defence Forces blew his *shofar* — a ram's horn — and the soldiers wept. Then the Chief Chaplain made a solemn pledge. "I, General Shlomo Goren, chief rabbi of the Israel Defence Forces, have come to this place, never to leave again." The soldiers sang *Hatikvah*, their national anthem of hope, offered a prayer for their fallen comrades and then ventured through the narrow alleyways of the Old City looking for snipers. For them, this was no conquest. It was liberation.

"I have set watchmen upon my walls O Jerusalem," Gita said, when she heard the city had been taken by the Israelis.

"What was that?" David said.

"It's from the Book of Isaiah. David, if anyone should be familiar with the Book of Isaiah it's you."

David had seen such a look of joy on Gita's face only twice before when their children were born. But now she wore it again.

"Right now Jewish soldiers are praying at the Wall," she said. "On the Temple Mount. Mount Scopus. The Mount of Olives. I can't believe it. Jews are in Jerusalem. Isn't it wonderful?"

"It's wonderful for Jews but the city is also holy for Arabs and now they've lost it. The Dome of the Rock?"

With that, a subdued rage took hold of her. "I don't understand why you're not elated about Israel regaining Jerusalem," she said.

"I think it's good Jews will be able to worship at the Western Wall again. But I wonder if Jerusalem is the kind of city that should belong to any one people."

"But Jerusalem *belongs* to the Jews, David. It's ours. It's our history. Our heritage."

"Gita, we've talked about this many times. Just because Israel's military might is superior to the Arabs' doesn't mean it's always right. The Arabs have legitimate claims to the land too. You forget that after the war the West set up all those Jewish refugees in Palestine which was a homeland to the Arabs. Palestinians were uprooted and kicked out."

"The Palestinians are always trouble."

"Look. The U.S. and Soviet Union are the real culprits here. The Americans helped set up a Western democracy right in the middle of the Arab world. A world supported by the Soviets. It's a front for the Cold War but with religious overtones."

"I'm sorry but I can't dismiss my love for the Holy City as religious overtones. It means something to me."

The war was short. On the third day, with Israel sweeping ahead on three fronts in the Sinai, Jordan and Syria, Egypt closed the Suez Canal and then broke relations with the United States. Israel captured the Old City of Jerusalem, Jericho and Bethlehem, prompting the pope's fears about the possible destruction of Christian shrines and his fears were well founded. The next day part of the Church of the Dormition, which was said to contain the tomb of the Virgin Mary, went up in flames. Standing next to it was a building reputed to be the site of the Last Supper. The shelling didn't spare Jewish history either with extensive damage to the Hebrew University and Israel Museum.

"I hope they removed everything of value from the museum," David said. "The Dead Sea Scrolls are in there." Gita nodded. "And a lot of Christian relics too."

"Christian relics? Who cares about that?"

"Gita, what kind of archeologist would say such a thing?"

"But the Jewish things are older and more important. Even from a purely archeological standpoint they're more important."

On the fourth day with the Gulf of Aqaba open, Israel agreed to a ceasefire, but only if the Arab countries would comply. Jordan said it would, but no one else did. On the fifth day Israeli troops reached the Suez and the ceasefire took a tenuous hold, but the battle with Syria still raged. On the sixth day of fighting Israel captured the Syrian front line and now had control of three strategic areas: the Golan Heights on the east side of the Jordan River including the eastern shore of the Sea of Galilee, the West Bank of the Jordan from the town of Mehola in the north to the Dead Sea in the south, and much of the Sinai Peninsula — all the way from the Mediterranean Sea to the Gulf of Aqaba and Strait of Tiran. Finally, on the afternoon of Saturday, June 10, 1967, the ceasefire was in effect. The Six Day War was over.

....

Glastonbury, 1967

After the partitioning of Palestine, David had taken his Dead Sea Scrolls to New York. With Israel's successful War of Independence the scrolls had found a home in Jerusalem. But what about the other scrolls? There were *hundreds* of them. Most of them had been found on Jordanian territory and remained for years in the hands of the Jordanian government, but Israel's victory in the Six Day War put East Jerusalem into the hands of the Israelis. That changed everything. The war over, Israel and Jordan agreed to have their teams of scholars prepare the scrolls for publication. The scholars began assembling thousands of fragments and translating them.

"I'm sure Israel will grant you access," Gita told David. "It's the Jordanians who cause trouble."

"Gita, archeologists in Jordan and other Arab countries want to study the scrolls too."

"But the Jordanians had those scrolls for years and did nothing. Now that Israel has them we'll see some action."

David loved Gita, but she grated him so. She was decidedly pro-Israel in everything and whenever he hinted that lands taken in the war would have to be returned she became hostile.

"No Arab countries would give them any land when Israel was created," she said.

"But their land is Palestine," he replied.

"No. Palestine belongs to the Jews." She looked at him. Glared at him. "It all boils down to one thing. We were there first."

The fallout from the Six Day War still fresh, they returned from their holiday in England. David went back to work while Gita tended to the children. But David couldn't get the monks of Glastonbury out of his mind. He immersed himself in the grail legends, which were composed between 1180 and 1230. Gita, always up on her history, explained that this was during the Three Crusades, a period of friction between Eastern and Western Christendom. She said a great upheaval between Church and State culminated in the Magna Carta in 1215.

"You must look at the time when these grail stories were written," Gita said to which David was about to make the same observation about the Old and New Testaments. But he held his tongue.

David wrote the Vatican Museum in Rome to say he was researching the grail legends. In his letter he asked where the goblet was reputed to be. When the reply came back stating that "according to folklore it is believed to be in Glastonbury," he knew he had to return. The opportunity came a few months later.

Researchers in Manchester had asked him to take part in experiments involving a CAT scanner. They were going to examine the famous bog mummies. The technology would let them photograph 'slices' of bodies, so instead of having only horizontal views of mummified remains, they would have cross-sectional pictures and be able to see inside the wrappings. It was the same process David would later use to study the mummy of Ankhpefhor. When the trip to Manchester was confirmed, David wired Brother Henry in Glastonbury to say he was coming.

He arrived in the fall when the air was cold and damp, leaving Gita with her hands full. Both children were sick with the flu. Glastonbury looked the same as before, but wasn't nearly as busy with tourists. It would be another two months before they would come en masse searching for the remains of King Arthur, the scourge used to flog Christ and the big prize. The Holy Grail. David asked about the old monk who guarded the till at the abbey ruins.

"It troubles me to tell you this, Professor Marr, but our beloved Brother Randolph passed away last December. He was eighty-two. He took ill just after you left."

Brother Henry still maintained the chapel in the church, and as before, it was devoid of anything more than a few hours of dust.

"I've been reading the Grail legends," David told him.

"Much like Hollywood I would think. Perhaps it is not a good idea for a religious cynic like you to read such things."

"I wrote the Vatican Museum. They told me the Holy Grail is here in Glastonbury."

"What else would they say? But how careless of me. I didn't ask about your family."

"Gita is fine thank you. But when I left the children were in bed with colds. Little Jennie had a fever. It was a bad time to go but I had commitments in Manchester. You've heard of the bog mummies? I'm working with some colleagues there and we're using a new technique to study the mummies. But that isn't what brought me here."

"I hope Jennie is feeling better."

"I called yesterday. Her fever is down. She's fine."

"Glad to hear it."

"The reason I'm here Brother Henry is that I want to see your grail."

"Oh dear I think that is not a good idea."

"Why not?"

"I believe we discussed that on your last visit."

David wasn't about to be let off so easily. "Look, I'm an archeologist. I work with science. When I was in Manchester we took computer-generated photographs of corpses. Mummies. First time this sort of thing has ever been done and it's amazing what we can learn about people who died so long ago. Their state of health … what they ate … how they lived."

"Fascinating."

"What's fascinating is that they were real people. They lived. They breathed. They waged war. Just like today. When you study the ages the first thing that hits you is how similar people are from one era to the next. You remember the Chalice of Antioch?"

"Of course."

"I knew it was Roman because I know Roman history. Because I concentrate on this period I am often caught up in religious history. Did I tell you I was involved in the discovery of the Dead Sea Scrolls?"

"You were?"

"I had some of the first scrolls and from them we learned about the Essene community at Qumran. We learned about the Hebrews in the first and second centuries B.C. and about early Christianity. Now I'm not a man who engages in conjecture or mythology. I'm an archeologist. I'm interested in this Holy Grail only from a scientific point of view. You say the replica of a grail from two thousand years ago is in this church and I want to see it. Let's put it this way. You and your fellow monks in Glastonbury attract a lot of tourists. The Church draws a lot of money here as it has for centuries. Isn't that right?"

"People are curious. I can't help that."

"But you don't deter it. You and the others claim to be good Christian men but think nothing of taking money from innocent people who come here looking for religious salvation and are willing to pay for it. So you stroke their imagination."

"I don't like the way you are putting that, Professor Marr."

"But it's true. The remains of King Arthur. The cross. The scourge. The grail. It's all the same. Just a commercial enterprise to raise money for the Church."

Brother Henry looked at David askance.

"What I'm trying to say is I've come here to see your precious grail and I'll be damned if you're not going to show it to me."

"I should think, Professor Marr, you may be damned if you *do* see it."

"I'm willing to take that chance. Provided it exists."

The monk threw up his hands in despair. "My dear sir you don't know how difficult you are making this for me."

"I'm only searching for the facts. You once called me a religious cynic. Well show me something. Maybe then I won't be so cynical."

Brother Henry sighed. "You have no fear of the consequences?" he said, and David shook his head. "All right. You give me no choice. Come back at midnight and I'll show you."

....

An autumn midnight in Glastonbury is cold. The air is heavy and eats right through the skin. After rapping on the church door, David was greeted with the voice of Brother Henry.

"Professor Marr, I wasn't sure if you were going to make it," he said. "Please come in."

David entered the pitch-black church as Brother Henry lit a solitary candle and covered it with a jar. Right away, a shadowy light swam through the dank air of the chapel.

"Are you sure you want to go through with this?" Brother Henry said. David nodded. "All right. Follow me but watch your step. I'm going to take you where it is very old and unsafe."

"Unsafe?"

"I was speaking in the material sense. We're going to descend a stairway that is more than fifteen hundred years old."

He led David to the back of the chapel. He took him through a pair of faded red drapes behind the pulpit and handed him the candle. He then lowered himself to his hands and knees, and rolled away a tattered rug. Under the rug was a square piece of flooring that had obviously been cut away. He pulled it off and there was an opening with barely enough room to squeeze through. Steps led below.

"Follow me," Brother Henry said.

"No lights down there?" David asked, peering into the dark

with the candle.

"My good Professor Marr, when this staircase was built electricity was still some time away. No one has seen fit to install any circuitry. But then no one ever comes down here."

"I thought you said people have seen it?"

"I must have been mistaken."

He led David down to the level below. The foundation was made of stone.

"Roman?" David said.

"You're the expert. You tell me. Now it gets a little tricky from here. Watch your step." He walked a few paces and stopped at another series of steps leading downward still. "This is a spiral staircase. Do be careful."

The candle in hand, David followed him down the winding steps and there were so many that he started getting dizzy with the constant twisting and turning. After descending twenty steps and more below the church, David could feel the air getting colder and damp.

"How far down does it go?" he said. "Are those Christian catacombs over there?"

"You say you have been reading the Grail legends, Professor Marr. Have you come across the poem *Perlesvaus*? Some suspect it was written by a Templar. The words talk about the effects of swords and knives on human flesh. There are references to children being mutilated and roasted alive." He stopped and turned to David who was two steps above him. "The Templars were accused of killing children and eating their remains. Some believe that the *curse* as you put it, the one about the replica's effect on children, stems from the Templars. From their stories I mean. I don't know if this is true of course but who knows? Who knows anything?"

David was getting uncomfortable with the bleak surroundings and his thoughts turned to his children, especially Jennie. He shouldn't have left her like that. He should have passed on Manchester. There would always be more mummies. But he wanted to return to Glastonbury. That was why he came.

"Tell me, Professor Marr," Brother Henry said, "do you believe in the spirit? The human spirit? Do you think it outlives the body?"

"I don't think so."

"You don't *think* so? You've never thought about it?"

"Of course I've thought about it. With every artifact I've ever found I've thought about it. But I've never seen any evidence to support that view."

"I see. You have obviously spent most of your time researching pagan civilizations then?"

"No."

"You mean you've also devoted yourself to people who believe in a superior being and a hereafter?"

"Of course. Almost every civilization known to man believes in the hereafter. And the concept of monotheism goes back to the ancient Egyptians."

Brother Henry resumed his descent, going lower and lower down the steps. "Robert de Boron's poem which was written about the same time as the *Perlesvaus* describes a grail made of gold and encrusted with gems. He said it was the cup of the Last Supper and that which caught Jesus's blood at the Crucifixion. But I've never seen a grail like that. The grail in the *Perlesvaus* is quite different. In it Sir Gawain is warned by a priest 'for behoveth not discover the secrets of the Saviour and them also to whom they are committed behoveth keep them covertly.'"

"What does that mean?"

"It means, Professor Marr, that the secret of the grail is entrusted to a select company."

"I once heard that the Grail is descended from Solomon."

"Close reading of *Parzival* traces the genealogy of the Grail family back to a man called Laziliez which some think to be a derivation of Lazarus. But there is much uncertainty here. The stories are all so different."

David wasn't sure how long they had been walking, but he could tell they were constantly descending. He figured they could be a hundred feet down by now. Maybe more. It was bitterly cold. Brother Henry took the candle, his face little more than a shadow, his features fluttering in the thin air this way and that.

"The replica is not far from here. At one time there was another church on the same site above but the tunnel we find ourselves in now has been here from the beginning."

"The beginning?"

"A long time."

"You said fifteen hundred years."

"Yes which puts it in the same time as the grail in the *Queste del Sainte Graal*. That story was explicit about events taking place exactly four hundred and fifty-four years after the Resurrection."

Just then, David's foot kicked at something on the stone floor. Brother Henry lowered the candle so David could see what it was.

"It's a skull!" David said with a start. He straightened himself. "Did you plant that? To frighten me? All this talk about eating children and murder and now a skull. You don't want me to see your grail, do you?"

"To be perfectly honest I would much rather we turn ourselves around and go back."

David picked up the skull. "This is from a child," he said.

Brother Henry shrugged again. "I told you."

"Where's the rest of the skeleton? Whenever I come across a skull there are always lots of bones around."

Brother Henry swept the candlelight across the floor, revealing fleeting glances of bones. They looked like arms and legs and other body parts. Bones were everywhere.

"What happened here?" David said.

"Who knows? These bones have been here for as long as I know." Brother Henry's eyes were mere dots of white in the dim light. "We are very close now. But I want to give you one last chance to change your mind. For your children's sake."

David shook his head. "I suppose you arranged my daughter's fever too?"

"Professor Marr, I would do no such thing. Children are the most precious of God's gifts. They are the hopes and dreams of our future and unlike adults they retain a sense of mystery. It's a shame so many of us lose that as we get older. Mystery allows one to expand their mind. I'm surprised at your comment. Surely you must realize that I am but a simple custodian. A humble servant. I have no power. None at all. That comes from above."

"Where to now?" David asked, getting impatient.

Brother Henry led him further along. The air was cold.

"Are we still descending?" David said.

"You are very perceptive, Professor Marr. There is a slight incline. The tunnel was made that way by whoever it was that made it."

They walked another few minutes. It was hard to measure time. It was hard to measure anything. Finally, Brother Henry stopped. He held the candle to the floor, pacing about. David could barely see him, but he could hear him counting. A few steps forward. A few more to the left. David kept close behind. He didn't want to let too much distance pass between him and the light from the candle.

"Here we are," Brother Henry said at last.

"So where is it?" said David, shivering in the cold.

"At your feet."

On the floor was a metal box a foot high with a chain around it. It was the kind of chain the Romans would have used. Brother Henry put his hand under the collar of his robe and took a crucifix from around his neck. The bottom of the long horizontal piece, the *stipes crucis*, was uneven, and turned sideways it looked like a key. Brother Henry inserted it into the chain lock.

"Go ahead," David said. "Open it."

Brother Henry opened the front of the box. A chalice was inside, smaller than the Chalice of Antioch and not nearly as ornate. It was made of wood. David wrapped his hands around it and took it out. It was cold to the touch.

"Careful now," Brother Henry said, putting his hand on David's wrist. "Drop it and it will break into a thousand pieces."

David ran his fingers along the edges of the chalice that was only a few inches high. "It certainly looks old but how old I can't say."

"It's not quite two thousand years old."

"But I've seen things like this that were more than two thousand years old. In digs along the Nile valley. Going back to the time of King Solomon."

"*And he spake three thousand proverbs and his sons were a thousand and five. And there came of all people to hear the wisdom of Solomon, from all kings of the earth.*"

David looked up at Brother Henry whose face was glowing.

"The Old Testament, Professor Marr. *Kings I*. I am not as ignorant as you might believe. But this chalice in your hands actually belonged to a descendant of King Solomon."

"I thought it was a replica."

Brother Henry smiled a weary smile. "There is no replica," he said. "*This is the Holy Grail*."

"This is the Grail?"

"Yes."

"Then I want to examine it. In a lab."

"I'm afraid that won't be possible. You should be grateful I have brought you here."

"I am but it doesn't prove anything. I see an old wooden goblet. It has to be tested."

"It has been tested."

"By who?"

"Trust me."

David applied his fingertips to the top of the cup. "I trust no one," he said.

"That is your problem, Professor Marr. You have no faith. It is a sorry man indeed who has no faith."

"You say this is the Holy Grail from the Last Supper and expect me to accept that? By your word alone?"

"My good Professor Marr, if you can't accept the word of an old monk who has absolutely no purpose in life other than to mind the chapel of a common church in Somerset whose word can you believe?"

David rested his eyes on the goblet. "I don't know what to believe."

"It is written, Professor Marr. '*And as they were eating, Jesus took bread and blessed it and brake it and gave it to the disciples and said 'Take, eat, this is my body'. And he took the cup and gave thanks and gave it to them saying 'Drink ye all of it*.' This is that cup. One and the same."

"Is it? Really?"

"I should think they should have named you Thomas after the disciple who chose not to believe. But we shouldn't tarry too long. It is frightfully cold here."

David's fingers were still clasping the top of the little goblet.

He was about to move them down the sides, but they wouldn't budge. There was no feeling in his fingers. They were numb. Was it the cold? But it couldn't be. Yes it was cold, but he could move his arms and legs. It was just his fingers on the icy surface of the wooden goblet.

"Why can't I move my fingers?" he said.

"Here," Brother Henry said. "Let me help you." He put his hands on David's and started rubbing them softly. "Are you sure you're trying to move them?"

"Yes!"

"Strange. But of course there must be an explanation. The dark and the cold and the dampness can play tricks on you sometimes."

There was nothing but blackness and the fragile flickering from the candle. Brother Henry kept rubbing David's fingers, trying to pry them from the goblet.

"They do seem to be fixed on it, don't they? It's almost as if they don't want to let go. Shall I blow on them for you? Maybe that will help."

He blew short puffs through his lips, his breath hot on David's hands. Soon, David could feel the blood returning to his fingers. He started moving them. One by one. Finally, when his hands were free, Brother Henry grabbed the grail and returned it to its resting place inside the metal box. He closed the door, and reapplied the chain and lock. David stretched his fingers and his knuckles cracked out loud. It was a sound he knew well. It was the same sound made by old brittle bones — bones that haven't moved in a thousand years — *snapping.*

"Strange," David said. "How I couldn't move my fingers. It must have been the cold."

"Yes. The cold."

"Was it? The cold I mean?"

"Perhaps. I don't know. But one thing I have learned in my eighty-seven years, Professor Marr, is that sometimes it's better not to ask. We must go now."

"*You're eighty-seven?*"

"Yes of course."

"But you don't look anywhere near that."

"Quite a mystery, isn't it? And to think all I do is devote my life to God. I don't subscribe to riches or material things or even to finding the reason for every little thing that happens. I just accept it. Strange, isn't it? Maybe it works. Follow me." Brother Henry took the candle, which was now melted exactly half-way to its base. "We have just enough light to get back. You wouldn't want to be caught in here without the flame, would you?"

He led David through the tunnel. It was easy to feel the gradual upward grade back to the spiral stairway. Brother Henry planted his foot on the first step to begin the long climb.

"Here," said David, "let me help you."

"Thank you but I need no help. I might be old but I am still strong. You see I have never been one to waste my energy on things that sap the soul."

"Things that sap the soul?"

"Yes, Professor Marr. Like financial concerns. Mortgages and taxes. Never had to worry about things like that. Or toiling eight hours a day at a job I might detest. Or perhaps sharing my life with people I don't even love. Such things can wreak havoc on a man over time, don't you think? They tend to sap one's strength."

"I suppose they do."

"But not for me. All I do is keep my faith. That's all. It's very simple really. The good thing about it is that it makes you stronger. Not weaker."

David marvelled at how Brother Henry pulled himself up with the agility of a much younger man. "If that wasn't a replica then there isn't a curse?" David said, following close behind.

"My good Professor Marr. I am sure you're aware that much misery has been waged throughout human history over what you've just seen. That should be curse enough, should it not? The only thing I know is that whoever does hold the Grail must make an offering in the form of a sacrifice. Sometimes it's a small one and sometimes it isn't."

"A sacrifice? Why?"

"It is payment, Professor Marr. For lack of faith. Everyone must pay for lack of faith. Even *you* must realize that."

"I don't believe ..."

"You can believe whatever you wish. But I know. You need

proof before you can believe. I feel sorry for you, Professor Marr, to be a man with so little faith. You look at a man's body and see only skin and veins and bones but you don't see anything else. You see no *test* in the world can get inside a man's soul, Professor Marr."

Back they climbed up the stairway that Brother Henry said dated from the fifth century. Soon they emerged through the opening in the floor of the church and everything was placed as before. Brother Henry escorted David to the front door of the chapel. He was about to say good-bye when he grabbed David's fingers that moments earlier were still as death. Then he kissed those fingers and looked up into David's face. His eyes of eighty-seven years were rich and alive, and there was great joy at play in them.

"I do hope that those who judge are not severe with you, Professor Marr, for you are a good man and more than that you are a blessed man."

"A blessed man?"

"These hands," he said, still clutching David's fingers. 'These hands have touched the same cup from which drank Our Lord himself. Don't ever forget that, Professor Marr. One day it just may be your salvation. Godspeed."

CHAPTER TWENTY-ONE

TWENTY-ONE

Eliraz's lab wasn't as big as mine and I would've been the last person to raise this delicate subject with her since I knew it was a source of friction. Why would a guest lecturer have a bigger lab than a permanent member of the faculty and one with definite career aspirations at that?

But Robbie was right about her. She was a good worker. Tireless, dedicated, results-oriented. Not surprisingly, she had responded to my invitation of DNA testing with enthusiasm, probably thinking I had finally recognized her as a professional, but I didn't know about her background in cell structure and for DNA that would be useful. She was business-like and formal in her work, but then she shot me a glance from the corner of her eye. There was something about Eliraz that baffled me. I didn't know how to take her. Deep down I felt she was going to be one of two things — either a great help or a great hindrance.

"Microbiology is an unusual discipline for an archeologist, isn't it?" I asked her.

"Not really. It comes in handy. You'd be surprised. Well here it is." She handed me a petri dish with the sampling of dried blood that I had scratched away from the skin of the mummy.

"One thing, David. You never said how you managed to get blood from a skeleton. I've heard of taking it from a stone. But not a skeleton."

"I beg your pardon?"

"Your skeleton. Your *thing*. Whatever it is you have in your lab. This blood sample is from it. Isn't it?"

"I never said that."

"No. You never said anything at all. But this is the first time you ever asked me to look at a blood sample. What else could it be from?"

"Well ... it ... could ... be ..."

"It couldn't be from anything else. It isn't a skeleton, is it David?"

"Not exactly."

"Well whatever you've got there has a problem. I can tell you that."

"What do you mean?"

"Sickle cell anemia." I held the petri dish up to my eyes. "It's a blood disease. People who have it can't send oxygen to their tissues properly. How are you in chemical biology?"

"Try me."

"It works like this. The molecules in red blood cells, the cells that carry oxygen, are defective. They don't work right. Normal red blood cells look like little disks and even when they're infected with sickle cell anemia they start out like little disks but when these sick cells get into the capillaries and veins which have less oxygen they collapse. That's when the shape of the cell changes. It looks like a curved knife blade or a sickle. Sickle cell anemia."

"What are the symptoms?"

"Severe anemia. The body starts fighting to destroy the defective cells. Then the number of healthy red cells in the system is reduced which causes anemia. It's usually hereditary."

"Hereditary?"

"The disease is common in Africa among blacks. In some parts of Africa as much as forty-five per cent of the population has it and even in the United States about ten per cent of blacks have it."

"Wait a minute, Eliraz. You're saying this blood is diseased and it comes from *a black man*?"

"It does have a disease and it *could* be from a black man. What's so funny? Did I make a joke?"

"No. No."

"I didn't say it's from a black man but it could be. On the other hand sickle cell anemia affects other races too. Those who have it are *heterozygous*."

"Forget the technical terms. Just give me the facts."

"The facts David are that it's common in parts of Africa and it's been around a long time."

"How long?"

"I don't know."

"Where in Africa?"

"It's found all over Africa and the Arab Peninsula too. Yemen for example. It's not rare in Yemen."

"What does not rare mean?"

"That maybe ten per cent of the population has it."

"You mean ten per cent of the black population?"

"No. Ten per cent of the population period."

"But that's a lot. One in ten?"

"The incidence might be a little lower in Saudi Arabia. Maybe five per cent. And you find it right here in Israel too. Not as high as those other places but you find it. Maybe one in a hundred."

"One in a hundred?"

"Yes. It's easy to see under a microscope. You see the hemoglobin from normal cells and sickle cells is almost the same. The difference is in the amino acids. The sixth amino acid in normal hemoglobin is glutamic acid but the sixth one in the sickle chain is valine."

That was Eliraz. The scientist. Trying to impress.

"I don't follow you," I said.

"What I mean is whoever provided this blood sample was anemic or at least had a propensity for anemia. If it didn't develop at the time of death it certainly would have later. I don't imagine the donor was very old. What do you know about him?"

"About who?"

"The donor?"

"The donor?"

"Yes. Who was it?"

Eliraz was draped in her white lab coat, scribbling in her notebook. I glanced over her shoulder to see what she was writing, but it was Hebrew and hand-written Hebrew was impossible for me to decipher. She looked at me.

"Who was it?" she asked again.

"That's what I'm trying to find out."

"Look David. I know you've got a lot more than a pile of bones in your lab. Skeletons don't give blood. Why don't you just show me and we'll get it over with?"

"You've done DNA tests before?" I said, changing the subject.

"Yes," she said with a sigh.

"Where?"

"I've done them many times. When I was an undergraduate I was in a group that duplicated Sanger's experiment with insulin. He was the one who broke the insulin molecule into fragments and identified the amino acids. That was the first time protein was produced by man and it led to the synthesis of insulin. The study of insulin is important to DNA research. It's probably the best example of recombinant DNA being used to help people. Sanger is important for other things too. He developed the process of paper chromatography."

"Of what?"

"Paper chromatography. It's a way to separate tiny pieces of insulin on filter paper. That was how he identified the amino acids. It brought DNA research into the modern era. You should try it yourself some time. You get to see what we really look like. Up close. Here let's have a look at this blood."

She put the petri dish with the blood sample under a microscope. Then she pressed her right eye against the eyeglass, adjusted the magnifying lens and told me to have a look. What I saw wasn't clear. Just tiny ring-like disks randomly scattered all over the place.

"That's the sample you gave me," Eliraz said. "From your mysterious *skeleton*. It has sickle cell anemia. Now let's look at normal blood."

She grabbed a needle and pricked the end of her finger. She squeezed a drop of blood onto another petri dish and then removed the first blood sample, the one from the mummy which she said was abnormal. Then she inserted her own sample under the microscope.

"You see the difference?" she said.

"I'm looking."

"The normal blood cells look like fine rings, don't they?"

"Now I see. Yes you're right."

"Okay. Now let's put the first lens back in. Have a look at those cells. You see the difference?"

"There are some rings but some of them aren't rings at all. They look like ... like ... little crescent moons."

"Like a sickle. Right? That's where the name comes from. Why don't you try it with your own blood?"

Before I could say anything she grabbed my finger and pricked the end of it, capturing a drop of blood onto a third petri dish. A moment later and she had the sample — *my* sample — under the microscope. I looked and it was the same as hers, every cell the shape of a ring. Then, once again, she inserted the sample from the mummy. The blood cells were different.

"DNA technology has come a long way," she said. "Now forensic experts can use it to solve crimes. DNA typing they call it. Everybody's DNA is different. It's like a fingerprint."

"So the DNA from the sample I gave you is different from anyone else's?"

"You might say that."

I had an idea. It was crazy. But why not? "Eliraz, tell me, what if I gave you a sample ... another sample I mean ... and it looked the same as this one?"

"The same as this one? From your *skeleton*?"

"Yes," I said with a smile. "From my skeleton."

"Then I'd say you might have two samples from the same source. And in this case that other sample would also have to exhibit sickle cell anemia."

"All right, Eliraz. I'd like you to test another sample. Could you do that?"

"Of course, David. No problem. But on one condition. I get to see your ... whatever it is."

Eliraz had taken to calling the mummy *whatever it is* for lack of a better name. All she knew was that it was no skeleton, but if it could produce blood that didn't leave many options. Her curiosity was in high gear. I thought for a moment. I wanted that other sample tested right away and she could do it for me. On the other hand, I had serious reservations about showing her the mummy. But then I didn't have to tell her where I found it. Or about the C-14. Or the *titulus*.

"All right," I agreed. "But first you'll do the sample?"

"Fine, David. And what's the sample from?"

"Some material."

"What do you mean?"

"An old cloth."

"What old cloth?"

"You ask too many questions. I'll bring you the sample tomorrow. When you have the results we'll talk."

The next day I gave her a second sample. It was something I had kept for many years from my one and only visit to Turin, Italy. It contained a small stain of what appeared to be dried blood and it was from an old cloth.

The Holy Shroud.

Turin was a remarkable period that I'll never forget. It was a lesson in people — even scientists — getting so caught up in wanting to believe something that they shut their eyes to everything they saw. I had never bothered to analyze the sample before, but the stain always intrigued me. Besides, I never had another blood sample I wanted to compare it with, but now I did. Eliraz arranged the sample and later that afternoon she called.

"I have the results of that other sample you wanted me to do," she said. "Now I can hardly wait to see your *whatever it is*."

"I'll be right over."

"But first I have something to tell you."

"What's that?"

"The donor of this second sample?"

"Yes?"

"This donor also had sickle cell anemia."

"He did?"

"Yes. *He* did. And that's not all." There was a pause. A long one. "While I was at it I also extracted some DNA. The DNA from that old cloth of yours matches with the other one. From your first sample. The *whatever it is*. That means it's the same blood. From the same donor."

CHAPTER TWENTY-TWO

TWENTY-TWO

The food in the hospital cafeteria did little to satisfy the appetite of Jamil Hassad. He often told me about the hospital food. Most days at lunch he would buy two sandwiches and was especially fond of turkey. The food was delivered by truck every morning just when the sun was rising over the sleeping Sahara. Jamil once said there was something about hospitals that brought out the worst in food — for staff and patients alike — and maybe it was the rush and pulse of the environment. He said the food was prepared without taking the time that it demanded and that wasn't Jamil's way. He was a man who liked his food slow and deliberate. He liked everything that way.

On the day I called him he had already absorbed two turkey sandwiches and a helping of strawberry yogurt. He liked strawberry yogurt because it was sweet, but still he was far from satiated. During his meetings with doctors, patients and corpses — every day he visited with all three — he was quick to grab handfuls of nuts, raisins and chocolates. The long meetings, the ones with the doctors, were the most arduous for he couldn't very well bring a jar of sweets into the boardroom, so instead he brought coffee sweetened with sugar. Hospital coffee. From a machine. He said it tasted like *khara*.

Shit.

In the morning before lunch that day he had visited his local mosque to perform the customary ablutions. *Wudhu*. He did that every day. Three times he would wash his hands up to the wrists and three times he would rinse his mouth and then rinse his face, followed by his right arm and his left. Three times for each. After that he would remove his shoes and socks, and wash first his right foot and then his left. Up to the ankle. Three times. That done, he would face Mecca.

"Allahu-Akbar. Allahu-Akbar. Allahu-Akbar. Allahu-Akbar."

'God is the greatest.'

"Ash-ahdu-an-la-ilaha-illahah. Ash-ahdu-an-la-ilaha-illahah."

'I bear witness that there is no God but Allah.'

"Ash-hado anna muhammaden-rasulullah. Ash-hado anna muhammaden-rasulullah."

'I bear witness that Muhammad is the messenger of Allah.'

"Hayye-alas-salah. Hayye-alas-salah."

'Come to prayer.'

"Hayye-alal-falah. Hayye-alal-falah."

'Come to security.'

"Allahu-Akbar. Allahu-Akbar."

'God is the greatest.'

"La-illah-illalah."

'There is no God but Allah.'

His mid-day prayers and his lunch complete, he returned to his office, shut the door and planted himself on his chair. He loosened his belt and searched for guidance by reaching for a small measure of security that he always kept close at hand — the chain and pendant of Osiris. He wore it around his neck. Osiris. The God of the Dead who had suffered death and was restored to eternal life and who was worshipped by pre-dynastic Egyptians six thousand years ago. Long associated with fertility, Osiris was the spirit of the Underworld and the ultimate symbol of Resurrection. Jamil also summoned The Book of the Dead. In ancient times when the pharaoh died the spells from that book would ward off ill-intentioned spirits and assure the soul of the dead king safe passage into the next life. Eternal life. It was what every man longed for. It was what Jamil longed for. He had told me so. Many times. I knew I would find him in his office just then.

"David! How good to hear your voice," he said into the phone.

"Jamil, I hope I'm not interrupting."

"Not at all."

"There's something I have to tell you. We did blood tests."

"I thought I was going to do that."

"I couldn't wait. I had a colleague do them. But she doesn't know where it's from."

"She?"

"Yes. She's a professor here at the university."

"David, I told you not to involve anyone."

"I know but she's an expert in cell structure. Did an undergraduate degree in microbiology. And she's an archeologist."

"But ..."

"She doesn't know, Jamil."

"Are you sure?"

"I'm sure."

There was a long silence on the line. "You had her do blood samples?" he said.

"Yes and the samples match."

"What do you mean they match?"

"I had her check the DNA from the mummy and from the stain."

"What stain?"

"From the shroud. The Holy Shroud. And they match."

"David, that shroud was a medieval forgery. You proved that yourself."

"I know and I can't explain it but they match. They match Jamil! The stain from the mummy and the stain from the shroud. They match! It's the same blood!"

"But that can't be."

"It can't but it is."

Another pause.

"David, have you told anyone else about this? Besides her I mean?"

"Her?"

"That woman."

It was a trick question.

"Jamil ... I told you ... she doesn't know anything."

"This is the woman you wrote me about in your letter. Isn't it?"

"Yes."

"And you said she suspects something. But why would you involve her if she suspects something?"

I didn't know what to say. Even over the phone Jamil could be an intimidating presence. It was his voice and his certainty. About everything.

"Jamil, I know you're upset but believe me she doesn't know."

"Well she must know something. Have you worked with her before?"

"No."

More silence. "Listen," he said. "It was a mistake letting her do these tests but you can't do anything about it now. She is Israeli?"

"Yes."

"You must be careful. If only you were anywhere else but Jerusalem. It's a dangerous city. She's a professor? She has students?"

"Yes. Robbie used to work for her."

"David, I don't think you recognize the severity of what we have here. We have to keep this from people at the university. Your university. We have to keep it from Muslims. We have to keep it from the Church. If any of them learn about this …"

"Why are you so worried about the Church, Jamil?"

"Why? Because they're the worst hypocrites in the world but are to be feared for they have tremendous resources. Resources beyond your imagination. Their antiquities people have made a career out of thievery and lies. Do you know the obelisk in the middle of St. Peter's Square?"

"I think so."

"It's Egyptian and it was stolen by the Romans and then by the Christians. It was erected in the square in the sixteenth century and there's a cross on top with an inscription. '*Christus vincit, Christus regnat, Christus imperiat*'. How do you think Muslims feel about that? That obelisk is typical of all the Vatican collections, collections built on theft, and it's only one of countless artifacts they stole from Egypt. They raped my country, David. The Romans. The Christians. The English. They all raped my country and the Israelis are no different so don't tell me about your archeologist friend or anyone else who can jeopardize this. Do you have any idea what fundamentalist Muslims would do if they found out?"

I could sense his exasperation through the telephone.

"Remember the *Ka*, David?"

"What about it?"

"They would steal the mummy, take it to Egypt and wash it in the Nile. That's the custom."

"What do you mean?"

"For mummification. They would cut an opening through the abdomen and remove the liver. Then the lungs, the stomach, the intestines, everything. Then they'd place all the organs in jars and fill the spaces left in the body with spices and resins. Then they'd remove the brain. Through the nostrils. Bit by bit with a spoon. You know how it's done. Then they'd fill the brain cavity with mud and preserve the features of the dead so the *Ka* doesn't disintegrate. They would leave the heart intact and keep the body in oils and resins. Just like the pharaohs. There would be no natron or quicklime. Not for this man. Then they'd put a scarab over his heart for eternal life. The four sons of Horus would be put beside him. There would be clothing, a mask, food and wine to provide nourishment for his passage to the next world. That's what they would do. And one more detail you should know."

"What's that?"

"They wouldn't think twice about eliminating anyone who got in their way." Jamil stopped to let it sink in.

"But why do all those things to the body?" I asked him.

"They would do all this if they believed the man was a *prophet*. We're talking about sacred lineage here."

"Jamil, sometimes I don't know if I'm talking to Jamil the pathologist or Jamil the Muslim. Jesus ... Christianity ... it all comes from Egyptian mythology. It's all there in the Temple of Luxor. Jesus is Horus and Horus is Jesus. They're one and the same. And just like you said the Catholic Church has been stealing from Egyptian culture since before the Church existed. Since before Christianity existed. The story of a Jesus figure goes back thousands of years."

"Twenty thousand."

"Twenty thousand?"

"Yes. In 18,000 B.C.E. there was a reference to Iusu who was defined as 'the coming divine Son who heals or saves'. That would grow into the god Horus. His mother was Isis."

"So Horus is Jesus and Isis is the Madonna. What's the difference? Horus was an ancient Egyptian god and the story of Jesus is derived from that. The virgin birth. The twelve followers. Isn't the raising of Lazarus from the dead in there too?"

"Actually his Egyptian name was El-Asar but the story is the same."

"So there was no Jesus. It's a myth. Like all religion."

"David the cynic as always. You are too dismissive of the human condition. So where does this Qumran mummy figure in your scheme of things?"

"There's only one answer. It's a forgery. But a very good one."

"What about the markings that correspond to the scriptures?"

"They could have mummified a corpse after they drove spikes into the wrists and feet. Same thing for the wound in the side. They did it so everything would match the scriptures."

"And the *titulus*?"

"That too. They doctored it up and planted it near the body."

"What about the matching of the blood? With the stains on your shroud? DNA doesn't lie. How do you explain that?"

"I can't. But there must be an explanation. The only thing I know is whoever did this went to a lot of trouble."

"David, you're missing the point. It doesn't even matter about Horus and Isis and Jesus. The only thing that matters is what people *believe* and that's why this is so dangerous. Now I'm coming to Jerusalem as we agreed. Did you book the CAT scan at the hospital?"

"Yes."

"What did you tell them?"

"Only that we have a mummy to examine. It's all arranged. I booked the equipment for four hours on a Saturday. During the Sabbath."

"The Sabbath?"

"It will be quiet then."

A pause.

"Have you told Gita about this?"

"No."

"Nothing?"

"She doesn't know."

"She's with you in Jerusalem, isn't she?"

"Yes. She was away at a conference when we found the mummy but she's back now."

"And she doesn't know? I find that hard to believe. Your wife is a very perceptive person."

"You don't have to tell me that."

Quiet. Jamil was thinking.

"David, has it ever crossed your mind that we were *chosen* for this mission? You and me?"

"What do you mean?"

"Don't you have a sense of being observed?"

"As a matter of fact, Jamil, I do feel like we're being watched. It's weird."

"We are being watched and you know why? We're part of a story unfolding as it was meant to be and it was a story written long ago. The Jews have been waiting for their Messiah for thousands of years and the Christians have been waiting for the second coming of theirs. But what they don't understand is it's the same Messiah. One and the same. And all the while Muhammad is watching over us. Following our every move. There is no room for mistakes. By either of us."

"I never associated you with mistakes, Jamil. *You* of all people."

"Believe me never before have I felt so mortal. I'm a Muslim who subscribes to the everlasting life of the soul and all the science in the world isn't going to change that. But the only way to everlasting life is through mummification. It means every detail from the embalming of Osiris must be duplicated or the dead are not granted passage."

I could hear him sigh over the phone.

"If only I could be a true Muslim and ignore the part of me that is physician and scientist. Why then the gods might have selected *me* ... Jamil Hassad ... to perform these ancient rites myself."

"You would do that?"

"Yes. But the physician in me makes that impossible. But what an honor it would have been."

"An honor?"

"A few nights ago I was thinking. What if Muhammad asked me to perform these rites to correct the terrible wrong of an improper burial? Such an indignity to be buried as a simple pauper in the sand. But what if I was the one to rectify this? Then maybe the gods would remember me but there's a problem. Muhammad has tied my hands into a knot. He's given me options. One of them is to be a good Muslim and the other is to be a human being who places the value of all mankind above any race or faith and that means we must be circumspect. So I think I've become a more whole person with this experience and that can only be a good thing. I hope it happens to you as well."

There was another silence, but not an uncomfortable one.

"Jamil, I have to go but I'm glad we talked. I hope you're not annoyed with me."

I detected a chuckle.

"You're a scientist, David. That means you're curious and impatient. A human being with human frailties. As for me I think I'm going to do some reading about that Holy Shroud of yours. This business about the blood matching just can't be."

CHAPTER TWENTY-THREE

TWENTY-THREE

November 1972

The museum's new Ancient Egypt Gallery would show how Egyptians mummified their dead. The exhibit was due to David's field work in the Nile valley. He had found a mummy from the seventh century B.C., its shrivelled body the size of a child's with an ugly opening in the neck and the mouth ajar. He had also found an older mummy, pre-dynastic, its remains surrounded by pottery. The usual sort of thing. The public always craved mummies and tombs, so David did his best to deliver. The new gallery attracted a huge crowd on opening day.

Gita was dressed in black, her back bare, her neck adorned with a necklace once owned by a housemaid of Cleopatra's. She looked like a goddess. The woman standing next to her, the curator of Vertebrate Paleontology no less, struck up a conversation.

"What do you make of that shroud everyone's talking about in Italy?" she said.

"The Holy Shroud?" said Gita. "Not much. Why?"

"I think it might be authentic. Most people think they're too sophisticated to believe in something like that. They're worried this shroud might have more than a grain of truth and if it does everything they stand for is in danger. But deep down most of us are looking for something spiritual that goes beyond the next paycheck or new car. The shroud is a wonderful opportunity."

Tabloids were writing about it and even scientific journals. It was the old story of religion and science mixing. The shroud was a hot commodity in Europe and now Americans were gaining interest. David knew that was dangerous. His old mentor Eli Solnik had called them a godless people, but David wasn't so sure.

"Did you hear how they explained that image that's confounded people for centuries? They said it was formed by a burst of radiant energy from the body during the Resurrection."

David joined the fray and upon hearing this story burst into laughter. But that didn't deter the curator of Vertebrate Paleontology. She told David about STURP. The Shroud of Turin Research Project. The Vatican was going to have scientists test the cloth.

"Do they have an archeologist?" David asked, but she didn't know.

He later learned that every scientist on STURP had ties to the Church. They called themselves scientists except they would begin with a conclusion and proceed to verify it. Not very scientific. It was the same reasoning used in Creation Science where people with letters and degrees after their names opted for biblical creation over evolution. Then some character in California did an experiment. He suspended himself from a cross of biblical proportions for thirty seconds in front of a TV crew and when his half-minute of suffering was over he concluded that Jesus had died of congestive heart failure.

"No one who was crucified died of congestive heart failure," David told Gita. "They died of asphyxiation." But it was on the news and David made his decision. He was going to get on STURP. "How can they date this thing without an archeologist?" he said, but Gita had an answer for that.

"Easy," she said. "They look at the Bible, trace the number of begats back to the time of Christ and then they have a date and millions of people accept what they say. But it wouldn't take much to see if it was from the first century or fourteenth century which is when it originated."

David wasn't up on the history of the Holy Shroud like Gita. She explained how in the Middle Ages there was an exhibit in

France. Pilgrims came to see it and a souvenir medallion was struck. A lot of money was raised for the Church, but a bishop said it was fake and the exposition was stopped.

"So at least one member of the Church had a conscience," David said.

"Not at all," said Gita. "His objection had nothing to do with science. He said since the Gospels didn't mention anything about a shroud there wasn't a shroud. Case closed. End of exposition. After that there are historical records and documents but where it was before that nobody knows."

"But if I date it I could prove the matter once and for all," David said.

"Good luck dear. You'll need it."

....

When Brian was almost thirteen Gita started planning his Bar Mitzvah. She had already given in to David's wishes about no Hebrew School, but now Brian needed lessons so he could read from the Torah. Gita called a rabbi who immediately expressed concern that the boy was only starting his lessons at this late date. "He's been held back but he can still have a sound Jewish education," the rabbi said. "He has a keen mind and is eager to learn. What would your husband say about him continuing his studies after the *simcha*?"

"He wouldn't like it. We agreed long ago that Brian would have a Bar Mitzvah but that was all."

"Is Brian having a confirmation too?"

"No. Why would we do that?"

"For his father. He's a Christian, isn't he?"

"Rabbi, my husband is the last man on earth who wants his children confirmed in the eyes of the Church."

When the guest list for the Bar Mitzvah reached one hundred, David balked.

"You can't deny me this," Gita said. "I've made sacrifices for you. When Brian was born we didn't have the *ben zakhar*. He never went to *shul*. He never went to Hebrew school and now that we're finally doing something you're putting a cloud over it.

It won't happen when Jennie has her *Bat Mitzvah* in five years I can tell you that."

Bat Mitzvah?

Jennie was the spitting image of her mother, but unlike her mother she was quiet and reserved. Her older brother Brian, who had inherited Gita's dark complexion and jet-black hair, was the spoiled one. Still, David was thankful for his son's interest in archeology. Brian had begun to comprehend the significance of large passages of time and how in some ways man had made great advancements, but in other ways no advancements at all.

David once gave him a book about the Sumerians of Mesopotamia, and the royal cities of Solomon and Pompeii. One photo in the book had a lasting impression. It was a shot of excavators in their Arab head-dresses probing near the ziggurat of Nippur. The thought of digging for things three thousand years old made Brian's eyes light up.

"They had trouble on that dig," David told him. "The great dune belt was always moving with the drifting sand and it still is. Finding things in conditions like that is hard."

"Were you at that one, Dad?"

"No. I never made it to Nippur."

"Then I'll go. I'll be the first member of the family to dig there. Maybe I'll find something."

David looked into his son's eyes and saw himself as a boy.

"I'm going to be like you, Dad," Brian said. "I'm going to be just like you."

....

October 1973

It was called the Yom Kippur War because the Arabs attacked on the holiest day of the Jewish calendar. The Egyptians crossed the Suez Canal in helicopters and boats, and laid down pontoon bridges as their armored forces poured across the narrow waterway into Sinai. Then Syrian forces attacked the Israelis in the Golan Heights and the plan was clear. Regain territories lost in the 1967 War by stretching the Israelis thin. The Arabs were well supplied with Soviet guns, tanks and planes, and in a few hours they had taken most of the eastern bank.

Israeli Prime Minister Golda Meir denounced the enemy for attacking on the Day of Atonement as thousands of reservists had to rush from synagogue straight to their military units. The next day the Israeli Air Force struck deep inside Egypt and Syria, severing bridges that had been erected across the Suez Canal, and isolating hundreds of Egyptian tanks and forces on the eastern bank.

But this would be no Six Day War. Things were going so badly for Israel that the state activated its hidden nuclear arsenal. Atomic bombs were assembled in an underground tunnel, rushed to air force units and readied for dropping from Phantoms jets. On October 13, a week after the war started, the Soviet Union dispatched nuclear warheads to Alexandria from its naval base at Odessa, so now Israel herself was a target for nuclear-armed SCUD missiles. In the second week of combat with no end in sight, there was real fear that a nuclear conflict might emerge. On October 24 U.S. forces around the world were placed on Defense Condition 3 — DEFCON 3 — also known as Red Alert. Not since the assassination of President John F. Kennedy ten years earlier had they been at that level.

The war came to an end with both sides claiming victory and with UN troops established between the two camps. Israel returned her nuclear bombs to their underground site and Moscow sent her nuclear warheads back to Odessa. After all the nukes were recalled, Egyptian President Anwar Sadat had to go to the morgue to identify the body of his younger brother who had been shot down in a dogfight over the Golan Heights. The Egyptian leader looked at the battered remains and wept. He clenched his fists and thought of the wars, all the wars fought and those yet to be fought, and he saw the face of Muhammad.

....

Egypt's second War of Attrition with Israel lasted from November 1, 1973 to March 17, 1974. Every day there were incidents of shelling, raids on Israeli patrols and full-scale attacks. When it was over the Americans and Soviets began airlifting out the supplies they had brought in to the area, but tensions remained high since Israel refused to give up even one inch of the occupied territories.

"I love the Holy Land," said David, "but I fear the Third World War will start there."

"It is written," Gita said. "Armageddon. Revelation. Chapter sixteen. *'And he gathered them together into a place called in the Hebrew tongue Armageddon. And there were voices and thunders and lightnings. And there was a great earthquake such as was not since men were upon the earth. So mighty an earthquake and so great.'"*

"Gita, I'm surprised. That's from the New Testament."

"There is the odd thing worthwhile. This comes from the Hebrew anyway. Everything from the New Testament is from the Hebrew except all that nonsense about Jesus. Armageddon comes from Megiddo. It's an important town. Many biblical battles were fought there and a big one in the First World War too. It'll happen. Some day it'll happen. But we'll win."

"Israel?" David said, and she nodded. "I see. So Israel can do no wrong and Israel can never lose. Right? Gita, sometimes I think you're going to make me an anti-Semite."

She glared at him. Such words, even in jest, didn't sit well with her. "I try to give our children some direction, David. Everyone needs direction. But what do you give them? People ask Brian what religion he is and he doesn't know. I'm a Jew and proud of it. What are you?"

"Just a man. But one who likes to dig."

Brian liked to dig too. He would come to the museum after hours with his father and David would show him artifacts not on display. As David learned more about STURP and the Holy Shroud of Turin, Brian got intrigued. He was the one who asked the question David hadn't even considered.

"What if it really is the shroud of Jesus?" Brian said.

"That's impossible."

"But why? You found things two thousand years old before."

"Brian, even if we date it to that time it could be any cloth. There's no way to prove it."

"But you said those people on STURP were wrong to

begin with their conclusion. Aren't you doing the same thing? Beginning with a conclusion that it's not real?"

Brian was his mother's son. No one but the two of them could get under David's skin like that and he wasn't asking the question to be smart or even to be difficult. He was asking because he wanted to know the truth. It was the hallmark of a scientist.

"Dad, you always say to take the middle road and weigh the evidence so why don't you start in the middle with the shroud? Accept its existence as a possibility. You believed the Dead Sea Scrolls were real? Why not this?"

....

At a meeting of STURP in New Mexico, an official with the U.S. Air Force planned to show a 3D model of Jesus. David wanted to attend, claiming to be studying the shroud from an archeological perspective, and they welcomed him. They didn't waste any time sending him literature supporting the work of those who had already pronounced the shroud as legitimate. The Vatican retained approval rights for all candidates to STURP, but there was one condition. You had to be a 'sindonologist'. It was the latest discipline in the classics — shroud studies. There was an International Center of Sindonology and everyone on STURP belonged.

Said the coordinator of the American unit of sindonologists: "Based on the scientific evidence to date, most of us would agree that this is the authentic burial cloth of Jesus Christ."

Said the bomb designer employed by the U.S. Air Force: "It is technically impossible according to our research for a forger to provide a perfect three-dimensional image on a piece of cloth. Therefore we can conclude that there was a body beneath that cloth."

Said the Swiss criminologist who had studied pollen samples taken from dust found on the shroud: "If the shroud is genuine, which I believe it is, it would be about two thousand years old."

Sindonologists all.

"This is crazy," said David. "STURP is going to spend a week studying the shroud and it will be a show trial for the public. But now before any studies have even taken place every member of the jury has already announced his conclusion."

"What do you expect?" Gita said. "They're all Christian fundamentalists. Your chances of getting involved in that thing are as good as a snowball in hell."

"But science has come a long way, Gita. If we had to develop a snowball in hell I'm sure we could do that. Provided we find the place."

....

In New Mexico the 3D image of the man beneath the shroud looked realistic. The only problem was the size. He was described as a taller-than-average Semitic male from two thousand years ago and at five-eleven he was — eight inches taller than average for the time. But there was no mention in the Bible of Jesus being a giant. There was no mention of his appearance at all. Those at the meeting spoke like men of science. Physicists. Chemists. Metallurgists. Medical doctors. Even criminologists were there. They all had credentials and every one of them said the Holy Shroud was the burial cloth of Jesus. Not a dissenting voice in the bunch.

But David wasn't convinced. During the two days of meetings he managed to get an interview with the head of the American contingent of STURP.

"Has the shroud been exposed to carbon 14 dating?" he asked.

"No. The Church won't allow it. A test like that would damage the cloth."

"Do you have an archeologist, someone familiar with carbon 14 dating, on your team?"

"No."

"I'm familiar with it and I can assure you the technology is available to provide accurate dating using very small samples. All I need is five or six centimeters of material. It's less than half the width of your thumbnail."

Still, the man said no. The next day, David met with a thermal chemist who told him how the image on the shroud had been imprinted by an intense burst of light. Flash photolysis, he called it. He said this meshed well with the traditional picture of a shining resurrected Christ emerging from the tomb.

"Are you Catholic?" David asked, and the chemist said he was. "Are you a member of the International Center of Sindonology?"

"Past president of the American chapter."

The chemist also belonged to the Bible-Science Association of America and the Creation Research Society. The latter was an organization of scientists, many of them with Masters degrees and doctorates, who conducted research supporting the creationist view, namely the principle message of the Book of Genesis. Verbatim.

"It's like the Hitler Youth," David told Gita. "The only difference is they're propagandists for the Bible."

But the chemist was also a member of the American Association for the Advancement of Science, an eminent professional organization and one of the leading scientific organizations in the world. David belonged to it himself.

"Professor Marr, like you I only want to get at the truth," the chemist said. "Is this really the shroud of Christ or not? I believe it is and we're going to prove it to the world."

David said STURP would enhance its credibility with an archeologist and the chemist agreed, but he said David must first acquire membership in the International Center of Sindonology. David said he'd apply.

"One more thing, Professor Marr. I don't mean to pry but what is your religious affiliation?"

"My religious affiliation?"

"Your faith."

David lied and said he was Catholic.

"And what church do you attend?"

David couldn't remember the last time he had set foot inside a church or any other place of worship for that matter. But he did want to be on STURP. He wanted to be on STURP very badly. "Why the Church of the Resurrection," he said.

....

The last time Jennie was this sick, David had been in Manchester taking pictures of the bog mummies with a CAT scanner. It turned out to be the flu, but this time she was worse. She had lost weight, and her arms and legs had become sticks. The doctor said her urine had a high sugar count. Then came blood tests and she was hospitalized. The prognosis wasn't good. "She has diabetes and will be insulin-dependent the rest of her life," the doctor said. The news stunned her parents.

"We did something wrong," Gita said, "and now we're being punished. There is a reason. Maybe it has to do with the scrolls or that grail you were after."

David said that was ridiculous, but there was no history of diabetes in their families. He remembered when Jennie was sick and he had gone to Glastonbury and touched what was reputed to be the Holy Grail. He remembered the warnings from Brother Henry, and his talk about sacrifice and payment for lack of faith, and now his little Jennie had diabetes. Was this David's payment for daring to venture where he was told not to go? Was this his sacrifice? He didn't know, but the guilt consumed him.

....

In 1898 the Vatican let a man take photographs of a cloth considered by many to be the most valuable possession in Christendom. The image on the cloth had attracted interest for centuries because no one could explain it. When the photos were developed the image appeared on the negative in reverse, assuming a new sense of realism. What had been a faded likeness suddenly became a human face. The negative triggered a fierce debate. In the 1930s public showings of the shroud were held in Turin, Italy, where it had been stored since the seventeenth century. New photographs were taken. A doctor who had experience with cadavers said the signs of wounds on the shroud were only possible from crucifixion. Scores of doctors and scientists studied everything from the apparent blood stains on the cloth to the impressions said to have been made by a human body. As before, some thought the shroud was authentic while others dismissed it as a fraud.

The shroud was an object of profound curiosity. David figured it was the work of a con artist from the fourteenth century, but the forgery theory presented a problem. It was that negative from 1898. Even if one accepted that the shroud was a medieval fraud, how could a negative image be produced before such technology was available? Turin would be the litmus test.

In the early 1970s interest reached fever pitch when European investigators claimed that the cotton used in the shroud had originated in the Middle East. They said they could tell by the number of twists in each inch of cotton fibres. A criminologist said that pollens found on the shroud could only have come from a salt-rich soil like that found near the Dead Sea and so, the argument for the shroud's authenticity continued to be built. Like an old fortification. Stone by stone.

The year 1978 would be the four hundredth anniversary of the shroud's arrival in Turin. It would be open to public view and examined. Scientists would be formally invited to Turin by the International Center of Sindonology and David would be part of it.

"But this whole thing smacks of the blind leading the blind," he said.

"Yes it does," Gita replied. "All the more reason a sighted person should be there."

CHAPTER TWENTY-FOUR

TWENTY-FOUR

It wasn't long after we had found the mummy, and the Bedouin shepherd was frantic. He kept blowing on his hands that were cold from the night air and in between the gusts of breath from his mouth he kept uttering garbled words that would have been unintelligible to me even if I knew Arabic. Robbie was having trouble understanding what he was saying too. In the few words he knew he asked the man to repeat himself. The frail little shepherd, anxious and fearful as he spoke, had more lines across his face than I had ever seen in a man.

"What's the matter, Robbie?" I said. "What's he saying?"

When at last he understood Robbie turned to me. "They have found something. A skeleton. He says it is old but he does not know how old. He says the man was murdered."

"How does he know that?"

"Because the skull is not with the body."

"That could mean anything. The bones could have rotted and the skull might have fallen off."

"No. He says there was a clean cut at the neck. Right through the bones. They found the skull several meters from the rest of it. And something else."

"What's that?"

"Well this is the thing, Professor Marr. He says it was buried in the sand."

"In the sand? But it's only a skeleton?"

"Just a skeleton. He says there was nothing buried with it. Just bones. That is all."

They talked some more and then the man tore himself away and threw himself on the ground. I didn't know if he was asking for forgiveness from Allah or what, but he was in a furious delirium of the kind I had often seen from his people.

"Buried in the sand?" I said. "Where exactly did they find the skeleton?"

"In Qumran but not where we found the mummy. It was closer to the ruins of the old Essene monastery."

I had long been puzzled by the monastery. It was an old building from antiquity that was buried on the shore between the cliffs and the sea. It was near the cave where the first Dead Sea Scrolls were found. According to the story, in the middle of the nineteenth century, a French tourist noticed the remains of a stone wall protruding above the ground and thought it might be the ruins of the biblical Gomorrah, but it was another hundred years before the site would be excavated. In the dig they found a tower and a number of rooms suggesting a community of some kind. There was a kitchen, an assembly area, a dining hall and also a potter's workshop, a stable and even an aqueduct and water system. It is believed the scrolls were written in a room called the *scriptorium.*

"Robbie, there's an old cemetery there with over a thousand tombs. A few of them were excavated twenty years ago and they were all buried the same way. With their heads facing south. The mummy. The head. It was …"

"Facing south, Professor Marr."

"There are only skeletons in that cemetery. Bones. That's all. But none of those skeletons was buried with anything either. No pottery. Nothing of value."

"So?"

"Why didn't I think of it earlier?"

"Think of what?"

"We better go see what they found, Robbie. Tell them we'll

pay them whatever they want to take us there. Tonight. And tomorrow I want to visit that monastery. At Kirbet Qumran."

"Tomorrow?"

"Yes. Tomorrow. In the morning."

"But you have a class tomorrow morning."

"The afternoon then."

"You have a faculty meeting."

"Then we'll go very early in the morning. Before my class. When is that?"

"Nine."

"All right. Let's go at seven."

"Seven?"

"Or six. That'll give us more time."

"Six? Six in the morning?"

"Yes. We'll go first thing. When the sun is rising."

"But the sun is not rising at six, Professor Marr. It is too early."

"We'll watch it come up then."

....

At six in the morning it is dark, but with the whisper of a sun about to climb over the tops of the white cliffs of Qumran. It is the best time for a dig because later it's just too hot, even in the winter months. Jerusalem was a short drive away and with my class at nine we had a good two hours. The night before the Bedouin had taken us to the skeleton they had found, with the detached skull, and as the old man said it looked like a decapitation. The neck had been sliced and I immediately thought of the Romans. None of the bones was missing. Everything was intact. Buried three feet below the surface on its back, hands crossed over the abdomen. The remains were facing south with no pottery of any kind, just like all the other Essene skeletons that had been dug up. Except for one thing. It was buried in the sand. Like the mummy.

"Why would they bury somebody like that?" Robbie asked me.

"Why would *who* bury it?"

"Whoever it was."

"Maybe they wanted to preserve him."

"But he was not preserved. There are only bones."

"Maybe something went wrong."

"Like what?"

"Well let's think. Because it's close to the spring maybe there was moisture in the ground and if there was moisture the body would decay. Bacteria would get it."

"But that did not happen to the mummy."

"No."

"Why not?"

"I don't know. Maybe the ground is drier where it was buried."

Right behind the monastery, which was a crude construction of grey stone blocks, there were scarred cliffs with caves and beyond the caves was the Dead Sea. Sometimes it was so dense there that a thick haze of blue hung over the surface. It was a mist, a blur that clouded time and logic together.

You could tell a dig had taken place and it looked like they had just left. They said the monastery was built between 136 B.C. and 106 B.C., and occupied by the Essenes until 68 A.D., the second year of the Jewish revolt against the Romans. The remarkable thing about the site is the fissure that runs through the steps, a stark reminder of the earthquake, which according to Josephus, rocked Judea in the spring of 31 B.C., taking thirty thousand lives with it. The tower in the main building block had been reinforced with stones around the base, probably after the earthquake. Coins found in the earth and in the caves nearby illustrate the different periods of occupation, so with all this it's possible to piece the historical fragments into a web of some kind and create the semblance of a story.

There was no entrance to the tower at ground level. The only way in was by a wooden bridge from the two-storey building to the south. This area was exciting because inside the building on the upper floor was the legendary *scriptorium* with two inkwells and a table made of plaster. On the lower floor was a room with a bench that ran around the walls. No doubt, it was where the manuscripts were assembled. All the evidence points to that. There were no sleeping quarters and since the cemetery indicated a population of about two hundred men at any one time, we figured the inhabitants lived in tents or even in the caves. An area adjoining the refectory or dining hall contained hundreds of plates, bowls and jars. This all made sense. The cemetery with the thousand graves stood between the monastery and Dead Sea, but bones were also found under potsherds in the open areas. Examination of the bones indicated a diet of mutton, lamb and veal, so it wasn't hard to reconstruct the daily life here. A peaceful community of men. Completely self-sustaining for they took in discarded children and any strangers who wished to join them. Showing no sign of belligerence to others and wanting only to go about their simple monastic way of life.

"The Essenes would have been a natural community for a man like Jesus to gravitate to," I said to Robbie as we trudged through the ruins of the monastery.

"*You* are talking about Jesus?" Robbie said.

"The biblical Jesus. A man like that could have adopted the ways of the Essenes. Don't you think?"

"I suppose that is possible," he said.

"And what about a man like John the Baptist? A man like John the Baptist could have been one of them too." I pursed my lips together and made that pensive look Robbie had come to recognize.

"What are you getting at, Professor Marr?"

"Just this. We're talking about the Bible. Consider for a moment the biblical Jesus and the biblical John the Baptist. Consider that they were both real. That they actually lived."

That was a first for me, but Robbie went along with it. For argument's sake.

"Now what if both of them were members of the Essenes? Important members I mean and then they were both executed. Isn't it logical to assume the Essenes would want their bodies?"

Robbie looked at me. "That is also … *logical*," he said.

"Do you know how John the Baptist died, Robbie?"

He didn't seem to hear my question. He looked off to the east where the sun was coming up over the horizon and it was something to behold — a great orange fireball ascending over a pall of blue mist that sat calm on the waters of the Dead Sea. I wondered if that mist held some of the mysteries we were searching for. For two thousand years we have been searching. Off to the west were the ancient cliffs with those caves that possessed secrets of the past. Come night and the sun would set upon them, disappearing once again over the rock, just like it has ever since that rock was first formed.

But Robbie did hear what I had asked him.

"According to the Bible he was beheaded," he said.

He stood there staring at the horizon. Then he released a mouthful of air from his lungs and watched the sun rise a little more before he kicked disconsolately at the dirt below. He started to head back, and then he stopped and turned around to look at me. He said nothing, but on his face was this great sense of foreboding.

CHAPTER TWENTY-FIVE

TWENTY-FIVE

We returned from Qumran smarting over our latest find. The headless skeleton unnerved Robbie as much as the mummy had earlier and he preferred to think the two weren't related. At least, he wanted to think that way. Because he was afraid.

I was afraid too, but for different reasons. I was afraid because someone obviously killed this man by decapitating him, just as someone took the trouble to mummify the body of another man who had been crucified. Crucified by the Romans, no less. Of that, we were sure.

But who were these men?

I left Robbie and returned to my lab at the university, locking the door behind me only to find myself staring at this dead man whose body lay on a table. He wasn't another Jehohanan. It would have been so much easier if he was, but Jehohanan was just a skeleton and only part of a skeleton at that while this specimen was a man with bones and skin and flesh. Even hair. He was a corpse, well preserved and dead for a very long time. But then people tend to believe souls have a way of returning.

That was the trouble.

The Lindow Man was dead, the victim of a ritual murder. Only the top half of him remained and just when he had been killed no one knew. Two different types of radiocarbon dating had been used — one of them pointed to the first century, and the other to three or four hundred years later — so we didn't know for sure. It was like my C-14 tests with the Holy Shroud. We didn't know the true date for sure. It was only an educated guess and in this profession educated guesses are the best we can do. But even when I first saw the Lindow Man — the garrotte around his neck, his throat cut, his skull cracked open — I didn't feel I was in the presence of something entirely dead. There was this sense that he still lingered. He was a man who had been wronged and I couldn't help but think that this poor soul in my lab had been wronged as well. He had been the victim of a Roman crucifixion. Why we didn't know. He could have been a runaway slave. A man trying to gain his freedom. Or he might have stolen something. Maybe a loaf of bread to feed his starving family. Who could blame him for that? And if you believed in God then you must ask how a just God could allow a man, maybe an innocent man, to die such a horrible death. But history is full of innocent men, never mind women and children, being killed.

It was the same with the Bronze Age hunter who was discovered a few years later. He was found in a melting glacier in the Alps. The Iceman they called him. I viewed his five-thousand-year-old body and saw the stark desperation on his face. It was still there after all that time. It was a look that cried out for understanding. How did this happen to me? And why? There were clues, of course. We knew he was in the mountains when he had died. Beside his body were a dagger and sheath, a quiver, a bow, a copper axe and backpack. One of his arms was bent at a hideous angle. He or what was left of him was only the size of a pygmy, but he was still a man — a man who once laughed and cried, who loved, who played with children at his feet. At the moment of death he had been on a precipice ten thousand feet high where the air was hostile and cold, and where it wouldn't take long for the elements to snuff the life out of him. Later we would learn about the arrow head lodged deep in his back. He had been killed, but who was he fighting and what was it about? These things we would never know.

Even with Ginger there was something about his remains

and how they were found that begged for answers. He had been clothed in skins and buried in a grave in the sand, his shrunken body frail and hopeless, but well provided with tools, weapons and food for his final journey. But who was he, how did he die and who did he leave behind? All we know is that he was a man just like this man.

Maybe another innocent man?

There was a look of peace on his face so unlike all the others. Peace as if in sleep. And there was a softness about him almost like that of a woman. He had been crucified by the Romans two thousand years ago. He wasn't a Nubian or a Roman. He could have been a Jew. I found the *titulus* with the words matching the gospel of St. Mark and it was the same with his gruesome wounds. They matched the holy book. Of all the preserved bodies I had ever seen this was the only one buried with no sign of identification. None. Pottery was the usual thing. It was even better than C-14 for dating the age, but there was no pottery and no clothing. Only animal skins. A simple loincloth. There were no coins. No weapons. No jewelry. Just the wounds and later the *titulus*.

I looked at the holes in his wrists and feet. He had been crucified like Jehohanan, but this wasn't Jehohanan. I lowered the sides of his plexiglass cage and touched his fingers just inches from where the spike had pierced his flesh. He took me back to every question I ever asked myself. Back to the Dead Sea Scrolls and the Teacher of Righteousness. Back to the monks of Glastonbury and that goblet which all those fools thought authentic. How could his blood possibly match that of the stain on the shroud? Both of those things were forgeries. Of course, they were forgeries. But still the blood samples matched.

I felt like falling asleep and in my depths of consciousness grabbed hold of his hand just as I had that first time in the desert when we first found him. I rubbed my fingers along his dried skin. I lowered my head near his face, my greying hair mixing with that of a dead man. I closed my eyes and thought of my children. My son. My daughter. And just then I swear I felt a movement, at first the insignificant touch of a fly, and then a fingertip easing along the edge of my ear and across the back of my neck. I could sense the gentle rise and fall of his chest. Was he breathing? And then he began talking to me, but in words I didn't understand. Suddenly, his body was no longer that of a dead man. His skin was turning pink. The dried pores of his hands were filling with blood. The color was returning to his face. He raised his hand and started to whisper.

Secacah.

That was the original name for Qumran. Then he said it again.

Secacah.

I opened my eyes only to see everything as it was before. A still and lifeless body frozen in death. Those horrible wounds in the wrists and feet. The dried lines of blood.

So, it was only a dream.

CHAPTER TWENTY-SIX

TWENTY-SIX

Turin, October 1978

For six weeks three million people would line up outside the Cathedral of San Giovanni Battista in Turin to see the Holy Shroud. But Gita didn't care. When the family was in line outside the cathedral, she let loose.

"These Italians are filthy. I saw a woman drop her kid's pants and let them pee on the sidewalk. Even Arabs don't do that! We stay in our hotel for three days and when I ask them to change our sheets they look at me like I'm crazy. And the way men stare at you the word 'rape' is practically on their lips!"

It was a constant source of wonder to David that Gita looked as young as she did. He was fifty, a year older than her and aging accordingly, but Gita seemed frozen in time. He wanted to tell her that a woman her age who attracted stares from men should be flattered. After waiting in line for an hour, she wanted to leave. David reminded her that this was the Holy Shroud.

"You of all people to say such nonsense," she said. "Look, Jennie and I could be shopping in Rome or visiting art museums in Florence but here we are with all these smelly people pushing and shoving us. They're all Jesus freaks and born agains. The burial shroud of Jesus Christ? Good God!"

Finally, the family of four reached the top of the church

steps and then went through the double doors to see saw what everyone was talking about. David was struck by how plain the shroud looked. It was a narrow strip of cloth, fourteen feet by three-and-a-half feet. Flood-lit. Mounted in front of the main altar of the cathedral. Guarded by its custodian, the Archbishop of Turin.

"I think it's pretty," Jennie said. "Who's that man on it?"

"It's a face," said Gita.

It was a face. Faint. There but not there and it made Gita stop for a moment. This cloth, this face that had baffled people for hundreds of years, was having an effect and it gave David a small sense of victory, which was sweet because there weren't many victories with Gita.

"You know," she said. "The only thing they're missing is a fan to blow it around a bit. That would add to the mood, don't you think?"

....

Now a member of the International Center of Sindonology, David was one of three dozen scientists on STURP. They were split into teams and his comprised chemists, biophysicists, pathologists and biblical scholars. The first test would involve blood, if that was what those dark streams on the shroud were, and his role would be to note the tests and results. Still, he hoped to subject a tiny sample to C-14.

"Let us pray," said the pathologist leading the group. "As scientists and sindonologists we are here to do the work of God. May He guide us and lead us to the truth." The pathologist, Dr. John Emerson, an American out to make the most of his position as team leader, led them through the Lord's Prayer.

The shroud covering was removed and despite David's doubts about the cloth being two thousand years old, he did feel a degree of respect for it. Even a fake from the fourteenth century was old enough to merit some esteem. The image was faint but got clearer the farther away you got. The face was foreboding with long hair down the sides, a full beard and eyes open. The arms were crossed over the stomach and the fingers were long, and there were only four fingers on each hand. No thumbs. Very clever, David thought. Whoever did this knew about the thumbs curling in and back in the fourteenth century yet, if that was when this forgery had been hatched.

They said the shroud was woven in a herringbone twill and that the hand-spun fibers and unique weave were from the Middle East. They said some of the pollens found on it were from the Dead Sea. They said the style of the cloth was from the first century.

"This is human blood," Emerson said, pointing to the dark stains that ran down the shroud in rivulets. "I can tell because of the flow. There had to be a crucified man under this cloth." He pointed to each spot and said the blood flow from the wounds was pathologically correct while a photographer snapped pictures.

"It's awfully red, isn't it?" David observed.

"Blood is meant to be red," replied Emerson.

"But not over such a great length of time. I've studied many corpses and always found dried blood to be more black than red."

"Not necessarily. When a person is badly beaten as we have here large amounts of bilirubin are formed." Emerson smiled. "I'm sorry but your name escapes me."

"David Marr. Archeologist."

"Oh the archeologist. How careless of me. Bilirubin. The chemical makeup is C33 H36 N4 O6. It's a reddish yellow pigment that occurs in blood, urine, even gallstones. There's no reason why it can't stay a bright red indefinitely. Our chemists will be able to help us with that. But what convinces me more than anything that it's human blood is the flow. We have a bleeding man, a man who has been crucified. There's no doubt in my mind that the natural flow of blood from the wounds in the head, the wrists, the ankles and the side would be like this."

Emerson said the signs of blood were consistent with wounds on parts of a body — stains near the head, a large flow at one side near what appeared to be ribs, another flow leading from the wrists and going down both arms, and more still leading from the feet. Just then a biblical scholar began speaking in Italian and an animated discussion ensued. Emerson asked for a translation.

"There is some debate as to whether iron spikes were placed

in the wrist or the palm of the hand," said the translator. "Most paintings of the Savior show wounds in his hands but what is evident from the shroud are wounds in the wrists."

"The flow of blood on the shroud is definitely from the wrists," Emerson said. "This is consistent with human anatomy. You will also notice the flow of blood across the back which could have spread from a side wound."

"In Roman crucifixions the spikes went through the wrist," David said.

"But the Gospels specify hand wounds," said one of the theologians.

"Yes but the word 'hand' has been translated from the Greek 'cheir' which can also mean the wrist and forearm as well as the hand. Because of the translation there's always been some discrepancy as to where the spikes were. But I can assure you it was the wrist."

"Thank you, Dr. Marr," Emerson said.

It was of some humor to David that anyone at STURP who possessed a doctorate was called 'doctor' at every opportunity. But Emerson wasn't offering the title as a compliment.

"What about these stains over here?" David said. "They're different from the blood stains."

"Water stains," Emerson replied. "From the fire of 1532. When the shroud was kept in Chambery, France. And you notice a small strip of material that was sewn by nuns to cover the most damaged area two years after the fire. You're familiar with the chronology?" David said he was. "Well let's get on with it then."

They would test for pollens. They wanted to verify conclusions of the Swiss expert about the pollens being Middle Eastern in origin, but they couldn't locate a single pollen, which immediately threw the whole project into an uproar. Someone said the Swiss researcher might have planted the pollens on the shroud before he had begun his testing. After a raucous exchange it was discovered that the testing process hadn't been done properly, so they tried it again and this time pollens were found. It was enough for several STURP members to smile with satisfaction.

Next came blood tests involving ultraviolet light and

low-energy X-rays. The idea was to see if any red paint had been used. It didn't appear that it had.

"But this only proves there is no red paint," David said. "That doesn't mean it's blood."

"Yes Dr. Marr," said Emerson. "But at least we know there is no paint. And pathological analysis which I'll do myself will determine if the flows on the shroud correspond to the flow of blood in a human body. A human body that has suffered certain types of wounds. If they do we'll be a little closer to a logical conclusion about the presence of human blood."

Then the threads of the shroud were examined through a microscope. If a forger had used powders and not paint to simulate blood, magnified viewing would show particles present in the powder. The test was performed and no particles were detected. Hence, no powders.

"But what we're doing is showing what the shroud is not. Not what it is," said David.

"Sooner or later we'll be able to conclude that it's blood, Dr. Marr."

"Human blood?"

"I think so."

David was the only member of STURP who was an expert on crucifixion and for this was held in regard, but not by Emerson. David was also the only member who ever questioned Emerson's observations and conclusions. Once the blood tests were finished and those present confirmed that it was human blood, the discussion turned to verifying the cause of death. That was when David told them about Jehohanan.

"And how can you be sure the man was crucified?" Emerson asked.

"We found one of the nails through his feet and it was definitely Roman. The cross fit the pattern for Roman crucifixions. The upright part of the cross ... which in Latin is called the *stipes crucis* ... ran up and down and the horizontal part ... the *patibulum* ... ran across. The victim's feet were nailed to the *stipes crucis* and after he was dead they cut off his feet. It was the only way to get the body down from the cross."

"But no one cut off the feet of Jesus," someone said.

"How do you know that?" said David.

"It's common knowledge. Besides you can see the feet on the image of the shroud."

It was enough to prompt Emerson to say "so much for your theory, Dr. Marr."

"Theory?"

"About the feet being amputated."

"In the case of Jehohanan I assure you his feet were amputated."

"In that case perhaps but not this one."

The blood tests done, a group of weary men broke for the evening while a second team prepared to work through the night. When bidding good night to his colleagues, David offered some suggestions. "There's a couple things I'd like to do," he said. "The first is to take a tiny sample of the cloth for radiocarbon dating."

"Impossible," Emerson said. "All tests must be non-destructive. They won't let you destroy any of the material."

"I only need this much," said David, raising his thumb and forefinger, a sliver of space between them.

"It's against the Vatican directive."

"But today we subjected the shroud to X-rays and ultraviolet rays."

"Not enough to harm anything."

"And you're telling me that taking a few centimeters of material is going to do harm? You wouldn't even know it's gone." Emerson shook his head. "Dr. Emerson, wouldn't you like to know if the shroud can pass the dating test?"

"Of course but I don't make the rules. What else did you want to do?"

"Examine the blood. The blood stains. We could take a small sample and examine it."

"Blood that's two thousand years old?"

"At this point we haven't concluded that it's two thousand years old, have we? But maybe we could help verify if it's human blood or not."

"And you ... an archeologist ... would want to do this examination?"

"Dr. Emerson, we archeologists are not the ignoramuses you

think. I know that deoxyribonucleic acids are the molecular basis of heredity and are constructed of a double helix held together by hydrogen bonds."

"Very impressive, Dr. Marr. For an archeologist, I mean."

"Do you know the chemical makeup of biliverdin, Dr. Emerson?"

"I don't believe I do."

"Well I am surprised. I mean for a pathologist. It's something of a cousin to your precious bilirubin except it's a green pigment. Not red. C33 H34 N4 O6. Like I say it's a green pigment occurring chiefly in bile. Which seems to be in great abundance around here."

....

On the second day of tests, Emerson told the media that the blood on the shroud was from a man. The night before he had tested stained shroud fibers for a substance called albumin, a component of blood. He said he found it. He had also performed a test with antibodies. Antibodies in animal blood attack human blood and this, he said, was what happened in his tests.

"But what about the blood of a primate?" said David. "Wouldn't that react like human blood to the invasion of antibodies from the blood of a pig or a goat?"

"Our learned friend here is quite right," Emerson told the group. "But gaze upon the image on the shroud and tell me we're looking at an ape."

End of discussion. The image was that of a man and the blood was human. Emerson had spoken. He initiated all the testing done by the team and determined what tests would be conducted. From the outset it was clear Emerson had the full support of the Vatican theologians. Every test he did and every comment he made pointed to the only conclusion anyone wanted to reach. The shroud was the burial garment of Jesus.

"Dr. Marr wants to conduct a carbon 14 dating test on the shroud which would destroy some of the material," Emerson said. "I told him this isn't permitted. He also wants to test a sample of the shroud for its chemical makeup but we have the same problem, I'm afraid."

The theologians all agreed, but David persisted.

"Radiocarbon dating would be the most conclusive test of all the tests done on the shroud," he said. "It's pretty reliable and can date anything under fifty thousand years old."

"How does it work?" asked one theologian. With the question David saw a glimmer of hope.

He told them how every living thing gets carbon-12 and radioactive carbon-14 from the atmosphere, but when it dies it stops taking in new carbon. C-14, being unstable, then starts to change to C-12. In five thousand, seven hundred and thirty years, half of the C-14 left behind in an organism is gone and in another five thousand, seven hundred and thirty years, half of the amount remaining will also be gone. David said this is why C-14 has a "half-life" of five thousand, seven hundred and thirty years.

"A test would show how old the cloth is within thirty to two hundred years," he said. "We could date the shroud and tell if it's from the first or second century or the fourteenth century and I don't see how a scientific team like STURP can avoid doing such a test."

"But Dr. Marr," said Emerson, "it's not infallible. What if you took a piece that was contaminated? The shroud has been touched by human hands for centuries. Contamination could be present."

"What kind of contamination?"

"Anything."

"Yes Dr. Marr," said another member. "It could be contaminated."

"I don't see how ..."

"But it could be."

"Look," said David. "Using this line of reasoning what about the blood ... what you claim to be blood ... that you tested? That could be contaminated too."

"No," said Emerson, shaking his head. "Blood is blood. Besides can you say with all honesty that C-14 is one hundred percent foolproof?"

"No."

"So what's the point?"

"But your tests are the same. They could be imperfect. Look, in any C-14 test a sample is prepared for lab analysis and submitted with samples from other substances. For something like the shroud we'd provide the lab with other pieces of material and date them all. The lab wouldn't know which material was from the shroud and which was from something else. The idea is to see how old the sample is. We do some of your tests. We do some of mine. And maybe no single test is foolproof but when taken together we can start to get some answers. Isn't that what scientific tests are all about?"

"And how would such a test explain the image?" one theologian asked.

"It wouldn't," David said.

Finally, the translator spoke. "Some archeologists have accounted for the yellow coloring of the shroud and possibly for the image. They found traces of limestone on the shroud and these traces match with limestone samples taken from burial chambers in old Jerusalem. Like the burial chamber where Jesus was kept. I was told the limestone causes the surface of linen fibers to change to the same yellow color on the shroud and that the process is speeded up by heat."

"Like heat from a human body?" Emerson asked.

"Yes."

"Dead bodies don't retain heat for long," David said.

"But maybe long enough for the image to be formed by contact with the body," Emerson said.

"How?"

"We don't know that yet but heat from a body could spread out somewhat."

"In this kind of detail?" said David.

"Dr. Marr, have you ever stopped to consider the image is something that can't be scientifically explained?"

"What do you mean?"

"I mean it may be a miracle."

"A miracle?" The translator explained to the Italians, one of whom crossed himself. "I don't find miracles very scientific," said David.

"Maybe not," Emerson said, "but that just may be the answer

any good Christian will have to accept."

....

"Dad, you've been testing the shroud for a few days. What if you date it and it turns out to be two thousand years old?"

"I'd conclude it's two thousand years old but that doesn't mean it belonged to Jesus."

"The odds would be pretty good."

"Brian, it's a forgery. There is no record of it before the fourteenth century."

"Both of you are forgetting something," said Gita who explained that the fourteenth century was known for relic mongering. But she gave credit to a French bishop who said the shroud was a forgery when it was displayed.

"Why was it on display?" she said. "To raise money for a church. It's an old story. Religion sells."

She told them about a French knight who was killed by the English in 1356. His widow thought it would be a good idea to display the shroud for financial gain — for herself and the local church. The shroud went on display the next year and souvenir medallions were struck. But the bishop said it was a fake, ending the display. It was then placed in storage.

"So no more money was made?" said Brian.

"Well the knight's widow was no dumbbell," Gita said. "She remarried a rich nobleman. Even then women had brains."

"And what happened to the shroud?"

"The knight's son had more expositions in 1389 and the pope of the time went along with it. But another thing both of you should know is that during the thirteenth and fourteenth centuries forty different shrouds were being peddled across Europe, all of them said to be genuine. And I guarantee you money was made from every one of them. That's the Catholics for you."

"Gita," David said.

"But it's true, isn't it?"

"Dad," said Brian. "I almost forgot. A cable came for you from Egypt."

It was from David's old colleague Jamil. David opened the letter.

"My good friend Dr. Hassad has some news. A book is coming out. It will be called *The Holy Shroud - Myth and Reality*. Color photographs. The works. The author is Dr. John Emerson."

....

It was the last day, the last shift, of STURP. The media entourage billeted outside the Cathedral of San Giovanni Battista was revving up for its final stand and Emerson would give them what they wanted. He scheduled a press conference to be held immediately after the tests were completed. His official statement was prepared. "The image on the shroud is not the product of an artist," he would begin before embarking on a journey that would ultimately tie the beginnings of Christianity to the present day.

The break between the second and third shifts was a long one, and the scientists were weary. On this last day of tests the three teams focused on how the image had been created. One theory said the body of Christ had been in contact with the shroud for no more than thirty-six hours because more than that and bacteria would begin to decompose the body, and there would have been signs on the shroud. But there wasn't. Thirty-six hours was also consistent with the scriptures. Another team, with one dissenting voice from the lone archeologist, concluded that the image and yellowing of shroud fibers came from the passage of heat generated by a human body.

Meanwhile, the Archbishop of Turin, custodian of the shroud, was nowhere to be found. But David knew where he was. He was celebrating with the other archbishops. The week of tests had been done and the Holy Shroud was confirmed as the burial garment of Jesus. All the clergymen were drinking brandy, making toasts.

The Holy Shroud lay uncovered on the table. No one was about. David ambled his way into the hallway and then the examination room. He took out a scalpel and looked for a place to cut his sample. "Only five centimeters," he said to himself. He lowered the scalpel to the far corner of the shroud where a small piece was missing near the long narrow strip sewn by nuns after the sixteenth-century fire. It was two inches from a red stain. Blood from the foot wounds perhaps? David thought he should take a sample of that too, but he needed a bigger piece. Well why not? Once he showed them it wasn't human blood and the shroud wasn't two thousand years old, they couldn't prosecute him. Not when he proved it was a fake.

David laid his left hand flat on the shroud and with his right pressed the end of the scalpel into the cloth. It cut like butter. He brought the blade down along a fine imaginary line. Three centimeters. Then four. Then five. Good. That was enough, but the more he took the better the chances of a reliable reading and he also wanted to get that stain, so he extended his cut to eight centimeters. That was about three inches. Then he turned the blade at right angles and cut another inch in width before coming back along the other side. It was better this way. Better than taking a tiny outside corner from the edge.

It was done. David had his sample. A three-by-one-inch strip. Plenty. Then he heard shuffling from the hallway. The scientists were returning. He took two steps back from the table and saw the image on the shroud staring at him — that haunting face, that negative no one could explain — and he thought he heard a voice coming from that face.

"Thief. Thou shalt not steal. Thief!"

He wrapped up his precious sample and slipped it into his pocket, but he kept hearing that word. *Thief! Thief!* He hurried from the examination room into the hallway where a man in a red robe was standing in the middle of the floor. A slight man with a long hawkish nose, thin lips and a face narrow and gaunt, he wore small round glasses and had a white skullcap on his head. His hands were folded over his abdomen.

"Can I help you?" he said, his words slow and heavy.

"I'm Dr. Marr," David said. "I'm on the examination team. Part of Dr. Emerson's group."

"I know who you are."

"I wanted to have a last look at the shroud."

"I see."

The man looked David in the eye. Unblinking.

"Forgive me," he said. "I am Cardinal Fiori." He bowed his head in a gesture of formal cordiality. "This has been a most memorable week. Has it not?"

It was strange how he talked, each word so distinct and separate from the others, almost as if they weren't connected in sentences.

"Yes it has."

David was anxious to get by, but the man wouldn't move to let him pass. Then this cardinal glanced over his shoulder in the direction of those now making their way back.

"You didn't join in the toast," he said.

"I thought it was only for clergy."

"Not at all. It was for all of us. Believers and non-believers alike."

He made David uneasy.

"Perhaps another time," he said. "When you aren't in such a hurry."

"Yes," David said. "Another time. If you'll excuse me."

David made his move. It was more of an escape. Then he did his best to lose himself in the throng of STURP members who were beginning to fill the hallway.

Emerson did as expected. He summoned the media and announced that the shroud was indeed the burial garment of Jesus Christ. It stood up to all the tests. "The image on the shroud is not the product of an artist," he said and related its storied history from the time of the Crucifixion at approximately 30 A.D. to the time of the Romans, the Byzantines, the Middle Ages and beyond.

....

The week-long tests of STURP done, the Holy Shroud was returned to its jewelled box. The box was placed inside a lead case and locked behind the altar of the holy chapel in the Capella Santa at the Cathedral of San Giovanni Battista. When it came time to say what he wanted, David had to be sure. He knew he'd never convince anyone on STURP, but he did need the backing of scientific authorities, so it wasn't only his word against the Church. He gave the lab at the Hebrew University in Jerusalem a cutting from his sample. Along with that were samples from other cloths — placebos — and he smiled when the calibrated radiocarbon results were in. Sometime between 1260 and 1390 A.D., the lab said, placing it in the same period as the French exposition Gita had told him about. Then he took two other pieces from his sample and sent them out — one to the University of Manchester in England, the other to a lab in Switzerland. The Swiss verdict came back first and it also pointed to the same period in the Middle Ages.

With two results saying the same thing, David published his findings in a scientific journal, which prompted the Vatican Museum to issue a statement about the fallacies of radiocarbon dating. But it didn't matter. David's results were largely ignored by everyone outside the academic community and then the Church got behind Emerson's book with an endorsement. Later, the third lab result arrived from England and why it took so long David didn't know, but this one said the sample dated from the first century. *The first century!* It was supposed to be from the University of Manchester, which was where he had sent the sample, but the lab that did the test was in Bridgwater College in the south of England — twenty miles from Glastonbury — and David never sent his sample there.

Emerson seized upon the result, allowing there might be something to C-14 after all. He said David was wrong to cut his sample from the Holy Shroud, but forgave him now that carbon dating itself had "sealed the proof," as he put it. David didn't care about Emerson and his lot, but he couldn't stop thinking about that clergyman who had seen him leave the examination room.

Cardinal Fiori.

It wasn't long before David's lone dissenting voice disappeared amid talk about blood from the Holy Shroud, pollens from the Dead Sea and the particular twist of the shroud's threads. And still there was that mysterious image and where it came from. No one had an answer for that. It was all grist for the mill.

CHAPTER TWENTY-SEVEN

TWENTY-SEVEN

Gita and I were lying in bed in our apartment in Jerusalem, neither one of us asleep. I was staring up at the ceiling.

"David, you never sleep anymore. What's wrong?"

I didn't know how to begin.

Of course, Jamil was right about her being perceptive, especially where I was concerned. She knew me better than anyone. We had been together so long. She knew me as a man who had a passion for history and that my whole life revolved around it. At the same time, she possessed an analytical mind. She was a beautiful woman who carried herself with a natural elegance and grace, always moving with an even certainty, knowing exactly what she was doing and why, especially when she was set on something.

These qualities would turn out to be very fruitful.

"What is it, David? I can see something is bothering you. If you can't tell me who can you tell?"

I looked at her and gave up. There was no keep point keeping it from her any longer. And so, I told her. She had been away at a conference when Robbie and I found the mummy, and it was a good thing too because those first few days I wasn't myself. Not that I was now. But I had started to internalize things, thinking what Jamil had said about the danger and all the fanatics in the Holy Land and what they would do if they found out about this.

What would they do? We had the Jews, the Muslims and the Christians. Each one of them thought they were right where God was concerned and each of them had their own brand of fanaticism. If a two-thousand-year-old crucified corpse turned up in the Holy Land, ultra-Orthodox Jews would have their own interpretation and might even be dismissive about it. Anything that wasn't distinctly Jewish had no significance for them. Besides, Jews never mummified their dead. But what about those extremists — the Levi Ashkols of the world — who wanted to get rid of all the Palestinians? What about them? There was no telling what they would do. They tended to act first and ask questions later.

And then there was Eliraz. I couldn't very well tell Gita about her, but she was always at the back of my mind. Still, Eliraz was a scientist — one with unbounding curiosity maybe — but she was no extremist.

I figured we had the most to fear from Muslims. The way I looked at it things were infinitely more dangerous with them because the whole concept of Jesus was central to Islam and to the Koran. Jamil had already told us about the rites of mummification and why it mattered. He even said what an honor it would have been for him to do it himself, and that from a man like Jamil yet.

I had never met another Muslim, or another person for that matter, who was as knowledgeable and rational as Jamil.

The thing about Muslims in the Middle East was the mob mentality that could run rampant and this is what differentiated them from the Jews and Christians. A great many of them lived in abysmal poverty and it was always easier to blame someone else for your own misfortune. History is full of that.

It had already started with this latest business. The *intifada* was growing by the day. What may have begun as nothing more than a horrible traffic accident, which took four Palestinian lives, had mushroomed into a movement with riots and demonstrations by Palestinians. It was happening in Gaza. It was happening in the West Bank. It was happening in East Jerusalem. Streets were being blockaded with burning tires. Palestinian youths were throwing stones at not only Israeli soldiers, but Jewish homes and businesses. There was a general strike. The Israeli army getting involved to try and quell things only made it worse.

And the media of the world was there to report on it. On one side you had footage of young Palestinian boys hurling stones and on the other the Israeli military armed to the teeth. It was the story of David and Goliath, but reversed.

Mahmoud was a young Palestinian, and I told Gita about him. I told her how I had found him on two occasions outside the door to my lab. But after hearing all this she was more concerned with the Church.

"You have a crucified man ..." she said.

"Mummy."

"A crucified mummy. And its wounds match what was written in the scriptures. In the Book of Mark."

"Yes."

"And you found a *titulus* with the same words from the Bible. And your DNA test showed blood that matches the stains on the Holy Shroud."

She thought that was crazy, but said there had to be an explanation. Then I mentioned the headless skeleton with the apparent connection to John the Baptist. For Gita that was the tipping point.

"All this was done for a reason," she said. "But who did it and when ... and why ... that's what we have to find out. And we have to find out before any of the nutcases do."

I told her about the dream I had and the mummy coming to life.

"You know, David, I've always wondered something," she said.

"You wondered what?"

"If there were any more scrolls in those caves at Qumran. Or

Secacah as your mummy likes to say."

Gita's mind was thinking. Calculating. Then she told me she wanted to visit the Ecole Biblique in East Jerusalem. It was an old institution devoted to the study of biblical text and it had a long history with the archeology of Palestine. Its scholars had been among the first to decipher the Dead Sea Scrolls. And why did she want to go there? Gita had absolutely no trust in anything to do with the Roman Catholic Church.

The next day she went to the Ecole Biblique. She spent the afternoon. When she got back she announced that she was going somewhere else. To Rome. To the Vatican Archives. I asked why.

"The Dominican Fathers of the Ecole Biblique had control over the Dead Sea Scrolls for years," she said. "Their ties to Rome are thick. Those archives are supposed to have records as old as the first century. It's about time one of us looked through them, don't you think? I elect me."

She didn't have to tell me how good she was with ancient languages, but I didn't want her to go.

"Why would the Vatican want to cooperate with you?" I asked.

"I'm not asking them to."

CHAPTER TWENTY-EIGHT

TWENTY-EIGHT

When Gita made up her mind about something, there was no turning back. She was determined to venture into the very heart of the Catholic Church and check out those old archives. Once it was clear that I couldn't talk her out of doing this, I persuaded her not to go as Gita Marr, but as Gita Levitt. That was wise. She would be armed with her maiden name to keep distant the identity of her archeologist husband. You can't be too careful. And so, we made a plan and prepared the necessary papers.

She was right about the Ecole Biblique, of course. The first seven Dead Sea Scrolls were discovered in 1947 at Qumran. The name Qumran was Arabic for 'two moons' and it was called that because when the moon came up over Mt. Moab a reflection was cast over the Dead Sea and you could see two moons. One of them was up in the sky and the other was over the water. But the original name — the biblical Hebrew name for the place — was *Secacah*. It was even mentioned in the Bible. In Joshua, chapter fifteen, verse sixty-one: *In the wilderness - Beit Ha'arava, Middin, Secacah.*

Until 1967 the many scrolls and scroll fragments found in the caves at Qumran and around the Dead Sea had been the property of Jordan, and under the watchful eye of the Dominican Fathers of the Ecole Biblique. But the liberation of Jerusalem in the Six Day War changed all that and the scrolls became the property of Israel. From 1947 to 1956 eleven caves were discovered at Qumran containing fragments of eight hundred scrolls from the Second Temple period. This was the most important archeological discovery ever made in the Holy Land. But not even two dozen of those eight hundred scrolls had survived in decent condition.

The first scrolls unearthed from Cave 1 were the complete Book of Isaiah, the Community Rule scroll and a commentary on the Book of Habakkuk. The Isaiah Scroll was the big catch. It had fifty-four columns and sixty-six chapters. A few days after the initial discovery four more scrolls were found in the same cave — a second manuscript of the Book of Isaiah, the War Scroll, the Thanksgiving Scroll and the Genesis Apocryphon. These seven scrolls were sold by the Bedouin to an antiquities dealer in Bethlehem who offered them to the Syrian Metropolitan of Jerusalem. The Metropolitan bought four of them for $100 and Professor Eli Solnik bought the other three. Later, Professor Solnik obtained all seven scrolls for himself and I wound up taking them to New York. Those scrolls eventually found a permanent home at the Israel Museum in Jerusalem.

But what about all the other scrolls? In the early 1950s the Jordanian Department of Antiquities conducted excavations at Qumran and at each dig was assisted by archeologists from the Ecole Biblique. It didn't take long before fragments of another seventy scrolls were found in Cave 1. Meanwhile, the Bedouin were busy doing some exploring of their own. They found Cave 2 with fragments of thirty-three new scrolls, including two fragments of Ecclesiasticus written in the original Hebrew, no less. This news brought more archeologists to the site, and soon two hundred and fifty caves were searched, but in only one of them was anything found. Cave 3. It contained pieces of fourteen scrolls and the Copper Scroll, which was an almost complete sample.

The Bedouin found more things. Fifteen thousand fragments, in fact. They found all this in two small caves designated as Caves 4a and 4b. The Jordanian Department of Antiquities then took action to prevent any scrolls from being smuggled abroad. It paid the Bedouin for fragments — the bigger the fragment, the higher the price — and the archeologists kept searching.

The cave just north of 4a — Cave 5 — had fragments of

twenty-five scrolls. This was where part of the Damascus Document was found and another part was found in Cave 6 where some thirty-one new scrolls were discovered. Cave 7, to the south of the other caves, had fragments written in Greek. In Cave 8 was a portion of the Book of Genesis, and part of the Book of Psalms and something else too — a hundred leather squares, each with a slit in the center. This had to be where all the scrolls were bound. Nearby in Cave 9 a single scroll fragment was found. Cave 10 didn't yield any scrolls, but was granted a designation since its floor was thought to have been connected at one time to Caves 4a and 4b, but had been washed away into the wadi. Cave 11, the last of the caves to produce any scrolls, was discovered by the Bedouin in 1956. It had twenty-five scrolls including the Book of Leviticus, an Aramaic translation of the Book of Job and the spectacular Temple Scroll — more than eight meters of it. It was the longest scroll ever found by the Dead Sea.

There were no other caves. At least, not that we knew of, but so many caves dotted the cliffs in and around Qumran who was to say that every one of them had been thoroughly searched?

The night before she returned from the Vatican, Gita called to say she had found something very important in Rome, but wouldn't go into details. She saved that for when I picked her up at the airport. The story of her visit goes like this.

She had entered the huge square of St. Peter's and passed the obelisk that stood in the middle — the obelisk Jamil had mentioned — and took a moment to admire the two fountains on either side of it. For all that Gita detested about the Roman Catholic Church, she still held an appreciation for the arts.

The Secret Archives were in a building next to the Vatican Library. As soon as she stepped onto the grounds, two Swiss Guards asked to see her papers. Security was tight and few passes were granted for the Secret Archives, but it was always easier for academics and scholars. The way we had planned it, Gita would pretend to be an American archeologist researching the letters of Pope Innocent III. His letters were housed in the Tower of the Winds in the oldest part of the archives. That is what her papers claimed and they were all in order with a letter from the associate director of the Library of Congress in Washington stating the purpose of her project. She also had a letter from an official at the U.S. Embassy in Rome, her passport had been issued in her maiden name and she had a photo. The name 'Marr' wasn't mentioned.

There was a brief encounter with the prefect. She told him about her interest in Innocent III and the lecture she was preparing. He checked her name against those on the list and studied her face, which matched the photo on her permit. Then he took the permit, she signed the register and in she went.

An escort led her along the corridor on the ground floor and she said this walk was eerie. Bleak. Without windows. The escort would turn on a light and with every section they passed he would switch on another, but each light lasted for only a few seconds before shutting itself off. And so, they moved in relative darkness.

She and her escort passed the Hall of the Parchments, a room where they kept the inventories and indexes, and then they reached the exit. From there they climbed a small circular stairway leading to the oldest section of the archives in the Tower of the Winds. Back in the early seventeenth century this area had served as an astronomical observatory. In fact, the signed confession of Galileo, which over the years had become an embarrassing document for the Church, was in this building.

Gita, with her eye for detail, said the cabinets containing the oldest documents in the archives were the most beautiful woodwork she had ever seen. These documents were housed in the Vatican registers and those registers also contained the papers of Innocent III, including his letters from 1198. She said these letters were written on parchment in huge books that looked like atlases, but the ink was now yellow.

She said the escort smiled — the first time he showed any emotion at all — and announced that she had reached her destination. She sat down at the end of a long table, the escort removing himself to the hallway outside the room in order to grant her some privacy while she worked. She opened the register of Innocent III and continued with the ruse. A moment later she closed the book and moved on to the next register. Then she got up and walked the length of the table and came across more cabinets. There was a narrow opening in the wall leading to another room and in that room was another long table with even more cabinets.

The escort remained outside in the hall.

Then she entered this room and the one after that. The last room, the third, was the one she wanted. Here were shelves of information — the earliest records from more than *twenty-five miles* of shelves in the archives. If there was anything from the first century, from the time of Saint Peter and Saint Paul, it would be in this room. It didn't take Gita long to find more writings on parchment, but this parchment wasn't like the registers of Innocent III. This was more than a thousand years older.

It was the same kind of parchment the Dead Sea Scrolls were written on.

Gita scanned the writings with her learned eye and was confident they had been prepared by early Christians. She knew about the story of Peter, that he was said to be buried on Vatican Hill, which according to the Vatican was confirmed by excavations and, in particular, by a Greek inscription from the year 160 A.D. There was also said to be a second inscription, a prayer addressed to Peter from Christians buried nearby. At one time, they say, bones were found. The bones of an old man wrapped in crimson cloth.

Gita unrolled these writings — scriptures — and didn't need any books or translations to decipher them. That was when she came across something. She found the words of Paul or of some unknown writer from the first century. The words, dated accordingly, had directions to a cave near the Dead Sea and then directions within the cave itself.

The cave of the Column having two entrances viewing to the east, an upper chamber with a large hole in the roof. And across from the opening a blue tel in the lower chamber, a back chamber with an opening down to a passage between the two like the tunnel of Solomon.

The passage described a cave at Qumran, but that cave didn't correspond to any of the eleven caves where the hundreds of Dead Sea Scrolls had been found. I knew all about those caves, so maybe there was another cave.

One that had been missed.

She wrote down the passage only to hear shuffling from the hallway. It was the escort. She quickly rolled up the parchment and rushed back to the first room. When she arrived there out of breath the escort was surprised to see her standing at the entrance to the next room. He asked if everything was in order and she said yes. He told her to follow him. He led her back to the old stairway, along the dim corridor where the lights went out one by one after they passed, then back to the register which she dutifully signed once again. As before, the same prefect was still standing there. He returned her permit.

"Thank you," Gita said.

"*Grazie*," the prefect replied.

Then she saw another man and I felt a chill when she described him to me. "He was a small man but obviously an important one," she said. "The others treated him with great respect. He was a man of authority. A cardinal. I got the impression he considered everyone's business his own and I swear I could feel his eyes all over me when I was leaving the building."

She told me what he looked like and I immediately thought of the cardinal who had seen me in Turin after I cut my sample from the Holy Shroud. Even though many years had passed, I never forgot his face.

Her mission accomplished, Gita disappeared through the entrance into the spacious grounds in front of St. Peter's Basilica. She said she didn't know exactly what happened after that, but it isn't hard to guess.

As we later learned, a meeting was held with three men — the prefect, the escort and the cardinal. He was a man who devoted his life to serving the Church and as one of influence he would summon the full power of the oldest organization in the world. The Vatican. It sustained itself through two ingredients — order and fear. Order was established through an iron-clad hierarchy where each member knew his position. Fear was established through authority placed in the hands of people who knew how to wield it. People like Cardinal Fiori.

CHAPTER TWENTY-NINE

TWENTY-NINE

"David, I have to talk to you. Right now. It's important."

Eliraz was agitated and it wasn't the type of agitation that I saw before with lovers not working out. This was different. She took me by the hand and led me to her office. She said to sit down and then she shut the door. She started to speak. Barely above a whisper.

"You know that DNA test I did for you?"

"Yes."

"I think it was compromised."

"What do you mean?"

"Well look. When you do a test like this ... from a blood sample ... you test the genetic markers."

"Go on."

"When you test for blood you use tubes and even for something like this ... blood from an old cloth as you put it ... you use tubes. Each tube is labelled with the name of the owner. In your case I labelled one of them *whatever it is* and the other one *old cloth*."

"So?"

"One of them was a blue label and the other one was a pink label. I know *whatever it is* was the blue one and *old cloth* was the pink one. I saw that the samples matched and called you right away. But later I realized something wasn't right."

"What wasn't right?"

"They got mixed up. *Whatever it is* was pink and *old cloth* was blue and I never labelled them that way."

"Are you sure?"

"Of course I'm sure."

The eyes of Eliraz the scientist were looking right into me. She wasn't the type to make a mistake like that.

"What could've happened then?" I said.

She put her hand over her mouth. To hide her whisper.

"Somebody compromised my test," she said.

"How?"

"I don't know."

"A student?"

"Maybe. Nobody but students go into my office."

"Without your knowing?"

She shrugged. "Don't students ever pick up papers in your office?"

I used to let them, but not anymore. Not since Qumran turned my life around. But I didn't tell her that.

"What are you saying, Eliraz?"

"I'm saying that somebody compromised my test. And it could only be a student. But none of them knew about this."

"Are you sure about that? Didn't you tell them about my ... skeleton?"

She let out a sigh. "Yes I'm afraid I did but none of them knew anything about a DNA test. Only you and me. And Robbie. He knew about it."

"You think Robbie compromised your test?"

"No. Someone else."

"Who?"

We both sat there saying nothing. And then it hit me.

"Eliraz, are all your students Israeli?"

"As far as I know but I don't go around asking them. Do you ask your students that?"

"No. But that's not what I mean. I mean ... do you have any ... who aren't Jewish?"

"Who aren't Jewish?"

"Christian."

"I'm sure I do. But what's that got to do with it?"

"I can't tell you but …"

"Well sooner or later you better because there's something else I didn't tell you. Yesterday I was followed."

"What are you talking about?"

"Believe me I'm not making this up. When I left here yesterday … it was late … everybody else was gone … but as soon as I drove out of the lot this car was behind me. I turned at the first light. It turned at the first light. I didn't think much of it but then I made another turn … not the way that I normally go … just to see … and it made the same turn. And then again. And again. You think that's a coincidence?"

She looked at me.

"Why was somebody following me, David? Why did somebody … a student … compromise my DNA test? And what does all this have to do with your … skeleton?"

CHAPTER THIRTY

THIRTY

Cardinal Fiori's job was to protect the interests of the Roman Catholic Church and as one of twenty cardinals in Rome he had tremendous resources at his disposal. In Rome the age-old battle between Church and State was alive and well, which was why the Vatican had extensive files on people it considered dangerous. There were many scientists on this list and I was one of them. It was incredible how far they would go to learn what they could about someone they deemed a threat.

They knew all about my work and reputation as an expert on the Romans. They knew I had written many papers in scientific journals, was connected to a prominent museum and university, and was widely considered a world authority on a subject that touched every Roman Catholic dearly.

Crucifixion.

They knew the place and date of my birth, the names of both my parents, the maiden name of my wife, and the names of my children right down to their middle names. They knew about the degrees I had earned, and every single citation and honor I had ever received from such organizations as the American Association for the Advancement of Science. Make no mistake, the AAAS was a long-time nemesis of the Church and anyone associated with that group was suspect.

They knew that in 1947 in Palestine I had taken part in a news conference organized by Professor Eli Solnik, an archeologist with the Hebrew University of Jerusalem, announcing the discovery of the Dead Sea Scrolls. Their file on me contained a newspaper account about that news conference from The New York Times. It also had a copy of my 1967 letter to the Vatican Museum asking about legends pertaining to the Holy Grail. It had the article I wrote in the Israeli Exploration Journal about the skeleton of a crucified man found in ancient burial caves at Giv'at ha-Mivtar. It had all my correspondence with Church officials through the 1970s concerning the Shroud of Turin Research Project. They knew I was a member of the International Center of Sindonology and STURP, and that I later denounced both those organizations, as well as the Holy Shroud, in a professional journal. They knew I was in New Mexico in March, 1977 when STURP scientists first met and that I participated in tests of the Holy Shroud a year later in Turin. But there was also something else in that file, a letter sent by special delivery to the Vatican Museum's Department of Archeology.

'I would like to request your assistance regarding DNA analysis with this sample blood stain enclosed in a petri dish. The sample was obtained by my colleague at the Hebrew University, Dr. David Marr, esteemed professor of archeology who is well known for his work with the Dead Sea Scrolls as well as digs at Herculaneum, Pompeii, Masada and many other sites. The sample is from an old preserved corpse which he recently discovered in Qumran. We have reason to believe this corpse may be of significance. I have analyzed the sample to the best of my ability and would appreciate ratification of my findings from tests at your laboratories. I believe this sample to be two thousand years old.'

It was signed 'Dr. Eliraz Shimron, Professor of Archeology, The Hebrew University of Jerusalem'.

I am sure the Vatican didn't waste any time doing its own DNA analysis of that blood sample and equally sure that the results prompted attention at the highest level. The letter would have gone straight to Cardinal Fiori and every name mentioned in my file would have been red-flagged immediately. When an official at the Vatican Museum caught the name 'Gita Levitt' on the visitor's list at the Secret Archives, Cardinal Fiori would have been told about it and then it wasn't difficult to connect the letter Eliraz wrote to Gita's visit.

As things turned out, the Vatican Museum's Department of Archeology never did respond to Eliraz. Cardinal Fiori made sure of that. But he did call the Secret Archives and ask about Gita. He learned about her alleged examination of the documents of Innocent III and that she had looked over those documents, but also that she had strayed into other rooms going back to the oldest records in the building. Back to the first century.

I have little doubt Cardinal Fiori went to see those things for himself and he was a man who required no pass to visit the Secret Archives. He would have immersed himself in those ancient writings where he found the reference to the Cave of the Column.

He left no stone unturned and made sure the last room of the Vatican registers was locked. No one, not even the Pope himself, could enter without Cardinal Fiori's permission. The letter from Eliraz, her blood sample, and the lab results from the Vatican Museum all disappeared. Then the local Bedouin in Qumran were questioned and paid handsomely for their answers, but it would be different dealing with archeologists. Archeologists were professional people — scientists — and they constituted a bitter pill for the Church. They always have. But Cardinal Fiori already knew of three archeologists who were involved in this thing — Eliraz, Gita and me.

CHAPTER THIRTY-ONE

THIRTY-ONE

"Hello David. There you are. Have you seen Eliraz? She wasn't in class today."

It was the head of my faculty at the Hebrew University. He often appeared when trouble was brewing.

"No," I said.

"I don't know where she is. That's not like her. Listen I have a problem. There's a reporter from *The Jerusalem Post* outside my office and he won't leave. Says he wants to ask a few questions but I don't know what he's talking about. Would you mind speaking to him?"

"About what?"

"He said Eliraz mentioned something about a discovery a member of the faculty made but I don't know where she is and I don't know what she told him. Would you mind? I have a lot of things to do and a newspaper interview isn't on my list. Thank you, David. I'll send him up to your office."

"No don't do that. I'll meet him in the faculty lounge. That will be more comfortable."

....

"Are you Professor Marr? From the archeology department?"

"That's right. And who are you?"

"My name is Yitzak Cohen. I'm with *The Jerusalem Post.* I was wondering if you can help me out."

"With what?"

"The other night I met Eliraz Shimron. She's a professor, right?"

"That's right."

"It was at a party of a friend. A friend of a friend. We were having a drink. She certainly can handle a drink or two. Maybe it was even three. I forget. But she told me about her work and I was interested."

"What exactly are you interested in?"

He took out a notebook. That wasn't good.

"She said something about a discovery ... a big discovery ... that someone in her faculty made. Something about a preserved man."

"A preserved man?"

"She said one of her colleagues ... and she was quite lavish in her praise of him ... found a mummy of some kind. Now I don't remember if she actually said the word 'mummy' but that was the impression I got. What other kind of preserved people are there?"

I said nothing.

"She said this preserved man ... this mummy ... is really old and nothing like it has ever been found before. Is that right?"

"I think you'll have to ask Professor Shimron about that. She's the expert."

"I don't think so. I think *you* are the expert."

"Me?"

"Yes. This morning I was doing a little homework so I'll get right to the point. Have you found a mummy that was *crucified*?"

It hit me right between the eyes. But how did he find out?

"I beg your pardon?" I said.

"Professor Marr, I've already spoken to a few people today and I think you're the first one who might know something about this. As soon as I mention to anyone the business about crucifixion all fingers around here point to you. They say you know more about this than anyone."

"I'm not at liberty to talk about a find we haven't studied yet. Well yes ... we ... I ... did in fact find something ... but a preserved man ... crucified ... that's stretching it a bit."

He waited for my jumbled reaction to sink in. He tried making eye contact with me, but I wouldn't let him.

"Is it?" he asked.

"What?"

"Stretching it?"

"I think so. That ... what you said ... sounds pretty wild to me."

"Aren't you the archeologist who found the skeleton with the spike through the feet?"

"The spike?"

"You know what I'm talking about. I read the article. They say you know more about Roman crucifixions than anyone."

"Well I've done a lot of research in that area."

"I bet when you found that spike it was a pretty wild discovery too. Wasn't it?"

"Well ... maybe."

"Right through the man's feet?"

"Yes."

"Have you found a crucified mummy? A crucified preserved man?"

"Where did you hear that? From Eliraz?"

"Not exactly. But she gave me the lead. Let's see." He looked through his notes. "She said ... here it is ... 'Someone in our department has found a human body with blood that could be quite old. Maybe even two thousand years old.' Those were her words. She said she did the blood tests herself. She said she couldn't talk about it but then she went right on and talked about it. You wouldn't believe some of the stories I pick up at cocktail parties."

"I bet."

"So she tells me something like that and then I learn about you. The world's top expert on crucifixion."

"I wouldn't go that far."

"No? How many people study this sort of thing?"

"Not many."

"I didn't think so. So it seems somebody here has found

something that's news and that means I want to write about it. Can you help me out or not?"

"I'd like to help you but like I said we're still doing tests ... lab work ... things like that ... and it's too early to make any conclusions."

"Is it a mummy?"

"Well ..."

"Is it or isn't it?"

"It's ... hard to say."

"Hard to say? You're the archeologist. Surely you know if you found a mummy or not."

"Sometimes these things aren't so easy."

"Can I quote you and say that yes you found a mummy?"

"I wouldn't want to say that."

"What would you want to say?"

"Well ... that ... we ..."

"You what?"

"Look. I can't say anything. It's too early."

The reporter, a look of exasperation on his face, put away his notebook. A temporary reprieve. "You know what? I think you're hiding something. What is it? And why are you hiding it? Just give it to me on background."

I wasn't that stupid. I shook my head.

"Is there something you can show me then?"

I shook my head again. The reporter, frustrated with me by this time, ran his tongue along his lip.

"Okay. What if we just say that rumors abound that an ancient preserved man, a mummy, has been found with blood that's very old? According to one source it may be two thousand years old. The person who discovered this mummy is reputed to be David Marr, a visiting professor at the Hebrew University. Professor Marr is believed to be the world's leading authority on crucifixion. How's that?"

The reporter didn't know what I was wrestling with just then. On one hand, I wanted to throttle him. On the other, I wanted him to disappear. At the back of my mind was Eliraz.

"I don't think that would be very good reporting on your part," I said.

"So give me something better."

He wasn't going to get anything from me. He could see how uncomfortable I was.

"Okay," he said. "You don't want to tell me and you don't have to. Fine. But I've still got a job to do. Tell me. Does this Professor Shimron have a drinking problem? A drinking problem that keeps her away from classes now and then?"

"Of course not. Why would you say that?"

"Why? She had a few drinks the other night. I guess she managed to drive herself home but then I learn the next day she wasn't at work and it's the first time she missed a class all year. She didn't even call to say she'd be away. Doesn't that seem a little odd?"

"How do you know it's the first time she missed a class?"

"I checked. I was told she works like a machine. That she's the biggest workaholic in the whole faculty. That doesn't sound like somebody who misses classes and doesn't call. Does it?"

"I guess not."

"So where is she?"

"How would I know?"

"Do you work with her?"

"Not really. Why?"

"She told me she did blood tests on your mummy. Did she?"

"I never said anything about a mummy."

"Fine, Professor Marr. On your discovery then. Did she do blood tests or not?"

"Yes ... she did some tests."

"And the blood ... this blood ... it's old? One … two thousand years old?"

"Is that what she told you?"

"Yes sir. It is."

"Then I guess you'll have to go with that, won't you?"

"Blood? From a mummy? A crucified mummy? Two thousand years old? Found in the Holy Land?"

He looked at me for a long time. Searching. Studying my face. I flinched.

"Just one more thing, Professor Marr. Your wife. She's an archeologist too. Is that right?"

"Yes."

"And you picked her up at the airport yesterday?"

"There's not much you miss, is there?"

"Can you tell me why she went to Rome?"

"What are you talking about? Who said she went to Rome?"

"Nobody. But if your wife Gita Marr is the same person as Gita Levitt then she went to Rome. Two days ago. She spent a day there and came back yesterday."

"What?"

"I've got her flights. She flies to Rome, stays one day and then flies back to Ben Gurion. But under the name Gita Levitt."

"How do you know it's the same person?"

"I don't but I think it is. She's staying with Mrs. Marr's husband here in Jerusalem and he's Dr. David Marr. Expert on crucifixion. Quite a coincidence."

"What's my wife got to do with this?"

Now I was getting angry, which is exactly what he wanted.

"She's not associated with the Hebrew University, is she?"

"No. Why?"

"So what's she doing here?"

"Is there something wrong with my wife being in Israel with me?"

"No but I wonder. That's all."

"You wonder what?"

"Well ... why would a man … a visiting professor … have his wife here when it could be a real problem for him?"

"What are you talking about?"

"Nothing. It's just that I wonder why a man who frequents the apartment of the woman he works with ... Eliraz Shimron ... would want his wife here. That doesn't make a whole lot of sense. Does it?"

CHAPTER THIRTY-TWO

THIRTY-TWO

It started simply enough with a story in *The Jerusalem Post* and it wasn't a long article. It said that a member of the Hebrew University's archeology department may have discovered a crucified body in Qumran. Eliraz was quoted. She said she had tested the blood of the corpse herself and that it was very old. I was identified as a world authority on the Romans who didn't want to be interviewed, but my involvement was implied. The next day another story appeared. This time the reporter had visited Qumran himself and wrote that "a mysterious pall" had descended over the Bedouin tribesmen, not one of whom was willing to talk to him. There was an interview with a high-ranking clergyman from the Roman Catholic Church in Jerusalem who discounted any possibility of a crucified mummy being discovered. But the story was quick to say that the skeleton of a man who had been crucified was once found in an ancient burial cave at Giv'at ha-Mivtar. I was mentioned again, and not only as the discoverer of that skeleton, but as an archeologist who wasn't returning calls. And I wasn't. Two messages from reporter Yitzak Cohen had gone unheeded. Then, after the second article appeared, calls started coming from other journalists.

I didn't want to talk to any of them because we still had unfinished business ahead of us. Gita and I wanted to find that missing cave, the Cave of the Column. Then there was Jamil.

He was in Alexandria now and we hadn't yet done our final examination of the mummy with the CAT scan. And what about Eliraz? She just disappeared. I called her several times, but she wasn't around. Two days went by and then another day and she didn't turn up. She didn't even cancel her classes, which wasn't like her at all. To make matters worse, the dean of our department was getting uncomfortable with all the unwanted attention from the media. He was getting calls too. He asked me point blank if I had discovered a mummy and I said no. Fortunately, this was over the telephone. If he had seen me in person my face would have branded me a liar.

Then came the mysterious phone call at the university. Right to my lab. Anyone could have gotten the number since it was listed in the telephone directory. The phone rang and I picked it up, but no one answered. I could hear them breathing on the line, only they weren't saying anything. I always answered the phone with my name, so whoever it was knew it was me and maybe that's why they had called. To confirm it. I don't know. I chose not to think about it, but when it happened a second time at my apartment, that was different. This was a residential number and wasn't listed. Anywhere. It was Gita who answered the phone.

"Hello?" she said.

Click.

CHAPTER THIRTY-THREE

THIRTY-THREE

I picked up Jamil at the airport on the day of our long-awaited CAT scan, but before I got him there had been trouble. Earlier in the morning I had driven to the university, through the gates and around the traffic circle like always, and was about to park my car when I saw a TV crew on the steps of the building. They were waiting for me so they could shove a camera in my face. I don't think they saw me and hoped they would be gone when I returned later with Jamil.

When we met at the arrivals area he had two black bags with him. In one hand he carried his briefcase, the one that said doctor on call. It was the same bag he had brought on his last visit. I didn't know what was in his other bag, but since he would be cutting through human tissue I figured his forensic tools must be inside it. He greeted me cordially, but without his usual warmth and aplomb, and looked to be on a mission. That was good. We were on a mission. But just the same, there was something different about Jamil this time. His sentences were short and without any trace of the wit and bantering humor I had come to expect from him. He made no references to his size or his work, and offered no sarcastic asides about my own discipline of archeology. He asked about Robbie's whereabouts and I said he was busy in the lab.

I didn't want to annoy Jamil since he was here to help me. He was the pathologist, the expert who had examined more mummies than anyone I knew. He was an Egyptian, a Muslim, a man familiar with the region and all the strife that went with it, and he certainly knew its history. Because of these things he had warned me not to involve anyone. He had warned me about that from the beginning.

I could see that he was uncomfortable in our drive from the airport to the Hebrew University. He glanced at me a couple times, but when I turned in his direction he just looked away. He sat there, rigid, his mind racing, and I could feel the waves of energy emanating from his body. Then at last he spoke.

"David, have you seen today's newspaper?" I said that I had. "You are mentioned in it. And in yesterday's paper as well."

"I didn't tell them anything."

"It doesn't matter. The less you tell a reporter the more he wants to know. We have a problem."

He was right. We did have a problem. But the press being on to us wasn't the only thing. There was more. I told him then about the decapitated skeleton we had found at the ruins of the old Essene monastery and about Gita's visit to the Secret Archives at the Vatican and the passage she had found about the Cave of the Column.

"So she knows?"

"Yes she knows. How could I keep it from her any longer?"

Jamil had always liked Gita. He admired her intelligence and spirit, but he said going to Rome was foolhardy. That was the word he used.

I was hoping, praying, that when we got to the university the TV crew would be gone. But no, there they were on the steps like before. I saw them from a distance, so I didn't park in my usual spot. Instead, I went to the visitors' lot. Of course, nothing escapes Jamil and he asked why I was parking in that lot, so I had to tell him. He said nothing and Jamil is the kind of man who can say more when he doesn't speak at all. We entered the building from the back and he kept shaking his head from side to side. He wasn't pleased.

Even without reporters around, moving the mummy to the hospital for the CAT scan would be difficult. It was Saturday, the day of the Sabbath, normally a quiet day in Jerusalem.

Saturdays were always a good time for research since there were no distractions, but thinking about that suddenly unnerved me. I realized that these media people were familiar with my habits. They knew I would be here on a Saturday morning and I wondered what else they knew.

We had to take precautions. Robbie normally wasn't around on Saturdays. He wasn't a particularly observant Jew, but never worked on the Sabbath. Yet, today he was here because this was an exception. Gita was with us too. We needed them both because moving the mummy from the lab required four people — two to handle the stretcher, a third person at the front, and a fourth at the back, the latter two serving as lookouts. Robbie went first. He opened the doors and cleared the halls with his eyes before telling us to proceed. Jamil and I then wheeled the stretcher along, Gita following close behind us.

But what about those reporters outside? What would we do with them? Jamil had an idea. He told Robbie to greet them and when they asked for me Robbie would say I was away for the weekend. Robbie did and it worked. The crew hung around for a few minutes, then packed up and left. When they were gone, Robbie brought a pickup truck to the back of the building. Still, the four of us were getting paranoid. Even Jamil. It was this business with Eliraz and the newspaper articles, and those phone calls at the lab and then at my apartment.

"We must be very careful," Jamil said.

Finally, we were on our way to the hospital. The biggest hospital in Jerusalem had one CAT scanner and we had booked it for the morning. A CAT scanner has an eerie side at the best of times and with our subject it was eerier still. After we arrived, we began. We exposed the mummy to a series of X-rays at different angles. Once the pictures were taken, they went into a computer which produced digital two-dimensional images. We had done the same thing before with Egyptian mummies and it was fantastic. We could actually visualize a mummy intact in its coffin and then peel off the skin electronically before examining the underlying bones and contents of the body. It was incredible technology and completely non-destructive. We didn't even have to remove the mummy from its protective case or take away the sheet on top, which was good because the medical radiation technologist assisting us wouldn't see it. But he would prepare the resulting photographic images and we were eager to study those images. It would be the first time that a victim of crucifixion had ever been examined in such detail.

The first pictures of the mummy's skull appeared on the monitor. When we saw them it was like studying a patient who had been suffering from brain cancer, only there were no tumors in this brain. We were in total awe when the pictures of the body were developed. They revealed a man with gaping holes in his wrists and feet. The technologist asked us how the holes got there.

"From arrows," said Jamil. This man was tortured before he was killed."

The marks of violence on the skeleton were limited to three areas — the bones through the wrists, the bones through the feet and the ribs on the left side. The skull wasn't damaged at all. Inside the mouth were twenty-eight teeth, all of them in relatively good shape. We calculated the height of the body to be one hundred and seventy-one centimeters or a shade over five feet, seven. That was taller than average for a Mediterranean man of the time. There were no outward marks of disease or nutritional deficiency. The overall appearance of the body revealed a man who hadn't been engaged in heavy physical labor and who had never been seriously injured.

Until the crucifixion.

But the injuries from the crucifixion were grave indeed. They weren't injuries produced by arrows, but thick Roman spikes. Nine inches long. Unlike Jehohanan, no nails were found in the subject, but the nails had left their mark. You could see bulges around the holes of the calcanean bones in the feet and a thick crust around the perimeter of those bulges. The same horrendous bulges were present in the bones of the wrists. This was further evidence of crucifixion. And there was more. You could see small wood fragments embedded inside the bones and in the side wound. It was very clear in the pictures. The state of the body made it obvious that death was due to asphyxiation from crucifixion. A Roman crucifixion. You could see the foot wounds between the second and third toes, the exact point where the bones begin to separate, and the wounds on the wrists. You could see the folding in of the thumbs, the collapsed shoulder blades and the blocked thorax. They all pointed to the one and only inescapable conclusion.

Jamil asked the technologist for more detail of the mouth, so the man went to his computer keyboard and prepared a reconstruction. Tooth by tooth. There were no serious abscesses. No impacted canines. No missing teeth or gum disease. In the end, we had three hundred X-ray *slices* of the body or cross-sections, if you will. The technologist took slices of the torso — each one of them only five millimeters thick — and then he took slices that were three millimeters thick of the head and as fine as one-and-a-half millimeters thick through the ears and eyes. That done, he stacked all these two-dimensional images on top of each other — electronically — producing a rough 3D image. But this wasn't a fabricated 3D image like the one I had seen at STURP long ago. This was the sum result of actual photographs. When it was all over, we were in a state of euphoria.

"The only thing left now is to take hair and tissue samples in your lab," Jamil said. "Then we'll be done."

CHAPTER THIRTY-FOUR

THIRTY-FOUR

Jamil opened his small black bag and took out his tools. It was the middle of the night and everything was shut down. He was going to cut away a few hairs and take a tissue sampling. The hair would then be examined under a microscope, which would allow us to study the tissue through electron microscopy. It was a process where mummified human tissue is restored with water, or as we like to say, rehydrated. When that was done we would take a series of micrographs and enlarge them with actual photos. This would let us study the makeup of the tissue and then we could search for infectious agents — viruses, bacteria, parasites. All this helps determine the state of the body when the person was alive and it also helps determine the cause of death, not that we had any doubts about that. But we had to do these things quickly. Time was a commodity that was fast running out.

Jamil had his traditional instruments for the incision and when he lined them up on a white cloth the light from above danced off their metallic surfaces. I was fascinated by his ancient cutting tools. They were primitive and crude. From another era. The last of his surgical knives was made of glass.

"What's that one?" I asked.

"An obsidian knife. It's Ethiopian. From biblical times. The Hebrews used it for circumcisions. It was also used for lacerations. Through tough skin. Makes an even cut."

It had been many years since I last saw Jamil perform his magic on a preserved corpse. When it came to forensic analysis the man was a genius and at his best with specimens from antiquity. He was more than a pathologist for he also possessed the knowledge of a historian and the sensitivity of an archeologist. He would cut into human tissue and from the extraction and examination of that tissue learn about the person it came from. His authoritative yet soothing voice had a calming effect as he began to work.

Once we had the samples we would do the electron microscopy. That would take place in the forensics lab at the university. Jamil would extract a tiny quantity of DNA from the hair and amplify it through what we called a Polymerization chain reaction. Then he would clone the sample by putting it inside a living cell. The technique had been used before on one of the Egyptian mummies. It would let us compare the genetic makeup of a man from two thousand years ago to people living in the Middle East today.

"David, I am finished," Jamil said. "We have more than enough samples. Now to your forensics lab."

He washed his hands and began putting his tools away when we heard a noise from outside the building. It sounded like someone was playing with the lock on the window. The blinds were already pulled down, so I peeked behind them to have a look. Sure enough, a small truck was parked outside, a dark figure behind the wheel. Another figure was moving around by the window.

The window of my lab.

Jamil motioned for me to check the lock on the door. A simple lock was on the outside and a dead bolt on the inside, so no one was coming through there. Still, the tinkering noises outside the window persisted. Jamil whispered to me that someone was trying to break in to my lab. But who? The next thing we knew the window opened. Just a crack. There was the soft humming of a truck.

"Who do you think it is?" I said softly.

Jamil put his fingers to his mouth. "Don't you have some bugs in here?" he whispered. "Insects? Spiders?"

"I have a tarantula. Why?"

He nodded his head and I realized what he was getting at. I tiptoed over to the cabinet where I kept my specimens and took out a small box with a tarantula inside. I put the box on the window sill and opened it. Very carefully. There was barely enough space for the tarantula to squeeze through the crack in the window and that is exactly what it did. It crawled out of the box and, once outside, scurried into the night.

A moment later we heard this garbled scream. It was immediately followed by footsteps and then panting. A lot of panting. Whoever had been playing with the window lock got back in that pickup truck pretty fast. Then the truck sped off.

"Well," I said when they were gone, "now there's a tarantula on the loose."

"Yes," said Jamil. "But at least it's on our side."

CHAPTER THIRTY-FIVE

THIRTY-FIVE

"David."

It was Eliraz.

"Eliraz! Where have you been? Everybody's been looking for you."

She called me on the phone. Just like that.

"I've been away," she said. "Thinking. Turning my life around. Making some changes."

"What are you talking about?"

"David ... *I know*."

Silence.

"You know what, Eliraz?"

"That first night when you and Robbie came in with your *whatever it is*? I was working late. My office light was off but I have a lamp on my desk and I saw you. I knew something was going on and after you let me do those blood tests and then after those tubes got switched I had to find out. So I did."

"You did what?"

"Shlomo helped."

"Who?"

"Shlomo. The doorman. After a little prodding on my part he told me he let you sneak in that night. No admission papers.

No nothing. But he didn't know much. So I came in one night myself. To your lab."

"You got into my lab?"

"Yes."

"How did you do that?"

Another pause. She cleared her throat.

"I borrowed your key and had a duplicate made."

"What!"

"I'm sorry, David. I know it wasn't the right thing to do but I just had to find out what you had in there."

For a long time she said nothing. There was only her soft breathing on the line. I was still trying to take in what she just said about the key. I couldn't believe she would really do that.

"You had a duplicate key made?" I said, still incredulous.

"Yes I did. So what does it mean, David?"

"I don't know what it means."

"But all this business going on. It has to do with that ... body ... you have in there. Doesn't it?"

I didn't say anything. I didn't have to.

"Look," she said. "There's something else I must tell you. I'm not coming back to the university. I tendered my resignation this morning."

"Whoa. Slow down, Eliraz. You're giving me more than I can handle. What do you mean you tendered your resignation? I thought you were going to be the department head."

"Not anymore. I decided to move from my apartment. Get something different. Smaller and not so elaborate. And I'm getting a new job too. Wait 'til you hear. I'm going to teach."

"Teach? You already teach, don't you?"

"You don't understand. I'm going to teach history to children. Palestinian children. At a refugee camp on the West Bank."

"But you're a Jew. They wouldn't let you do that."

"They are going to let me."

"I don't understand, Eliraz. Wouldn't something like that be dangerous?"

"Yes it could but they have a problem getting teachers. Good ones I mean. At first they didn't want to hire me but like I say they don't get many applicants from qualified people and certainly not from archeologists at the Hebrew University."

"A refugee camp? *A Palestinian refugee camp?*"

"Yes. I had to go before a committee and they brought up every possible reason why I shouldn't do it but I impressed them. I mean with my knowledge of their people. They said if they could find a Palestinian with my background that person would be running the whole camp. But they still didn't want to hire me. They didn't want a woman so that was the last straw. I laid out all my credentials on the table. Showed them my professional memberships. My publications. I even agreed to work for the same salary they pay everyone else. It's not much. Two hundred Jordanian dinars a month. That's about two hundred and fifty American dollars."

"A month?"

"Yes. I sold everything I have. All my furniture. Everything but my car. That's what I've been doing the last few days. So now I've got some money, enough to get me through, at least for a while."

"I still think it's dangerous, Eliraz. How many Israelis have taught at a camp like that? On the West Bank?"

"How many do you think? I'm the first. And you wouldn't believe the irony around this place. Take the wife of the man who runs the school. You know how she earns her living? She crochets woollen *yarmulkes* for the Orthodox Jewish settlers who live nearby and she's a Palestinian!"

"That is irony."

"The West Bank is full of it. During the day the Palestinians and Jews try to kill each other and at night they provide each other with goods and services. It's crazy."

"The Middle East has always been crazy."

"But this is a job with a purpose, David. That's what I lacked before. That's what my life lacked. Something with a purpose. So what about you? What are you going to do now?"

"What do you mean?" "You know what I mean. Your *whatever it is.*"

What could I say? She seemed to know everything.

"Eliraz, I'm glad you're excited about this teaching job even though it sounds very dangerous. But you created some big problems for me."

"I know I have and I'm sorry."

"That newspaper reporter. He keeps digging. He won't stop. What on earth possessed you to talk to a reporter about those blood tests?"

"I didn't know what I was doing that night. I was drinking and talking too much I guess. But I didn't know he was from a newspaper."

"And your letter to the Vatican. That wasn't a smart thing to do. You should have told me before you sent them anything. Those were *my* blood samples!"

"I thought they could help. I've dealt with the Vatican Museum before. Their people are good but I never heard from them. Listen if there's anything I can do."

"I think you've done enough, Eliraz."

Pause. Was there a glimmer of shame in that silence? I doubt it. She changed the subject.

"You know what's funny?" she said.

"What?"

"I don't think I'm going to miss working at the university one bit. All the in-fighting at the faculty. The power trips. I'm not going to miss that. But I'm really looking forward to working with these kids. I think I'm going to get more out of it than they will. The pay is a joke but I don't care. I don't even care. Can you believe that?"

I sighed.

"One more thing, David. Remember when I told you about that *hurt* you wear all the time?"

"Yes. I remember."

"It has to do with your family, doesn't it? Something deep and personal."

"As a matter of fact, Eliraz, it does."

"I thought so. Only a loss could affect someone like that. So you wear it everywhere you go."

"Do I? Wear it I mean?"

"Yes you do."

"So what was it about?"

I swallowed.

"It was my son, Eliraz. It was my son."

CHAPTER THIRTY-SIX

THIRTY-SIX

Jerusalem, 1984

Deep in the rock beneath the City of David is a tunnel where the air is cool. Buried, impervious to the penetrating heat of the desert sun, the tunnel snakes along for a third of a mile, and it seems never ending with only darkness and cold damp walls of stone. A long meandering journey awaits visitors in the bowels of this ancient kingdom, and the journey is worthwhile for it leads to that most precious of commodities. Water. The tunnel winds its way to a spring that has been known through the ages as Gihon, which means gusher.

In 1867 an explorer, Charles Warren, made a startling discovery in the rock. As head of an expedition mounted by the Palestine Exploration Fund, he was searching for answers to three compelling questions. Where on the Temple Mount was the Temple located? Where were the three city walls described by the historian Josephus? And where exactly did the Crucifixion take place? He never found the answers, but he did find something.

He sank seven shafts into the ground along the western side of the Temple Mount. At the bottom of his shafts, he found the foundations of a large pillar, along with a tunnel that had been cut from the bedrock. It was seventy-five feet below the present ground level. There was also a vertical access, a zigzagging, sloping corridor with steps that led from the City of David to below the city wall and then to an ancient shaft just above the waters of the spring.

The shaft was a hole a hundred and sixty feet long. It was there so the people of Jerusalem could draw up water from the spring even when under siege. The shaft — Warren's Shaft as it came to be known — was hard to find. Tons of soft fill had accumulated over the centuries since it was last used, but it was still there. People knew it was there. It was up to the archeologist to dig it out and reveal the history for all to see.

David knew about the spring. It was in the Bible. It was legend. The spring was a season-long source of water that had proved invaluable during the months without rain — April through November. How the people of the time managed to hack through the bedrock with their crude instruments never ceased to amaze him, and he knew it had more to do with human ambition and drive than the edges of their metal cutters. It had to do with survival.

"Donkeys?" a surprised Brian said when first he saw the dim-witted animals with empty canvas bags draped across their backs, ambling up the steep hills of the City of David. "You're going to use donkeys to bring all the rubble down from the shaft?"

"Yes," David said. "When you have to carry rubble down these hills donkeys are the best thing to use. Always have been. These hills are too steep for anything else."

Brian shook his head. He playfully slapped his father on the back and let out a laugh. "Donkeys," he said. "I don't believe it. It's the 1980s and we're using donkeys."

The purpose of the dig was to clear out the tons of soft till that filled Warren's Shaft. It would take time. The donkeys were slow. The party included mining engineers, mountain climbers, graduate students, and all sorts of archeological junkies. Some of them were kids who were still in school and others were people who just liked digging for relics. They were in love with history, and many of them lived a hand-to-mouth existence, scrounging up the money to fund their addiction which often meant travelling to exotic sites around the world. They shared a passion for the past and it joined them all as one despite the diversity of their backgrounds. And even though he was leader of the expedition, David was one of them, too, and so was Brian. The bug had infected them both. It had been passed down from father to son.

Brian was a graduate student on his first dig in the Holy Land. It was the opportunity he had been waiting for, a chance to get into the dirt and become one with the ancient earth below. David thought it might do for his son what the caves and Dead Sea Scrolls had done for him. He thought this dig might be the catalyst to forever bind Brian to the region. And it would, but not how he had hoped.

The group used donkeys to haul countless buckets of soil and stones up from the shaft, and there was so much it seemed the work would never end. Finally, when it was all cleared out, they could descend the shaft and follow the twisting path of the tunnel just as the people of ancient Jerusalem once did. Then the engineering miracle that had taken place so long ago became all the more remarkable.

"How did they do it?" Brian asked. "How in that time could they possibly have done something like this? It's incredible."

It was incredible. Brian had learned from his mother why Jerusalem was built here. The site was due to the Gihon spring at the foot of the hill in the Kidron Valley. Gita had told him that the original Canaanite inhabitants sunk a shaft down to the spring from within the city walls. It gave them access to the water supply without having to venture outside and expose themselves to hostile invaders. It was this same shaft, she had said, that David's men penetrated when they first conquered Jerusalem. The shaft was the key. It would always be the key.

"Some people say the shaft was built after King David's time but they're wrong," Gita had told him. "The proof is in the Second Book of Samuel. It's all there. And the Second Book of Chronicles tells about King Hezekiah, the King of Judah, and how he prepared for the siege by Sennacherib in the eighth century B.C. He built up the wall that was broken down and then an act of pure genius. He built a tunnel right through the rock. Under the city. And diverted the water supply to a reservoir giving access to his people and at the same time denying it to Sennacherib. It was brilliant!"

Standing in the tunnel with the water up to his thighs, Brian imagined the women of the City of David carrying pottery on their heads, and he had to marvel at the ingenuity of the ancient Hebrews. But while his mother filled him with biblical quotations telling of this masterful work, it was his father who posed the question of how the tunnel got built. The two of them, father and son, were the first archeologists to ever walk the entire length of the tunnel.

"It's six hundred yards from one end to the other," David said.

"Not quite," said Brian. "Five hundred and thirty-three meters. Or five hundred and seventy-seven yards to be exact."

David stood there looking at his son who had just corrected him. "Who told you that?" he said. "Your mother?"

Brian nodded.

"Then it must be right."

They both laughed. Gita and Jennie weren't with them since they were spending the day in Tel Aviv. David had wanted them to join in the dig to make it a family affair, but Gita would have none of it. The engineering miracle of the old Hebrews might be something to behold, she had said, but inhaling all that damp air, never mind the precarious descent into Warren's Shaft, was better left to the men.

"But going down the shaft would be easier for you than anyone else," David assured her. "It's a narrow opening and you're small."

"I don't think so," Gita said. "Besides Jennie and I would get awfully dirty in that sewer, wouldn't we?"

"Sewer?"

"You know what I mean. And we'd get wet. You're walking in water in the tunnel, aren't you? I'd probably have to wear a bathing suit to do something like that. Wouldn't I?"

"Not really ... you could ..."

"You want me to put on a bathing suit in front of all these men?"

"I didn't say anything about bathing suits."

"Okay dear. Let's say we don't wear bathing suits. What if we just wore ordinary clothes and they got wet? Jennie and I have these tops on and shorts and we get soaking wet and ..."

"All right. I get the point. If you don't want to join us then don't."

"Listen the idea of getting my feet soaked doesn't appeal to me at all. No. Jennie and I will pass thank you. If you don't mind we'd rather visit Tel Aviv and do a little shopping."

"So that's it!"

"Of course. What do you think? We are women you know."

Gita and Jennie had left early in the morning for Tel Aviv, which was thirty miles from Jerusalem. That would give them a full day to sample all the textiles from the finest shops in town. Fine, David thought. He and Brian would probably be better off without them anyway.

Once down the shaft and inside the tunnel, they began to dwell on how Hezekiah's amazing creation had been built. They reasoned that two teams must have dug the tunnel from opposite ends. Simultaneously. Exactly how they met at all was a mystery, but Brian had an answer for that.

"Remember Hoopoe and his tunnel? From *The Source* by James Michener. This is where Michener got his idea."

David scratched at his chin. It was bristly because he never shaved regularly when on digs. "And what did Hoopoe do?" David said. "It's been a long time since I read that book."

"Don't you remember? From inside the city walls Hoopoe and his men put up flags in a line. Forming a range. The range gave them an orientation. With that as their guide they dug their shafts. Then they dug their tunnels toward each other. It was quite a trick."

The dark bleak tunnel dulled the senses. David and Brian needed flashlights to see where they were going. At first, they tried candles, but the candles always went out and they spent so much time fumbling around with matches trying to re-light the candles that they gave up. And what about the sounds? They weren't sharp sounds at all, but they could hear things. Every word was echoed through the long hole in the rock. The musty smell and dampness would pour through your nostrils where it would sit and collect in your lungs.

“That’s probably what they did,” David said. “When you think about it it’s really something. They had nothing more than pick-axes which would account for the zigzags in the middle of the tunnel.”

“How’s that?” Brian asked.

“Well you have two teams working from opposite ends.” David stretched out his arms to either side and pointed his fingers. “But how did they find each other? That’s the mystery. Think about it. When they got close they probably heard each other and from then on it was strictly trial and error. They went this way and that, hewing and chiselling the rock according to the sound that they heard. Finally after a long time they met.”

Brian nodded. “That must have been some meeting. And it’s all because of the spring. Mom said the Gihon spring produced hundreds of cubic yards of water every day but the water source was never in danger until Sennacherib attacked. So Hezekiah built his tunnel, Warren’s Shaft was blocked off, the source of the Gihon was covered up and all the water flowed to Shiloah, an artificial reservoir. And lo and behold the people could get their water in a time of siege. It was brilliant.”

David only had to look at Brian’s face to see that the wizardry of the old Hebrews was leaving an indelible impression on him. It was hard to explain since you had to feel it yourself. David had felt it. Many times. Any archeologist felt it. It was something that took you back. Back through the ages.

Whenever he was at Masada, David could sense the steadfast courage of the Jews resisting the Roman hordes. It was etched in his blood. When he was at Pompeii, he could relive the tragedy, death and destruction that the eruption unleashed as if it had just happened and he was witnessing it with his own eyes. And at Givat ha-Mivtar, when he first found what was left of poor Jehohanan, he could feel the pain of spikes ripping through flesh and bone, and could see before him a man with the very life breathing out of him. Now here with his son the two of them couldn’t escape the euphoria at two teams of workmen digging through the rock in one last attempt to preserve their city and then meeting, at long last, after months and even years of toil.

What joy they must have known.

"The original Hebrew name is *Breichat HaShiloah* which means 'pool of the conducted waters'," Brian said.

"Your mother?" David asked.

"Yes. But Shiloah was later changed to the Arabic *Siloam* which means 'spring of consolation.' They say anyone who is sad and who drinks from the spring is consoled because the spring gets its waters from the Garden of Eden."

"I wouldn't take that literally, Brian. No one has ever found the Garden of Eden."

"Well if it does exist it must be around here somewhere. This is the Holy City, isn't it?"

"So you think I should drink? Here? From this water?"

"Sure. If you want to. But only if you're sad."

"What's there to be sad about?"

David looked down to the water and swept his fingers through it. He knew it was drinkable. The tunnel owed its history to that fact, but the setting wasn't conducive to lapping up spring water. Everything seemed dirty and damp. The air. The rock. And the water seemed dirty, too. So instead of drinking it, he cupped his hand in the water and raised it to his face, then splashed his mouth in the cool freshness. The water felt good and soothing, but he didn't drink.

"It was here where they say Jesus cured the blind man," Brian said.

"Your mother didn't tell you that part, did she?"

"No. I learned that for myself. '*And as Jesus passed by, he saw a man which was blind from his birth. And his disciples asked him, saying Master, who did sin, this man, or his parents, that he was born blind? Jesus answered, neither hath this man sinned, nor his parents, but that the works of God should be made manifest in him. I must work the works of him that sent me, while it is day. The night cometh when no man can work. As long as I am in the world, I am the light of the world.*'"

"Where did you learn that?" David asked him, surprised at his son's quotation.

"Chapter Nine, the Book of John," Brian said with a shrug. "The first time I read it was when Jennie got her diabetes. I was looking for something and found it with that passage. I liked it because it tells you there doesn't always have to be a reason for everything. You know the way Mom says all the time. Sometimes things just happen. Like Jennie. It just happened. When I read it I remember thinking if only there was a Jesus who could cure her then she'd be all right. I would have given anything if it was me and not her. I even prayed I would get it so she wouldn't be alone. We could take our insulin shots together and then it wouldn't be so bad for her."

David thought about the Dead Sea Scrolls and the Holy Grail. He thought about the warnings given him by Brother Henry. He thought about the sample he had taken from the Holy Shroud.

"I remember telling her it wasn't her fault," Brian went on. "She thought she did something wrong. But she was just a kid and I kept asking myself why this happened to my kid sister. But there was no answer. Then I read her that passage from the Bible and told her to remember that things could be a lot worse, that other people have worse things than diabetes to put up with. I told her to consider herself lucky that she lives when she does."

"You were right to tell her those things, Brian. It helped. I know it helped. You've always been a good brother to her."

Brian shrugged. "This spring is also called The Virgin's Spring," he said.

"Do you know why it's called that?"

"The Bible says it's where Mary washed the clothes of Jesus. So this spring, this shaft, this well, it's all very important … to Jews ... to Christians ... and Muslims too."

David shook his head and smiled. "You impress me, Brian. You really impress me."

"We're explorers, Dad. We should know what we're exploring shouldn't we? We should know about the people … the history … the legends. It goes with the territory. Doesn't it?"

"Yes. It goes with the territory."

"Any archeologist who studies the Middle East should know the Bible. That's why I've been reading it and I've learned a few passages. From both books. The Koran too. There's a lot of good ideas in there. Food for thought. I guess I'm just a citizen of the world."

Brian was indeed a citizen of the world. He wasn't only a Jew or a Christian or any other single entity. He was something more, something richer, a union of composite parts in one glorious whole. He was a man, but a man who with the benefit of insight and impartiality would one day take all this blessing and become a great archeologist. Even better than his father. No one was more aware of that than David himself.

In the weeks leading up to their final descent into Warren's Shaft and their trek through the tunnel, they had uncovered a rich historical legacy. The stratigraphy had some twenty-five layers of settlement. Twenty-five layers! There were the remains of ancient walls built as far back as the eighteenth century B.C. Almost four thousand years ago. There were the ruins of buildings from the days of the kings of Judah, and a burnt room from the destruction of the First Temple, and from that burnt room a major archeological find. Fifty-one clay seals and on one of them the name 'Gemariah son of Shaphan.' Shaphan was the scribe of King Jehoiakim, spoken of in the Book of Jeremiah. Yes, it was a dig that David would long remember.

Only the two of them were in Hezekiah's Tunnel now. Together they trudged through the water and walked the full length. It seemed so much longer than five hundred and thirty-three meters. The going was slow and tedious in the narrow tunnel with its low ceiling, and soon they found themselves in water up to their knees. But finally they reached the end, and it was time to ascend Warren's Shaft and return to the surface. This was the hard part. The narrow vertical shaft climbed straight up through the rock, about forty feet, before reaching into another cavernous tunnel above. That tunnel, in turn, would take them back to the entrance, but it was the shaft, Warren's Shaft, that was the most difficult to navigate. Not only did they have to pull themselves up, but do it in a tight space.

A line with light bulbs attached at ten-foot intervals ran down one side of the shaft, and a thick rope ran down the other. You literally had to pull your way up the wall of rock against the forces of gravity, always hanging on to the rope with your feet inching their way up. Bit by bit. The steps once forged in the rock had long been eroded, so it wasn't secure. Not even for a toe-hold. It was a climb. You had a hard hat on your head and work boots on your feet. The rest was muscle and David thought just then that maybe it was a good thing Gita and Jennie were not with them.

David would go up first. He spit into his palms and rubbed the spit in. He reached up, placed the soles of his boots against the rock, and hoisted his body two feet closer to the surface. There wasn't much room. It was a narrow shaft. With his legs bent and his body tucked in tight like a ball, it was a slow painstaking way to climb. But he couldn't let go. It was the only way. He reached up, planted his feet against the rock, and lifted himself again. Every now and then he would stop for a moment to rest — David was fifty-five years old but in good shape — but always there was the constant pull on his arms. Yes, he thought, Gita wouldn't have liked this. She wouldn't have liked this at all and neither would Jennie. When he was fifteen feet up, he looked down and called out to Brian so he could begin his climb.

Brian always liked to copy his father. He spit into his palms, rubbed his hands together, and began hoisting himself up. On his way he passed through the levels, the oldest ones first for they were at the bottom. Back to the Bronze Age when this shaft was first used. Back to the early Canaanites. Back to King David. Back to King Hezekiah and Sennacherib and the stories his mother had told him. Ever since he was a little boy, she had told him, and now he was here with his father travelling through time. That's what they were doing. Travelling through time. Brian could hear the chiselling of Hezekiah's workmen carving out the rock as they made their tunnel. He could hear the feet of the women swishing through the water-filled passageways leading one way to the Gihon spring and the other to the Siloam pool, and he could feel their smug confidence knowing that the precious waters were theirs and theirs alone. Travelling through time was an adventure and what made him love the work. It had been passed on from father to son, but sometimes sacrifices had to be made. Nothing comes easy for time travellers and the sacrifice was climbing up Warren's Shaft.

It was hard to breathe and the air Brian took in wasn't fresh. In a few seconds the sweat began to soak him through. Forty feet of upward vertical climbing. The only sounds in the shaft were the grunts of two men, grunts that magnified themselves over and over down the shaft before dying in the dark below.

Brian's hands were wet from the dampness and from the constant pulling up of his body weight. Up. Up. He was a solid a hundred and ninety pounds on a six-foot frame. Bigger and broader than his father. There was less room for him to maneuver and weave his body up through the hole. Up. Up. His black hair, Gita's hair, mopping wet with sweat. This was worse than being under the hot sun in the desert. At least, his arms and legs didn't ache in the desert. It was just the heat. His eyes, Gita's eyes, were moist and it was hard to see. Harder than before. Halfway up he stopped for a rest and filled his lungs with air. Cold dank air. Putrid air. He longed for the surface. How much farther? He couldn't tell where his father was. He looked straight up and all he could see was a shadow grappling above. But he could hear. The echo was so loud that the most insignificant sound of David's boots kicking at the rock filled the shaft.

"Dad! Are you at the top?" Brian cried.

"Almost! Almost!" came the echo.

Three-quarters of the way up the shaft, more than thirty feet from the bottom, Brian tried to stretch out as best he could when his back rubbed against something in the rock. Something hard. A small sharp edge that had escaped the chisels of all the stonecutters through the ages caught him square in the middle of his spine. He let out a yell. A terrifying yell. It shot up the narrow corridor like an electric current. David was just finishing his climb and about to step out into the upper tunnel, the tunnel leading to the entrance, when he stopped and pressed his feet on the best hold he could find in the wall. He looked down.

"Brian? Are you all right?"

He couldn't see. There was a flickering light from the nearest bulb below him, but it was hard, impossible, to make anything out. All he could do was turn to the side and try to look over his shoulders. But there was nothing to see.

"Brian! Are you all right? Are you all right?"

Then panic. The pain that began in the small of Brian's back filled his legs and they went limp. He tried to massage his aching back, so he let go of the rope with his right hand and reached around himself so that he was hanging on by only his left. His fingers were wet. The rope was wet. It wasn't enough. All David could hear was a slow exasperated sigh followed by the piercing sound of a shrinking scream. And for six horrible seconds — an eternity — the click-click-clicking of something. Boots. Hands. Arms. Banging against rock. Then nothing.

David stopped. He went cold.

"Brian?" he asked softly. "Brian?"

Then louder.

"Brian. BRIAN!"

Back at the entrance the workmen knew something was wrong. They peered into the hole, but there was nothing to see. All they could muster were faint voices groping in the unknown. David released his hold on the rope and half-climbing, half-falling his way down the shaft, he descended. He didn't feel the scraping of his elbows against the rock as he flailed his way and dropped.

"Brian!" he screamed, but there was no Brian.

It took him less than a minute to get to the bottom. His hands were bloodied from the rope burns, but he didn't feel pain, and he didn't see anything. Not until his feet kicked at something that was too soft for rock. It was him. Brian. He had fallen. All the way down. There was a bulb just a few feet overhead. David grabbed the line to steady the light and kill the moving shadows. Brian's body was in a heap in the shallow water at the bottom of the shaft. Where the shaft met Hezekiah's Tunnel. His head was bloodied and scraped. The skin on his arms was ripped apart. There was a sense of broken bones.

"Brian," David whispered.

He released the rope that ran up Warren's Shaft and through the upper tunnel to the surface. It hung loose and free. There was one, then two abrupt jerks on it from above. He tugged it three times in response. The signal for help. In a moment there was the jumbled sound of a commotion from the other end as men began dropping into the opening one by one. David cradled his hand under Brian's battered head and laid him down flat on the watery rock bed of the tunnel.

For a moment, one solitary moment that would stay with

him forever, the eyes of his son, his one and only son, opened half way. But the rest of him was still. As still and lifeless as the rock. Brian gazed into the face of his father and lingered. Like a photograph. Then his eyes closed.

It wasn't long before the others arrived. They had a first aid kit with them, and water and bandages. One of them pushed Brian's chin forward, pinched his nose and started applying mouth-to-mouth. When that didn't work, he began pounding him on the chest.

"Don't do that. I think all his ribs are broken," another one said.

"You can live with broken ribs," was the reply.

But it was no use. The men looked at each other saying nothing. Then all eyes descended on David. He was their leader. He was the archeologist. The one who made decisions. Showing no sign of emotion, he told the men to go up and call an ambulance. How they would get a stretcher down here he didn't know. But they had to call an ambulance. Then one of the Israelis began to cry like a whimpering child. He buried his face in his hands, sobbed through his tears, and wiped the wetness from his eyes. He lowered his head and started chanting.

"Yis'ga'dal v'yis'kadash sh'may ra'boo ..."

The Mourner's Kaddish.

"No!" David screamed, grabbing him by the collar. "No!"

The man looked into David's face and saw rage. Explosive rage. More rage than David had ever shown before.

It was thirty minutes before two medics were able to descend the shaft with their medical supplies, and forty-five before a harness was tied to the body so it could be hoisted by pulley back to the top. How limp it was. How limp *he* was. Hanging from the hoist like a slab of meat. But this was Brian. His son! David watched the lines pull him up, and he thought of Gita and Jennie. He thought of the book with the ziggurat of Nippur, which had first whetted Brian's appetite for things old. He thought of the day, that wondrous day when he was born, only to end like this. He watched the lines pull him up. Up through the dark of Warren's Shaft. Up past the layers of time. Back to the surface and the present day.

The last one to leave the tunnel was David. He walked the

same steps he and Brian had walked not an hour earlier. Not an hour earlier. His boots disappeared into the waters said to be fed by the Garden of Eden, and a slow shiver worked its way through his body. He lowered his hands into the water and it was cold. Deathly cold. He remembered Brian's words about the spring of consolation. *Siloam.* He raised the sustenance of life to his lips where it mixed with his tears and he drank. He drank deeply. So deeply he thought he would never stop drinking. He drank until the spring was dry.

CHAPTER THIRTY-SEVEN

THIRTY-SEVEN

Gita and I hadn't been to the caves for forty years, but it seemed like yesterday. From the road leading to Qumran I could see Cave 4 out the corner of my eye and then it all came back to me. It was the biggest cave, once filled with hundreds of scrolls. Near the ruins of the old Essene monastery, it was easy to spot. Cave 5 was close by and Cave 6 was off to the west with Caves 7 to 10 on the other side of the ridge. The caves where the first discoveries were made are a mile and a half north of the ruins while Caves 3 and 11 were another mile beyond that. They were just a few of the hundreds of caves in the area and I had long believed that all of them had been thoroughly searched. But maybe one of them wasn't.

I knew there were more caves around Cave 11. From a distance they looked like black holes with openings of various sizes. They all faced east, but one of them was different since it had two entrances. It was in the middle of nowhere. Gita and I decided to head for that one.

The walk took me back to our first trip to Cave 4 so many years earlier and just like then it was difficult negotiating the rock face up to the entrance. Even more difficult because I was older. It had been so much easier for Muhammad adh-Dhib's goat. But the cave with the two openings was relatively easy. We got in through the lower opening. According to the reference Gita had found about the Cave of the Column, there was indeed an upper chamber with a gaping hole in the roof. Could this be the cave she had read about in those scriptures at the Vatican?

We searched the lower chamber and before long found the bluish mound the words had referred to. The tel. What secrets would it reveal? My eyes darted this way and that. The back of the cave was narrow and the ceiling so low you had to tuck your head. Even Gita, as short as she was, couldn't stand up straight. But then the cave just stopped. I thought again of the ancient words she had read. By this time I had committed them to memory.

The cave of the Column having two entrances viewing to the east, an upper chamber with a large hole in the roof. And across from the opening a blue tel in the lower chamber, a back chamber with an opening down to a passage between the two like the tunnel of Solomon.

With a flashlight to guide me I crouched and started scratching away at the cave wall with my fingers. White particles began dropping like fine crumbs, and the more I scratched and scraped, the more they fell, and then whole pieces started coming apart.

"Gita, I found a hole," I said.

The pieces kept falling, and the hole got bigger and bigger. When it was big enough I stuck my head through only to see the hole leading to another opening. A cave within a cave. So this must be the back chamber. We clawed our way through the rough edges of the wall and that wall was gone in less than a minute. It crumbled onto the floor, kicking up a flurry of dust particles that filled the air. We waited for the air to clear and then crawled inside. This cave was even bigger than the first one, about fifteen feet long before tapering to a corner at the end. There was a small opening at the corner, a crack just a few inches wide. Did it lead to another cave? I laid down flat on the ground and reached inside the crack. I couldn't see what I was doing, but could feel my way. Sure enough, something was there.

"I think it's a scroll," I said.

"The missing scroll!" Gita exclaimed.

I eased it out of the rock into the protective confines of

my arm. Then Gita and I edged our way into the wider space of the cave where we both stood up on our feet. Even with our flashlights, it was still dim, so we retraced our steps, went back through the first cave and stepped out into the open sunlight. The air, though very hot, was refreshing. The scroll was wrapped just like all the others had been with a strap around the outside. I unravelled it and the first words became visible.

"It's Hebrew!" Gita said. "Let me see! Let me see!"

It was the same voice of that young archeology student catching her first glimpse of the Dead Sea Scrolls many years ago. All this time and her enthusiasm hadn't waned. But now Gita wasn't a student. She was an archeologist and a master of old languages. If this was written in Greek or Aramaic she could decipher the words without trouble, but because it was Hebrew — ancient Hebrew — it was even easier for her. She wasn't able to read those words in 1947, but she could now. Her voice grew soft as her finger followed the letters from right to left.

"But I say until you I will not drink henceforth of this fruit of the vine until that day when I drink it new with you in the kingdom of my Father."

"The Book of Matthew?" I said.

I didn't know St. Matthew word for word, but was familiar with parts of it.

"When the Son of Man shall come in his glory, and all the holy angels with him, then shall he sit upon the throne of his glory."

"What's the Book of Matthew doing here?" I said, bewildered.

We unrolled the scroll and found something else. A smaller piece of parchment was wrapped inside. We spread it out. It was also written in ancient Hebrew, but in a different hand from the rest. Gita did the translation.

"And ye shall come to the community at Secacah and there ye shall take the earthly remains of the prophets and bury them to a depth of two cubits in the sands of the desert, with no urns nor remnants of material things, and there shall they be kept."

We looked at each other. A shudder ran down my spine.

"Two cubits?" Gita said.

I raised my arm and bent it. "From the elbow to the tip of the middle finger. A cubit. It's about a foot and a half."

"Three feet," Gita said. I nodded. "And your mummy was buried three feet below the surface?" I nodded. "Now I get it. Whoever perpetrated this thing went to a lot of trouble."

"What do you mean?"

"Look! It says right here in this scroll. Take the bodies of these two men ... whoever they were ... and bury them three feet below the surface in the desert ... and that's what they did."

She read the passage from the scroll again.

"One of the graves took and one of them didn't," I said.

"That's right."

"And the beheaded skeleton?"

"Like I said, David, whoever did this went to a lot of trouble. They wanted to validate the story of Christ and John the Baptist. Look at this scroll. It's from the New Testament. But that doesn't fit with anything else found around here. Does it? But here it is. Someone hid it in this cave long after those other scrolls were stashed away. These two bodies were buried later too."

She was thinking.

"David, what does the New Testament say about where John the Baptist was executed?"

"It says Herod had John beheaded at Machaerus on the other side of the Dead Sea. Just a few miles south of Qumran. And that he was baptized by Jesus in the Jordan River. Right over there somewhere."

"So now it all makes sense, David. And this missing scroll explains it."

"Not quite," I said. "We still don't know who wrote this missing scroll. We have to do some tests on it and date it."

I thought about the Dead Sea Scrolls and what they said, and the similarities between the Essenes and the first Christians. The rituals of baptism. The communal meals. The sharing of property. I thought how both these groups had organized themselves in much the same way. The old Hebrews had divided themselves into twelve tribes and the early Church had twelve apostles. And now we had another twelve. At *Secacah*.

Cave XII.

But deep down I was suspicious about this scroll. It looked authentic, but I had seen lots of things over the years that looked authentic and weren't. A simple C14 test would give us a good idea about how old it is.

"Whoever did this did it so everything follows the Bible right down to the last detail," Gita said. "As far as frauds go it makes the Piltdown Skull look like nothing."

"Fraud or not they were still murderers, Gita. They killed these two men."

She just shook her head.

"There were lots of murderers in those days," she said. "Just like now. Not much has changed, has it?"

That was when she noticed we had company.

"People," Gita whispered, pointing over my shoulder.

Four men were about fifty yards away on the lower ground. They were standing there watching us and then they started coming closer. We had nowhere to go. All we could do was wait. The man at the front of the group waved at us to get our attention.

"Hello!" he said. He kept walking toward us, the others following behind. "I want you to give that to me."

He pointed to the little scroll in my hands. His English was good and my first thought was that he might be a journalist. They seemed to be coming out of the woodwork. I immediately tightened my grip on the scroll. There was no way he would get it from me and he caught the determination in my eye. When he was only a few feet from us he stopped and the three other men came up beside him. I couldn't tell if they were armed, but in the Holy Land lots of people carry guns. Journalists too. But now I realized these men weren't reporters at all. I could tell by their faces. They wore too much conviction for that. The man stuck his hand out.

"Professor Marr," he said. "Give that to me. We don't want any trouble."

"You know my name," I said.

"Yes."

"You better do what he says," Gita said.

Still, I hesitated. Two of the men started talking. I didn't know what they were saying because it was Hebrew.

They were Jews.

Then one of them put his hands on his hips to show that they meant business. He was the biggest of the four, a good three or four inches over six feet. Solid. Square. Broad shoulders. His head was shaved.

Gita nudged me and said to give them the scroll. Reluctantly, I handed it over.

"Wise decision," said the one in front. He unrolled the scroll. "What is this?"

His eyes met mine. He appeared to be in his mid to late twenties, a young man with sharp features. Not the type who liked small talk.

"What is this?" he said again. "And why is it so important to you?"

He looked at Gita.

"It's a scroll," she said.

"I can see that. But what language is it?"

"Old Hebrew."

"Old?"

"Ancient."

He opened the smaller scroll inside.

"And this?"

"Same thing," Gita said.

"What does it say?"

She said nothing. He was getting impatient.

"What does it say!"

Gita and I just stood there. I didn't take kindly to men, especially men I didn't know, yelling at my wife like that. But they were four and I was one and not only that, I was old enough to be their father. Then just like that he changed his approach. He smiled and spoke softly.

"I'm going to find out what it says anyway. If not from you from someone else who can tell me." He started to examine the scroll in his fingers. "It's parchment of some kind. Goatskin. Sheepskin. Cowskin." He looked at me. "Parchment was used as a substitute for papyrus. Right? And this is where the Dead Sea Scrolls were found. No?"

He looked about.

"You seem to know something about this," I said. "Who are you?"

"My name is Levi Ashkol."

He seemed very proud of himself.

"You're right, Professor Marr. I do know something about this. I used to study archeology. Just like you. But I don't know what this says and you're going to tell me. Aren't you?"

I took a long breath.

"The first scroll ... the bigger one ... is from the Book of Matthew," I said.

"But that's Christian. What about the other scroll? The little one inside? What's that?"

"We don't know. We have to test it. Do a C14."

He looked at me.

"You're lying," he said. "You know what it is. You know exactly what it is."

"Why would I be lying?"

"Because it's something important. Why else would you be here? In this place. Where the Dead Sea Scrolls come from. Hmm?"

I said nothing.

He rolled up the small scroll, put it back inside the other one and rolled that up too. Then he reapplied the strap to the outside.

"Thank you for this," he said.

"What are you going to do with it?" I asked him.

"You don't have to worry about that."

"But what if it's not real? What if it's a fake?"

"You are asking the wrong question. What you should be asking is what if it's real. And I'll tell you. It's a Dead Sea Scroll that's been missing all these years. It was written by Jews. Jews who used to live here."

He swept his hands out to either side.

"Right here in this very place. Two thousand years ago ... more than that ... they lived here. The land is ours. All of it. This is just more proof."

"Proof of what?"

"Our cause."

"And what cause is that?"

He smiled and took a step closer to me.

"We don't want strangers living in our home."

Then without another word he turned around and started walking away. The others followed suit. We watched them head down to the lower ground where they jumped into a car and sped off in a trail of dust. They didn't look back at us.

"They're Israeli," Gita said.

"I know who he is," I said. "Robbie told me about him. Anything that shows the Jews have been here a long time they use. For their own purpose. And that's to get rid of all the Palestinians. All Arabs for that matter."

"They look like thugs to me," Gita said.

"They are. They come in all shapes and sizes, Gita. Religions too."

We decided to follow them, so we got into our jeep. We saw them hit the main highway, which ran along the shore of the Dead Sea, and then they turned west on the road to Jerusalem. It was a thirty-minute drive to the city. We tried to keep some distance from them, but managed to stay on their tale. There weren't many cars on the road. When they got to Jerusalem they turned south toward Bethlehem and still we followed behind, but on the way to Bethlehem we had to stop outside the town for the border patrol because we were now entering Palestinian-controlled territory. The four of them were a few cars ahead of us.

The *intifada* was still growing and tensions were high. Higher than normal even. First we had to go through the Israeli checkpoint. None of the Israeli soldiers looked more than eighteen. Wielding their ever-present Uzis they eyeballed us and then one of them stuck his head in the window asking for identification. I showed him our passports and my badge from the university. He said to go ahead, but warned us about the trouble from the day before. He said rocks had been thrown at Jews who were passing through. Thirty seconds later we got to the other side of the border patrol. The Palestinian checkpoint. These soldiers looked even younger than the Israelis. Once again I showed our passports and my university badge. They waved us through and I stepped on the gas.

Gita had never been to Bethlehem. Not once. It wasn't a place for Jews and not a single Jew lived there. Ever since the Palestinians gained control of the area, tourism had been taking a beating and few foreigners came anymore. It was too dangerous. Then we heard a church bell. It might have been from the Basilica of the Nativity. It dated from the fourth century and, according to Christian lore, had been built on the very site where Jesus was born. They say the family of Muhammad adh-Dhib, the young Bedouin shepherd who discovered the first scrolls, still lived in town.

The car with the four Israelis drove along the main street — Manger Street — right into the heart of Bethlehem. The road wound its way through an array of biblical sites before straightening out near the bus terminal. The basilica, the main attraction in town, was just up the road. Then their car stopped. I watched as the man who took the scroll from me — Levi Ashkol — got out. Then there was another man. In a robe. He looked like a clergyman. He handed Ashkol some money and, in return, Ashkol gave him the scroll. Gita and I stepped out of our car and tried to follow the man in the robe on foot. We watched as he went into the spacious courtyard around the basilica. People were there, a lot of people, and just like that he disappeared in the crowd.

CHAPTER THIRTY-EIGHT

THIRTY-EIGHT

The bustling market of Ben Yehuda Street is a short walk from the gates of the Old City. Its coffee shops, restaurants, boutiques and food markets are always teeming with life. This was where young and old came together to mingle, and to sample the wares of local merchants. I was walking through the crowded markets of Ben Yehuda, just as I had done many times before, on my way to see Eliraz. We had arranged to meet one last time at a popular pita shop before she would leave for her new job at the refugee camp. I still had a problem with that. It was a dangerous thing to do.

But that was Eliraz.

No cars were allowed on Ben Yehuda Street and as I strolled about amid the throngs of people it was hard to imagine the turmoil the Holy Land had been going through. Still, life was peaceful here, even flourishing.

I was late for our meeting. Just as I was leaving my office, a student had stopped me in the hall to ask about his paper, so I had to stay and talk to him. When I finally tore myself away, I had to rush to my car and speed off to the market.

After parking nearby, I was on foot across the road from the pita shop where Eliraz and I were supposed to meet. There were people everywhere, busy, laughing, enjoying their lunch at the outdoor tables spread about the roadway. I could see a young man and woman seated at a table, beside them a baby in a stroller, and an older couple, no doubt the doting grandparents. The baby, a little girl in a bright yellow dress, had ribbons in her hair. Her grandparents were making faces and giggling at her. Then I spotted Eliraz. She was standing on the street outside the entrance to the pita shop.

In the split second before the blast — for all I knew it could have been an earthquake — Eliraz saw me. She called my name out loud and waved.

"David! David!"

I waved back. From the corner of my eye I could see a man rushing across the roadway through the crowds. Heading straight for the pita shop. Then came the most horrible sound I had ever heard. An explosion. Even though I was across the street, it threw me right off my feet. At first, I couldn't see a thing for all the smoke and dust and those searing waves of heat. I tried to clear my eyes and that was when I heard the distinct soft sound of voices moaning. For thirty seconds or so it was like that. Shock. Relative quiet. And then mass hysteria.

Scores of people were screaming. Then there was the bellowing rage of sirens coming from everywhere and the mad rush of feet going in all directions. I saw then that my shirt was ripped. People were running into me and I was knocked down. I got up and called for Eliraz, but couldn't see her. Finally, I got my bearings. I looked across the street to where the pita shop had been. But now there was no pita shop, only a bombed-out building and the surreal sight of arms and legs and body parts all over the pavement. I looked closer. The baby girl was intact — I could tell because her body was so tiny — but she was dead. Both her parents were dead too. There was no sign of the grandparents.

I called Eliraz again, but my voice was lost in the frenzy because people were screaming names from all over the place. The sound of sirens got louder. It was like a war zone. Two Orthodox Jews were scraping bits of flesh from the still-standing wall of the building next to the pita shop. Human remains were splattered on the trees nearby and soon they were taking that too. For burial. At the same time an angry gang of young Israeli men started shouting in Hebrew and this Hebrew I could understand.

"Death to Arabs! Death to Arabs!"

I didn't know then how many people died in the market that day. The only thing I knew was that it was the work of a suicide bomber. We found out later he had wired himself with sticks of dynamite, and bolts and nails to serve as shrapnel. He was a young schoolboy of sixteen whose father and older brother had been arrested earlier. The family had lived in one of the refugee camps. To the Israelis he was a terrorist and to the Palestinians a martyr.

Then we learned something else about him, something that was never reported in the press. It was Jamil who found out. A few days before his death the boy had moved out of his parents' home and into the home of a friend, and it wasn't the home of a Palestinian or even that of a Muslim. It was the home of a Christian. The boy had converted to Christianity. When he died he had a cross around his neck. He had traded his life for the lives of Jews he had never met. A whole family was wiped out and scores of people were injured.

One of the dead was Eliraz.

CHAPTER THIRTY-NINE

THIRTY-NINE

It was told to me like this. A priest rapped on the front door, which was answered by a little boy, and he was a beautiful little boy. His dark hair was tousled on top, his face full and round with the rosy cheeks of a cherub, his lips the color of mischief.

"Good morning," the priest said.

"Hi," said the boy.

"Is your mother home?"

In a moment she appeared. "Can I help you?" she said.

"I am Father Anthony Smith. I live at the rectory down the street. At the church. We're doing a fund-raising drive for an expansion of our church. There is a new subdivision going in and we're expecting ... hoping ... for some new members. I was wondering if you might be able to make a small donation."

"A donation?"

"Anything would be appreciated."

"Fine." She opened the door.

"My name is Michael," the boy said. "I'm three."

His mother laughed.

"Father Anthony Smith. Fifty-nine years old. Pleasure to meet you."

"What's that around your neck?" the boy asked, staring at the white collar.

"You don't know?"

The boy shook his head. His mother told him to run off and play, but he didn't move.

"He's never seen a priest before?" the man said.

"We're Jewish," said the woman.

"Oh. And you're going to make a donation?"

"Sure. Why not? Just a moment. I'll get my purse."

"You're old," the boy said, his eyes still fixed on the white collar. His mother returned and handed the priest some money. "You're almost as old as my *zayda*," the boy said.

"Who?" the priest asked.

"Michael is talking about my father," the woman said. "His grandfather."

"Oh," said the priest. "Here. Sign this and we'll send you an income tax receipt. And I'd like you to have one of our cards. So I take it the boy's grandfather must be pretty old?"

"Not at all. Michael thinks everyone is old. Everyone who's more than three."

The boy was still looking at the priest. "He's an *arkee ... jist*," he attempted, his head jerking with the last syllable the way it always did when he tried to say that word.

"A what?"

"An archeologist," his mother said, as she signed the form.

"Really? What's his name? If you don't mind my asking."

"David Marr. He's in the Holy Land right now with my mother. She's an archeologist too."

"Both of them? Really?" The priest struck a relaxed pose. Comfortable. "So what are they doing there?" he asked nonchalantly. "Digging?"

"I don't know."

"Maybe they found something. Did they? Find something?"

"Why do you say that?"

The priest shrugged. She looked at him. He caught the glance and changed his tone. "Are you an archeologist too?" he asked.

She thought that was funny. "Hardly. I'm busy enough with Michael thank you. But I teach part-time."

"Archeology?"

"No. English literature."

The priest smiled. "Well it's been very nice meeting you. And your son." He glanced at the name she had signed. "Jennifer ... Glass. Thank you very much Mrs. Glass. We appreciate your contribution."

"If we're going to be neighbors you should call me Jennie. Everyone calls me Jennie."

The priest gave her a friendly nod and she shut the door. Then he walked across the street, but didn't stop at the next house or any house at all for that matter. He ambled along the sidewalk, looking over his shoulder to make sure he wasn't being watched. But why would he be? His eyes constantly on the house, he turned around and waited at the corner. Soon the little boy came out as the priest knew he would and he was alone. Jennie should have kept her eye on him, but any mother knows you can't watch your children every minute of the day. It just wasn't possible. He jumped onto his tricycle and started peddling madly. It didn't take him long to build up speed. He passed the first house, then the second and then the third. His feet were peddling with great motion, but he wasn't travelling that fast. Not fast for a fit man of fifty-nine. After all, it was only a tricycle.

CHAPTER FORTY

FORTY

I wasn't awake when Jennie phoned or asleep for that matter. It was some state in between, but just the same I was emotionally spent. A wreck. I kept thinking about the bombing in the marketplace and its aftermath. The little baby and the human limbs everywhere. I couldn't get the picture out of mind. And Eliraz. We were supposed to meet at the pita shop.

It could have been me.

When Jennie's call came I was in the living room watching TV — they were profiling the victims — and the moment I heard her voice I knew something was wrong. My first thought was her diabetes. Jennie never had any serious complications since she had always been meticulous about her condition, even as a child, but there was always the potential for danger. And so, I thought the worst. I could sense the panic in her voice and then she said something about Michael.

My grandson.

"What happened? Is he all right?"

She said he was fine, but she had an awful scare. Michael had been missing for almost an hour. It was any mother's greatest fear.

"That was the longest hour of my life," Jennie said. "I went crazy. He was out on his bike and we couldn't find him. I called the neighbors. His friends. Nobody knew where he was. I was all set to call the police when he turned up at the door with a priest."

"A priest?"

She said it was the same man who had come to the house earlier collecting donations for his church. I don't know why, but I had a flash of Brian just then. In the tunnel. Below the Old City. I had been thinking a lot about Brian lately. At that moment the possibility of something happening to my grandson was the worst thing I could imagine.

"I wanted to call the church to thank him for bringing him back but I didn't know his name," Jennie said. "But he did give me a card. The writing was in Latin."

Jamil had been staying with Gita and me at our apartment, and it was the ringing of the phone that woke all of us up. The two of them were standing beside me when I was talking to Jennie, both listening intently.

Jennie started reading the Latin words to me. I grabbed a pen and scribbled down what she was saying. She said there was a telephone number on the card and she read that to me too. Then Gita had a few words with Jennie and a moment later she hung up. Meanwhile, Jamil was busy studying the Latin words I had written on a slip of paper.

Solum in ecclesia christi domi davidis verus pacis invenitur.

Jamil gave me the gravest of looks. "David," he said. "Now your family is being watched. On the other side of the world."

The Latin words meant 'Only in the church of Christ will the House of David find true peace.' For the first time in my life that I could ever remember I saw fear — true fear — on the face of Jamil. It was there in his eyes. I looked at the phone number Jennie gave me, and dialed.

CHAPTER FORTY-ONE

FORTY-ONE

Jamil once told me there is no due process in the Vatican. He called it an absolute dictatorship. "Not a military junta but a religious one," he said. The Church's influence had spread to more than a billion people around the world and to someone like me with an ear for history it was as if the legions of the Roman Imperial Army had conscripted them. A department called the Sacred Congregation for the Doctrine of the Faith had once dared to call itself the Holy Inquisition and an inquisition it was. It would weed out heretics and undesirables, and it didn't matter if they were inside or outside the Church. It would deal with Protestants and Jews, and anyone deemed an enemy. It could silence any priest or nun with the threat of excommunication, but how it actually worked had long been shrouded in mystery.

I made the call. There was a momentary delay before someone came on the line. I identified myself. Another delay and then a different voice.

"Professor Marr?"

There was an accent. Italian. The voice was heavy, deep and slow as if great time was at hand.

"What do you want with me?" I said.

"With you? Nothing." A pause, a clearing of the throat and

what sounded like a sip from a drink. "I won't waste my words. You are walking on dangerous ground. We want to examine what you found. Strictly for the cause of science, Professor Marr."

"Science?"

"It is important that we make a proper identification … of what you found … in the desert."

"We already did that."

"And who from the Church was involved in this procedure? I don't think you understand. You see archeological items of interest to the Church belong to the Church. It's as simple as that."

Each word he spoke weighed on me as if it were a piece of rubble from an ancient tel.

"Did you have Eliraz killed?" I asked him. "In the market?"

"That was the work of a suicide bomber."

"Who died with a crucifix around his neck."

"Maybe he saw the light before he did his deed."

"Did you ..."

"Enough questions. Now you listen to me. You would be wrong to underestimate us. It would be a very bad mistake. I want you to listen and listen carefully. I am asking for your cooperation."

"What are you talking about?"

"We know about you and how you stole from the desert and we also know about your past. You are meddling in things that don't concern you, Professor Marr."

"They don't?"

"No. Now I will only tell you once. We will make an exchange. You will give us what we want and in return we will grant you peace. *Pacis*."

Jamil was next to me listening to everything.

"An exchange?" I said.

"That's right."

"And where will this exchange take place?"

Before there was time for a response, Jamil whispered something to me. I nodded in agreement.

"How about the desert?" I said. "At Qumran. At the ruins of the Essene monastery by the Dead Sea."

Another pause. There was more talking. Two other voices were in the background.

"Fine then. When?"

At first I suggested the next day, but Jamil shook his head and raised two fingers in the air.

"Better make it the day after tomorrow," I said. "But it must be late. After it gets dark."

"The stroke of midnight?"

"Yes. Midnight."

"Fine, Professor Marr. Until Qumran then."

CHAPTER FORTY-TWO

FORTY-TWO

We were ready for the final step in the forensics lab. Electron microscopy. Jamil had wanted the extra day so we could extract DNA from the hair sample and clone it in a living cell. It was the last thing to be done. We were in my lab and he was busy washing his hands in the sink preparing for the task when we heard something from the hall.

It came from outside the door and sounded like the shuffling of feet. Jamil lifted his head and instinctively reached for his obsidian knife. Taking that as a cue I raised the sides of the plexiglass enclosure of the mummy, closed it up and reapplied the white sheet on top. Then there was more noise. I didn't want to believe that someone was trying to break into my lab — and not through a window this time. But there was no mistaking it. Some person was out there in the hall working the lock. Jamil motioned for me to move against the wall, while he stationed himself just inside the door.

The tinkering noises from the hallway persisted. The inside lock on the door — the dead bolt — was what they were after.

The first lock was solved quickly and the door opened a fraction of an inch, the dead bolt still in place. Then they started working away on that one. At that moment Jamil and I weren't even breathing. We were frozen stiff. Waiting. Waiting for what we didn't know. Then my telephone rang and it shook both of us with a start. The noise from outside stopped. The phone rang once. Twice. Three times. On the fourth ring the after-hours recording kicked in and the phone went silent. For the longest time there was nothing and I thought maybe they — whoever they were — had decided to leave. But then I heard a noise unlike anything I had ever heard before. It was a long sharp whistle, only quieter, and with it the dead bolt just exploded along with a sizeable chunk of the door.

When the intruder burst in Jamil was flat against the wall inside the door. He immediately swung himself around and his huge square fist caught the man flush in the middle of the face. In boxing they call this a roundhouse and it's very effective, especially for someone as strong as Jamil. He broke the man's nose on impact, likely in several places, for the sound of bone crunching is unique. The air erupted from him, but there was a gun. With a silencer on the barrel.

So much for that strange whistling noise.

After the blow from Jamil, the man fell to the floor in a heap and dropped his gun. Jamil screamed for me to get it, but I was useless. Even more than useless. I couldn't think straight. I had never touched a gun in my life. A few seconds more and the man started coming around. He struggled to his knees, his fingers grappling with his face, feeling around to see what remained of his nose. He tried to breathe, but could only do it through his mouth. A pool of blood was on the floor below him.

"Who are you?" demanded Jamil, his hand wielding that little knife of his. Then with a nod he motioned for me to get the gun. This time I managed to pick it up.

The stranger didn't say anything. There was only a look of shock and incomprehension. Jamil then switched to Arabic and now the man began to talk. He was still rubbing his battered face. It was all covered in blood.

"Keep the gun on him!" Jamil cried.

I pointed the gun uncertainly. Nothing seemed real. There was an instant of eternity when I stared into the eyes of this person and he stared into mine. He was young and dark, an Arab

I think, and then I looked a little closer. I had seen him before. Was it Mahmoud the cleaner?

"*Mahmoud!*" I said. "You!"

He was full of fear and I don't think it was because of me even though I was the one with the gun.

"You know this man?" Jamil said.

I told him who he was and about our two earlier meetings and how he had been snooping around outside my lab. I told him about the Ateret Cohanim and Levi Ashkol.

That was enough for Jamil. He took out his obsidian knife and showed Mahmoud its fine edge. He cut through the air with the blade, little swipes going this way and that. Mahmoud was terrified. He forgot about his nose and started pleading for his life. In Arabic. It was a scene of heated confusion and words I didn't understand. There was an exchange between the two of them and then Jamil explained.

"Another man is outside. In a truck. You can guess what they came for."

Jamil spoke to him again, this time in English.

"I have a bad temper and you've brought out the worst in me. Your face is in bad shape and you're losing a lot of blood. I'm a physician and can fix you up or I can just let you bleed to death. But first you better tell me who sent you."

Mahmoud replied in Arabic.

"What is it?" I said. "What did he say?"

"They want to take it to Egypt and wash it in the Nile and do their business," Jamil said.

Then Mahmoud screamed "*Allahu-Akbar! Allahu-Akbar!*" He looked at Jamil.

"If you are a true Muslim you will not stop me," Mahmoud said.

"If I am a true Muslim!" said Jamil, and with that he got very angry. He slapped Mahmoud across the face with the back of his hand.

More blood splattered onto the floor. Mahmoud's face was getting worse by the second. It was swelling in front of my eyes. His twisted nose, what was left of his nose, was hanging on by threads of flesh. I thought I could make out bone.

"You see this knife?" Jamil said to him. "It's thousands of years old. It was used by Ethiopians and you know what they used it for?" Mahmoud shook his head. "To slice open the skin of a man's penis. For circumcision."

Now the look on Mahmoud's face was one of pure horror. He stared at Jamil, and the sheer ferocity in Jamil's eyes left precious little doubt about him using that knife of his. Then Mahmoud turned to me. He saw how unsteady I was with the gun and he made his decision. He could surrender to his fate or go after one of us.

He chose me.

It happened quickly. I could have shot him if I had reacted right away, but no. He rushed into me and knocked the gun from my hand. Then Jamil made his move. Jamil wasn't a young man, but he was a bull. He lunged for Mahmoud's neck, his hands in a stranglehold, squeezing the life out of him. Mahmoud choked and gasped. His face was turning blue. But just when I thought he was going to black out he kicked Jamil in the groin. Jamil doubled over and fell on top of him. The two of them were grappling with each other, but I couldn't tell who was doing what.

Jamil was much bigger than Mahmoud.

There was a grunt and then blood. Jamil had been stabbed with the obsidian knife! The blood started pouring from a gash in his arm and a fever took hold of him. He became possessed. A raging madman. He made a fist and smashed Mahmoud in the face. Once, twice, three times, four times he hit him. I thought he would never stop hitting him. Mahmoud's face turned into a bloody pulp, as if there were no bones holding it together.

I had never seen so much blood.

Finally, Jamil stopped. Mahmoud lay on the floor. Jamil asked me for the gun and I handed it to him. But maybe that was a mistake. Jamil was still so enraged that I thought he might use it, and so did Mahmoud.

When your life is hanging in the balance you can summon the power for a last stand. This was Mahmoud's last stand. Somehow he found the strength to climb to his feet, a steady stream of blood and flesh dripping from his face, and with a terrifying scream he bolted straight into Jamil. The two men fought again. Amid the grunts and groans there was a sharp whistle, and then one of them dropped to the floor in a thud. At first I couldn't tell who. Then Jamil raised his head and looked at me in numb silence.

"Are you all right?" I asked him.

He nodded in between his hurried breaths. It took me a few seconds to realize what had happened. Mahmoud was on the floor. He wasn't moving. Jamil turned him over and felt for a pulse.

"We have to get rid of him," Jamil said, and it was so matter of fact.

I was in shock.

"Is he dead?" I said.

"Your mortuary ... your morgue ... we'll take him there … and clean up the mess … remove every sign of it."

"Is he dead?"

"Yes he's dead damn it! Now listen to me! We don't have much time. We have to take his body to the morgue … and make him look old … very old."

I didn't know what Jamil was talking about.

"Shouldn't we call the police?" I said.

"The police? And have them come here and take photographs? Come to your senses man! We can't do anything of the kind."

"But he could have killed us!"

"Yes. We're fortunate how things turned out, aren't we? Now are you going to help me or do I have to do this by myself?"

Maybe it was because Jamil had so much experience with corpses, but he was so cool it was frightening. He moved quickly yet methodically, and began to clean up the room. I glanced out the window and saw a small pickup truck driving away. It was the other man, the driver Jamil had mentioned. Undeterred, Jamil went to work on Mahmoud's remains and never before had I realized what a fine line it was that separated life from death.

Jamil took out his cutting instruments and didn't waste any time extracting the bullet before washing it down the sink. I had a key to the room he wanted — the morgue, the forensics lab — and soon he was ready.

"Why did you take the bullet out?" I asked him.

Jamil looked at me. "It's one thing to find a mummy from ancient times, David, but it's quite another to have one with a bullet inside. Tell me. How would you explain that?"

We carried Mahmoud's lifeless body to forensics and it wasn't long before he became a nameless commodity. It was like a dream. Jamil asked me where the chemicals were stored. I told him. Then he grabbed a syringe and injected the body with an arsenic solution. I had no idea what he was doing. Then he added more preservatives and doused Mahmoud's remains with a mixture that gave him an aged appearance. It was remarkable how quickly he managed to achieve this effect. The corpse — that's all it was — looked dried out and *ancient*. Like a mummy. No one would know that Mahmoud was alive just a short time ago. I looked at Jamil and he could see the terror in my eyes. It was the second time in the space of a few days that I had witnessed death.

"David, it was either him or us," he said, putting away his tools. "Besides … he was a thief … a common thief … like Barrabas."

"Barrabas?"

I didn't know what he was getting at.

"The man who was freed by Pilate," he said. "There was a choice to be made. It was either him or Christ. The people chose Barrabas and we're going to choose him too."

CHAPTER THIRTY-THREE

FORTY-THREE

The last word of the Old Testament is 'curse' and it is something Gita had mentioned many times. The fourth and final chapter of Malachi begins with the judgment of the wicked and the rising of the sun of righteousness.

'Remember ye the law of Moses my servant, which I commanded unto him in Horeb for all Israel, with the statues and judgments. Behold, I will send you Elijah the prophet before the coming of the great and dreadful day of the Lord. And he shall turn the heart of the fathers to the children, and the heart of the children to their fathers, lest I come and smite the earth with a curse.'

Gita said it was an omen, a warning for all humankind to amend its ways and set itself free on the road to salvation. I thought it a strange way to end such a book.

"It's the best way," she said. "It holds out a vision, a vision of what's ahead unless we change our ways. It's the same with the New Testament. The Book of Revelation ends with the devil being loosed upon the earth after being bound for a thousand years. He goes forth to do his evil all over the world and all those who are deceived are cast into Hell."

Both the Old and New Testaments are ominous in their final message, and it was something to hear Gita quoting the New

Testament. But ever since I had told her about my discovery, and her visits to the Ecole Publiques and the Vatican Archives, and then our return to the caves of Qumran, Gita's edges had become more rounded. She even said that no single work possessed all the answers, that they all "begged and borrowed" from each other, and she included the Koran.

Night was falling and Jamil was making the final preparations. This whole thing was his idea, and while it was dangerous doing nothing was even more dangerous. He told us what to do, starting with hiding the body of Mahmoud in the university mortuary. That was where we had always kept corpses for study. But now that mortuary possessed in its midst a well-disguised creature of antiquity. Then Jamil said he would take this corpse and *crucify* it.

He was a pathologist who knew human anatomy and I was an archeologist who knew about the Romans. He asked me about the skeletal remains of Jehohanan and the Roman spike found in his foot, so I gave him the exact dimensions. Then he took out his many knives along with a very large screw, and proceeded to cut openings in the wrists and feet of poor Mahmoud. It wasn't long before this dead man, this *mummy* he had just created, was turned into something else again.

"We must give every impression that *this* is what you found in the desert," Jamil said. "The exchange will buy us some time."

We had agreed to make the exchange with Cardinal Fiori at twelve o'clock midnight. The plan was to pass off Jamil's hastily mummified body — the body of Mahmoud — as the thing they so desperately wanted.

"Do you think it will work?" I said.

"What do you mean?"

"Those people in Rome. At the Vatican. They have scientists. They will study this."

Jamil just shook his head.

"David, if someone is a real scientist why would they work at the Vatican? The place has nothing to do with science. Of course this will work. Trust me."

I found it incredible how Jamil could be so relaxed and calm at a time like this. I didn't know how anyone could be after what we had been through, never mind the procedure he had just performed on a human body. But he was. He excused himself to go speak with Robbie and then Gita came in to join me. We shared a private moment together. She talked about a dream she had.

"It was a message from Brian," she said. "He was reaching out to me. I think he was trying to tell me something."

"What was he telling you?"

"That I should leave something behind here. In this land of trouble. Palestine."

"What do you mean?"

"A contribution. I keep thinking about that woman from the university who was killed in the marketplace. I keep thinking about the children she wanted to teach. Those children at the refugee camp."

"What about them?"

"Who will teach them now?"

"I don't know."

"But don't you see, David? The value of a Jew in the same room with these Palestinian children? Showing them that we're all really the same people? And we are. We're all Semites. Isn't it foolish to raise these children to hate and despise Jews? How will any peace ever come to the Holy Land from that? So I was thinking ..."

"You were thinking what?"

"About teaching them in her place, at least, until they can find a permanent instructor."

"You!"

"Yes. And maybe they can teach me a little about themselves too. I'm going to do it, David."

"But Gita ..."

"Just for a little while. It won't be for long."

"It's too dangerous. I won't let you."

"Aren't you planning to do something very dangerous yourself tonight?" I had no answer for that. "I already made up my mind. Or maybe Brian made up my mind. I know he would want me to do this."

I didn't know what to say.

"I'm not afraid," she said. "Really I'm not."

Just then Jamil returned. "It's time," he said. "We have

to go now."

I squeezed Gita's shoulders. "I don't think you should come with us," I said. "We'll be all right."

"But you need me, David. You need me."

"This will be no place for a woman."

She pressed her fingers against my mouth. "My place is with you."

CHAPTER FOURTY-FOUR

FORTY-FOUR

It was as dark as any night could be and the sky was clear with countless stars. There were more stars than I had ever seen before. It was so beautiful. The heavens were parading their majesty in a spectacle that only the desert night can unveil and it was all there for the four of us. Me. Gita. Jamil. And Robbie. We were in a small pick-up truck. Jamil looked to the cosmos and pointed.

"That is the constellation Orion," he said. "It's unusually brilliant tonight. You see those three stars in a row and the two bright ones at the bottom? The brightest of them is Rigel."

I followed the line of his finger and searched among the millions of stars in the night sky. Then I saw it. One star was shining brighter than all the others.

"To the Greeks it was Orion the Hunter," Jamil said. "The three stars in the middle were his scabbard but the Pawnee Indians saw something else. Three deer. And the Egyptians saw something else again. Osiris."

I tried to imagine the shapes he was talking about.

"What you see is in the eyes of the beholder," Jamil said, as much to the night air as to me. "If only man could look at the world with a wider vision then maybe we would have peace. Peace in the Middle East I mean."

I turned my head and stared into the savage emptiness of the desert. Above was the black sky filled with a vast array of glistening stars, and below the sand and rock of the desert. Both of them — the sky and the desert — went on forever. There was nothing else.

"Rigel is a massive star," Jamil said, his eyes still wandering above. "And it will surely be something when it dies. The carbon will burn into oxygen and then iron and then gravity will take over and she'll just collapse and it will happen quickly. Very quickly. Just think of it, David. Why a star like that has been around for billions of years and then in a few seconds it dies. Poof! You see over there?" He pointed to another corner of the night sky. "In the year 1054 there was a super nova so bright that Chinese astronomers recorded it for weeks. Its remains are still visible as the Crab nebula in Taurus. Imagine. We can see light that takes billions of years to reach us and then you think back two thousand years and it's only a blip. Nothing. Absolutely nothing."

Gita joined in. "Sometimes I think whenever someone dies they leave a star behind," she said. "That's why there are so many of them. One for every person who ever lived."

"Then there is a star for your son," Jamil said. "Who knows? Maybe it's Rigel."

"Maybe," Gita said.

She smiled and looked so beautiful. I could see Brian's face in her and sensed that he was with us. I could feel his presence. The mood was abruptly broken by Robbie.

"I see them now!" he said with one hand on his binoculars and the other on the steering wheel of the truck carrying us.

I could make out images in the distance. It was a few minutes to midnight and we were on the road to Qumran. There wasn't far to go.

"I see vehicles," Robbie said, peering through the binoculars. "There is a small truck in the middle and a few jeeps in the front and back."

"How many?" I asked.

"Four jeeps I think."

"Four jeeps and a truck?"

"Yes. They are a ... a parade ... a con ... a con ..."

"Convoy," Jamil said. "It's a convoy."

"Yes," said Robbie. "A convoy. That was what I meant to say."

We didn't know what to expect. Only that they were determined, very determined, to get what they wanted.

"They have guns!" Robbie said.

I was in the back of the truck with Gita. When she heard that she took hold of my hands.

"Should we go back?" Robbie said.

"No," Jamil replied. "That would only invite their fire."

Jamil turned to face Gita and me in the back. He showed us the revolver he had brought. Just in case. He opened the chamber. It was fully loaded. I threw my arms around Gita and thought about her safety. About her being here. I thought about Jennie and our little grandson Michael back home.

"How many men do you see, Robbie?" I asked.

"Two. In each jeep. They look like Arabs."

"Bedouin," Jamil said. "Of course they have brought Bedouin. They know the desert well."

"So that would be eight men," I said.

"Eight men with guns!" Robbie replied.

Robbie looked at Jamil again, his eyes doing all the explaining necessary when it was eight guns against one.

"What about the truck? Who's in there?" I asked him.

"There are two ... no ... three men in it. They are dressed different than the others. Not Arabs. One of them is in uniform. He looks like a soldier. Another man is in street clothes. And the one in the middle is wearing a robe."

"That would be our man," Jamil said.

We were approaching the ruins of Qumran, a two-thousand-year-old ghost town. Jerusalem was twenty miles to the west, a short drive, but then everything in the Holy Land is close. The Dead Sea came into view, and the plain cut by the wadi that drained the Buqeia valley, and the caves where it all began. As the distance narrowed between those jeeps and our truck, my mind drifted to the real meaning of this place. I thought not only of the Essene ruins, but the Holy Land, this *space* that was so contested through the ages. I was consumed by its history and its endless passion for violence. There had been so much bloodshed in so tiny a space — Jerusalem to the west, Bethlehem immediately south of that, and further along, Hebron and Masada. The Dead Sea, from one end to the other, is barely thirty miles long, and a smaller body of water still is the Sea of Galilee with the Jordan River connecting the two of them. I thought of the towns and the camps and the death. The sheer volume of death through the years is enough to numb the senses. This region has known more turmoil than anywhere on earth and all because of a prize that can never be won.

Jamil was right. They were Bedouin in those jeeps. Eight of them. Two to a jeep. And inside the truck were three men, one of them a member of the Swiss Guards who kept close to the cardinal. I glanced over my shoulder. Our precious cargo was rocking gently in the back. The air was cold, the silence overpowering.

"We have done all that we can," Jamil said. "Now we're in the hands of God."

Jamil's Hebrew was perfect and his skin dark like the color of an Israeli. He could pass for an Israeli. He could pass for the Egyptian that he was or a Jordanian or a Saudi. He knew all the people like the back of his hand — their language, their customs, their history. Beside him was my young assistant Robbie, an Israeli who only wanted to bring his country into a new era of peace with its neighbors, if that was possible. He was full of a naivety common to the youth of Israel, but deeply committed to his homeland. In the back of the truck with me was Gita, who had always looked at the world with a fine edge and who had always brought a fierce energy to anything she tackled. She had been with me for so long and she insisted on being with me now.

The convoy stopped. The Bedouin tribesmen stepped out from the jeeps, each of them with a menacing Israeli uzi slung over the shoulder. Just then I thought of the irony Eliraz had mentioned about the Palestinian woman who spent her nights crocheting woollen *yarmulkes* for the Orthodox Jewish settlers, the same enemy her husband would face by day. And I stared for the longest time at those uzis. There was a moment of silence and then the military officer emerged from the truck. He crossed his arms with an unbridled self-assurance and looked at us. The man in the robe appeared next, a large crucifix around his neck.

"I am frightened," Robbie said from behind the steering wheel.

"We are all frightened," said Jamil, concealing his gun under his jacket. "But you can derive strength from fear."

Jamil and I stepped out from our truck.

"You are David Marr the archeologist," said the man in the billowing robe. It was the same voice I had heard over the phone and the same man I had seen in Turin. There was no mistaking him. I nodded. "We meet again," he said. Then he turned to Jamil. "And you must be the Egyptian doctor Jamil Hassad. I have heard much about you." Jamil lowered his head respectfully. "I am Cardinal Fiori."

I was afraid. We were so vulnerable. But Jamil remained calm.

"We have brought what you asked," he said.

"We shall see."

Cardinal Fiori waved his hand. The man in street clothes stepped out of the truck and so, now there were three men in front of us. Cardinal Fiori didn't move anywhere without his Swiss Guard beside him. He walked with a slow methodical cadence, his red robe flowing in the air as if he wasn't even walking but gliding across the sand and rock. All the while, those uzis were perched on the shoulders of the Bedouin. We escorted the cardinal and the two with him to our truck. Jamil released the catch and the back gave way.

Cardinal Fiori immediately raised his hand to his mouth and gasped out loud. His face went white. He came closer, looked at me and then back at the two men with him, and then fell to his knees and crossed himself many times. He cried out in Latin. I didn't know what he said for he spoke very quickly. It was as if one long word had poured from his lips. A moment later and the other two helped him to his feet, the officer obediently dusting the sand from his clothes. Then Cardinal Fiori looked off toward the sea.

"Is that the old monastery over there?" he said. "The ruins?"

"Yes," I said. "The Essene monastery."

"I have never seen it before. You believe the Dead Sea Scrolls were written there?"

"Yes I do."

He looked at me full of curiosity, but curiosity embedded with dread and scorn.

"Would you like to see it for yourself?" I asked him.

"See it?"

"The monastery. The *scriptorium*."

"The *scriptorium*? The room where you think they were written?"

"Yes."

He appeared to be studying my invitation and then he said yes, he would like to see it. He nodded to the officer who immediately began to frisk me. I hoped he wouldn't do the same to Jamil. Thankfully, he didn't. The officer told Cardinal Fiori that I was clean and said he would come with us, but he was told to stay behind.

"Leave me with the archeologist," Cardinal Fiori said. "Alone. I wish to speak with him."

We walked over to the ruins, just the two of us, and once we were beyond earshot of the others he began talking to me.

"I remember you from Turin," he said. "I could have had you arrested for what you did but in the end it didn't matter. So I let you be. Usually I am not so forgiving."

I thought it strange to hear such a man speak words like that.

"But that stunt your wife pulled at the archives was something I couldn't let be. And I didn't."

The words were slow. Deathly slow.

"Tell me, Professor Marr. You are an educated man. You have spent much time in the Holy Land. Do you think there is a possibility that Jesus was a member of the Essenes?"

I had to be careful. Very careful.

"I don't know," I said. "Maybe he was."

"I fear that you attach too much importance to the words of Philo Judaeus and Flavius Josephus. You have read the *refutatio omnium haeresium* of the writer Hippolytus?"

"I'm familiar with it."

"Then you are aware that there are some contradictions to Josephus in his writings."

He wore this air of supreme confidence. I was compelled to

reply to what he had just said.

"There are contradictions in all writings," I said.

I wasn't sure of the look he gave me then, but it was anything but warm. He said there wasn't any mention of the Essenes in the New Testament. Not one. He was full of doubt about the importance of this community and I had the distinct impression that he would go see the ruins if only to prove me wrong. I took up the challenge. I told him when the monastery was built and when it was occupied, and about the Jewish revolt against the Romans, but he was oblivious to it all. However, once we were near the ruins and I pointed out the fissure running through the steps to the monastery, he seemed to gather interest.

"There was an earthquake here in 31 B.C.," I said. "Thirty thousand people died."

"Remarkable," he said, examining the crack in the stone with his foot. "And you know the date from Josephus no doubt?"

I didn't give him the satisfaction of an answer. I explained that the site was founded in the eighth century B.C. and had been inhabited until the destruction of the first temple.

"In 586 B.C.," he said, demonstrating his knowledge of Jewish history.

I told him about a fortress being built and that its cistern was the only structure from the first temple that survived. I told him how the site had been abandoned for five hundred years only to be rebuilt. By the Essenes. I showed him how the tower in the main building block had been reinforced with stones around its base after the earthquake. I told him about the many coins that had been found here, their dates stamped clearly. Then we entered the ruins and I led him to the long chamber of the *scriptorium*. I showed him the plaster tables, the debris remaining from the old ink wells and the bench that ran around the walls. I explained that the ancient manuscripts were assembled here in this very room. I pointed out the cemetery with the thousand graves nearby. Finally, he raised his hand.

"I have seen enough," he said.

"What do you think?" I asked him.

He looked at me with conviction. "I think this place should be steamrolled by bulldozers and buried for all time. It proves nothing. These ruins could be from any time. Anyone could have lived here. Maybe the Romans lived here. Scholars themselves are anything but unanimous in their views. Some say the scrolls were written in Jerusalem. Some say this place was the home of a wealthy nobleman."

"I think those people are wrong. Most scholars agree that the Essenes lived here and wrote the scrolls. But there are many similarities between passages in the Old Testament and the New Testament and ..."

He raised his hand again, imploring me to stop. "Conjecture. Innuendo. Allusion. But very dangerous. If I had my way this place would not be here tomorrow."

He lifted the edges of his red robe off the ground and shook the dust free.

"So what will you do now?" I asked him.

"What kind of question is that?"

"A simple one."

He stepped up to me, his lips mere inches from my face. His eyes were steely and cold. I could feel his hot breath on my skin.

"I'll tell you what we *could* do," he said. "We could erect a display at our museum in Rome. It would be a display of the only preserved body of a crucified man ever to come down through the ages. It would illustrate the abhorrence and finality of such a horrible execution. And why? To show the world the true power and meaning of the Resurrection. We could do that."

"I gather you will do many tests."

"Tests? What tests?"

"Your scientists. You want them to examine it, don't you? To see for themselves?"

He smiled again, but this time it was a different smile. "There will be no tests."

"But ..."

"You are a fool, Professor Marr. What do you think we're going to do? When I'm through with this there will be nothing left of that corpse. Nothing! It won't even exist. It will be as if it never existed. Never."

He spoke with a smug sense of pride and accomplishment. Then he turned and headed for the truck. The officer looked pleased to see him and Jamil was relieved to see me, but at the same time he had this great sense of urgency on his face. All the Bedouin appeared restless.

"We have a problem," Jamil said, pointing to the man in the street clothes. "He is a medical person with the Vatican and he did a brief examination of the mummy. But he only looked at it. He must have crossed himself a hundred times and then he said he wanted us to hand over the truck. Our truck! I told him we can't do that."

Cardinal Fiori exchanged a few words with this man and then he spoke to me. "You have delivered what you promised but Francesco here doesn't want to touch anything. He would prefer if you would just let us have the vehicle."

Jamil raised his hands. "No. That was not the agreement. This is our truck. We can't let you have it."

"We will pay you for it."

"That's not the point. It is our truck. Besides how would we get back from the desert?"

"We will take you."

Jamil looked the cardinal in the eye, his face revealing how little trust he had in him. Cardinal Fiori was not amused. He glanced behind him at the eight Bedouin standing with their uzis draped over their shoulders.

"I don't think you are in a position to bargain, Dr. Hassad."

"I'm afraid we can't give you the truck," Jamil repeated. "We had an agreement."

Cardinal Fiori spoke again to his man who repeated his unwillingness to move the body from our truck and then he shook his head impatiently. He wasn't a person who was used to waiting for things. The orders he gave just then were in Italian and after he said them the Swiss Guard cried out in Arabic. Immediately, all the Bedouin raised their guns to eye level. The guns were pointed at us.

Were they just going to kill us like that? Here? In the desert at Qumran? In the black of night?

At that moment, nothing was real. The past weeks had only been a dream. There was no mummy. There was no warning from Jamil. No one was hurt or dead. People weren't watching us or looking for us. There were no Arab tribesmen standing thirty yards away with uzis. The only thing real was the sound of the wind rolling through the desert. You could hear it and feel it. You could inhale it. It was a soft enduring whistle with no beginning and no end, and it just went on and on and on like always.

The world had stopped.

"Wait!"

The soft voice of a woman broke through the air. It was Gita. She had been sitting in our truck and came out of nowhere. Her face, except for her eyes, was covered by a kerchief that was tied into a knot below her chin. A shawl was draped over her shoulders and around her neck.

"They wouldn't dare shoot a Muslim woman," she whispered as she hurried by me before turning to the east where she flung herself onto the desert. She raised her hands above her head and spoke. In Arabic.

"Allahu-Akbar. Allahu-Akbar."

"Ash-ahdu-an-la-ilaha-illahah."

"Ash-hado anna muhammaden-rasulullah."

"Hayye-alas-salah."

"Hayye-alal-falah."

"Allahu-Akbar. Allahu-Akbar."

"La-illah-illalah."

The Bedouin tribesmen looked at each other. Then, one by one, they all dropped their guns and threw themselves on the sands. Praying. Cardinal Fiori and his two accomplices watched.

"Who are you?" he said to Gita when she got to her feet.

"One who knows that some men are not willing to risk the wrath of the *Ka*," she said.

"What are you talking about?"

She turned around to face the same Bedouin who a moment earlier had their uzis pointed at us. And she spoke to them in their own tongue. Then they picked up their guns and returned to their jeeps.

"These men would sooner shoot you than me," she said to Cardinal Fiori. "You have what you want. Now take it and let us go."

"Who are you?" he asked her again.

She didn't reply, but instead motioned for Robbie to bring our truck alongside theirs. Then the two of them, Robbie and Gita, transferred the body we had brought — our mummy, the remains of Mahmoud — from our truck to theirs.

"There," said Gita confidently, her face still covered by the kerchief. "Now you can go. You have your prize."

Just then I had the distinct feeling that Cardinal Fiori wanted only to satisfy his curiosity and grab the kerchief from Gita's face to reveal her identity, and if he had done that he wouldn't have seen a Muslim woman at all. But he did no such thing. His hands clasped together in the manner of a pontiff, he told his two men to get back inside their truck.

"You are a courageous woman," he said to Gita and then he stepped into the vehicle.

In a few seconds the four jeeps and truck were turned around and on their way. We watched them disappear until they were a thin line crawling along the white sands of the desert.

"If I didn't know better I would've thought you were a Muslim woman myself," Jamil said to Gita as she tore away the kerchief and shawl. "*Allahu-Akbar,*" he said.

"*Allahu-Akbar,*" Gita said with a smile.

CHAPTER FORTY-FIVE

FORTY-FIVE

We could have told them just as Professor Solnik had once told them. That we had found a crucified mummy in the desert that was two thousand years old and that someone or some group had gone to great pains to ensure its wounds matched the words written in the Book of St. Mark. But even with Professor Solnik it had taken years before anything concrete happened with the Dead Sea Scrolls and even then there were those who wanted no part of the truth. It was the same with the mummies of the pharaohs. There were people who wanted no part of the truth and it would have been the same this time as well because one thing that remains true throughout the ages is that people believe what they want to believe.

"Homines quod volunt credunt," Robbie once said to me.

Deep inside I still wanted to tell the world what we had found. A remarkable discovery — the mummified remains no less — of a man who had been crucified. It was something that had never been found before. We had done all these tests and literally risked our lives to do them. Some had already paid with their lives. But no. Gita and Robbie said we had to take it back. Return it to the desert. And Jamil agreed with them. He said there was nothing else we could do now.

"But what about science, Jamil?" I said. "What about science?"

Jamil did everything he could to make Mahmoud's corpse look like a victim of crucifixion. He made a cut in the chest cavity as if it were a sword wound. He made holes in the wrists and feet that were the right size for a Roman spike. He added arsenic and chemicals to make the holes look much older than they were. He did everything that was necessary to create enough time for us to do what we had to do. Give it back to the desert. It was funny because this was what Robbie wanted to do from the very beginning. But my curiosity got in the way.

Jamil put everything into perspective.

"Surely you of all people, David, know that feeble minds will never see if their eyes remain closed. No matter what you show them people will always have a choice. When you found the Dead Sea Scrolls they had a choice and many chose not to believe. It was the same when Galileo said the world was round and it was the same with every discovery ever made that didn't fit the doctrine of the day. This is a battle that will always be waged. Let us give thanks for those with insight and common sense to question their existence for without them the world would be an even more frightening place than it is."

How I wanted to tell everyone what we found at Qumran. How I wanted to tell about the tests we did and the headless skeleton and the missing scroll and what it told us about the secrets of bodily preservation in the desert sand. How I wanted to be the scientist that I always claimed to be. But I couldn't. We couldn't.

Jamil's words about the Dead Sea Scrolls took me back to that day long ago when we told them what we had found in the caves. It had been so difficult for Professor Solnik with those bombs going off everywhere. But he was a man of courage who didn't care what might happen to him because the scrolls were more important. *They matter more than me and they matter more than you,*" he had said.

It was the same now.

....

It was early morning and no one was about when Robbie and I were driving along the highway as we passed the ruins once more. We passed the caves east of El Buqeia and the Valley of Achor west of the Maritime Plain. We looked at the stilled waters of the Dead Sea and made our way to the sands where we first found it. But not back to the same spot. The Bedouin knew this place now and they would find it again, so we went two miles farther south until we came to a flat area full of emptiness.

Robbie and I didn't say a word to each other. We didn't have to. We disappeared into the black night, eased the mummy from the back of our truck, dug deep into the dirt and parted the sands with our shovels. One last time I looked at the face of this man, this mysterious man about whom I knew so much, yet so little, and we gave him back to the earth.

He would remain a secret known only to scientists who were too vulnerable and fearful to go any further. There was too much danger. Especially here. And so, our secret would remain a secret. The first sandstorm and no one would ever know what lay beneath the desert.

Jamil returned home to Alexandria, while Gita was busy preparing for her first morning at the school in the refugee camp. Her class would begin at eight o'clock sharp. I remember thinking of the Palestinian children she was going to teach and wondered how they might receive her.

"How I fear for this land," she told me just before she left. "I fear for all its inhabitants and especially for those leaders who have the courage and conviction to stand up against the violence. They are in great danger not only from other people but their own."

History would prove her words prophetic. With all the talks and speeches and years, there were times when peace seemed near, but it would always evaporate when the cauldron reached a boil. There was never peace in the Holy Land because of the deep-rooted anger that sank into the earth like the roots of a great tree that can never be toppled.

"Well Robbie," I said, "our adventure is done. Whatever work awaits us at the university will seem so mundane now, won't it?"

"What?"

My mistake. He wouldn't know that word. *Mundane.*

"I mean what should we do now?"

"Well I am going back to my studies," Robbie said. "As for you I think I know what Dr. Hassad would want you to do."

"What's that?"

"He would tell you to get in your car and drive up to the camp to be with your wife. She needs you. There is still time."

He glanced at his watch. I smiled at him and nodded, then turned and started to walk away.

"Wish her well for me," Robbie said. "It is a difficult mission she has taken for herself. But an admirable one. I wouldn't want anything to happen to her."

I took a few steps and stopped. Did I just hear right? Did Robbie really say what I thought he said?

"Robbie. You said '*wouldn't*'. That's a contraction."

"I did?"

"Yes you did. I think that's a first."

"Hmm. It must be your influence. I … *I've* been hanging around you too much I guess."

I got into my car and drove north out of the bustle of Jerusalem and into the wilderness where according to scripture the prophets once walked. From the road I could visualize time as it was for in many ways this land hadn't changed at all. It was just as bleak and coarse as ever. Hilly terrain with little greenery and even less water. *Jeshimon* the Hebrews called it. Desolation. A forbidding place where the snakes and scorpions thrived. A place which Gita once said could produce only monotheism.

Many years have passed since that time and yet, things remain much as they were in Palestine in 1947. You had two sides wrestling for the same land, two peoples still clinging to what they feel is their historic right. It was like that on the day when Robbie and I went back to Qumran and it will be like that tomorrow. It is the one certainty in the Holy Land.

On my way to the camp that day I drove through the Israeli settlements in Ramallah and Hallamish. Hallamish was a peaceful community. It stood on top of a picturesque hill and was so lovely that the residents called it *Neve Tzuf*, which means 'place of nectar.' Here before me was the stark contrast of the West Bank in full abundance. While the Arab settlements of the region were ramshackle at best, Hallamish was a modern community with homes of wood and stucco. The roads were paved with street lamps at the sides and the vision was that of a prosperous post-war America. But a little further along was the deadly refugee camp. I had never been to such a camp before, and the squalor and destitution were everywhere. In broken Arabic I asked where the school was and got directions with uncomfortable stares. A man who looked like a police officer asked for identification. I showed him everything I had. My driver's license, passport, work permit, university card. When he was satisfied, he let me proceed.

The school was a simple building and I hoped they had running water for many children were there. The mix was half Muslim, half Christian. Unemployment in the area was over fifty per cent and it was easy to see why the young grew up to hate Israelis.

Gita would have her hands full.

She didn't see me at first. I crept into the back of the room, while she was busy helping some of the younger ones ready themselves for the morning. For sure there would be a language problem, but Gita was very good with languages. Even though I had spent more time than she in the Holy Land, her knowledge of Arabic was much better than mine. Using her best colloquial Arabic she extended greetings and introduced herself, and was pleased to find that some of the older students had a rudimentary knowledge of Hebrew. But only the Christians. Not the Muslims. She set out to do her job using both tongues of the region, along with a smattering of English. She said she was an archeologist from America and then told them she was Jewish. She asked these young Palestinians what they knew about Jews.

"They eat children," said one of the girls to which some of her classmates grimaced in horror.

"Who told you that?" Gita asked, and the girl said her uncle.

Gita said this wasn't true, that Jews cherish children as much as any people. Then she showed them photos of Brian and Jennie, and said who they were and with that she began to discuss the holy books. The Koran. The Old Testament. The New Testament. I watched from the back of the room. Her ease with such Arabic words as '*ibada*,' which means the worship of God and '*najat*,' which refers to salvation gained in the hereafter seemed to pull the young Muslims to her. She told them the Koran was the most recent of the scriptures and that it incorporates the word of Muhammad, as well as the words of earlier prophets, going all the way back to Abraham. She then recited whole Koranic passages and I think they were impressed.

She told them how long ago we had found the Dead Sea Scrolls in a cave in Palestine and how she felt when she saw Roman coins with the words 'Judea capta' stamped on them. She told them about me and the many digs I had been on. She told them how our son Brian had died in a tunnel below the Old City of Jerusalem and how we mourned him still. She showed these tender children that she wasn't only a Jew, but a wife and mother. And they listened.

"My own husband is not a Jew," she said. "And his closest friend is a Muslim."

Then she saw me at the back of the room and a look of joy erupted in her face. She stopped for a moment and smiled. She told the children about the monastery at Kirbet Qumran and how important it was. She even called it "the birthplace of Christianity" and said how the Essenes had written the scrolls on that very site more than two thousand years ago.

"The Old Testament is a wonderful book," she said. "It was the seed of the New Testament and in time both these books led to the Koran. So they are all part of each other. All part of the oneness that they preach. The oneness of God."

I think they were all on side then, but just to make sure she had brought along the three holy books. She tossed me a smile as she looked at me from the corner of her eye. Within that smile was our whole life together. Our home. Our discoveries. Our children and our tragedies. I felt so much for her at that moment that I wanted to leave my place at the back of the room and take her in my arms and hug her close to me. But I couldn't. We were in a school and the children were there. Young faces already tarnished with despair. It was tragic and sad, I thought. Some of them were so young. But what if Gita could paint their faces with the brush of knowledge? Then there might be understanding and after that maybe even hope.

A little Palestinian girl, one of the youngest in the group, raised her hand. Gita addressed her and probably thought as I did, that she wanted to be excused. I wondered again about the bathroom facilities for many homes in the camp had no running water. But no. The girl had a flower in her hand. She carried it to the front of the class and put it on Gita's desk. Then she stopped and spoke in Arabic.

"This is for you," she said, and even I could understand her.

The face of that little girl was with me when I left the camp later that morning. She had put a smile in my heart and given *me* hope, a hope that remained when I decided to take a short drive to Qumran before returning to Jerusalem and begin making the final plans for our trip back home. I longed for home now, but was compelled to see Qumran one last time.

When I arrived I got out of my car and gazed up to the skies. The spirit of Yahweh was there. I could feel it in my bones. It was a spirit embracing the wisdom of Moses, the compassion of Jesus and the perfect simple balance of Muhammad. And I clung to them all. As one. For they are one. I turned in the direction of the Western Wall and prayed. I faced Mecca and made a silent plea for the mutual understanding of men. And I looked back at the ruins of Qumran where to this day a spirit still soars. It soars over the hills of Judea and across the desert of the Sinai. It soars through the rock of those ancient cliffs and into the caves where the word was first born. And just then I felt something, a comfort deep within my soul, so comforting that it made me raise both my hands into the heavens as high as they would go. So high that I actually touched whatever spirit was there.

And I was not alone.

Author's Note

What if? With those two words just about anything is possible, and for a writer they are the key that opens up the imagination. The idea for *QUMRAN* came to me many years ago when I first heard about the preserved body of a man found in a melting glacier in the Alps. Not only was he remarkably preserved, but he was 5,000 years old! So … what if your protagonist is a renowned archeologist who is teaching in the Holy Land and makes this incredible discovery that has the potential to turn the world on its edge? Thus began my research into the Dead Sea Scrolls, which were discovered at Qumran just off the Dead Sea back in 1947. It also began my personal journey studying the legends of the Holy Grail and Holy Shroud of Turin, not to mention the wonders of the Old City of Jerusalem and the tumultuous wars of the Middle East. As a writer who is deeply interested in archeology, I found that writing this novel was not only an adventure, but an education that allowed me to explore science and religion, and those touchy areas where the two intersect. I hope the same journey is true for my reader.

Dear Reader,

Without you none of this would be possible, so I want to thank you for reading *QUMRAN*, and I would be eternally grateful if you would take a minute or two to review the book on Amazon. No matter what authors tell you, we do want to know what our readers think.

Sincerely,
Jerry Amernic